KU-154-490

THE TRANSLATOR

Harriet Crawley

BITTER LEMON PRESS
LONDON

BITTER LEMON PRESS

First published in the United Kingdom in 2023 by
Bitter Lemon Press, 47 Wilmington Square, London WC1X OET

www.bitterlemonpress.com

© Harriet Crawley, 2023

All rights reserved. No part of this publication may be reproduced in any
form or by any means without written permission of the publisher.

The moral right of Harriet Crawley has been asserted in accordance
with the Copyright, Designs and Patents Act 1988

A CIP record for this book is available from the British Library

HB ISBN 978-1-913394-80-6
PB ISBN 978-1-913394-83-7
EBook 978-1-913394-82-0

Typeset by Tetragon, London
Printed and bound in Great Britain by CPI Group (UK) Ltd, Croydon, CRO 4YY

PRAISE FOR

THE TRANSLATOR

"There's no shortage of suspense, but also room for a vivid portrayal of everyday life in Moscow."

Sunday Times **Best Thriller Books of 2023**

"Wonderfully realised. Highly readable."

The Times **Thriller Book of the Month**

"Engaging spy story…in a Moscow full of menace."

Financial Times **Best Summer Thrillers of 2023**

"A classic thriller of the new Cold War."

Antony Beevor, author of *Stalingrad*

"A gripping, prophetic and ingenious novel of love and political intrigue in the new Cold War. A real page turner."

Owen Matthews, author of *Overreach* **and** *Red Traitor*

"Prescient and pacey, this book sizzles with the author's expertise."

Edward Lucas, author of
The New Cold War: Putin's Threat to Russia and the West

"*The Translator* is an intricate, stylish political thriller brimful of poetry and love. Audacious and irresistible."

Rachel Polonsky, author of *Molotov's Magic Lantern*

"Fast-paced thriller with a chilling ring of authenticity and an eerie closeness to present events in Ukraine. Unputdownable."

Xan Smiley, *The Economist*

"Brimming with intricate detail on Russia today, it is both moving and terrifying – a compelling combination."

Daily Mail

"The plot is clever, the writing elegant, the characters sympathetic and the action exciting."

Literary Review

"It's filled with intrigue, loyalty, betrayal and romance. If you like your political thrillers to be plausible with plenty of heart, this is definitely a book for you."

LoveReading

Harriet Crawley has been a journalist, writer, and art dealer, worked in television and radio, and she stood for the Westminster and European Parliaments. A fluent Russian speaker, Harriet was married to a Russian and sent her son to state school in Moscow, where she worked for almost twenty years in the energy sector. She speaks five languages and this is her fifth book.

To my beloved son, Spencer,
who believed from the start and saw me over the line.

In memory of Julian, who lit up my life.

Ищи ветра в поле, а правду на дне морском.

———

Seek the wind in the field and the truth at the bottom of the sea.

A TRADITIONAL RUSSIAN PROVERB

1

Clive was panting heavily as he reached the top of a peak in the Scottish Highlands. Sweat streamed from his forehead to his upper lip where he tasted its saltiness. The heart monitor was tight and damp around his chest. He slipped the backpack from his shoulder and pulled out his phone to check his performance. In case he had forgotten, the phone reminded him it was Saturday, 9 September 2017, and on that morning his running time had been 2 hours 42 minutes. Average heart rate: 152 bpm. Calories burnt: 2,100. Not bad for a man of forty-one, and every bit as good as last year.

For Clive Franklin, hiking up a Scottish Munro in September had become an addiction, something he did every year when the craving for stillness and solitude became overwhelming. And here he was on the summit of Na Gruagaichean, surrounded on all sides by jagged Highland peaks, triumphant, king of the castle, holding his ground, wind blasting in his face. There were fierce white clouds scudding above his head, so close he could almost touch them, and an eagle wheeling high above the purple heather, which seemed on fire in the morning sunlight. His legs were scratched to ribbons. Far below, he could see Loch Leven and the village of Kinlochleven, where, with a bit of luck, he would spend his Saturday evening in The Green Man, watching Mollie Finch play her cello.

Clive had plucked a broad leaf and was mopping the trickle of blood from his calf when he heard a high-pitched tinkle coming from the pocket of his backpack. The sound filled him with dread and had no place on Na Gruagaichean. He ignored the ringtone for as long as he could until there was no mistaking the frantic whirring of Rimsky-Korsakov's "Flight of the Bumblebee" in all its dizzy gaiety. On his phone he saw the words: No caller ID. I don't *have* to take this call, he told himself. I can choose *not to pick up*. Then, with a deep sigh, he pressed "accept", and, as he did so, the wind dropped; the reception was good.

"Where in God's name have you been, Franklin? I've been calling you for the past two hours and forty minutes!"

"Who is this?" Clive said, knowing right away that it had to be some nerd at the FCO who had tracked him down and was about to spoil his day.

"Martin Hyde. Prime Minister's Office."

"I'm afraid there must be some mistake," said Clive. "I work for the Foreign and Commonwealth Office."

Clive knew he was being pompous by calling the department by its full name, but he was irritated.

"No mistake, I assure you."

"Then why the 'No caller ID'?"

"Fair point. Stay where you are. I'll ring you right back."

Clive stood facing the wind, noticing a bank of dark clouds on the horizon. His phone rang again.

"There!" said the peremptory voice. "Now you have my number. Right, let's get on with it. You've been seconded to the Prime Minister's Office. It says here you're one of the best interpreters in the country."

Clive winced at the word "interpreter". He thought of himself as a translator, for arcane reasons of his own, but it hardly seemed the right moment, standing on the side of a mountain in the Highlands, the wind ripping across his face, to go into detail.

"Russian into English," shouted Hyde.

"And vice versa," Clive shouted back, thinking of Mollie and her flaming red hair.

"Yes, vice versa. That's what it says here."

"With all due respect, Mr Hyde. I'm on a sabbatical. With three months to go."

"You *were* on a sabbatical," said Hyde, spitting out words in bursts. "We need you. Important meeting. Tomorrow. In Moscow. With President Serov. We're flying out tonight. Not using embassy interpreters. Taking our own team."

So that's it, thought Clive. My day is ruined. And my evening with Mollie Finch, watching her play Brahms as if her life depended on it. Or is it?

"Mr Hyde," said Clive. "With all due respect you really *don't* need me. You've got Martin Sterndale. He's first-class."

"He may be first-class," Hyde snapped, "but he's lying in a coma in St Mary's, Paddington. He was knocked off his bicycle at seven o'clock this morning in Hyde Park. Franklin, your country needs you! Leg it down that Scottish Munro of yours and be on the Kinlochleven quayside at two o'clock this afternoon. A helicopter will pick you up."

Clive scowled as he heard these instructions.

"I'm sorry but... how... how... how do you know where I am?"

The wind dropped suddenly, and so did Hyde's voice.

"Don't be a bloody fool, Franklin. We always know where you are."

Whatever they say, going down is much easier. Clive fairly skipped through the heather. Now and then he would reach out to touch the purple flowers. They were part of his childhood, part of him. He thought of his father who had first brought him to the Highlands when he was six years old. And then he thought of Hyde and what lay ahead: an end to his peaceful, productive existence in the company of his favourite Russian writer, Anton Chekhov; an end to the solitude he loved. He would step out of the shadows and into the limelight, and the chaos, and the bad temper of international affairs. He knew exactly what he was going back to. Clive had served God knows how many Foreign Secretaries, attended dozens of top-level meetings, from Helsinki to Hangzhou. He was a Russian specialist: English into Russian or vice versa, whatever the occasion demanded. At a pinch he could do the same in French, but French specialists were two a penny, and, in any case, Russian was his thing. He loved the Cyrillic alphabet, the byzantine grammar, the soporific, sensuous sound of the Russian language. And once, he had loved a Russian woman.

By one o'clock Clive was back in Kinlochleven, a village of twenty cottages with a pub and the B&B on the waterfront where he was staying. He stopped for a moment and listened to the soft sound of water lapping against the quay and looked at the glittering reflection of boats on the choppy surface. This place had been kind to him. He'd found inspiration everywhere – in the Highlands, in the sky, in the heather. He was working better than ever, long hours, sometimes late into the night. And now this slow, pensive life was being snatched away. He felt like shouting out, "Leave me alone! Let me be!"

Back in his lodgings Clive caught sight of himself in the hall mirror. He was a tall, long-limbed man with a mop of black curly hair, melancholy dark eyes and a face bright red from the hike. He was staring at his crumpled T-shirt and the glistening skin on his face and arms, when a thought occurred to him which just might keep him right here in Kinlochleven. He had nothing to wear! Just hiking boots and shorts and an old T-shirt, one pair of jeans and a sweater. How could he meet the Russian president looking like this? Clive picked up his phone and called the last number.

"Mr Hyde?"

"Franklin?"

"I'm afraid you'll have to find someone else. I only have hiking clothes. Nothing smart."

"We have everything you need, Franklin. Shirts, ties, suits: the lot."

"But… I can't just wear any old clothes. I mean… How do I know they're the right size?"

"They are, Franklin," Hyde said wearily. "The clothes will fit you perfectly. Trust me."

"And my insulin? I can't go without my insulin. I'm a diabetic, you know."

"I know everything about you, Franklin. We've got your insulin. A month's supply, but of course you won't be away that long. A week at most."

Only a week! Clive's mood lifted. His cottage was rented until the end of the month, so he could give the owner of the B&B a quick call, explain he would be away for a few days, leave his belongings behind and send a WhatsApp to Mollie.

"A week," said Clive. "After which I can go back to my sabbatical. Is that agreed?"

"Agreed. Everything's settled then. Oh, and thank you for coming on board at such short notice."

"Do I have a choice?"

"Let's not get existential," said Hyde, in a new, lighter voice. "There is just one other thing… *Why* are you on a sabbatical? I mean, what on earth *for*?"

Clive bridled. The question was an intrusion into his most private world. Still, it deserved an answer.

"I took a sabbatical," Clive intoned solemnly, as if he were saying a prayer, "to translate twenty-seven short stories by Anton Pavlovich Chekhov."

"Good grief," Hyde said under his breath. "The ultimate student of the human soul. Is that also you, Franklin? Mankind in all its complexity. Et cetera. Well, perhaps your insights will come in handy at the negotiating table… We shall see."

The quayside at Kinlochleven was crowded with locals and holidaymakers with children, all curious to see what the noise was about, pointing up at the whirling blades of the AgustaWestland 109S as it landed nervily on the end of the jetty. As the rotor blades came to a stop, an FCO staff officer unbuckled himself from the co-pilot's seat and jumped to the ground. He was a jovial, stocky man, and he introduced himself as John, before taking Clive's holdall and canvas book bag and putting them into the side hold.

"Seems a pity to drag you away," said John, glancing down the quay at the neat row of white houses, and then the sunlight dancing on the loch. "Just a formality, but I need to see some ID. Security is super tight these days."

"My passport's in London. In my flat. 18 Gilbert Place. Behind the British Museum. How do we pick it up?"

"We don't," said John. "Driving licence?"

"I don't drive."

"Not a problem." John took a close-up of Clive's face on his phone, then turned away. While John whispered urgently into his phone, Clive took a moment to admire the flying machine: snow white with a red stripe banded in dark blue running along the side. Suddenly John spun round.

"All good. You're clear," he said with a broad grin. "Not everyone gets to fly in this little bird, I can tell you. It's reserved for VVIPs. In case you don't know, that's Very Very Important

People." As he spoke, John looked dubiously at Clive, at his tousled hair and crumpled clothes. "For whatever reason, you're getting the red-carpet treatment, my friend."

John pushed back the small crowd of curious holidaymakers and locals who were standing too close to the helicopter, then he showed Clive into the passenger seat at the back and told him to buckle up and put on his headset with its built-in microphone. Finally, John jumped into the cockpit alongside the pilot, and, against the roar of the rotor blades, he issued one last instruction.

"Enjoy the ride."

2

Would it really be just a week? Clive wondered, as they refuelled in Carlisle and then flew up into a soft September sky, the sun low on the horizon. At a certain point you have to stop worrying, he told himself. Let events take their course. Think of something else.

Before he knew it, there it was, right below, York Minster, rising up like an imperious sea monster above the low buildings of the city; no central spire, instead a massive tower proclaiming power and faith to the medieval world.

"I grew up in York," Clive said into his microphone, against the deafening shudder of the helicopter.

"Lucky you," said John.

Not really, thought Clive.

He could still hear it: the sound of his own ten-year-old treble voice soaring up effortlessly into the highest reaches of the Minster's nave as he sang solo, his eyes fixed on the floating hands of his father, Barry Franklin, choirmaster and conductor, who now and then nodded with approval. Those were the happy years. Later, it was all downhill. His mother developed Parkinson's, and it was agony to watch her decline, inch by inch. She was gentle and patient to the last, but unable to move and almost without a voice. The letter from Cambridge offering him a place at Trinity arrived the day of his mother's funeral. "I know you'll get in," she had whispered, the day before she died. "I believe in you."

As the helicopter left York Minster far behind, Clive stared down at the land he loved, his England, at the patchwork landscape of harvested fields and yellow straw stubble; at the villages with their country churches and narrow spires pointing like needles into the balmy late-summer air; and here and there, on a village green, he spotted tiny white figures playing a last game of cricket before the end of the season.

Time to shift gear, get your head into the right place, Clive told himself, as he leant back in his seat and shut his eyes. So long, Kinlochleven. Hello, Moscow. How long had it been since he had set foot in the place? Two years? Really? Two whole years?

In Moscow, Clive had been a diplomat, a member of Her Majesty's FCO. On paper, he was married; in practice, he was getting a divorce and lived alone in a bachelor flat. At the British Embassy, Clive had held the rank of second secretary, then political councillor. And then nothing. After Moscow, he announced that he no longer wanted a career in the diplomatic service, but would be happy to keep working for the FCO as a Russian interpreter and translator. The FCO gave him work around the clock: a G20 here, a G8 there, a meeting of foreign ministers, the Olympic Committee, the Winter Olympic Committee, the UN climate-change conferences, until he thought he was going mad and demanded a sabbatical.

Of course, the job had its perks. At the last G20 in Hangzhou a year ago, Clive remembered how exhilarating it felt to be sitting in a room with the most powerful men and women in the world. President Serov had shaken his hand and congratulated him on his Russian. Clive was flattered, just as he was flattered that morning when Hyde told him he'd been seconded to the Prime Minister's Office. This was a first. He'd never been seconded before. Sharpen up, he told himself.

As the helicopter came into land at RAF Northolt, the sun hit the horizon and turned the sky blood red. On the tarmac,

Clive was met by a young man in a bow tie and a three-piece suit who introduced himself as "George Lynton, from the Prime Minister's Office", and who insisted on taking Clive's holdall as he led the way to the VIP terminal. Passing through various checkpoints, he brandished a special pass with an air of self-importance, while Clive was searched and searched again.

"All very tedious," said George, who was no more than twenty-five years old and yet seemed to belong to another century, with his exaggerated self-confidence, languid gestures and upper-class accent which didn't seem quite real. Clive decided within minutes, in fact, that George's posh drawl had been learnt as you learn a foreign language, laboriously and with intent.

The VIP terminal was almost empty, except for two separate groups of people huddled together in different corners of the lounge. In one group, Clive spotted several people of Chinese origin.

"Changing room number one is all yours," said George. "You'll find a new set of clothes on the hangers. Everything else is in the suitcase, including a washbag with toothpaste, razor, the lot. And a four-week supply of insulin. Humalog."

"*Four* weeks?"

"That was my idea. They said two weeks, and I thought: Why not four? Better safe than sorry," George said breezily. "Have a shower. Oh, and anything you leave behind will be washed and cleaned. All part of the service. And no hurry. We'll be here for a couple of hours."

Clive knew better than to ask who was on the flight, so instead he said:

"When do we take off? And in what?"

"In the RAF Voyager. There's a special cabin up front for the big cheese, whoever that may be. The front twenty rows are all pretty luxurious, and the rest is fairly normal. We're at the back, of course. As soon as I get a departure time, I'll let you know. Newspapers are over there by the bar. Oh, and before I forget, you'll need this."

George handed Clive his brand-new passport, issued that same day with last year's photograph, which was kept on file at the Foreign Office.

Clive opened the stiff pages of the burgundy passport and was relieved to see that he'd kept his diplomatic status.

"Diplomatic passport," George confirmed. "Could come in handy, especially in Russia."

George tried a tired smile, then gave up and handed over a neat little stack of business cards. "These are for you. Sir Martin said they might come in handy."

"*Sir* Martin?"

"Yes... You didn't know? How odd... You didn't google him?"

"No time," said Clive, staring at the business card.

CLIVE FRANKLIN
Translator
Foreign and Commonwealth Office
King Charles Street
London SW1A 2AH

"I was told it had to be 'translator' and not 'interpreter'," said George. "Any reason?"

"Yes," Clive said, looking at George, at his Adam's apple straining against the white shirt and cobalt-blue tie. "The accepted wisdom is that you're either an interpreter who interprets speech, or a translator who translates text. But in Russian there's only one word for this skill: *perevodchik*. Translator. You're either an audio translator, *ustny perevodchik*, or a written translator, *pismenny perevodchik*. I'm both. So 'translator' suits me best. Does that make sense?"

"Sort of," said George, who was staring at Clive as if he were a rare specimen of butterfly.

In the changing room, Clive opened the small suitcase and found three neatly folded white shirts, an assortment of socks and boxers, a pair of jeans, three T-shirts, a couple of casual shirts and two sweaters in sober colours, dark blue and dark grey. He liked them both. On a hanger was a Marks and Spencer suit, which fitted perfectly. He took a shower, put on the jeans, a shirt and a sweater and emerged, feeling fresh and thirsty. He was helping himself to a glass of Rioja when George reappeared and asked if everything was all right. "Perfect," said Clive, and he held up his glass, inviting the young man to join him for a drink. George muttered he was on duty, then glanced around the lounge to see that he was not needed elsewhere before pouring himself half a glass of red wine and letting slip that he'd never been to Russia and was, well, quite excited. Meanwhile, Clive pulled out his laptop and googled Martin Hyde.

"He spent twenty years in MI6," said Clive, looking straight at George.

"Yes. And?"

"You know what they say…"

"No, what do they say?"

"Once in MI6, always in MI6."

"Really? Well, these days Sir Martin is special adviser to the PM on Russian affairs."

There was a blankness on George's face which told Clive everything he needed to know: this man was one hundred per cent loyal. Any leaks from the Prime Minister's Office were not coming from George Lynton.

"Tell me about yourself," said Clive, trying another tack. "Where are you from?"

"Meaning?"

"Born. Where were you born?"

"Wales. Anglesey. Famous for sheep."

"And once upon a time you had a strong Welsh accent?"

"I did… I had a very strong Welsh accent… How did you know?"

"It's still there, buried under your very proper English vowels."

"Really?" said George, suddenly flustered. "I thought I'd covered my tracks. I dumped the Welsh when I was at Oxford, that first summer… That's when I decided to try for the Civil Service and this friend of mine, Rose, well, she's sharp, and she told me I sounded like a provincial Welsh git, and to ignore all the stuff about diversity and inclusion, because if I was to have even the faintest chance of passing the exams, then I needed to get my tongue round those cut-glass English vowels. So, I did."

"How?"

"From the telly. Tom Bradby and a few others."

George got to his feet, twisting his neck as if his collar were too tight. Clive could sense the young man was embarrassed at having divulged so much.

"For Russia, we take no personal devices," George said, once again his cool self. "So, before you board, you'll be asked to hand over your mobile and laptop. MI6 insists. It's a bore, I know, but everything will be waiting for you when you get back. The embassy will give you a new mobile, nothing fancy. Pay as you go. But it'll do the job, and if you need a laptop, just ask the embassy for one. Anything else I can do for you? No? Well, if you'll excuse me…"

Clive watched as George drifted off to another part of the lounge, to make himself useful to another set of people. He opened the contacts app on his phone and scribbled down a few numbers, then typed "Meduza" into Google. It was time to get up to speed with the latest news in Russia and find out what was left of the political opposition. Clive had moved onto the Yandex news bulletins to get the Kremlin take on the world, when something made him look up, and he saw a nervous George Lynton holding open the door into the lounge for Mrs Maitland, the third female prime minister of the United Kingdom. Everyone stood up, including Clive.

Clive had never seen Martha Maitland in real life and was surprised how small she was, and how smart, in a well-cut burgundy suit. He watched with admiration as this petite woman in her fifties worked the room, exuding energy and optimism, her chief of staff by her side, while minions fussed about, introducing the prime minister to various people in the lounge. One man stood apart, tall, broad shouldered, with a strong jaw line and thick reddish-brown hair with white tufts at the temples. He came in with the prime minister but distanced himself at once and headed straight for the bar, where he poured himself a neat whisky. Clive knew at once: this had to be Martin Hyde.

It was Clive's turn to shake hands with the prime minister, who had a very direct stare.

"Mr Franklin, can I say how grateful I am that you interrupted your sabbatical to come on this trip? Sir Martin will brief you on the flight."

"I am delighted to be of service, Prime Minister," said Clive, and he meant it. As he stood face to face with his prime minister, he felt a solemn sense of duty. What had Hyde said? Your country needs you. Well, thought Clive, here I am.

Sir Martin Hyde stepped forward, hand out. Clive noticed that he wore cufflinks, and that his eyes were the palest blue and as hard as pack ice.

"Good to meet you, Franklin. I like to put a face to a voice. Franklin likes Chekhov," Hyde added, looking at the faces around him.

"Doesn't everyone?" said the prime minister, with that easy charm which, according to the press, had contributed greatly to her unexpected victory.

Clive had followed the election in the first month of his sabbatical. At the time, journalists across the board had agreed that Martha Maitland was more than the sum of her parts: a widow with centre-left leanings, she believed in God (she was an Anglican) and had a rebellious teenage son who had been expelled from school for taking drugs. That was her trump card, Clive recalled. The moment the scandal broke, Mrs Maitland's ratings went up by twenty per cent. Every parent in the country was sympathetic, and millions voted for her. So did Clive, but for a different reason. He was tired of men destroying the planet and murdering their fellow human beings. He voted for Martha Maitland because she was a woman.

It was almost midnight when the RAF Voyager took to the air, heading due east. The prime minister and her team sat in the forward section of the aeroplane, shielded by a beige curtain. Clive and George sat at the back, but, as soon as the seat belt signs were switched off, George got up and left, only to return moments later.

"Sir Martin invites you to join him. Won't take long. Quick briefing."

Martin Hyde was sitting in a business class seat in front of a table, his hand holding a glass of neat malt whisky. The surface of the table was cluttered with papers and files.

"Sit down," he said, pointing to the empty seat in front of him. "Drink?"

"Water's fine, thank you," said Clive, who'd already had a couple of glasses of Rioja and needed to keep a clear head.

"Suit yourself," said Hyde. "I want to apologize for being rather brusque on the telephone this afternoon. We needed to get hold of you in a hurry." He took a gulp of his whisky and leant back against the headrest of his seat.

"This trip is... how shall I put it? Unexpected. A whim of our dear prime minister. She wants to deliver her message to President Serov face to face, eyeball to eyeball. And why not? Things between our two countries could hardly be worse, except when it comes to the arts. In matters cultural, we are still the best of friends. By the way, this meeting is hardly costing the taxpayer a penny. It's a stop-over on the way to China. After the meeting tomorrow, the PM gets back on this plane and heads for Beijing. As for you, well, I'd be most grateful if you could stay in Moscow for the rest of the week and join our trade negotiations at the Foreign Ministry, which are going nowhere. Perhaps our people are losing the plot? Or just missing something? I think it's time we got a new slant on these talks, and you seem to be just the man for the job. You probably know this already, but Monday's a holiday when Moscow celebrates its eight hundred and seventieth birthday, so you'll have the day off. The trade talks resume on Tuesday." Hyde let out a deep sigh and leant back in his seat. "I'm not asking for the moon... Or perhaps I am?" Hyde was now bolt upright and staring at Clive. "As an interpreter —"

"Translator," Clive cut in. "If you don't mind. I know it's not the usual terminology but I —"

Hyde waved a hand, to indicate that he could not care less about the explanation.

"As a translator," Hyde resumed, "you're in an exceptional position, because... how to put this? You're invisible. No one notices you. No one remembers you. You melt into the background and stay there. From where you can watch and listen. And who knows what you might hear?"

"I'm not a spy, Sir Martin. I'm a translator."

"Yes, but you *are* ready to help, are you not?" Hyde said, urgently. "We need help, Franklin. We need it badly. It's all hands on deck."

"Of course, I'm ready to help, but, with all due respect, I don't know what you're talking about."

"I'm about to tell you. For the past few months, the Russians have been putting up dozens of new micro communications satellites. Each one is less than a thousand kilos in weight and about two metres in diameter. We don't have a precise number, but we think they've put up at least eighty. It could be more. Why? Our Ambassador – good man, Luke Marden – has put out feelers. Oh, say the Russians – and this is all over the Russian press by the way – we need new communications satellites, because we're such a big country. Must get fast broadband to Siberia, or some such rubbish. As far as I can see, even the *FT* has swallowed the propaganda." Hyde leant forward and tapped the pink paper on the table in front of him. "There's an article in here that goes on and on about the *size* of Russia. Six-point-eight million square miles, seventy times the size of the United Kingdom. Russia, the biggest country in the world even *after* the break-up of the Soviet Union, et cetera, et cetera. So, what are these eighty-odd micro communications satellites supposed to *do?*"

"Spy on *us?*"

"But why put up eighty then? It's too many."

"Spy on everybody?"

Hyde shook his head.

"As you know, Serov is ex-KGB, so we can assume that he's methodical and does everything for a reason. He's got something up his sleeve."

Hyde paused and pulled up the window blind. Clive found himself on a level with a crescent moon so close he could almost touch it.

"If we take a step back," Hyde continued, "Russia is struggling economically. The Western sanctions we imposed after it took Crimea are biting, and my feeling has always been that when the bear is cornered, he'll attack. Not in any conventional way, of course. Warfare today is *asymmetric*. Undercover. Difficult to detect. Cyber and all that. The Russian digital footprint was all over the last election. You know that as well as I do. The Russians bombarded our social media with fake news, bot attacks and God knows what else. They did everything they could to sow doubt and confusion, with one aim: that we would begin to doubt ourselves. And once that happens, our social and political cohesion falls apart. Suddenly we're at each other's throats, and divided we fall."

Clive ran his fingers through his thick hair.

"This isn't really my world."

"It *is* your world, Franklin. There's no escape. Not for you, not for anyone," Hyde said curtly. "I've read your file. You met Serov a year ago at the G20 in Hangzhou. That's good! He might even remember you."

"I doubt it," Clive murmured, shaking his head.

"Look, Franklin," Hyde said, leaning forward and staring straight at Clive. "All I'm asking you to do is to keep your eyes and ears open. You never know: you might hear something helpful. As I said earlier, it's remarkable how people relax in the company of interpreters, let their guard down, say things they shouldn't…"

Hyde smiled and finished his whisky.

"I'm staying with the ambassador," he said. "You're at the Metropol Hotel. If you need to reach me, here's my card. My brand-new mobile will be bugged of course, and so will yours, so just mention trade talks. If it's urgent, give a brand name like Range Rover or Tiptree jam. No, skip Range Rover. It's now owned by Tata. Just say Tiptree. Or JCB. Or Dyson. You get the idea. You must remember all this from your days at the embassy…"

"I do remember."

Hyde was looking sharply at Clive.

"There's something I'd like to ask you, Franklin. After your stint in Moscow, which, by the way, you did extremely well, you packed it in, left the diplomatic service and became a full-time interpreter... All right, all right... translator. Why?"

"The job was too political. As I just said, not my world. And I missed Chekhov."

Hyde seem satisfied with the answer and leant back in his seat.

"You know, I read Russian and French at Cambridge, just like you. My French is still pretty good, but my Russian... Well, it's vanished into thin air! Can't remember a thing. Still, now you're here, we can all relax. It's good to have you on board, Franklin. Is there anything you want to ask *me*?"

"Am I doing English into Russian?"

"Yes, yes, that's what it says in the briefing book," said Hyde, tapping a file on the table in front of him.

"Good," said Clive. "That's how I like it."

Clive waited for the inevitable question: But why? Surely it's easier to translate from Russian into your native tongue? He had his answer ready: No, because it's all about controlling what the other side hears. This answer was on the tip of Clive's tongue, but it stayed there, because Hyde merely yawned and said, "Anything else?"

"Do we know the name of my opposite number? The Russian translator?"

"Not a clue. Does it matter?"

"Not really. Just curious."

"Let's get some sleep," said Hyde. "Tomorrow... sorry, make that today, you need to be on top form. The briefing book is right here." Hyde tapped the file on the table. "Are you up to speed on the current jargon? Post-truth and alternative facts and all of that? What's fake news in Russian?"

"*Feykoviye novosti*," Clive said without missing a beat. "But the purists are up in arms. *Feykoviye* is not a Russian word. It's an anglicization. They think it should be *lozhniye novosti*. Lying news."

"Either way, the Russians are very good at it."

Clive was getting up to leave when Hyde put a hand on his arm; his grip was iron.

"The FSB will be watching you, morning, noon and especially night, so no high jinks. Is that understood?"

Before Clive could say anything, Hyde thrust the weekend *FT* and the briefing book into his hand and murmured, "Bedtime reading."

At the back of the aeroplane, Clive found George sitting upright in his seat, looking unusually glum. "Bad news," he said. "While you're at the meeting with the PM and Serov, I'm stuck in the airport all day with the Chinese team. I don't even get to set foot in Moscow."

George's voice trailed off. His urbane mask had fallen away, and he looked like a disappointed little boy.

"This *is* a pity," said Clive, with genuine sympathy.

"Can I ask you a favour?" said George. "Will you take this? Leave it with reception at the Metropol?"

George handed Clive a nicely wrapped parcel; it felt like a book.

"What is it?"

"*Under Milk Wood*. Dylan Thomas. It's a birthday present for my friend Rose. The same Rose who told me I was a Welsh git. She's in Moscow, working for the British Council."

"Rose what?"

"Friedman. Rose Friedman. Sir Martin can't stand her. No idea why. Will you take it? Thanks. Thanks a lot. I'll send her a text when we land. She's a great friend. Don't get me wrong..." he added, suddenly flustered. "There's nothing between us."

George decided not to finish the sentence. Instead, he handed over the parcel, cursed his luck once more and went to sleep.

Clive stared through the window into a forever expanding black universe. He was back where he didn't want to be, in a world of ringtones and deadlines and WhatsApp and political intrigue. In other words, he was back in the game.

Pressing his face to the aeroplane window, Clive watched dawn breaking over the vast megalopolis of greater Moscow, home to sixteen million people. Flashes of early-morning light bounced off the opaque surfaces of the lakes surrounding the capital; now and then the same dawn light exploded with a blinding flash on the aluminium roofs of the spanking-new, red-brick, three-storey houses built in their thousands, hidden from view by high walls, electric gates and the dense black woods of greater Moscow. Here and there Clive spotted an old, surviving village with those hand-carved wooden dachas, and he could almost hear the creak of faded blue shutters, feel the crunch of fallen apples in the orchard, smell the roses and lopsided lupins by the broken porch and hear the cocks crowing. But, even from ten thousand feet, he could see that these old villages were few and far between. Wood had given way to brick, mud tracks to asphalt, and satellite dishes sprouted like mushrooms on every aluminium roof. Clive pictured, somewhere far below, the armed security guards and their guard dogs patrolling the high wire perimeters of the mansions of Russian oligarchs and fat-cat bureaucrats. Now, at first light, they would be glancing at their watches, counting down the minutes to the end of their night shift.

They were coming in to land. Clive glanced at George, who was sleeping soundly, then leant back against the seat and closed his eyes. Due north was the old capital, Saint Petersburg. Four hours on the fast train. Only four hours. Did she ever give him a thought?

Don't be a fool, he told himself. What makes you think she's even there? She's probably remarried and lives in Berlin or Paris, or even Istanbul. How many languages does she speak? So many. Forget about it. Forget about *her.*

3

Marina Volina was in her running shorts and tank top, staring out of her kitchen window as she watched the first light of dawn break across the Moscow sky. Another day. One that her foster son, Pasha, would never see. Ten days ago, she had found him dead on the floor of his flat near Dynamo, eyes open, a syringe in his hand. Yesterday, on the ninth day after his death, she'd visited his grave and cried. She blamed herself for Pasha's death. She could have, she *should* have done more to save him from his addiction.

On the kitchen table was a fortieth birthday card from Lev, the president's private secretary and her only real friend in the Kremlin. Inside were the printed words: *Like wine, you only improve with age.*

Such nonsense, Marina thought, as she caught sight of Sasha, the handyman and caretaker of the building. He looked like an Old Believer with his long white hair and wispy beard, prowling among the parked cars in the courtyard below, followed by his emaciated wolfhound, Ivan the Terrible. Marina started at the chime of the Swiss cuckoo clock: it was five o'clock. She hated five o'clock. From the age of five, her father had dragged her out of bed to go swimming at that hour. He had wanted her to become a champion. Well, she never did become a champion. But she did take up running. Marathon running. And over the past few days, when she thought she was losing her mind, it was the running that had kept her sane.

Time to stretch, Marina thought. Crossing the octagonal hall with its four old-fashioned glass bookcases, she went into her front room, which overlooked Mamonovsky Lane and the 24/7 Taiga bar, and, further to the left, Tverskaya, Moscow's main thoroughfare. She swung a leg up onto the polished dining table. She always stretched here, in this room where her grandfather, a famous Bolshoi tenor, had sung romances to a select Soviet audience. The pull on her hamstrings felt good. Marina brought her head down to her knee, feeling the burn. Suddenly a raucous laugh erupted in the street below, and Marina caught sight of a drunken young man tottering across the street, while his girlfriend tried to keep him steady. The Taiga bar, she remembered, boasted thirty-three types of vodka, and it was there, just a few months earlier, that she and Pasha had watched the Victory Parade on 9 May. The entire Russian army had rumbled down Tverskaya in front of their eyes as they sat drinking Caipirinhas through a straw, gaping at the endless procession of tanks, rocket launchers and intercontinental ballistic missiles as they filed past, heading for Red Square. It had felt surreal.

And now Pasha was dead. That also felt surreal.

Time to focus, she told herself. Time to run. As she put on her Newton running shoes, which she always left by her front door, she noticed the knee-high black boots that she had worn to the cemetery the day before. They were still caked in mud. She stared at the boots and above all at the mud and remembered the clammy brown earth heaped on top of the freshly dug grave. Pasha's death hit her, once again, with brutal force, but a lifetime of discipline kicked in, and she fought off the surge of grief that was about to engulf her, sucked in one deep breath, and headed out of the door.

.   .   .

At Vnukovo airport, the British prime minister and her party were met by the ambassador, Luke Marden, a small, trim man with thick grey hair and a bushy grey-white beard. He was bristling with energy and news. There was a change of plan, he explained. The meeting with President Serov would not be taking place inside the Kremlin, but at Villa Novo-Nikolskoye, his official country residence outside Moscow. They were not expected before noon, which meant they could all get a few hours' rest and "freshen up".

Before he knew it, Clive found himself alone in the back of an embassy Range Rover driven by Fyodor, an embassy driver, speeding into Moscow hard on the tail of the VIP flag car, a brand-new purpose-built Jaguar with an extra row of seats and a Union Jack fluttering on the bonnet. Through the Jaguar's rear window, Clive could see the back of the prime minister's head. Next to her sat Hyde, and facing were the ambassador and the chief of staff. It was the first time Clive had found himself in a VIP convoy, and the details amused him: the four police outriders on BMW motorbikes with flashing blue lights and three police cars – all Fords, Clive noted – which now and then unleashed their sirens and shattered the peaceful dawn.

He pressed his face to the window, eager to see how much his beloved Moscow had changed. There seemed to be more of everything: more high-rise apartment buildings, more expensive cars, more 24/7 supermarkets. The convoy split into two somewhere near the Kremlin. The police escort followed the flag car, leaving the Range Rover to make its way to the Metropol Hotel. There, Clive was greeted by a doorman in a top hat, black cape and white gloves who stood to attention as he held open the heavy bronze door. But Clive kept him waiting. He wanted to savour the moment of his return and lingered outside the hotel, looking for those landmarks which meant so much to him. The Bolshoi Theatre was whiter than he remembered;

the granite statue of Karl Marx blacker, but the inscription was surely still there, in gold: *Workers of the world, unite!* The traffic was definitely louder, and the art nouveau mosaics beneath the roof of the Metropol were brighter. Above the rooftops, he could just see the twin entrance towers to Red Square, with their double-headed eagles glinting in the rising sun. It felt good to be back.

As he turned back to the waiting doorman, only then did he take in the banging and hammering that was going on all around him, the dozens of workmen clambering over scaffolding as they put up some giant edifice.

The Metropol had lost none of its absurd opulence, Clive thought, climbing the malachite staircase to the lobby. He could almost see his face in the marble floor. In his embassy days, he was in and out of the Metropol, looking after VIP visitors, and now, several years later, he was glad to see that nothing had changed: cascading chandeliers above his head, huge black leather armchairs, gold and green standard lamps, three metres high, blazing with a hundred lightbulbs. Excess, he said to himself. Russia is a country of excess.

Clive handed over his passport to a receptionist whose name badge read "Liza", and asked if he could have a room with a view. Liza looked at his passport and then at him.

"From the way you spoke, I thought you were Russian," she said, flashing her shiny vermilion smile. "Let me see… Yes, your room – it's on the fifth floor, and it does have a view. Sort of. You can see the Bolshoi. Just. And the giant screen, all part of the celebrations tomorrow… Moscow City Day! They've put up stands in Red Square… There's seating for forty thousand. All free! No one pays a penny! We've got a veterans' choir, a children's choir, a Cossack dance troupe. There's even an exhibition of yoga from our Russian champion! And speeches, of course, from the mayor… He's —"

"I used to live here," Clive interrupted, but kindly, not wanting to dampen Liza's spirits. "I love Moscow City Days. Russian choirs are the best... Can't wait for tomorrow."

Meanwhile, he had a favour to ask. Could Liza find out which Chekhov plays were playing, and where? He would like to see them all. And did she have a map, yes, a good old-fashioned paper map, of the new park, thirty-two acres in the city centre, just behind the Kremlin? The Zaryadye Park – that's the one! He needed to explore this huge green space. In fact, there was a lot he needed to do. He thought of all the museums and galleries he would visit and the walks he would take in the evenings down the old familiar streets. It almost felt like a holiday.

In his room, Clive took a shower, made himself a cup of black coffee and lay down on his bed, glancing up at the ceiling and wondering where the CCTV cameras were hidden. Or maybe there weren't any. He was probably considered a low security risk. Even so, best to assume that every gesture might be recorded. Don't pick your nose, he told himself, as he used the telephone in his room to dial a Moscow number. There was no answer, so he left a message. Then he focused on the job in hand. The mental preparation was always the same, a limbering up of the mind, a rigorous testing of himself. He went through various linguistic exercises, tossing English words and phrases into the air like tennis balls, then hitting them across the net in Russian. It was natural, effortless; he felt completely at ease in either language. Above all, he needed to be fresh. He glanced at the briefing book. The prime minister was not in a conciliatory mood; she was going to stick it to President Serov and object to Russian behaviour, on and off British soil. Clive's job was not to translate words, it was to translate *meaning* – and for that, he needed to be sharp. Take a nap, he told himself.

He was dozing off, with the taste of coffee in his mouth, when he noticed a two-page print-out, in English, which Hyde had slipped inside the briefing book.

Summary of a speech given at the Russian Academy of Military Science, Moscow, by General Kurnikov, and published as a Ministry of Defence background briefing paper.

"Non-military, asymmetric methods of confronting the enemy are being developed as a priority. The best procedures are as follows: first, it is important to destabilize the enemy through information and psychological warfare, so that the lines are obscured between what is truth and what is a lie. When the enemy is weakened in this way, we should advance simultaneously on several fronts, using all means to penetrate and influence the politics, economics, transmission of information (television, social media, etc.), and the overall psychology of the targeted nation. The aim here is to create an atmosphere of chaos and a loss of control.

"We, in Russia, surpass the West in our non-military capabilities and insights. Our new and improved resources – thanks to President Serov – mean that we are capable of waging this new type of warfare from all corners of the planet and even from space."

Clive read the last sentence twice.

4

Marina ran what she called "the short circuit": through Red Square, down to the Moscow River and back past the Bolshoi, up Petrovka, then left onto Kuznetsky Most to rejoin Tverskaya. She was back home by eight o'clock, pulling open the heavy mahogany door of Tverskaya 25. In the entrance hall, Marina checked her flimsy tin mailbox, pulling out a handful of letters, and was about to climb the chipped marble staircase when she heard a familiar voice ring out from the landing above.

"Is that you, Marina Andreyevna? Back from your early-morning run? Come and tell me about yesterday. How did it go? I'm so sorry I couldn't be with you."

Oxana Denisovna Belkina was a "lift lady", a plump, white-haired woman in her late sixties with alert brown eyes and several moles on her round face; she also had a bad back and arthritic fingers. Oxana spent her days on the landing at the top of the entrance stairs, right by the lift, sitting in an old swivel chair next to a rickety table and a narrow bed, where she slept at night. She worked in shifts with Nadia, the other lift lady, both pensioners, both grandmothers who took turns to keep watch day and night and make sure that no "undesirables" came into the building. In winter it was so cold they were used to sleeping in their coats, until Marina supplied them both with thick blankets.

"Nine days…" murmured Oxana, her eyes on Marina, who was climbing the stairs.

"I don't believe in all that religious nonsense," Marina said, sinking onto Oxana's bed in her running shorts and holding her water bottle. "The soul is lost... It's trying to find heaven... So, on the ninth day, you go the graveside and give it a nudge! It's absurd."

"But you went all the same," said Oxana.

Marina stared down at her hands.

"He was so young, Oxanochka. Twenty years old."

"Drugs are such a curse," murmured the lift lady.

"I should have done more..." Marina whispered.

"Now, don't go blaming yourself... We've talked about this before. You did everything you could for that boy and more! It's not your fault he took an overdose of... What's it called? Such a long, difficult name..."

"Methamphetamine."

"Yes. That's it. Tragic, absolutely tragic. But *not* your fault."

Oxana was staring hard at Marina, who sighed and turned her face away.

"So, where's that brother of his?" Oxana asked sharply.

"I don't know. He's always on the move, but he came to see me a couple of months ago... It was May, I think... You were away... He told me he was into online poker, and I said he was an idiot. He spent the night and left his clothes all over the floor, and I said he was too old to behave like that. He got furious and said I was a control freak and disappeared."

"After all you've done for him! He's a bad apple, if you ask me!"

"No," Marina said emphatically. "He's a lovely boy. So is —" She checked herself. "So was Pasha. Both lovely boys."

Sitting on the edge of Oxana's bed, Marina thought back on her life with Vanya and Pasha. She had known them for ten years. Almost all of that time had been in Saint Petersburg, when she lived on the Fontanka with her husband, Alexei, who was fighting his cancer every inch of the way. They had a big flat on the first floor of an old building. Right at the top was a woman who never seemed to be at home, with two wild boys who raced down the stairs, knocking into people, screaming with laughter, swearing. One day they knocked into Alexei. He grabbed Vanya and carried him up to their flat screaming, sat him down and fed him ice cream. That was the start of the friendship. All the grubby details came out: the father had walked out; the mother worked in a nightclub and was never at home. The children played truant. It was Alexei who sorted them out. He had no children of his own, and Marina had discovered she was infertile, something she blamed on the relentless swimming of her youth, so Vanya and Pasha became "our boys".

Marina took a sip from her water bottle. "What worries me," she said, "is that I have no way of contacting Vanya, and he may not know that his brother is..." Marina had to steel herself to say the word. She took a deep breath and then murmured: "Dead." Then she reached across and took Oxana's gnarled, arthritic hand. "I wish I could stay here with you, Oxanochka, but I must take a shower and go to work."

"Go to work! On a Sunday! You should be at your dacha getting some fresh air... The pollution rates here in Moscow are terrible at the moment."

"The president needs me," said Marina, getting to her feet.

Oxana looked impressed.

"Well, of course... for *him*... that's different... If Nikolai Nikolayevich needs you, then of course you must go... We all owe our president so much! Goodness me!"

Back inside her flat, Marina lay on her bed and shut her eyes.

The funeral had been a strange business: so many software engineers from the troll factory; young people crying openly as they looked at the childish face of twenty-year-old Pasha Orlov in his coffin; a big bunch of white lilies from General

Varlamov delivered by FSB goons. But no family. No brother, no mother, not even the ex-girlfriend.

Marina tossed the handful of letters she had pulled out of her mailbox onto the kitchen table and took a shower. Wrapped in a towel, her hair still wet, she returned to the letters. A flyer from a plastic surgeon. An appeal for donations to an orphanage. A white envelope with no name. Inside was a postcard of Gorky Park and, written in capitals on the back, lines in Russian from Pushkin's *Ruslan and Ludmila*:

> У лукоморья дуб зелёный;
> Златая цепь на дубе том:
> И днём и ночью кот учёный
> Всё ходит по цепи кругом...

> *Near the shore a green oak stands,*
> *A golden chain upon its boughs:*
> *And day and night a learned cat*
> *In fetters round and round it goes...*

For the first time that day, Marina smiled. She held the postcard between her thumb and forefinger, feeling its texture. Gorky Park was the giveaway, even more than the poem. Somehow Vanya had sneaked into the building unseen. What did she used to call him as a child? A cat. An alley cat.

Only then did she notice, tucked inside the same blank envelope, a white card with a black border – and a message. "PASHA WAS MURDERED. BY YOUR LOT."

Marina let out a cry, like a wounded bird. And yet, deep down, she had known it all along.

It was 09.55, and Clive was in the lift, heading for his rendezvous with an embassy car at ten o'clock, when he remembered

George's book. He hurried back to his room and noted with some satisfaction (he was never late) that it was exactly ten when he stepped into the lobby, looking for Liza. He saw her at the reception desk, but she wasn't alone; in front of her stood an agitated young woman in tight black leather trousers and a red biker jacket. A helmet at her feet, she was remonstrating.

"It *has* to be here. Please, have another look," the young woman pleaded, pushing her hand through her messy blond hair, which had one distinguishing feature: a flaming red streak on one side.

"Rose?" Clive asked loudly and clearly.

The young woman jerked her head round and stared. She was in her mid-twenties, with the face of a child, round and wide-eyed. Clive handed over the book.

"You must be Clive," said Rose, taking the book and smiling. "My friend George told me about you. Said you were *reliable*. Which I am not." Then Rose leant forward and, rolling her eyes from the floor to the walls, she whispered. "What do you think? All this marble… That wall's pink alabaster, and the stairs are porphyry! And d'you see the Chinese vases? So bloody big, we could hide inside! And what about those leather chairs? More like beds, don't you think? It's crazy. This whole place is so un-cool… I mean… Well… It's too fucking much! Thanks for the book. See you around!"

Clive slid into the back seat of the embassy Range Rover and warmly greeted Fyodor. The car lurched forward.

"New pavements," said Clive. "Very smart."

Fyodor smiled into the rear-view mirror, and Clive caught sight of his broad, flat face and friendly eyes. He knew, from his time in Moscow, that all Russian drivers who worked for the British embassy had to report daily to the FSB, so he always tried to make their lives easier by saying something positive.

This wasn't difficult on that particular morning, when the city looked so clean and majestic.

"We've got a good mayor… He takes care of the city," Fyodor said. "Our president, Nikolai Nikolayevich, now there's a true patriot. He takes care of Russia! And you're going to meet him today… What an honour!"

"It is indeed. Your president is a man of considerable stature. A world figure. And you know something? I've met him once before."

Fyodor raised an eyebrow. He looked impressed.

As they crossed the Kammeny Bridge, Clive asked Fyodor to slow down. This was his favourite view of the Kremlin: the mighty fortress with its blood-red walls and green towers looming above the Moscow River, and, standing on the opposite bank, an elegant white mansion, the residence of the British ambassador.

In the front courtyard, a large Union Jack fluttered on its flagpole. Clive handed his passport to the duty officer and waited. Moments later he was shown into an oak-panelled library. He barely had time to glance at the books on the mahogany table, which, judging by the titles – *Great Country Houses, Royal Palaces, The House of Windsor* – had been carefully chosen to impress the Russians, before the door flew open and Luke Marden appeared with his hand outstretched.

"Sorry to keep you waiting," he said, shaking Clive vigorously by the hand. "So glad you're with us… We need somebody with perfect Russian… Wish mine was… Oswald has your mobile… Bet you feel lost without one… Everyone does… The cars are outside… We're off… Need to take a detour… There's a demonstration… Quite a *rare event* these days… God help the demonstrators… The villa's quite something… Wait till you see it."

Clive was only half listening to what the ambassador said; he was more interested in *how* he said it. He knew that Marden was fluent in Russian, but the ambassador was bound at some point to switch to English out of respect for the prime minister. Then what? He knew it would be tricky, keeping pace with the staccato tone, the unfinished sentences, the rushed speech. But he would manage.

Clive was no longer alone in the Range Rover. Beside him sat the political counsellor, Oswald Martindale, a spare man with thinning hair and a tired, sarcastic smile. From the moment they were introduced, Clive guessed rightly that Martindale was head of station. A spook. Languidly, Martindale handed Clive an old iPhone. "Clean as a whistle," he said. "And no cameras." The number of the phone was stored in the contacts under his name. The FSB would be listening in, Martindale added. Of course.

They headed out of Moscow along Kutuzovsky Prospekt, in order to avoid being caught up in the demonstration, so Fyodor explained. Clive saw a steady stream of young people heading towards the Kremlin, holding banners with the slogan: Free Nikita Strelnikov.

"Who's Strelnikov?" Clive asked Martindale. Then he checked himself as he glanced at Fyodor. "Maybe tell me later."

"I can tell you right now," Martindale said, avoiding eye contact with Fyodor and staring out of the window. "He's the new rock star of the opposition… Used to sing pop. Now he sings protest songs and posts his videos on WhatsApp and Telegram and VK. Apparently, he's really got under Serov's skin. They've banged him up on a trumped-up charge of tax evasion… He's facing years in prison. It's all part of a new crackdown."

At the word "Serov", Fyodor glanced into his rear-view mirror, but Martindale went on talking.

"God knows why they had to drag you off a Scottish mountain for a meeting that's going nowhere… They should have left you there, smelling the heather."

"You don't like it here?" said Clive.

"What's to like?" Martindale countered, his voice weary.

"People. Art. Literature."

"Oh, *please*. This country is corrupt from the top down. Everyone who can leaves. Have you noticed? And no wonder... The stories I hear... The people I meet... You don't know the half of it."

"I do. I do know the half of it. And I'm glad to be back."

Sirens wailing, the convoy with the police escort drove past miles of new apartment blocks towards the outer ring road, the MKAD. Sometime later, the Barvikha Luxury Village flashed by, along with some of the world's most expensive shops – Chanel, Ermenegildo Zegna, Bulgari – as well as a brand-new concert hall in the shape of a giant whale bone. Clive caught sight of a billboard announcing a forthcoming concert with Vanessa-Mae.

"You know the average wage in Russia?" Martindale said suddenly. "Three hundred pounds a month. And the average state pension? Fifteen thousand roubles. That's one hundred and ninety pounds. In the villages, a lot of people only get eight thousand roubles a month. That's a hundred pounds. You can't live on a hundred a month. Meanwhile, the president and his cronies are robbing the state blind."

Fyodor had his eyes trained on Martindale in his rear-view mirror.

"Lovely weather," said Clive.

The convoy left the main road and swerved into a dense forest where black fir trees blotted out the September sun. There were electric fences on both sides of the road, and Clive noticed CCTV cameras every twenty metres. They passed through seven security checkpoints.

"I understand you've met the new tsar," said Martindale. "Full of peasant cunning. On the surface, he's a chummy sort of bloke who cracks jokes, pretends to have friends. Which he doesn't. Basically, he's a loner."

"He likes cats," said Clive. "On his official website, there's a photo of him and a Kurilian bobtail."

The Range Rover pulled up right behind the Jaguar in front of an impressive nineteenth-century villa, which, according to Martindale, had been used as a hunting lodge by Nicholas II. From the back seat of the car, Clive had a perfect view of the marble steps, at the top of which the Russian president and his entourage stood waiting.

The cameras flashed as a smiling Nikolai Serov welcomed Martha Maitland and her party. Clive and Martindale brought up the rear, which gave Clive time to observe the president. Serov was a big man, over six feet, with the broad shoulders of a boxer and white hair combed straight back. He was in good shape, and his smooth skin made him look considerably younger than his seventy years. Suddenly it was Clive's turn to be introduced to him. He held out his hand. Serov kept it.

"I know this man!" said the president with a laugh. "We met at the G20 in China. You did English into Russian. Very impressive. Your name is…?"

"Franklin. Clive Franklin."

Clive was not a man to blush, so his face gave nothing away, but he felt uncomfortable being the centre of attention. His job was to translate, not to converse. He was relieved to see the ambassador whispering into the prime minister's ear, no doubt translating the president's comments.

"Are there many more like you, Mr Franklin?" the president persisted. "We'd better watch out! This man speaks Russian with no accent. Can we match that? I'm not sure! How many of our interpreters speak English with no accent?"

The president glanced at his officials, who were not sure how to react.

"Where *is* everybody?" the president asked, turning to Lev Ignatiev, his private secretary, a tall man in his late twenties with a bald head, who stepped forward and whispered something in his ear. "Really? And Dmitri?"

"Please, apologize to your prime minister," Serov said to Clive. "We're waiting for my translator and also for our foreign minister. They're both stuck in traffic. And on a weekend!" Serov then turned to Martha Maitland and laid on the charm. At this point, Clive came into his own, took over from the ambassador and translated every word seamlessly.

"In life there are forces outside our control," Serov said urbanely. "What's the hurry? We're among friends! You and I can get to know each other. Coffee? Tea? Or something stronger, perhaps?"

The prime minister decided that now was the moment to show off. Was President Serov related to the illustrious Russian painter, Valentin Alexandrovich Serov, whose picture, *The Girl with Peaches*, she would dearly love to see in the Tretyakov Gallery? (Hyde had thought up and carefully researched this line of small talk and even shown the PM the painting on his laptop.) As Clive translated, he guessed that the answer would be a "yes" and that the answer would be "a cousin", since every Russian called even the most distant relation "cousin". Clive was right. The president was indeed related, on his mother's side. A distant cousin.

More importantly – and, of course, this was Hyde's intention – the president was impressed.

The delegation was then offered refreshments in the main reception room, which was opulently furnished with gilded sofas and chairs and portraits of Russian rulers – Peter the Great, and Catherine, and Alexander II – all interspersed with still lives and hunting scenes, mostly Dutch.

President Serov suggested to Mrs Maitland a tour of the paintings, with himself as guide. It was the Landseer that caught the prime minister's attention: an imperious stag with magnificent twelve-point antlers, standing on a craggy mountainside surrounded by bracken and looking out at a kingdom that was rightfully his – the Scottish Highlands.

Mrs Maitland turned to Clive. "I wonder how this painting got here. Do we know? Perhaps we can ask the president?"

"It was a gift," Serov said smoothly, happy to show off his artistic knowledge, "from your King George V to his cousin Tsar Nicholas II. According to your director of the National Gallery, who was here last month, it's one of Landseer's best."

The president then invited Martha Maitland for a stroll on the veranda, from where she would have an excellent view of the Italian gardens. The British ambassador suggested to Clive that he might like a short break while he held the fort for the next five minutes. I wonder why, thought Clive. Perhaps the prime minister and the ambassador had a secret to share? Maybe, and maybe not. In any case, Clive was glad to get back to the Landseer. The more he looked at the painting, the more he felt himself back in the Highlands, the wind on his face, the heather scratching his bare legs. Then he heard a deadpan voice.

"Can't stand animal paintings, alive or dead," said Oswald Martindale, chewing on crisp celery, his dark-grey suit hanging loosely on his spare frame. "In case you're interested, over there is the head of Gazprom, so we can assume that BP and those vast oil deposits in Sakhalin will be on the agenda. Otherwise, the place is stiff with FSB."

"Of course," said Martin Hyde, who had joined them. "What do you expect? There's too much gold leaf in this room, don't you think?"

"Over there," Martindale said abruptly. "Varlamov. The Wolf."

In the far corner of the room stood a tall man in his early fifties, immaculately dressed. His wiry black hair was cut very short and sprouted straight up. His hairline was unusual, coming to a peak in his forehead, above a long and pointed face, a narrow nose and thin lips. His eyelids hung low over his dark eyes, giving him a deceptively sleepy look – and, yes, he did look like a wolf. He reminded Clive of Cassius: a lean and hungry man.

"And the Wolf is…?" Clive asked.

"General Grigory Varlamov, deputy director of the FSB. Tipped to take over the organization any day now. The president is godfather to his daughter."

A hush fell in the room as President Serov and Prime Minister Maitland returned. From the British side and the Russian side, delegates fell silent and stared. The tension was palpable.

Clive was familiar with this febrile atmosphere. He had encountered it many times and always found it disturbing. He could never understand why people changed their behaviour so dramatically in the presence of power, why they allowed themselves to be so overawed, paralysed, unable to speak. But it was always thus, and Clive observed a familiar scene as everyone stood around in a sort of trance, waiting for something to happen. And something did happen. The Russian foreign minister, Dmitri Kirsanov, arrived with no fuss. Excusing himself in Russian to the president, he turned to Martha Maitland and offered her an elegant apology in convoluted English, craving her indulgence and repeating "mea culpa". Then he noticed Clive.

"We know each other," said Kirsanov. "A thousand apologies, but I forget your name…"

"Clive Franklin," interjected the ambassador, with a courteous bow of the head.

"Mr Franklin! Of course!" said Kirsanov, throwing up his hands. "We meet again! You have Russian roots, I seem to remember?"

"Latvian," said Clive, not happy where this was going and grateful to the president, who suddenly took charge.

"I don't think we can wait any longer," Serov announced. "My translator is stuck in traffic! But do I really need my own translator when we've got Mr Franklin in our midst? Let's get down to business, my friends!"

As if on cue, a side door opened, and in walked a woman with a flat Slavic face, eyes set far apart, and auburn hair coiled in a bun. She carried herself very erect, like a dancer.

Marina wore no make-up, and she'd made no attempt to hide the grey hair around her temples. Her clothes were dull – a grey suit and a white blouse – chosen with care, to make herself as anonymous as possible. She was in no mood to be noticed, to stand out.

And then she saw Clive.

"Prime Minister," said Serov, waving extravagantly at Marina, beckoning her to hurry up. "This is Marina Volina, our version of Mr Franklin. You see, we're not so chauvinist after all! We, too, have women in important positions! Ambassador, will you make the introductions?"

Clive translated mechanically, all the while telling himself to stay in control, not to stare too much, not to let on. But a voice inside his head was crying out. Is this Marina? Is this *really* Marina? She looked so thin, so drawn, so sad. What had happened to the beautiful young woman he had fallen in love with? What had life done to her?

Marina shook hands with each member of the British delegation, repeating, "Marina Volina, nice to meet you," until she came to Clive, at which point she hesitated and turned, puzzled, in the direction of Lev, the president's right hand.

The ambassador understood at once and stepped forward. "Perhaps you were expecting Martin Sterndale?" he said in English. "Unfortunately, he's had an accident and is in hospital. Mr Franklin stepped in at the last moment. He's one of our finest interpreters."

Marina turned to Clive and smiled, and Clive knew at once *why* she smiled, because she had remembered how he hated the word "interpreter" and could feel his irritation. Her smile was complicit; more than that, it was a sign. And something else happened in that moment, when Marina stood before him, smiling her wonderful smile; her tiredness and her sadness fell away, and Clive found himself staring into the face of the young and beautiful Marina he had once loved to distraction. The illusion lasted only a second before the beloved face vanished. All Clive could see were dark circles under Marina's eyes as she offered him her hand and looked right through him without a flicker of recognition. Turning to the ambassador, and for the benefit of the British prime minister, Marina spoke in English.

"Please send Mr Sterndale my best wishes and tell him I do hope he makes a speedy recovery."

Clive thought he saw something mischievous in her eyes as Marina turned again to face him.

"Have we met? You look… familiar."

Clive was speechless. It's a game, he told himself. She always loved games.

"The marathon!" Marina said, her face lighting up. "We ran New York marathon together when we were both working at UN, all those years ago…"

It was Clive's turn to smile. Marina had just made her first two mistakes: she'd forgotten to say "the" before "New York marathon", and again before "UN". She's nervous, he thought.

"Who got the fastest time?" Serov asked.

"I didn't finish," said Clive.

"Really?" said the president. "Well, Marinochka always finishes."

Marinochka! The word jarred with Clive. He had never called her that. His name for Marina was "Marisha".

"And then she's onto the next race," the president went on. "She's about to run the Moscow marathon… When is it?"

"Two weeks today," Marina said evenly, looking at no one in particular.

"Maybe Mr Franklin would like to take part?"

The president's suggestion caught Marina by surprise. For a moment she was flustered.

"With all due respect, Nikolai Nikolayevich, you can't just run a marathon... You need to train."

"He looks fit to me," Serov countered. "How about it, Mr Franklin? Extend your stay and join our Moscow marathon! It will be good publicity for closer cooperation between our countries! You'll be on television, running side by side with Marina, two experts in the noble art of translation. But this time you have to finish!"

"I'm only staying till the end of the week, Mr President," Clive said firmly, longing to put an end to this pointless banter. "But thank you for the invitation."

Clive understood perfectly that this absurd time-wasting exchange about the Moscow marathon was a deliberate ploy by the Russian president to unsettle, even belittle Mrs Maitland, who retained an icy calm. Tribal loyalty kicked in, and Clive, resenting the discourtesy, felt a bristling hostility towards his host. But his face gave nothing away. He was relieved when he followed President Serov and the prime minister into the conference room, where oak-panelled walls were hung with hunting trophies: wild boar, roebuck and deer. For a moment, Martha Maitland stood in front of a full-size stuffed brown bear, its mouth wide open and showing off the sharpest teeth, its paws raised with long, threatening claws.

"That's not the original," said Serov. "The original was moth-eaten and had to be replaced. Luckily, Russia is full of bears. Please, take a seat."

5

"A waste of bloody time" was Oswald Martindale's verdict. The political counsellor muttered this under his breath as the meeting ended and they headed for lunch in the gilded reception room. Martin Hyde disagreed. The PM had put her marker down, he wrote that evening in a confidential, encrypted email. She had gone on the offensive from the start. In an even, unemotional voice, she told Serov that her government was fully aware of Russia's efforts to meddle in UK elections and the Brexit referendum, and that, even though these attempts had largely failed, it really was time to stop the cyber attacks altogether against UK institutions and political parties. Surely the president could see that such behaviour was most unhelpful if the two countries were to build a better relationship? The PM even mentioned a new troll factory in Moscow to show she was in the know.

At this opening burst of criticism, President Serov and Foreign Minister Kirsanov looked surprised, even aggrieved, exchanging puzzled glances but remaining silent.

The prime minister moved on to her second point of contention: the regular incursion into UK airspace by Russian bombers, which she called "harassment". The latest incident, she noted, was only last week, involving a Tu-95 skirting the Shetland Islands. Granted, it was good practice for the Typhoon pilots to be scrambled so regularly, but did we not all have better things to do?

Now Franklin's Russian had a harder edge, to match the prime minister's growing irritation. The president and his foreign minister exchanged more glances but still said nothing.

Martha Maitland's third point was to demand, in the strongest possible terms, an end to assassinations on British soil by Russian agents.

The gloves were off, and Clive Franklin was talking tough. His Russian was greeted with anger from President Serov, and Marina conveyed her president's "astonishment", even "outrage", at "such baseless, fanciful accusations". The foreign minister weighed in, speaking in Russian for the benefit of his president, but at this point Marina toned down the rhetoric in the interests of diplomacy. "This is pure fantasy, amounting to provocation" became "This is pure fantasy." The omission was not missed by Clive, who turned to his prime minister and completed the sentence in a whisper.

"Did you say provocation?" Martha Maitland shot back. "And what do you call your invasion of Crimea?"

Hyde had always predicted they would come to blows over Ukraine. President Serov banged the table and referred to Ukrainian opposition as "ultra-nationalists"; Martha Maitland hailed them as "democrats" and said Ukrainians had every right to demand a cessation of all hostilities and the restoration of Crimea. Russia had invaded the sovereign territory of Ukraine, she insisted, and usurped the rights of its people. Clive chose his Russian words very carefully, selecting the harshest terms. "The usurpation of rights" became "the violent suppression of rights". Both the president and the foreign minister bridled, but Mrs Maitland had hit her stride, and she went on to denounce the war in the East, and the hundreds of Russian soldiers posing as "separatists". Her words hit home. The Russian president stabbed the green baize table with the tip of his pen, got to his feet and declared the meeting over.

"Shall we have lunch?" Serov asked, without enthusiasm.

The prime minister turned to Clive and, with a gritty smile, said that she really didn't need him, sitting as she was at a small table between the British ambassador and the Russian foreign minister, who was fluent in elaborate English. So, Clive was momentarily redundant. He was also hungry.

He headed for the buffet and took his time selecting from the sumptuous spread of lobster, sturgeon, caviar and oysters served by chefs in white hats, and, when his plate was full, he found a table on the veranda overlooking the Italian gardens with their baroque fountains. He could both see and hear water spurting from the marble mouths of dolphins. Clive was hungry and needed to eat; only then could he think straight about Marina. He was cracking a lobster claw when Martin Hyde sat down beside him.

"Well done, Franklin. I see you filled in a few gaps. What was Volina up to?"

"Trying to lower the temperature, I imagine," said Clive, extracting the plump white meat from a lobster claw meticulously and with ease. Hyde watched, transfixed. Neither he nor Clive noticed the slender shadow that fell across their table.

"May I join you?"

Hyde got to his feet and offered Marina Volina a chair.

"I feel I owe Mr Franklin an apology," Marina said, smiling at Hyde and sitting down. "Clive, I'm so sorry I didn't recognize you right away…"

"Well, it was all so long ago," Clive said casually, looking down at his plate. If only Hyde had not been there, he would have confronted her, asked what she was playing at. Was it her idea of a joke? Or was it Marina's way of telling him something?

"Clive was member of our Russian book club on the fourteenth floor of the UN," Marina said, looking at Hyde.

"I was," said Clive, looking straight at Marina and taking in every detail of a face he had done his best to forget for over a decade. He had also forgotten the particular musicality of her English, which gave her away as a foreigner. Now and then her "o" was slightly too long and her "r" was a little too hard, and sooner or later she would forget an article, just as she had a moment ago. Her English was almost perfect. But not quite. It was all part of her infinite charm.

"The British were on the twelfth floor, and we were on the fourteenth – and so was our book club," Marina explained. "Clive was a regular. The only Brit. I wonder if it still exists. The book club, I mean."

"I can't help you there, I'm afraid," said Hyde, watching Marina with his trained eye.

Clive held the silver lobster crackers in his hand and was about to crack the second claw when he hesitated, then glanced at Marina, who sat demurely at the table, a thin smile planted on her impassive face. So you want to play games, Clive thought. I'm up for that.

"Your friends tried to recruit me as a spy, remember?" Clive said, shattering the pink bone with the pincers.

At the word "spy", Martin Hyde tilted his head back slightly and narrowed his eyes, keeping them fixed on Marina, whose expression had changed. She seemed amused. Her face had relaxed, and her eyes were laughing.

"Really?" said Marina. "I don't remember that at all."

Of course you do, thought Clive. Look at you, the consummate liar... And you do it so well, so convincingly. I should know... But, in spite of everything, I don't hate you. No, I don't hate you at all...

Of course, he knows I'm lying, Marina was thinking, but

does he know *why*? It's the one way I can get his attention… He must guess. He's so clever. She studied the face she had once known intimately and felt a sudden tenderness towards Clive, a tenderness mixed with admiration, that he had got over her, moved on, reached the top of his profession. After all, she reminded herself, I broke his heart.

Clive had a sudden urge to reach out and touch Marina's thin, sad face. Of course, he did nothing.

"I remember you liked Chekhov," Marina said in a new, gentle voice.

"I still do."

Clive searched her eyes, light brown flecked with green, and thought he saw sympathy, affection even, but before he could be sure, Marina's attention had been caught by Lev, who was waving at her from across the room. It could mean only one thing: the president needed her. She left in a hurry, while Hyde headed over to the buffet to get some lunch.

"Of course they tried to recruit you," Hyde said, returning to the table with a plate piled with crab, blinis and caviar. "The only Englishman in the book club…"

"It was a half-hearted attempt," said Clive, dimly remembering the Ukrainian girl who had pressed herself against him in the lift. Everyone knew she was FSB, even Marina, who had warned him to be careful. "The Russians could see that I wasn't remotely interested. I told the ambassador. He said they were trying to recruit everyone…"

"So you and Marina Volina are old friends?" Hyde said, rolling himself a plump pancake filled with caviar and sour cream.

"I haven't seen her for, what, ten years? She didn't recognize me."

"Or perhaps she did? But had a momentary lapse and was lost for words? What happened in the New York marathon? Why didn't you finish?"

Clive pushed his plate to one side.

"The three of us were running together: Marina, her husband, Alexei Ostrovsky, and I. About ten kilometres before the finish line I went into diabetic ketoacidosis, which happens when you're diabetic and don't know it. Unless you get insulin immediately, you die. When I collapsed, Marina noticed straight away a fruity smell on my breath, like pear drops. That was the giveaway smell… And she knew what it meant."

Clive fell silent. He remembered it all perfectly. He had drifted in and out of consciousness, Marina bending over him.

"How?" said Hyde. "How did she know what it meant?"

"Because when she was at school, her best friend had the same seizure… And then she read up on it."

"So, what happened then?"

"She told Alexei to get some insulin right away. Alexei sprinted over to the nearest ambulance… Paramedics came running. I don't remember. But they saved my life, Alexei and Marina."

Clive could feel Hyde watching him as he stared down at his plate.

"Where is he now, this model husband?"

Clive resented the sarcastic edge to Hyde's question, but he kept his voice neutral.

"Dead. He was diagnosed with lung cancer in New York. Not altogether surprising, since, like most Russians, he smoked like a chimney. The first treatment was successful, and they left for Geneva, where Marina got a big UN posting, revamping the school for interpreters, but then Alexei's cancer came back. I saw them in Geneva about ten years ago. Alexei told me he wanted to die in Saint Petersburg. Which he did, a couple of years ago."

"You didn't look them up, Marina and her husband, when you were stationed here in Moscow?"

"No. I spoke to Marina just once. They'd moved back to Saint Petersburg, but Alexei didn't want to see anyone. The chemotherapy made him feel terrible. I was back in London when she posted a video of the funeral on VK, and someone sent it to me. I can't remember who."

Clive would never forget Alexei's handsome face in the open coffin, and Marina, solemn but not weeping, bending over to kiss his forehead.

"So Volina is her maiden name?" said Hyde, with a casual indifference that Clive found unsettling.

"It's Volin without the 'a'," Clive said, about to add that "Volina" was the feminine form, but then he remembered that Hyde had studied Russian. "Her father, Andrei Volin was a Soviet general and a close friend of Serov's in Berlin and Dresden before the collapse of the Soviet Union."

"I see-ee," said Hyde, stretching the vowels like elastic and wiping the corners of his mouth with a napkin. "Now I understand! They go way back… So we can assume that Mrs Volina is part of Serov's inner circle."

"I wouldn't know," said Clive.

"Oh, I am sure. I am one hundred per cent sure," said Hyde. " When they're alone, I wouldn't be surprised if she didn't call him Uncle Kolya."

An empty smile crossed Hyde's face. Then he got to his feet to rejoin the prime minister.

Reuters reported that the meeting had been robust. In the group photograph that circled the globe, a grim British prime minister was seen shaking hands with a stony-faced President Serov on the steps of the Villa Novo-Nikolskoye. Next to the Russian president stood a good-looking but unsmiling woman in a nondescript grey suit; next to the British prime minister stood a man with curly black hair who seemed slightly bewildered. (One Russian photographer thought he looked just like the poet Alexander Blok.) The Englishman was not looking at the camera; he was looking at Marina Volina.

"So that's why she came," Serov murmured, as he stood on the steps of the villa, holding Rurik, his honey-coloured Kurilian bobtail, and watched the flag car disappear into the forest. "To give us a ticking-off. You know what *really* gets under my skin? The way these bloody British act so *superior*. They're hypocrites, all of them! The City of London is the money-laundering capital of the world… For years… *for years* the British have been only too happy to take *our* Russian money. *No questions asked.* As for Maitland, she's an opinionated bitch. Did you see how she lectured me?"

Marina was always taken aback when the president spoke in such crude terms. But, as he told his many biographers, he was the son of a peasant who fought on the Eastern Front and died on the same day as Stalin. The young Serov had spent his first years in a remote village, living in a small wooden house with electricity but no running water. After his father died from a heart attack at forty-one, he and his mother moved to a run-down housing estate in Chelyabinsk near the Urals, where he learnt to fight for his life from the age of three.

"They're all like that, these women politicians," Serov fumed, as he walked under the marble colonnade with Marina by his side. "Power brings out the nanny in them. Everything's black and white. No grey. And no jokes. When did you last hear a woman politician make a joke?"

The president looked out at the endless forest and sighed.

"These people are *not* our friends. Britain, America, the EU, the whole bloody lot of them… They don't *want* a strong Russia. Crimea! They bang on about Crimea! Don't they know that Crimea was Russian till Khrushchev gave it away… When was that?"

"Nineteen fifty-four," said Marina.

"There you go! Yesterday! Khrushchev gave away Crimea only yesterday, and now we've got it back. What's all the fuss about? But the West wants to punish us, humiliate us. Look at them piling on the sanctions. It's ridiculous! I tell you, Marinochka, we have no choice. We have to fight back. Defend ourselves. And the best form of defence is attack, right?"

"If you say so."

Not once in the past year had Marina voiced a political opinion, and she was not about to do so now. Her policy had always been to keep under the radar.

"I do say so, Marinochka. Soon, very soon, we're going to strike where it hurts. Don't look so alarmed. No tanks. No invasion. No bombs. In fact, not a single shot fired. But trust me, we'll knock the wind out of their sails!"

They walked on in silence; the only sound was water gushing from the fountains below. Suddenly, Serov stopped and turned to Marina, saying, "So, how come you failed to recruit the British translator, Franklin?"

"He wasn't interested. Not everyone wants to be a spy, Nikolai Nikolayevich."

Serov burst out laughing.

"That's what I like about you, Marinochka! You stand up to me! Not like all these other fawning idiots." The president caught sight of Lev leaning against the balustrade, his back to the gardens, staring at his phone. "Not Lyova," said Serov. "He doesn't fawn. He's got some spunk, like you."

"Nikolai Nikolayevich, all that business about me taking Clive Franklin running... You were joking, right?"

"Of course I was joking... On the other hand, why not? He might collapse again, and then we can have a photograph of Franklin gasping for breath... Britain on its knees!"

Serov let out another hearty laugh; his bodyguards, burly

men from the Federal Protective Service, looked up, and so did General Varlamov. The president was talking to Marina Volina and *laughing*? How was this possible? Marina Volina had *no sense of humour*. Or had he underestimated her?

"Now, what's this I'm hearing about your foster son, that clever young man? What *was* his name? Orlov, yes? Pasha Orlov. He had a heart attack and *died*? From an overdose of methamphetamine?"

"Apparently."

Be careful, Marina told herself. Be very careful. *Pasha was killed by your lot.* The words written by Vanya on the scrap of paper were booming inside her head. *Your lot* meant who exactly?

Be very careful, she repeated to herself as she stared into the president's face.

"And you found his body," Serov continued sympathetically. "That was hard on you, Marinochka. Very hard. I'm sorry for you. I know you were very fond of the boy. He was like a son to you, yes? This is a personal tragedy…" The president placed both hands on Marina's shoulders and looked into her tired face. "But life must go on. And you're brave, just like your father. You need a holiday. You're too thin."

"A holiday?" Marina said in genuine surprise. "Well, once I'm done with the Moscow marathon, that would be nice. I'd like to go to Italy."

"What's wrong with Crimea? Don't you like your little house near Yalta? Overlooking the sea?"

The "little" house in Crimea had been another gift from the president, which, according to Lev, she could not possibly refuse. It came with its own beach and speedboat, a housekeeper, a gym and three guestrooms for friends.

"You can use my helicopter to come and go," Serov continued. "Who needs Italy?"

Serov picked up the cat which had been meowing and rubbing itself against his leg.

"I'm very grateful to you, Uncle Kolya... You've been so kind."

Serov smiled. He liked the sound of those two words: Uncle Kolya. They took him back to happier times when his wife was alive, and so loving, and this woman beside him was a child, wide-eyed and innocent, and so grateful for the smallest present.

"I gave your father a promise that I'd take care of you, and that's exactly what I'm doing, because your father took care of me, all those years ago, when I was a young man, learning the ropes. Loyalty, Marinochka. It's all about loyalty."

Suddenly Serov threw Rurik to the ground. "Damn that cat!" he said, licking a spot of blood on the back of his hand. His bodyguard lurched forward, but Serov waved him away as he sucked his hand. Lev came forward in long, lazy strides with a clean white handkerchief, which Serov took.

"Come to Crimea this weekend," Serov said to Marina. "We fly on Friday afternoon, back early Sunday. It's my birthday... There'll be a nice lunch... Just a few close friends... In the morning, I'll need your help for a couple of hours... The rest is holiday... Lyova, fix it, will you?"

"Not a problem," Lev drawled, smiling at Marina, who smiled back. In that moment, she thought to herself, how strange it was that this tall, tattooed young man with a bald head should have the face of a child.

The president led Marina back into the villa, where in the domed entrance hall he broke away to speak to Varlamov. There was nothing casual about their conversation; this was urgent business, and, as they conferred, their heads were almost touching. They only broke apart to let Foreign Minister Kirsanov into their midst.

Marina watched from a distance, as three of the most powerful men in Russia huddled together. Vanya's words kept pounding in her head: *Pasha was killed by your lot*. What could Pasha have possibly done that was so bad? *Your lot*. Meaning who? The president? Did you kill Pasha, Nikolai Nikolayevich? Look at you, laughing, tossing back your head, showing a row of perfect white teeth – all yours, as you told me once over dinner. Or was it you, Foreign Minister Kirsanov? Did you kill Pasha? Or you, General Varlamov? Or has Vanya made the whole thing up?

"What a bloody awful way to spend a Sunday," Oswald Martindale remarked to Clive as he stood in the entrance hall, examining the painted ceiling above his head, counting a dozen plump cherubs holding wreaths of flowers floating upwards into a rosy sky.

"Sunday!" Clive said, suddenly flustered. "I forgot it's Sunday. What time does the Bolshoi start on a Sunday?"

"Haven't a clue. I never go there if I can help it. Can't stand all that glitter... I'm always blinded by the gold paint... Tell you what, let's go and ask your friend Marina."

Oswald Martindale led the way through the open French windows to a balcony overlooking the garden. They found Marina Volina standing next to General Varlamov, who was sucking hard on a vaporizer.

"So very sorry to interrupt you, Mrs Volina," Martindale said in his most unctuous voice, at the same time acknowledging the general with a polite nod, "but Clive here wants to know what time the Bolshoi starts on a Sunday."

Marina turned sharply. "Six o'clock. Why? Is he going?"

"Yes," said Clive. "I am."

"I told you Marina Volina would know," Martindale said to no one in particular.

"It's *The Queen of Spades* tonight," said Marina, looking past Martindale at Clive. "I've got a ticket, but I was thinking of giving it a miss. The reviews have been terrible. Let's hope they're wrong for your sake. Oh, and remember to take some cash. They don't take credit cards in the upstairs bar."

Clive didn't move. In New York, he and Marina had developed endless strategies to outwit the FSB. They were always playing literary games, passing on information using their own codes or just dropping hints.

"We are such stuff as dreams are made on, and our little life is rounded by a sleep," Marina said out of the blue. Her face was solemn, as well it might be, because all those years ago, in New York, any quotation from *The Tempest* was a red alert; it meant, we have to meet. Now.

How? thought Clive. Where? He searched Marina's face, but she avoided eye contact. And then he understood: she'll fix it, she'll find a way.

"You'd better leave now if you want to make it on time," Marina said, glancing at her watch.

"Chop-chop," said Martindale, taking Clive's arm.

From the loggia, Marina and the general watched the Englishmen drive off in the Range Rover. Marina could feel Varlamov's irritation.

"So, what was *that* all about?" he said.

"I was just humouring Mr Franklin with a bit of Shakespeare."

"Next time, make it Pushkin."

General Varlamov took a deep drag on his vaporizer, wishing it tasted more like the real thing.

"That political counsellor," said the general. "He's got 'spy' written on his forehead. He even dresses like one. Did you see his suit? And his shirt? The collar was frayed."

"I'm afraid I didn't notice, Grigory Mikhailovich."

Marina was always scrupulously polite and respectful to the general. Once she had overstepped the mark and called him "Grisha", and his rebuke had been final: "No one calls me

'Grisha', except my wife, my mother and the president." From then on, it was always "Grigory Mikhailovich".

"And did you see the so-called special adviser, Martin Hyde? *Sir* Martin Hyde? MI6 through and through. It's no secret, of course. We know, and he knows we know. He's staying for a week. I wonder why... He must have a hidden agenda. Perhaps the Englishman does, too? Mr Franklin, isn't it? So, what's his first name?"

"Clive. Clive Franklin."

It feels so strange, Marina thought, to say his name out loud after so many years. I thought I had buried it forever.

"You know what the president said to me just now? Word for word?" Varlamov said, heading back into the villa. "He said, 'Grisha, be sure to keep an eye on that Clive Franklin. I don't trust anyone who speaks such good Russian.' My thoughts *exactly*."

"But you'd be keeping an eye on him anyway, surely?"

"Of course. And Hyde. From the moment they arrive to the moment they leave. When it comes to surveillance, our resources are... How can I put this? Infinite. Per capita, we have more intelligence officers than the Chinese."

"Grigory Mikhailovich, there is something I've always wondered... And I'm sure you can enlighten me. In this era of artificial intelligence, why do we still need to tail people? Take Clive Franklin. Why not track him through his mobile phone?"

"And what if he chooses to leave his mobile behind? Or gets himself a burner that we can't trace? Or uses someone else's mobile? And tracking is only part of it. We might want to know who he's meeting... who he's talking to. A mobile won't tell us that. Dear me, Marina Andreyevna, you're not thinking clearly today. Tails are indispensable. So, while we're on the subject, what else can you tell me about your friend, Clive?"

"He's not really a friend..."

The general wasn't listening. He had slipped his vaporizer into his pocket and was typing something into his phone.

"Clive Franklin," he said reading off the screen. "Let me see... Was at the UN from 2003 to 2005. Part of the British translating pool at the UN. Then joined the Foreign Service. Married Sarah Woodall in 2006, divorced in 2007. Was in Georgia 2009 to 2011, then London, then Moscow from 2013 to 2015. He's been seconded to the Prime Minister's Office for this trip. They must think very highly of him."

General Varlamov put his phone into the inside pocket of his smart and very expensive midnight-blue Italian suit and looked at Marina.

"Odd you didn't recognize him."

"Is it?" said Marina, remembering her sense of bewilderment then panic when she had first recognized Clive. "I haven't set eyes on Mr Franklin in over a decade. I just drew a blank. It happens."

"Not to me. Never to me. So, all those years ago we tried and failed to recruit him. Maybe you should give it another go? Take him running. Sound him out?"

"I don't really have time. The marathon is two weeks away. I'm in serious training, Grigory Mikhailovich."

"Talking of appearances."

"Were we?"

"Like it or not, Marina Andreyevna, you're in the public eye. Today you were photographed by the world's press on the steps of the villa, next to the president. And, well, may I be frank? You used to be reasonably well turned out, but in the last few months, you've let yourself go. I'm speaking to you as a friend now, Marina Andreyevna."

"Could you be a little more specific?"

Marina knew the irony in her voice would be lost on Varlamov. But she also knew that the general was a man who spoke his mind and who had the trust of the president.

"Your hair. It's bad luck for you, my dear, that you are prematurely grey, but you are, and so you really must take steps to remedy the situation. This means, and I hope you don't feel I am being too personal... This means that you really *must* dye your hair. Grey hair makes a woman look old and, well, rather dowdy. It's certainly not the right look for a top translator who's in the public eye, who's photographed next to the president. I'm sure you can see that."

"My appearance is *my* business, surely?"

"No. I'm afraid not. You're part of a *team*, Marina Andreyevna. Please remember that. And please don't take offence. As I told you, I'm speaking as... as a friend. I have your best interests at heart, believe me. We must all put our best foot forward for the sake of Russia."

"Dying my hair would be a patriotic act?"

"Well, you could put it that way."

Marina let out a burst of laughter to hide the intense hatred she felt at that moment for General Varlamov.

"I don't see what's so funny," he muttered, turning his back on Marina and looking out over the Italian gardens. "The president agrees with me. You need to smarten up."

Marina could hear the anger in Varlamov's voice and she braced herself for what might come next. The general turned and faced her and spat out three words.

"Pity about Pavel."

Varlamov never used diminutives, even with subordinates; he liked to keep a distance. Pavel was never Pasha, always Pavel: alive or dead.

"The boy was such a fool, to throw his life away like that!" the general continued. "Pavel Orlov was the star of our Moscow research institute. He had a great future as our most inventive..." Varlamov hesitated.

"Hacker?" Marina suggested.

"Software developer. He was the most inventive software developer we've ever had. I put him in charge of the UK referendum on Brexit. Your boy was such an asset… He stoked the fires, right and left. So easy when you know how. Those were his very words. And he covered his tracks, *our* tracks… The British suspect us, of course! You heard them today letting off steam, huffing and puffing, but they can't prove a thing thanks to your boy Pavel, who left no trace. Well, almost no trace. They know about our little Moscow operation… I wonder how. I suppose there's always some digital footprint… Anyway, your Pavel was outstanding. Then he ruins it all… takes an overdose of some recreational drug. Methamphetamine, if I remember rightly. What a pity."

"Pasha told *me*," Marina said slowly, taking her time, "that he didn't *do* drugs." She was looking directly at the general, weighing up what he had just told her, asking herself why she had this feeling in her gut that General Varlamov was lying. "He told *me* that he only smoked weed, which, according to him, doesn't…" Marina stopped herself. "Didn't count. Grigory Mikhailovich, I have a favour to ask. Could I possibly see the pathology report? I am…" Marina checked herself. "I *was* his foster mother after all. Maybe not officially, but de facto."

The general shook his head.

"The pathology report can only be seen by the *legal* next of kin. Your relationship with Pavel had no legal basis. You were not *officially* anything. Just a friend. A very close friend. Do correct me if I'm wrong…" The general gave Marina a condescending smile, as if to say, "I've looked into this and I know what I'm talking about."

"He told me I was like a mother to him," Marina blurted out, close to tears.

"Yes… well…" said the general, turning away to suck on his vaporizer. "Where are they, by the way, his next of kin?

His birth mother? And what about his brother? What's his name?"

The question was asked so casually, but Marina knew she had to answer. There was no escape.

"Ivan… Vanya."

"Someone was sleeping on the floor of Pavel's flat. Any idea who?"

"No idea. But surely your people can find out?"

"We know a man was in Pavel's flat, but none of the neighbours could give a description. It seems he always wore a hood. Maybe it was Ivan?"

"The last I heard, Vanya was in Vladivostok, working for the mafia."

"What mafia?" Varlamov scoffed. "You've been reading anti-Russian propaganda."

"Yesterday," said Marina, "I went to Pasha's grave. It's was the ninth day. I'm not religious, but I wanted to go. I wondered if Vanya would turn up, but he didn't. I left flowers."

"You left sunflowers. But someone else left a bunch of yellow tulips. Any idea who?"

"You were *watching* me?" Marina felt a coldness on the back of her neck.

"Not you. The grave."

Marina remembered a young man in a raincoat who had walked unsteadily over the duckboards between the muddy graves. He'd looked so out of place.

"Who could have left those flowers?"

"Maybe a friend? Pasha had a lot of friends… remember his funeral? It was packed…"

"My operative was at the cemetery when it opened at seven o'clock. The flowers were already there, so someone got in before daybreak. How? Why?"

"I've no idea, but in all honesty, Grigory Mikhailovich,

does it really matter? Pasha is dead. Nothing will bring him back."

Marina felt a surge of grief, but nothing would make her cry in front of Varlamov. Not a single tear would fall.

"Ah, I remember Ivan now," said Varlamov. "We gave him a job in the Petersburg office, when he was just sixteen. Then he chucked it in and disappeared. Yes... that boy was clever. Almost as clever as his brother. If Ivan contacts you —"

"He won't," Marina said, a little too quickly.

"I don't want you to think I'm heartless, Marina Andreyevna, but Pavel was not a team player. He was a rebel... He resented authority. I'm told they're all like that, these developer whizz-kids, They've always been unruly. Undisciplined. They don't like being told what to do. They think they know it all... and anyone over twenty is a dinosaur..."

"You have to make allowances for these brilliant young developers, Grigory Mikhailovich. They live in another world."

"You're right. They're a breed apart. I've had to learn a whole new language: 'spear-phishing' and 'phishing' and 'smishing' and 'vishing'. Not to mention 'malware' and 'ransomware' and 'brute-force attacks'... All very stimulating. When I took you round the Internet Research Institute, it was nothing special... just a couple of rooms full of computers. It was you who noticed there wasn't a coffee machine. Well, you'll be glad to hear things have changed. These days, the institute takes up three floors and, as for coffee machines, there are six!"

6

What was it about the fourth pillar from the left at the Bolshoi? Why do people always want to meet there? Clive wondered as he grabbed his rouble notes from the cash machine by the metro, hurried across Theatre Square, past the fountain and the benches, and ran up the steps of the Bolshoi. Latecomers and ticket touts stood beneath the portico, which was supported by eight huge pillars. There, at the fourth pillar on the left, stood an elderly lady, staring at her phone; she was in her eighties, her white hair cut short, her brown eyes bright with energy. When she saw Clive, her face lit up with a beautiful smile, and she threw out her arms.

"My Clive!" she exclaimed. "My handsome English son… I was so thrilled to get your message… I called your mobile, but you didn't answer. I've been here for half an hour, waiting."

"So sorry to be late, a thousand apologies," said Clive, bending low to hug Vera. She was so small, and so precious. "I've got a new mobile, just for this trip. I'll give you the number."

"It's not like you to cut it so fine," Vera scolded, presenting her tickets to the Bolshoi doorman, explaining to Clive that they were a present from a student. Inside the hall, they passed through security, and Clive just had time to buy two programmes.

As they took their seats in the tenth row of the stalls, Clive felt entirely at home, in his red plush armchair, facing the world's largest velvet stage curtain emblazoned in gold thread with the double-headed eagle and the word "Russia". He looked up at the seven rows of balconies, all gilded to extinction, and decided that maybe Martindale had a point.

"I'm so pleased to see you, Vera," said Clive, putting his arm around her, glad to have her close by once again. They were in regular contact on WhatsApp. Only last week, he had sent her photographs of the Highlands, and he always remembered her birthday. Now and then he called her, just to hear her voice.

Vera Seliverstova had been Clive's Russian teacher, but in fact, from the very start, she was much more than that. In his gap year, after the death of his mother, Clive had spent the summer with Vera and her daughter, Anna, in their dacha outside Moscow, and it was in those balmy months, in between swimming in the local pond and playing tennis on the bumpy court overgrown with weeds, that Vera had educated him, not only in the Russian language and its literature, but also in politics. Vera understood exactly what was happening inside Russia; she saw the growing censorship, the creeping dictatorship, and she denounced it, never giving up the fight for what she called "a normal life". But above all, she loved Clive and called him her "English son", and he loved her back. Vera's daughter, Anna, was a well-known human-rights lawyer; Clive followed her on Instagram.

"How is Anya?" Clive asked.

"Annushka's at a police station, trying to get some students out of jail…" Vera dropped her voice. "A lot has changed since you were last here. Not for the better, I'm afraid."

Vera glanced at her watch. "Why does the Bolshoi never start on time?" She took Clive's hand and held it tightly. "Tomorrow's a holiday. Come to the dacha, and we'll pick mushrooms."

The lights dimmed, and a voice reminded everyone to turn off their mobile phones and refrain from flash photography which was *strictly* forbidden.

The new production of *The Queen of Spades* was set in a lunatic asylum, and before long a man in a side box close to Clive and Vera took to shouting "Rubbish!" every few minutes and laughing out loud. He was given a stern ticking-off by a torch-bearing usher, who threatened him with immediate expulsion if he continued to disturb the performance. He persisted, however, and before long two security guards escorted him from the theatre. But even as he was leaving, this opera-lover, red-faced with indignation, shouted, "Shame on you, shame on the Bolshoi for allowing such rubbish!"

At the first interval, Vera turned to Clive. "That man who kept shouting… He's right! This production is *dreadful…* Why did they have to bring in a German guest director? No Russian would put on something like this."

"We need a drink," said Clive. "Let's go upstairs."

The bar on the seventh floor was crowded, and Clive was pleased to see that people still dressed up for the Bolshoi – in sequins and tight dresses, and in suits – and that little girls still ran around in organza with bows in their hair. Clive bought two glasses of Russian champagne and two open sturgeon sandwiches and looked around for a place to sit.

That was when he saw her, as he knew he would, sitting alone on a red bench in front of a long table beneath a mirror, sipping a glass of red wine, wearing the same grey suit she had worn at the villa.

When Marina saw Clive, she waved at him and smiled. Instinctively he looked around, knowing that somewhere in the noisy, excited crowd, a tail was watching. Then he headed towards Marina with Vera by his side.

"I thought you were going to give this a miss," he said, putting his tray down on Marina's table.

"I wish I had," said Marina, shaking her head. "Vera Petrovna! What a surprise to see you here!"

"I'm often at the Bolshoi," Vera said stiffly.

"Vera Petrovna and I are neighbours in Peredelkino," Marina said to Clive, slowly and distinctly, and Clive understood at once that she was playing the same game of cat and mouse they had perfected in New York. It was important to talk loudly about ordinary things, so the tail could report back. "We meet now and then in the lanes, when I'm walking my dog. I've asked Vera Petrovna round for tea several times, isn't that right?" Now she was looking directly at Vera. "But you always find some excuse not to come."

Vera sat straight-backed and stony-faced, steeling herself against Marina's charm. It was her duty to dislike this woman.

"Once upon a time," Marina continued, "I was best friends with Vera's daughter Anna. We went to the same school in Moscow, sat next to each other in the same classroom. That's when I came to stay in Peredelkino for a whole week. Do you remember, Vera Petrovna? I must have been about fourteen. It was such a happy time. Anna and I played endless games of tennis on that terrible court in the woods… You couldn't see the lines and there were holes in the net… But we had such fun. And we picked mushrooms. And you let us watch American films until one in the morning."

Still Vera refused to smile; instead, she took a bite of the sandwich and a sip of the champagne.

"I can't believe how many mushrooms there are this year," Marina persevered. "The woods are stuffed with them."

"It's a bumper crop," Vera said to Clive, still avoiding eye contact with Marina. "You'll see for yourself when you come tomorrow."

"We've had a terrible summer, haven't we, Vera Petrovna?" Marina continued, determined to establish some sort of dialogue. "Nothing but bulldozers and builders… Our village is being completely ruined by the rich."

"Your friends," said Vera.

"But, Vera Petrovna, they are *not* my friends," Marina objected with a smile. "I avoid them like the plague. I find most rich people pretentious and immensely boring."

Marina picked up Clive's programme, fat and glossy. "These programmes cost a fortune. I never buy them any more. And tonight, what a waste of money! Such a diabolical production. Have you ever seen worse, Vera Petrovna? Tell me honestly…"

Vera could feel her resistance ebbing away. To avoid defeat, she excused herself and went in search of the ladies. Clive leant forward, looking hard at Marina, and spoke in English.

"How are you?" he said.

"Older. Wiser. And you?"

"Older, definitely. I don't know about wiser."

"So, what was all that about… At the villa… Your pretending not to know me?"

"I was caught off guard… They told me it would be Sterndale… And suddenly it's you, standing there. I couldn't think straight. It was such a shock. And then I realized it was my *sudba*, my fate… And everything fell into place."

"You've lost me there… I don't know what you're talking about."

Clive saw the flecks of green in her light-brown eyes. He also saw fear.

"Are you all right?" he said.

The question hung in the air.

"Why do you ask?"

"You look so… so different…"

"You mean old."

"I mean sad. Do you believe in *sudba*?" he asked suddenly.

"Doesn't every Russian?"

Marina opened the programme and turned the pages till she came to a photograph of the guest director, an avant-garde German from Wuppertal. She showed the picture to Clive, who drew closer. Their heads were almost touching when Marina murmured:

"I can't live here any more. I want out."

"Ah," said Clive, and contained in that little puff of breath was a world of understanding. He leant back against the red plush banquette and stared straight ahead. At this point Vera rejoined the table, muttering about the disappointing standard of dress these days at the Bolshoi. Now in *her* day...

"I won't be a moment," Marina interrupted, getting to her feet, taking the programme with her as she headed for the ladies.

The first bell rang, and a metallic voice reminded everyone that the performance would continue in five minutes. But not for Marina, who reappeared and announced that she was leaving. "I can't take any more. This is the worst production I've ever seen. Apologies to all, but I'm off." Casually, she dropped the programme on the table and flicked it towards Clive, then she spoke loudly and clearly in Russian. "Would you like to come running one morning? The president suggested it, if you remember..."

Clive had noticed the lone male drinker wearing a navy suit and a red tie sitting at a corner table, looking in their direction.

"I think that's going to be difficult, time-wise," said Clive. "I'm here for work. But thanks all the same."

"Call me if you change your mind. Here's my card."

Marina was handing over her card when it fell out of her hand. Bending down to pick it up, she noticed Clive's shoes. "They could do with a polish," she said, then coughed and through a half-closed fist mumbled, "Try the Armenian at the Metropol, first left inside the entrance."

Marina was on the point of leaving when a striking young woman in a bright-green silk shirt and black leather trousers hopped off her bar stool and marched over.

"Well I never! Clive bloody Franklin! Purveyor of Dylan Thomas and my new best friend!"

With a warm handshake, Rose Friedman introduced herself to Marina and Vera as a beacon of British culture, followed by "My name is Rose, and I'm delighted to meet you," pronounced in excruciating Russian, but with verve. In case anyone had a shadow of doubt, Rose explained that it was her mission in life to promote Shakespeare across Russia's eleven time zones. Then she handed everyone a business card.

THE BRITISH COUNCIL, RUSSIA

Rose Friedman

Cultural Projects Officer
Email: rose.friedman@britishcouncil.ru
Mobile: +7 985 766 8321

"Don't get me wrong," she said, addressing everyone. "I *love* Russki culture. Which is why I'm here. Got my ticket from a tout right outside. So glad I came! It's such a *great production*, don't you think?" Vera, who was clearly amused by Rose, shook her head vigorously. Rose looked dismayed. "No? How come? What's not to like? Tchaikovsky? Pushkin? It's magnificent on every level! *The Queen of Spades* is about an addiction – gambling. Now *that* is a form of insanity, so *obviously* the story has to take place in an insane asylum."

"It's not obvious to *me*," Marina said kindly, not wishing to be too hard on this ebullient young woman and admiring her for holding her ground.

At this point, Vera felt the need to speak up. "Miss Friedman," she said, "I respect your opinion of course, but I cannot agree with you. I am offended by this production! Yes, seriously, I am offended!"

"And you, Clive?" Rose said. "Are you friend or foe? Oh my God! It's foe! I can see from your face! I'm outnumbered, three to one. How can I make you understand? No time! The second bell's going to go any minute. How can I make you think outside the box? You have to open your mind! Let in fresh air!"

The three-minute bell rang urgently.

"No time to make you see the light!" Rose lamented. "Clive, my friend, one of these days… I mean nights… we should go clubbing." With that, Rose hurried off to her seat in the gods.

Vera couldn't find her glasses, and by the time she did find them the one-minute bell was sounding and there was a rush for the lift. Clive, Vera and Marina were the last to squeeze inside. Marina kept an eye on the young man in a suit who was running down the steps, frantically trying to keep pace with the glass lift. As it hissed down the seven floors, an American was telling a story about a Texas rodeo, filling the lift with bursts of raucous laughter. Marina was inches from Clive's face.

"I know how these things work," she whispered. "Ask your people what they want."

People spilt from the lift, while the solitary drinker in the red tie stood panting right opposite the lift entrance, his eyes trained on Clive. By the open door leading to the stalls, Marina held out her hand to Vera, who, in spite of herself, took it. Then, looking at Clive, she said in sing-song voice, "And all our yesterdays have lighted fools. The way to dusty death."

Seconds later she was gone.

Macbeth… What did a quote from *Macbeth* mean? He couldn't remember, but she'd said the word "death", which had to mean danger. And yet, she had delivered the lines in such a light-hearted way. Was that for the benefit of the tail? Or was all this a bit of fun, for old time's sake? Or a trap?

Back in his seat, Clive tried to focus on the second act, and failed. All he could think about was Marina, what she'd said, how she'd looked, and when, in the second interval, Vera confessed that even she had had enough of this diabolical production, Clive was only too happy to leave and walked Vera to the metro station.

"See you tomorrow, my precious, beloved Clive," Vera said, stroking Clive's hand in front of the ticket barrier. "You really should get together with my Annushka… You two would make such a lovely couple…" Vera rummaged in her handbag for her pensioner's free travel pass, found it and waved it about triumphantly. Then she gave Clive a parting kiss and looked him in the eye.

"I understand everything… You have no secrets from me, my English son. I know you loved that woman all those years ago in New York… But just remember: these days, Marina Volina is *one of them…*"

Five minutes later, Clive walked through the lobby of the Metropol to the bar, where he sat down at an empty table. The room was crowded, but he noticed, sitting alone in a corner, an elegant redhead nursing a vodka and orange, looking expectantly at every newcomer. She didn't have to wait long. Two blond giants – Finns, Clive decided – walked over and offered to buy her a drink. Clive ordered a whisky sour and then leafed through the Bolshoi programme. In the centre pages there was a torn-off corner of a white napkin. Marina's message was brief: *Monday, 8 p.m., by fence at back of V's orchard.* Below were Russian capital letters – ЮРБФ – and a crude drawing of a foot.

Clive couldn't help smiling. She was playing the alphabet game. Very simple and very handy. Except she'd added a drawing. She must think I'm losing it, he thought. The English equivalent of ЮРБФ is URBF: U = you, R = are… So what's Б? and what's Ф? Clive looked at the foot. Of course! Being followed.

What, here? Now? At the Bolshoi? Here in the bar? Upstairs in my room? Suddenly, he felt too tired to care. He rolled the napkin scrap into a ball, which he would flush down the lavatory in his room, and took the lift to the fifth floor, where he barely noticed the blonde in a short silver skirt sitting on the landing. When Clive walked past without so much as a backward glance, she spat out the word "pederast".

Clive lay in bed, too troubled to sleep. Was it really only yesterday morning that he had been in the Highlands, the raw wind whipping across his face? What he would give to be back there without a care in the world! Instead, he was holding an imaginary conversation with Marina in his head. It's no use, Marisha! Forget it! Whatever you've got in mind, it isn't going to happen. There was a time when I would have walked on burning coals for you, but that time is long gone. You're barking up the wrong tree.

Inevitably – he couldn't help himself – Clive wondered how to translate "to bark up the wrong tree". All he could think of was the Russian expression, "to turn up at the wrong address", which, somehow, did not carry the same punch.

That's that then, he told himself. Nothing doing. But even as he came to this conclusion, he knew that it was one thing to make up his mind about Marina when she was *not* in front of him, and quite another when she *was*. Her presence unnerved him and aroused in him… what? Nostalgia? Pity? No, not pity. Never pity for Marina. Tenderness? Yes! An overwhelming tenderness. He could see the anguish in her light-brown eyes, and he wanted to take her by her thin shoulders and press her to him and tell her everything was going to be all right.

Really? Was that all? his sarcastic inner voice challenged. You feel nothing more than *tenderness*?

Then from nowhere, ringing in his ears, Clive heard the voice of Byron sounding the alarm: "Tread those reviving passions down…" Passion? Who said anything about passion? Clive knew that he was deluding himself if he did not acknowledge that his feelings for Marina, which had lain dormant for so long, had flared up, taking him completely by surprise.

He began to wonder if he was going mad. Breathing heavily, he threw back the covers and walked over to the window, where he could see the Bolshoi – just. Will you *never* learn? asked his own scathing alter ego. You danced to her tune in New York, and she dumped you for another man. Now she wants your help! *Please*.

"Enough," Clive called out aloud, surprising himself at the sound of his own voice. He threw himself back onto the bed, his head throbbing. I need to cool down, he told himself. I need to detach myself from this world. He picked up the volume of Chekhov he always carried with him and began to read "The Steppe". Even though he had read the story countless times before, it took no more than a few sentences for Clive to find himself sitting in a rickety carriage next to a nine-year-old boy, his uncle and a priest, on a journey across Russia in another century. The descriptions were so vivid, so meticulous, so alive, that Clive could smell the hay on a passing cart, touch the uncut grass waving in the wind, hear the rattle of cartwheels on a muddy road. He even saw dark clouds massing on the endless flat horizon, even though there was no mention of them, because the storm came only much later. But Clive didn't get that far: on page twenty-eight, he fell asleep.

7

Did I really say that? Marina asked herself as she walked home from the Bolshoi. Did I really say, "I can't live here any more. I want out." She stopped in a café for an ice cream and went over every word of her conversation with Clive in the bar and in the lift. From his body language, she could tell that he didn't trust her. And why should he? She had turned him down, made her life with another man, and she never did get to tell him the real reason why. Still, Marina had no regrets; she didn't do regrets. But still, she couldn't help wondering, *What if?* At the Bolshoi, looking into Clive's face, she was struck by the gentleness, the sympathy shining in his dark eyes. Russian men didn't have eyes like that. Certainly not Alexei.

It was just after ten o'clock when she pushed open the heavy mahogany door to Tverskaya 25, climbed the chipped marble stairs, careful not to disturb Oxana, who was snoring gently in her bed on the landing by the lift, and walked up one more floor to her flat, where, in front of her door, she almost tripped over the crumpled, sleeping figure, head resting on a backpack.

"Vanechka," Marina whispered, stroking his head. "My darling Vanechka."

Vanya woke with a start, and for a moment he didn't seem to know where he was. Without saying a word, he followed Marina into the flat, but when Marina tried to hug him, he stood stiff in her arms.

"I was so happy when I got your card," Marina said. "I was so happy that I would see you... Then I saw your postcard... My God, if it's true..."

"What d'you mean, 'if it's true'?" Vanya said furiously, moving towards the door. "I'm telling you that my brother was murdered by your lot, and you don't believe me? I'm outta here..."

"I do believe you, Vanechka, I swear I do... I shouldn't have said that. Please don't go. I'll cook you a nice supper."

Vanya relented and headed straight for the shower. Marina made herself a cup of coffee, Turkish, a taste she had acquired on a trip to Istanbul with Alexei, during one of those false dawns between bouts of chemotherapy. She drank it slowly and waited; she knew that her relationship with Vanya hung in the balance. When he returned, his thick blond hair was dripping wet. Without a word, he sat down at the kitchen table, downed a beer and then tucked into a huge plate of pasta, now and then muttering that it was good, very good, and could he have some more cheese? Marina sat opposite, so happy to hear his deep voice and his particular soft pronunciation: Vanya couldn't say his Rs. He had grown a beard, which made him look like everybody else, but underneath all that blond stubble was a very young, smooth face with a high forehead and a flat nose. He was painfully thin, but, to be fair, he always had been. His blue eyes were more wary than ever, darting all over the place; exactly what you would expect of a nineteen-year-old hacker who works for the highest bidder.

"Oxana didn't stop you?" said Marina.

"No one stopped me. No one was there... And the back door was open. Great security."

"Oh, Vanechka..." Marina reached out and put a hand on his arm. "I'm so miserable about Pasha... I loved him, Vanechka. I really loved him. Just as I love you."

"Pasha came to Moscow because of you."

"Yes. Because of me. And that makes me feel so terrible. I blame myself… for… for everything. But don't you remember how he hated Petersburg, how he said it was so boring?… He kept begging me to find him a job in Moscow, and so I did. A really good job. Well paid. Right up his street. He was so pleased… And then, one morning General Varlamov called me and said that Pasha hadn't turned up at a meeting, which was very unlike him, and he asked if I knew where he was. Well, I didn't. In fact, I'd hardly seen Pasha all month. He'd been working round the clock. Anyway, I went round to his flat… I had his keys. And that's when I found him lying there on the floor. Later, they told me he hadn't been dead that long… Only a few hours. I closed his eyes, Vanechka."

It was a moment she would never forget. It was still so painfully vivid: in one gentle gesture, using her thumb and middle finger, she'd pulled the cold skin of Pasha's eyelids over his open, lifeless eyes. Remembering all this, Marina hid her face in her hands.

"Here," said Vanya, pushing his unfinished coffee in front of her.

Marina wiped her eyes and drank it. Then she reached out and touched Vanya's face, and, as she did so, she saw tears in his eyes.

"They told me he'd died from an overdose of methamphetamine."

"He never touched it," Vanya said contemptuously. Then he got up to make another coffee, which he drank standing up.

"Vanechka, how did *you* find out that Pasha was… was… dead?"

Vanya didn't answer. He stood with his back to Marina, facing the sink.

"I missed you at the funeral," Marina said quietly.

Vanya spun round, furious.

"No way was I coming! Not with all those FSB goons sniffing around, reporting back to your friend Varlamov."

"He's not my friend."

"I know that shit Varlamov," Vanya said with sudden vehemence. "I worked for him in Petersburg, remember. For a couple of weeks."

"And Varlamov remembers you. Why didn't you come to the cemetery yesterday, Vanechka? For the ninth day?"

"I did. I came and went. Made sure they didn't see me, those FSB idiots. I left yellow tulips. Don't tell me you didn't notice."

"How did you manage…?" Marina's question petered out. Perhaps he had gone to the cemetery before dawn? Anything was possible with Vanya. "Vanechka, forgive me, but I don't understand… Pasha told me you'd moved to Baku?"

Vanya didn't seem to hear the question. He was restless; he left the kitchen to prowl in the octagonal entrance hall, opening drawers and the glass doors of the old-fashioned bookcases, looking up at the ceiling, then into the dark dining room. Lit only by a beam of yellow light from a streetlamp outside, Vanya was shaking his head.

"This place gives me the creeps… You bugged?"

"Of course not." And then she wondered. According to Lev, she was under the very lightest surveillance, but things could change in the twinkling of an eye.

"You got my postcard, right? So, you knew right away it was from me? Pushkin!" Vanya laughed. "You wouldn't give me my pocket money till I knew that poem by heart. Do you remember? I got someone else to write out the verses, just in case… Gotta be careful. Can't trust anyone, can you?"

"Vanya, your note… I don't mean the verses, I mean your note… How can you be so sure?"

Marina stopped speaking. Vanya was staring at her with a look of anger, even fury. Then his wary eyes looked up at the ceiling.

"It's hot in here," said Marina. "Let's go out onto the balcony."

Marina turned on the kitchen radio, loud. She picked up two glasses, took a bottle of Beluga vodka from her fridge and went out onto the balcony, where she sat in an old plastic chair facing the playground and the parked cars. Vanya positioned himself with his back to the courtyard, his backpack at his feet and his hood pulled down, so Marina couldn't see his face. Marina poured out the vodka. He knocked his back in one and wiped his mouth with the back of his hand. His voice was low and tense.

"I know exactly how Pasha died. I was *there*."

"Tell me everything," Marina whispered. "Please."

"I was in Baku for a couple of weeks, then about a month ago I got this job in Moscow and needed a place to sleep, just for a couple of nights. Pasha said I could stay at his. He'd been working day and night for that shit Varlamov on some pet project of his, all hush-hush, tracking down some stolen money. They were after some oligarch. Needed to get into his emails, bank accounts, all that shit. Those FSB developers hit a brick wall. Not Pasha. He cracked it. Then he had nothing to do. He was bored so he nosed around the FSB headquarters. You been inside the Lubyanka? Pasha said it was a dump. Anyway, he nosed around and told General Varlamov to his face that his in-house FSB security was rubbish. Pasha had a special word. *Vulnerable.* 'General, your security is *vulnerable*.' That's what he said. Varlamov told him to zip it and get on with his job. Pasha got offended. Said Varlamov had been disrespectful. He got so fucking angry. Said he was gonna get his own back, make Varlamov look really stupid. And he did. And now he's dead."

Vanya broke off. Marina didn't move. The glass of vodka in her hand was untouched. In the silence, she could hear cats fighting.

"Pasha got some time off," Vanya went on. "They told him he could work from home. That's when I turned up, and we hung out together for a couple of days. Played Fortnite... Pasha was just the same... always laughing his head off. Everything was one big joke. He told me a couple of things he'd done... So crazy... so scary... I said, 'You're nuts.' But he didn't care. He thought he'd live forever."

A black cat jumped onto the balcony from nowhere, startling them both, and then ran off again.

Vanya leant forward. "It was Friday afternoon. We'd run outta beer, so I said I'd go down to the bar and get some. He said he'd join me. Just had something quick to do. For his job. I waited for the lift. This guy comes out wearing an MGTS uniform. With a ladder. I clocked the guy. He's gonna work on the distribution box, which is on the landing outside Pasha's flat. 'Don't cut off his internet,' I say to him, as he climbs up the ladder and opens the box. 'Don't worry,' he says. 'I'll take care of things.' So, I go to the bar opposite and sit on a stool, and I ring Pasha and tell him to hurry up, and, by the way, there's a telephone guy on the landing. And as I'm talking, I hear Pasha say, 'Shit, no internet.' I ring him maybe ten minutes later, but he doesn't pick up. Then I see the MGTS guy coming out of the building. He's got a bag on his shoulder, and the ladder. He walks off down the street. I wait another five minutes, buy some beer and go back to the flat. Take the lift."

Vanya held out his vodka glass. Marina poured him another.

"Thanks," he said before tipping back his head and once again drinking the shot in one. "Pasha was lying on the floor. Eyes open. Hand out, holding a syringe. I went over to him and took his pulse... You taught us that first aid stuff when we were kids, remember? Nothing. I put my hand in front of his nose, mouth. Nothing. I looked at his arm. There was trickle of blood from his vein. That bastard had injected him with something."

Vanya was speaking so softly now that Marina had to move closer to hear him.

"His two laptops were gone. And his mobile. I got down on my knees, right beside him, and then I… then I put my head on his chest… It was still warm… and I said goodbye… I made him a promise. I swore to Pasha that I'd get General fucking Varlamov. Then I got the hell out before anyone saw me."

Vanya dragged his sleeve across his face.

"Vanechka," Marina said slowly. "Are you saying that General Varlamov sent someone to kill Pasha?"

"Not someone. He sent a pro. What's the big surprise? The FSB does it all the time. You know that. You live in Moscow. You *work* with these guys…"

Marina leant forward in the darkness.

"I don't work *with* those guys. I work alongside them. I keep my distance. I'm an *interpreter*. But, Vanechka, it was General Varlamov who rang me and told me that Pasha hadn't turned up at some meeting. He was worried about him. He asked if I'd seen him…"

"He set you up."

"No," said Marina, shaking her head. "No." A sickness rose in her throat.

"He had it all planned. He made sure Pasha's death looked like an accident. Made sure it was *you* who found his body."

"Vanechka, *why* would Varlamov want Pasha dead? He was the golden boy, the hero…"

"Why?" For the first time that evening Vanya laughed, short and sharp. "Because your friend the general got it into his head that maybe, just maybe, Pasha had hacked into his private email account. And he was fucking right."

"What?"

"Yeah. Pasha did a superhack and got loads of emails from your friend the general…" Vanya fumbled in a pocket and waved a USB stick at Marina. "Over six fucking months of emails, right here. He made a copy... gave it to me... just in case... That's what he said. 'Just in case.'"

Marina gasped.

"I need money. I'm broke. These emails... What d'you think? Maybe they're worth something? Maybe quite a lot... to some dude who wants to bring the bastard down? Maybe you can find me a buyer?"

Now it was Marina's turn to take her vodka glass and drink the shot in one go.

"It all depends on what's in the emails."

"Personal stuff."

"Can I see?"

"Not here. At my place. Come tomorrow... No, not tomorrow. I'm heading out of town. Come on Tuesday. After dark. And come by metro. No fancy Prius..."

"How do you know my car's a...?" Marina stopped herself. The boy was always one step ahead.

"I'll come on foot. Don't worry. Eggs don't teach the hen."

"Proverbs!" Vanya grinned. "You and your proverbs..."

"In English it's even better. Don't teach your grandmother to suck eggs."

"You and your bloody English... You read me bits of *The Happy Prince* and even some fucking Shakespeare... I couldn't understand a word, but you said, 'Language is music: listen to the sound.'"

"Alexei read you Pushkin."

"He had a great voice... And he made the scary bits really scary." Vanya looked away. "I miss him," he said quietly. "I miss him a lot." Then he turned back to Marina, his eyes bright. "Alexei had this thing about grammar. Said I had to speak clean Russian. *Clean...* That was his pet word. 'Use the instrumental and not the fucking accusative.'"

"You had a brilliant memory... You were the quickest learner."

The light in the next-door flat went out, and now they were sitting in total darkness as a black cloud covered the orange moon.

"You'll need to remember this," Vanya said, glancing around in the darkness. He pulled out his phone and typed out his address in a text message. Marina memorized it and nodded. Then Vanya cleared the text.

"Vanechka... Before you go, tell me: how did Pasha pull it off, this hack? Do you know?"

"Of course I know. He couldn't stop talking about it. He was so fucking pleased with himself."

Vanya dropped his hooded head, and for the next five minutes he spoke so softly that Marina had to ask him to repeat the odd sentence. She was shivering from cold, but nothing would make her move inside and break the spell.

"So, now you know," Vanya said, getting to his feet, picking up his backpack. "If only he'd kept his mouth shut."

Vanya stopped by Marina's front door. "Thanks for the shower, and for the grub and the vodka."

"Do you want to give me your mobile?"

"No point. I change it every week. Sometimes every day."

"Wait, Vanechka... Wait just a moment!" Marina said, her voice pleading. "Let me hug you, just once. Please."

The young man hesitated, then he allowed himself to be hugged.

For almost an hour, Marina sat in her darkened dining room, the parquet floor lit by a shaft of yellow light from the street, while she listened to the odd drunken laugh from the Taiga bar below. In the darkness, she made up her mind once and for all that she no longer wanted to call Russia her home and would do whatever it took to get out. She had told Clive as much, but did he believe her? More importantly, would he help her? She had to prove to him that she meant business, that she was deadly serious...

When the cuckoo clock reminded her that it was three in the morning, Marina decided to get some sleep.

8

That Monday morning, Clive woke early, and, for a moment, he had no idea where he was. The beige curtains were unfamiliar and so was the picture on the wall – a rocky shoreline with an old boat tipped sideways on the sand. And then he remembered. He was in Moscow. And so was Marina.

He decided to wear boots. He would be picking mushrooms with Vera – that much he knew. But the leather boots, which had made the journey from the Highlands to Moscow, were grubby and needed a shine. Clive skipped down the stairs, trailing a finger along the cool malachite wall, and took a seat in the high chair to the right of the revolving doors. This was the workplace of the Armenian shoeshiner, Narek Arkapyan, a short, muscular young man with black hair and eyes, fresh from Yerevan, so he told Clive in a burst of friendly information. He had spent the summer in Moscow, living with his uncle and working at the hotel and doing all sorts of odd jobs. The money was good, twice as good as anything he would have earned in Yerevan, where he was a student. But soon he would be heading home. Which was sad, because, well, he had developed a crush on Liza, the receptionist. Narek let out a deep sigh when he mentioned her name.

Sitting in the high chair, with Narek crouched at his feet, Clive was about to open his copy of the *Financial Times*, given to him by Hyde and still unread, when Narek handed him the new Metropol in-house magazine. Clive looked around. As far as he could tell, his high chair was not in the vision of the two CCTV cameras that were clearly covering the entrance. Nevertheless, he had to assume the tail would be watching. While Narek polished furiously, he turned the pages of the glossy booklet. Next to "Katya, expert masseuse… home visits", there were two words scrawled in the margin: "What news?"

Without the slightest sign of hurry, Clive laid the booklet to one side and casually turned the pages of the crumpled newspaper, as if he hadn't a care in the world, when in fact his mind was racing. He had no idea what to do next. Then the article about Russian broadband, mentioned by Hyde, caught his eye. Clive pulled out his pen.

"Are you any good at crosswords, Narek?"

"No good at all," he replied, working the boots to a glorious shine with his cloth.

Clive turned back to the article, ringed a word with his pen, then scribbled something in the margin. Then he turned more pages, his eye skating over headlines.

"Done," said Narek, with a final flick of his cloth.

Clive tossed the well-worn newspaper onto his seat, pulled out a thousand-rouble note and told Narek that his boots had never looked better.

The moment he stepped out of the Metropol, the full force of Moscow City Day hit him in the face: across the giant screen scudded the number 1147 for the benefit of Muscovites who had forgotten, or never known, how old their city was. Very old indeed. Founded in 1147 by Prince Yuri Dolgoruky. The smiling face of the mayor of Moscow, up for re-election in a few short weeks, shot across the screen at three-minute intervals, wishing sixteen million Muscovites a happy Moscow City Day!

Even though it was only nine o'clock, Clive noticed a steady stream of people filing into Red Square, where, according to

Liza, they could listen to a veterans' band and an army choir, watch Cossack dancers and even take part in a yoga session. Good luck to you all, thought Clive, as he headed for the main road, determined to take a "gypsy cab". Clive stuck out his hand and waited for a car – *any* car – to stop. Only then did it occur to him that perhaps the era of gypsy cabs was over, and he was wasting his time standing by the kerb. Before long, though, an old Ford drew up, and the driver asked him where he wanted to go. "Novodevichy Cemetery," said Clive. They agreed a price, and Clive slid into the back seat. It had always been one of the great perks of Moscow that you could stop any car and strike any deal. Also, it was a simple way for ordinary Muscovites to earn some extra money. I mustn't forget to buy white lilies, thought Clive, as he scanned the street for a flower shop. I've got a date with my hero. He's dead, but very much alive, inside my head.

Half an hour later, Clive made his way down the central pathway of the cemetery, carrying a large bunch of white lilies. As he walked, he nodded to the life-size bronze statues which adorned the graves of famous Soviet scientists, writers and artists, all long dead: the tap-dancing comedian with his boater and his dog; the ballerina in her tutu; the bleary-eyed, bespectacled writer smoking a cigarette. Good morning, all!

Chekhov's tombstone was typically modest. It reminded Clive of one of those old canal houses in Amsterdam: a narrow block of white marble two metres high, topped with a grey slate roof and a name in black letters: Anton Pavlovich Chekhov. Flowers lay scattered over the grave, some fresh, some wilting and some plastic.

Solemnly Clive laid his white lilies at the foot of the tombstone, then he glanced around: nearby, a gardener was digging the soil with his hoe, while a young woman holding white roses scurried between the graves, checking inscriptions, nervous and lost. Was she his tail? Or was it the gardener? Suddenly he didn't care. In a loud and ringing voice, Clive addressed the tombstone in Russian.

"Anton Pavlovich, I am here to say, 'Thank you.' My debt to you is immense. You have changed how I live my life, how I think. Truly! That is no exaggeration. You have given me the most precious gift: a deeper understanding of human nature. You have made me laugh and made me cry within the space of a few pages. And there's something else… For me, your characters are not creatures of fiction: they are real, and they are my friends. At times, they have been my *only* friends. May you rest in peace."

The man with the hoe looked up and smiled.

From the cemetery, Clive went straight to Kievsky station, where he bought a ticket to Peredelkino, a town twenty-seven kilometres west of Moscow. Only that morning, in his hotel room, Clive had watched the mayor of Moscow on TV boasting how much money he was spending on upgrades to the Moscow transport system. This most definitely does not apply to the suburbs, Clive thought, as he sat on the hard wooden bench of the commuter train – the *elektrichka* – and stared out of the grimy window at the dismal landscape of greater Moscow: the piles of litter by the railway track, postage-stamp allotments and decaying tower blocks of the Brezhnev era.

This *elektrichka* was no different from the one Clive had taken when he first came to Russia as a fifteen-year-old boy. In those early days of the Russian Federation, traces of the Soviet Union were everywhere. How well he remembered the main roads lined with kiosks selling ice cream and tobacco and warm Coca-Cola and *shashlik*, kebab cooked on charcoal fires; the local shops, which sold yogurt and sour cream by the ladleful; no wrapping paper for presents, but beautiful hand-painted Christmas baubles, which cost nothing. He remembered village after village of dilapidated dachas with surprisingly neat kitchen gardens, mud roads full of potholes, overgrown lupins and rose bushes pushing against broken fences. To Clive, who at that age had barely left York, it all seemed impossibly exotic.

And it still did.

Sitting in his carriage, he ignored the plaintive cry of a hawker selling air-freshener, fixed his eyes on the dirty window and slipped back in time, fifteen years or more, to those heady days in New York when Marina Volina had been his lover.

They had met in the lift of the United Nations building in New York. He had been so engrossed in a book of Chekhov's short stories that he overshot his floor, the twelfth, home of the British translation service, to find himself on the fourteenth, home of the Russian translation pool. The lift doors opened to reveal a young woman in her early twenties with light-brown hair and wide-set hazel eyes staring straight at him.

"Going down?" she asked in English. Clive nodded, as he felt himself jolted out of Chekhov and into the present by this beautiful face. Her mouth was wide, her manner uninhibited.

"Ah, Anton Pavlovich," said the young woman, this time in Russian, looking at the book in Clive's hand. "So, which is your favourite story?"

"'About Love'," he said, and with those two words he felt as if he had bared his soul to this stranger, told her everything she needed to know. It was his turn to find out something about her. "And you?" he said. "Let me guess. 'The Lady and the Lapdog'?"

"Not at all!" she exclaimed. Her tone was playful. "It's too gloomy. And everything takes too long. I like 'Gooseberries'. It shows us as we really are. Stubborn and not very nice. By the way, your Russian is perfect."

The doors opened at the twelfth floor, where Clive needed to get out, but the young woman held the door open with her foot and they went on talking.

"And how do you know I'm not Russian?" said Clive. "Did I make a mistake?"

"No mistake, but you've got the *Financial Times* in your pocket, which sort of gives you away." Then she held out her hand. "Marina Volina. Interpreter for the UN Russian service. I think we need you at our book club. Our lot are… well, 'lazy' would be putting it kindly. Will you come? This Friday at seven. Fourteenth floor."

At first, they were friends. No, that's not true. He was in love with her right from the start. She was friends with everyone and intimate with no one – or so it seemed. He was dazzled by her, too dazzled; he felt out of his depth. They went running together most mornings, early, through Central Park and down Riverside Drive, ending with breakfast at Sarabeth's in the Hotel Wales between 92nd and 93rd. It was spring, and they ran over petals from cherry blossom trees. Now and then they went to dinner with friends, and occasionally to the movies, where Clive sat with his hands folded on his lap, longing to reach out and hold her hand but not daring to make a move. Every week they met at the book club on the fourteenth floor.

Then one day, three, maybe four months after they had met, Clive stopped on the Gapstow Bridge, by the pond, and told Marina that he was in love with her. He confessed everything: he was desperate, couldn't sleep, couldn't eat and, above all, couldn't go on just being her friend. Marina burst out laughing and kissed him.

They escaped to Maine for the weekend and shared a double bed in which Clive proposed.

"Why the rush?" Marina said.

"Why not? What's the point of waiting? Let's get married and go and live… anywhere!"

Marina moved into Clive's building, renting a flat on the top floor. We have to be careful, she told him. Your lot and my lot will be watching. Everything must be discreet and behind closed doors. For a month, Clive walked on air. They were together almost every night. After making love, they would lie in bed and smoke and talk about their favourite writers. They showed off to each other, Marina reciting Pushkin, Clive quoting Shakespeare, and then vice versa, switching effortlessly from English to Russian and back again. They chucked proverbs and abstruse words at each other until they dissolved in laughter. On clear nights, they would sit on her balcony and look at the stars. The smell of her. The sweet smell of her... It all came back to him in the dirty *elektrichka* as it rumbled on to Peredelkino.

Six months later, Clive was back in London and Marina had left for Geneva. That was almost the end of the story. But not quite, Clive remembered, staring through the grimy window of the train. There was a New York marathon followed by a wedding. Hers. Not his.

One evening at the book club, Marina brought an old friend from Moscow along, Alexei Ostrovsky. He'd been a Russian TV journalist who had worked for the channel NTV in the good old Yeltsin days. Under President Serov, NTV had been purged and become another government mouthpiece. Alexei had given up journalism and opened a fitness centre in Moscow, then a second, and a third. Instead of music through your earphones, he insisted on extracts from self-help books to keep the brain working alongside the body. The idea caught on, and soon everyone wanted to be part of a discussion group on community-led audio apps while they ran on the treadmill. Alexei was thinking of going global, so naturally he turned up in New York.

Clive liked him immediately: he had big blue eyes and a mop of thick blond hair, spoke English with an American accent and was always laughing. The three of them went running together. Alexei would leave Marina and Clive behind: he was faster and fitter.

In less than a week, Clive understood that the idyll was over. Suddenly, Marina was busy all the time: too busy for late-night dinners with Clive, too busy for love, too busy to explain, but never too busy for their morning run. On a beautiful spring day in Central Park, Marina said they should all run the New York marathon. It would be Clive's first full marathon, Alexei and Marina's second. Clive agreed, only because it meant he would see more of Marina.

He thought he was losing his mind. All he could think of was Marina. His heart quite literally ached. He couldn't eat or sleep. He struggled with his translation work, the daily news bulletins which demanded his full attention: the first joint Russia–China military exercise, Hurricane Katrina wreaking havoc in New Orleans and the US Gulf Coast, terrorist bombings on the London tube... It all meant nothing to him. Nothing at all. And then he cracked. One evening, over dinner with Alexei, he poured out his heart.

"Marina's avoiding me," he said in a miserable voice, staring down at his plate of untouched food. "She says she's busy, always busy... I don't know what to do. Have I done something wrong? Offended her in some way? What should I do, Alexei?"

Alexei put an arm round Clive's shoulder.

"I'm the last person you should ask, my friend."

Clive threw off Alexei's arm and faced him, eyes full of hurt.

"You... *You* and Marina?"

Alexei gave a sorrowful smile.

Clive went to ground for a month, like a wounded animal, not answering texts or calls, until Marina and Alexei dug him out of his apartment one glorious sunny day and took him for a run in the park. They had lunch in their old haunt, Sarabeth's, and drank Rioja until, abruptly, Alexei made himself scarce.

"I owe you an apology," Marina said, alone with Clive. "But you must understand, this is not a new story. It's an old story."

Marina and Alexei had been lovers in Saint Petersburg, but Alexei was married, and, when he told her he would never leave his wife, she broke off their relationship, came to New York and got on with her life. Then, out of the blue, Alexei turned up a free man: his wife had left *him*, and he and Marina took up where they had left off. Of course, she felt badly. Very badly. She had never meant to hurt her gentle English friend who spoke such beautiful Russian. Clive was not convinced. Had she ever loved him? Was it all a lie? Marina had looked away, shaking her head, saying that he was too hard on her, that he didn't understand. She was Russian, he was English... The situation was impossible. There was so much more to this than met the eye... She was truly sorry. Could he forgive her? Please?

He could not. Nor did he want to hear any more excuses, any more of her convoluted explanations. Clive spat out a casual observation that Alexei was not the marrying type... The man had a roving eye. Then he walked out of the restaurant, only to be stopped at the door by Alexei himself, who took Clive by the arm and led him back to the table, noisily ordering vodka, then toasting everlasting friendship between the three of them.

The wedding took place a few days before the marathon at the office of the city clerk on Worth Street. Marina wore white, Alexei wore a red rose in his buttonhole, and Clive was their witness. They drank champagne on the roof garden at the top of the Peninsula.

Together they ran the New York marathon. Not long after, Alexei was diagnosed with lung cancer. Wait, that's not right. Clive didn't run the marathon. He collapsed. Alexei and Marina saved his life. And just as Clive came out of hospital, Alexei went in. Out of nowhere, they found a tumour in his lung. After six months of chemotherapy, the doctors gave Alexei the all-clear, and he and Marina moved to the UN offices in Geneva.

. They had a house on the lake, and two years later Clive paid them a visit one rainy autumn day, but it was not a happy occasion. The gaiety had gone. Marina was aloof, and Alexei was ill and tired; they talked of moving back to Saint Petersburg. The conversation was oddly stilted. Marina knew that Clive was married and asked to see a photograph of his wife. Clive produced one on his phone, but he didn't mention they were getting a divorce. Marina told Clive that her father had died, the Soviet general, and that she didn't miss him at all.

Years later, while Clive was working in the British embassy in Moscow, he heard that Alexei had died and that Marina had a job in Saint Petersburg. Every time he went there, he wondered if he would run into her, perhaps leaning over a bridge on the Fontanka or looking at some half-lit mosaic in the gloom of St Isaac's Cathedral, but he never did. *Sudba* had kept them apart. Until now.

On the platform in Peredelkino, where several women were selling mushrooms, cucumbers, apples, blackberries and potatoes, Clive noticed a tall young man haggling over some fruit. Was this his FSB tail? Clive bought deep-pink roses from a flower-seller and went over to the line of taxis and asked to be taken to Old Peredelkino, the writers' village. No one calls it that any more, the driver muttered. The place is much too expensive for writers! You need to be an oligarch to buy a house around here. Anyway, you can walk. It's just down the hill. "I know," said Clive. "I'll give you a thousand roubles. Just take me."

In the car, Clive leant back against the seat. First mushroom-picking with Vera, then Marina. And then what? He knew instinctively that his meeting with Marina would change his life. But there was no turning back. It was his fate, his *sudba*.

For the first time, Clive saw the new church in Peredelkino, big enough for over a thousand worshippers, and he winced at the in-your-face, garish cupolas in flaming red, vibrant green and cobalt blue. He pressed his face to the window urgently. Damn it! Had he missed it? No, it was there! The stone arch leading to the cemetery where Boris Pasternak was buried. As the taxi hurtled down the hill, Clive tapped the driver on the shoulder and asked him to stop at the Boris Pasternak Museum. The car pulled up outside a large white wooden dacha set in an apple orchard.

He wouldn't be there. Of course not. How could Alyosha be in the same place after all these years? But he was. The gaunt-looking Alyosha with his long hair and wild eyes, who knew every verse of Pasternak by heart, was standing by the porch, smoking.

The men embraced warmly, not once but twice. Alyosha begged Clive to stay. "We drink, we talk," he promised. Clive explained that, sadly, he couldn't, not this time, but he'd be back.

"Where are you living?" Clive asked.

"Where? Here, of course," said Alyosha. "Where else?"

As the car drew up outside Lermontov Street 2A, Clive noticed that the big green gate was still hanging on its hinges. But the orchard and the garden were meticulously neat, and there were new blue shutters on the old wooden dacha. Vera was delighted with Clive's pink roses; she clapped her hands like a young girl and placed them carefully in a vase. Inside the dacha, everything was as Clive remembered, rooted in the past, down to the red plush sofa, the lace tablecloths and the silver samovar. On the wall, Clive recognized the photograph of Vera's mother, who had written a book on heroines of the French revolution. It had been dedicated to Stalin, who gave her a plot of land in the writers' village in 1936, but a year later she was denounced and had to spend eight years in the gulag. She never once blamed Stalin, though. (It was those wicked men around him.) After the war, like thousands of others, she was rehabilitated and the Peredelkino plot of land was restored to the family.

Over a sumptuous lunch of pickled cucumbers and ice-cold vodka, "Olivier" salad (Clive's favourite), chicken noodle soup, blinis with red caviar, and apple pie made from her own apples – all of which had been prepared in a minuscule kitchen – Vera fired questions at Clive about his work, Brexit and the Queen. Then she told him about the rich Russians who had ruined Peredelkino with their brick mansions, and the property developers who kept pressuring her to sell – "No way!" – and the ludicrous new laws that made it illegal to burn old branches in your back garden, which, of course, she ignored.

"And that's Volina's house," Vera said suddenly, nodding towards a wooden dacha less than fifty metres away, beyond the apple orchard. She then handed Clive a bucket, and they headed for the woods.

Clive tried to keep his mind on mushrooms – which were poisonous, and which were not? – but he didn't even notice when his bucket was almost full. He kept looking at his watch, thinking about the hour of his meeting with Marina, which was fast approaching.

They walked back to Vera's dacha on a carpet of dead birch leaves, still soft from the rain, while the light from a warm September sun filtered through the trees. The gate onto the road was open, and Anna was standing by her car, talking into her mobile. She waved to her mother, smiled at Clive and went on talking.

Clive had forgotten how small Anna was: not as small as her mother, but she couldn't have been more than five feet. She was slight but athletic, with big dark eyes and jet-black hair cut in a bob with a sharp fringe. Somehow Anna always manages to look elegant, Clive reflected, even now, in black jeans and a black shirt rolled up above her elbows. But he also noticed a difference: she was graver, more imposing.

Over the years, Clive had followed Anna's career in the Russian and British press as she defended musicians and pop stars and rebellious young people. As a result, she was one of the most famous human-rights lawyers in the country, revered by the younger generation. "A thorn in the side of the Russian state" – so one German magazine had written.

Inside Vera's dacha, the three of them sat round the small table, which had been meticulously laid for tea. Vera was reaching for the teapot when she noticed the bruise on Anna's forearm.

"Where did that come from? Yesterday? At the demonstration? Let me see your arm." But Anna pulled down her sleeve.

"Mamochka, don't fuss. You know I can't stand it. It's Nikita Strelnikov I'm worried about. He's lost eleven kilos in three months. We're trying to appeal the sentence, but if we lose, then I don't think he'll survive. Not as a gay man in a Perm prison. That's our holy Russia for you. Meanwhile, Serov is tracking teenagers on social media… In case you haven't noticed, Clive, we live in a police state."

"He's noticed," said Vera, as she poured three cups of tea. She then placed a bottle of red wine and a corkscrew in front of Clive, as well as a bottle of ice-cold vodka, and disappeared into the kitchen.

"I do admire you, Anya," Clive said. "I followed you in the Russian press. I'm afraid I don't do social media, but I gather you're —"

"Please," she said with a wave of her hand. "I don't like compliments."

Anna pulled her chair closer to him. Her face softened.

"I'm glad to see you again, Clive. You're a nice man. And you're very kind to my mother... She loves you like a son. Before you arrived, I was remembering that first summer when you came here... What was it? Twenty-five years ago? Even more? You fell in love with my cousin, Anastasia. You kissed her under the cherry tree, right over there! I saw you. And do you know something? I was jealous!"

"Really? I can't remember a thing about Anastasia... But you, you were so nasty to me, giving me all the worst jobs, like making a compost heap..."

"I was a cow. I'm sorry." Anna put her hand on Clive's arm. "My mother said —"

"What did I say?" asked Vera as she carried in her *pièce de résistance* – a sponge cake bursting with strawberries and cream. Vera began to cut the *tort* with great care, licking her finger now and then.

"You said that Clive was to help in the garden," Anna resumed. "In return for the Russian lessons that you gave him for free, because he was your favourite right from the start. He could do no wrong! God, how that used to annoy me!"

Anna was smiling broadly at Clive, making it clear that she had forgiven him long ago. She hardly touched her cake, while Clive took greedy mouthfuls, then wiped the cream from the corners of his mouth with his napkin.

"You two should spend an evening together," said Vera, pouring out three glasses of red wine.

"I don't have free evenings, Mamochka," said Anna as she raised her glass. "Clive, welcome back to Russia! Here's to you!" They all clinked glasses. "By the way," she added playfully. "The FSB guy sitting outside in the Ford Escort... Is he here for you or for me?"

9

That same Monday afternoon, about seventy kilometres away, Marina was a guest at a wedding party being held at the Lakeside Country Club. The bridegroom was Igor Golikov, a flamboyant Russian oligarch and a friend of the president and his inner circle. He was also a friend of Marina, from her Geneva days. Igor had called her personally to invite her to his wedding – his third – to twenty-one-year-old Nastya, who was floating around in a billowing white dress. She was superbly spoilt and had already thrown her first tantrum of the day after Igor gave her the keys to a Jaguar instead of a Porsche. The bride was surrounded by maids of honour in pink taffeta, all young and beautiful. The champagne was Salon, and the caviar was black. So it was that Marina found herself among the most powerful men in Russia and, by definition, the richest of the rich. With a job to do.

That morning Marina had dropped by the Metropol after her early-morning run. (Her time was good: 15 km in 1 hour 35 minutes.) She had hoped to leave a pair of old shoes with her friend, Narek, the Armenian shoeshiner, but he shook his head and said they were beyond repair. However, he did have a small gift for her, a used copy of the *Financial Times*, which someone had left behind. Foreign newspapers in print were hard to come by these days, he said.

Sitting behind the wheel of her Prius, Marina turned the pages of the newspaper, searching for a response from Clive to her "What news?", but she found nothing. She took a deep, despondent breath. He was turning his back on her. And who could blame him? Marina opened the paper one last time, and there it was, tucked away in an interview with Viktor Romanovsky, Russia's deputy prime minister, proclaiming to the world that Russia had just launched a new generation of communications satellites that would bring high-speed broadband to every corner of the Russian Federation.

The word "satellites" had been circled in black, and, next to it, Clive had scribbled four words in the margin: "How many? Why now?"

Marina leant back against the headrest. Here it was: her first task, a test she mustn't fail. More than that, she had to prove how good she could be; she needed to act fast and present Clive with the intelligence at their meeting that evening. The timing was perfect, she told herself, glancing at the gold-embossed wedding invitation on the passenger seat. Viktor Romanovsky was bound to be there, and, as we all know, people get drunk at weddings and say too much.

By the time Marina arrived at the Lakeside Country Club, the wedding party was in full swing. Guests were filing into the huge tent, passing through a five-metre-tall heart made out of a thousand red roses, while waiters carried trays of champagne across a lawn of artificial grass imported from Miami. At the end of the jetty, a Chinese gin palace bobbed on the man-made lake, a resting place for those too drunk or too tired to go home, while the children from Igor's two previous marriages ran along the white sand. Rumour had it that both ex-wives were present, although no one could be sure. What was beyond a shadow of a doubt was that the marriage between fifty-one-year-old Igor and twenty-one-year-old Nastya had taken place that morning in the main registry office in Moscow and at noon the couple had arrived by helicopter.

Marina glanced up at the clear sky and spotted at least six drones taking pictures of the wedding of the year. Inside the tent, she joined the queue to greet the married couple. While she waited in line, she realized that she was seriously under-dressed in her dark-blue suit with a shocking pink blouse, whereas all the other women wore evening dresses, even though it was two in the afternoon. But Marina didn't care. The ostentation amused her: diamond earrings, sapphire brooches and ruby rings were two a penny, yet Marina, who wore no jewellery at all, felt just fine. She knew that all this flaunting of wealth would please her friend Igor, the host and bridegroom, and the vice-chairman of a state-run oil company on an official salary of $23 million a year, which everyone knew to be a gross understatement.

Igor looked the part in his grey morning suit and white carnation. He was a fit man with reddish hair and designer stubble, and when he saw Marina, he threw out his arms and embraced her. He then introduced her to Nastya, who turned her pretty, heavily made-up, blank face in Marina's direction and faked a smile.

Right, thought Marina, I've said hello. Now I can focus on the matter in hand. He's here somewhere, the man who can tell me what I need to know. She moved among the guests, looking for the deputy prime minister, but instead she caught sight of General Varlamov, urbane and confident, standing in the centre of the tent and surrounded by sycophants.

As Marina stared at Varlamov, a hatred rose in her throat that almost choked her. According to Vanya, he had ordered the assassination of Pasha. Was that really so surprising? she found herself asking with the cool detachment that was at the core of her being. She had been in the Kremlin long enough to understand how the general would see things. Pasha had broken every rule in the book, and from Varlamov's point of view, all that mattered was to limit the damage. A trial would be too messy and reveal too much; assassination was much neater. She could almost hear Varlamov defending his actions.

At the same time, she felt nauseated by the thought of her dead foster son and decided to splash cold water on her face. Marina headed for the ladies, where she found herself standing in front of a basin next to one of the maids of honour in her clouds of pink taffeta.

"Oh my God, look at me," said the girl, staring at her face in the mirror. "I look horrible. My mascara is running... I don't believe it. Non-run – that's what it says on the packet... Nastya will kill me... Oh my God."

Marina studied the girl. She was exquisite: a perfect oval face, high cheekbones and eyes of the palest blue. Her lustrous blond hair was almost white, her voluptuous figure was brimming with youth and health, and she had very long fingernails, perfectly manicured, the colour of plums.

"Did you *see* the bowls of black caviar?" she said, peering at her face in the mirror. "And the champagne? I've never had French champagne before. I'm a country bumpkin."

Marina warmed to this girl with her open, friendly expression and held out her hand.

"My name is Marina Volina. I'm an old friend of Igor's."

"Katya Bogdanova," the girl replied, taking Marina's hand and smiling gratefully. "Sister of the bride, except I'm not. I'm her friend. But Nastya says I have to go around saying I'm her sister. That way people will pay more attention, and that way I'll find a... a..."

"A what?"

"A sponsor. I'm here to find a sponsor. Once I've got him all sorted, then I'm going to get into films. I'll be the next Scarlett

Johansson." The girl giggled in a charming, self-deprecating way.

"Why not go straight for film?" Marina asked.

"It doesn't work that way. You need money... You need money for everything. I've only got five thousand roubles in my purse and not a copeck more. To get into films, you have to look smart, wear nice clothes and get to know all the right people. That costs money. And I don't have any."

Katya seemed keen to share her life story. She and Nastya had grown up together in Khabarovsk, been classmates and shared one dream: to get to Moscow. Nastya got there first and hit the jackpot. She married a millionaire.

"Billionaire," corrected Marina.

"Really?" said Katya with just a flicker of envy in her voice. Then she stared at her beautiful face in the mirror and let out a deep sigh. It was all right for some, she told Marina, confessing that she was always short of cash and that to save money she'd come by train. All the way from Khabarovsk. Endless cups of tea. And these men who kept pestering her. Six whole days and nights.

"Russia's so big... too big... Don't you think Russia's too big?" Katya asked, as she applied a glutinous layer of lipstick.

"Russia is what it is," Marina said kindly. "But Moscow's an unforgiving city, and I can understand that a young person might well feel lost here. How old are you, Katya?"

"Nineteen. But Nastya says I have to say twenty-one."

"In my opinion," Marina said, staring at the reflection of her own face next to Katya's in the mirror, "you don't need a sponsor. You need a job."

"But a sponsor *is* a job," Katya said, opening her blue eyes wide.

The two women left the marble washroom together and went their separate ways, dissolving into the crowd.

Marina was sitting on a bar stool, scanning the bobbing heads of the guests crowded inside the tent for Viktor Romanovsky. She examined the faces of government officials and top civil servants, bankers and captains of industry, and, of course, the heads of the security services – above all, the FSB, the "new nobility", as they were called these days. Everyone here looks pretty happy, and why not? In Russia, life at the top is good. As long as you don't break ranks. Stay loyal and you'll stay safe. Break ranks and anything can happen.

Marina turned to the barman and asked for a Virgin Mary. She was about to add that she liked a lot of lemon when she felt hot breath on the back of her neck.

"Have I told you that you're a very attractive woman?"

She spun round to find herself inches away from the very man she was looking for: Deputy Prime Minister Viktor Romanovsky. The sex pest.

"Viktor Dmitrievich, it's good to see you," Marina said, offering her best smile. "And yes, you have. Several times, in fact. But you're in a minority. Apparently, I've let myself go."

"If only, if only you'd let yourself go! I can't even get you to have dinner with me! I'm a widower, you're a widow… We're made for each other!"

"You think so? You *really* think so?" Marina's eyes were bright, expectant.

"I do! I most certainly do…"

"Well," said Marina, thoughtfully. "Maybe."

The man is so conceited, she told herself. Keep going.

"Really?" said Viktor, looking genuinely surprised. "This *is* a change. A volte-face, as they say in France. I am… well… most encouraged!"

The deputy prime minister was tall and youthful-looking,

with wavy salt-and-pepper hair and the blatant self-confidence of a practised seducer. He took Marina by the arm, his grip strong, proprietorial.

"So, let's not delay... Let's make a date *this week*... I'll get my secretary to call you."

"Talking about this week, I've just read an article in the *Financial Times* on Russian broadband. And you get a mention."

"Don't let's talk shop, *please*. Not *here*, not *now*," Viktor pleaded.

"But I found it so *interesting*... And you were so *articulate*... Do tell me —"

Marina was not able to finish her sentence. Her words were blown away by the deafening sound of a helicopter coming in to land, silencing not just the guests but also the master of ceremonies and the band. The helicopter made its descent with a certain predatory grace, plunging down to earth and then bouncing ever so lightly on the artificial grass lawn, until it nested, like a huge, sated bird, on the grass helipad by the beach. Whining, the blades slowed to a standstill; the engine was cut.

Guests who had put their hands to their ears and kept well away from the blast of the rotor blades now surged forward to welcome Nikolai Nikolayevich Serov, who emerged from the helicopter flanked by bodyguards and holding a stupendous bunch of peonies. By his side was the unmistakable figure of Marina's friend Lev Ignatiev, tall, young and bald.

With dismay, Marina realized that in all the clapping and cheering, Viktor Romanovsky had disappeared. The bridegroom, Igor, and his new wife, Nastya, stepped forward. The bride's mother lost a shoe in her excitement as she took a video of her daughter with the president of the Russian Federation. Someone handed Serov a microphone.

"I am very happy to join you here for my good friend Igor's wedding... Not his first, but let's hope his last – and on Moscow

City Day, when we celebrate the birthday of our great city, the capital of our nation, the largest country on Earth. Igor Ivanovich, this is my wedding gift to you and your beautiful bride."

The president handed over the envelope, which Igor opened.

"I give you an oak seed," Serov continued. "One oak seed. From this one seed a great oak will grow. This seed is a symbol of faith in our great country, and of renewal."

The master of ceremonies introduced a band of Cossack dancers and singers. As they took to the stage, Igor invited the president to step to the front, but he declined; he had to leave in fifteen minutes. He would watch from the back, then slip away.

Marina found herself next to Lev.

"Lyova, is that a new tattoo?" she said, staring at the side of his neck. "The head of a lion?"

"My star sign," Lev said in his deep bass voice. "Do you like it?"

"Yes," Marina said with a smile. "Yes, I do."

Marina was about to go in search of Romanovsky when the president spotted her and, with a wave of his hand, summoned her to his side. The security men parted to let her through.

"I thought you didn't like parties, Marinochka."

"I don't. But Igor was very kind to me when Alexei got cancer. You never forget those things. I felt I should be here… for him."

"You're a loyal friend. That's the quality I admire above all others…"

The president took Marina by the arm and walked towards the beach of silky sand.

"I've been thinking about that boy of yours," Serov said sympathetically. "Such a waste! He was brilliant. I told him so to his face. He was in line for a medal. I told him that, too. My little investigation was going nowhere till Pasha Orlov came on the scene."

Marina knew all about these "little investigations", which had become something of an obsession with the president as he delved into the suspicious activities of those he did not trust. Several times she had been asked by Serov to translate sensitive documents, sometimes straight off the computer screen as he sat alone in his office. She had discovered there was a system in place. Vertical. Top down. And it worked. Step out of line and, well, there would be consequences. Unpleasant consequences. Long ago, Serov had made it clear to his inner circle that he had no objection to those around him getting rich, but only with *his* knowledge and *his* approval and according to *his* rules, unwritten, of course, but understood by everyone. Well, not quite everyone, because some people were still cheating behind his back, and so brazenly! Fifty billion had gone missing during the 2014 Winter Olympics. Serov was seriously put out. He'd summoned General Varlamov and told him to investigate. Nothing happened. The FSB technical team hit a brick wall of Swiss bank accounts. It was Varlamov who said there was a new boy in the research institute who might shed some light. Enter Pasha Orlov, who got to the bottom of things fast and confirmed the president's worst fears – that he was surrounded by liars and cheats.

The president and Marina stood for a moment on the jetty, staring at the golden dragon on top of the Chinese gin palace, surrounded by the FSO close protection team. Someone brought a tray of champagne. The president took a glass, while Marina chose water.

"Have you seen my latest approval ratings?"

Marina nodded and said, "Seventy-two per cent."

They clinked glasses.

"But you can never sit back and relax, not in *my* job. There are people out there who'd like to see the back of me. Oh, yes! They say I've been in power too long, that I'm getting old. Do

I look old? Do I? Don't answer." Serov twirled his hand in the air. "I'll let you into a little secret, Marinochka. Getting old is going to be a thing of the past."

"What exactly do you mean?"

Serov signalled to Lev, who was hovering close by.

"Ask the professor to come over," he said, before explaining to Marina that Professor Olga Tabakova was the director of a stem-cell research institute that had his personal backing. This was the last person in the world Marina wanted to meet, but she was trapped. Minutes later, they were joined by a glamorous brunette in her mid-forties in a white Prada trouser suit that showed off her muscular yoga figure. With no preamble, Tabakova launched into a well-rehearsed sales pitch: her institute had the most brilliant scientists in all of Russia, and the five-year plan was way ahead of schedule. Any minute now, there would be a tremendous breakthrough: men of ninety would pass for forty.

Marina turned to Serov and asked, "Nikolai Nikolayevich, may I ask if you're planning to live forever?"

"Not forever, of course not," said Serov. "But if I look young and have energy, then maybe I can serve my country for another decade or two…"

"You must, you must – for the sake of Russia," Tabakova insisted, giving Marina the coldest of Siberian smiles. She turned her adoring gaze back to Serov and, with more breath than voice, murmured, "Our President *must* continue to serve!"

Marina held her smile in place.

"Forgive me, Professor Tabakova, but I didn't catch the name of your institute?"

"The IfL."

"The IfL. Now let me guess… Could that be the Institute for Longevity?"

"Exactly," the professor conceded sourly.

"My brilliant Marinochka!" said Serov, raising his glass of champagne.

"I must look you up online," said Marina.

"You won't find us online," Tabakova replied tartly. "We remain in stealth. Now, if you'll excuse me…"

The president watched as the professor melted into the crowd, then under his breath he murmured, "I've given her millions. Let's see what she can deliver."

Serov drained his glass, then he stopped; he had reached his limit. It was water from now on, he informed Marina. Lev came loping across the lawn in big ungainly strides to remind the president that it was time to leave.

"This weekend, Marinochka, I want you to look smart," said Serov. Then he turned to Lev. "Lyova, Marina Andreyevna needs some money for expenses."

"Not a problem," said Lev, giving his stock-in-trade answer to most presidential requests. He raised an eyebrow and smiled at Marina, as if to say, "Lucky you."

"Give her anything she wants," said Serov. "She's going shopping."

Instead of saying "thank you", Marina quoted her favourite Russian proverb: "On arrival, you're judged by your clothes: on departure, by your mind." Instinctively, she searched her mind for the English counterpart. "Don't judge a book by its cover" came closest.

Serov dismissed the proverb with a wave of his hand. Then, flanked by bodyguards with earpieces and dark glasses, and with Lev loping behind, the president hurried across the grass to the helipad, where his host, Igor, was waiting to see him off.

Marina watched as the helicopter soared towards the sun.

Trumpets announced that lunch was served, and, for the next hour and a half, Marina made polite conversation at a table with bankers and oligarchs, who, mercifully, talked across her, assuming, as they so often did with women in Russia, that she had nothing to add to the conversation, which suited her just fine.

She kept looking around for Romanovsky. Suddenly she saw him leaning against a pillar, flirting with the bride. Marina slipped away from her table and took her place at the bar, a few metres away from her quarry. She caught Viktor's eye and smiled, whereupon Viktor was dislodged by the bridegroom, no less, who came over to claim his bride for the first dance. Dozens of guests surged forward to watch, but not Romanovsky, who sauntered over to Marina.

"No dancing? Not even with me?" he asked, holding out a hand, which Marina ignored.

"I don't like dancing… I like talking, and we were having such an interesting conversation before the helicopter drowned us out. The interview you gave to the *Financial Times*… Well, it just blew me away. I had no idea that ultrafast broadband is being delivered to the remotest parts of Russia, all thanks to these new microsatellites… Dozens and dozens of them. Why so many? I'm really curious."

"You're curious, are you?" said Viktor Romanovsky, looking sharply at Marina. Beneath all the flirtation was a cool head. "Well," he said with a neutral smile, "allow me to be curious as to why *you* are so curious about microsatellites. I would have thought poetry was more your thing."

"I have to keep up to date with all the latest terminology. That's part of my job. How can I translate things like 'full fibre coverage' if I don't know what I'm talking about?"

"All right, all right!" said Romanovsky, taking a glass of champagne from a passing tray. "Officially, it's all about broadband. We're a very big country and we need a lot of microsatellites. Unofficially, now that would be telling! They'll chop my head off if I breathe a word. However, because it's you, my dear Marina,

I can tell you that these microsatellites will give Russia the edge *when the moment comes*. And that moment is coming soon. And, for your ears only" – and here Romanovsky dropped his voice – "I had a hand in the planning. A *big* hand. You might even say I was the architect of this bold little adventure. Our dear president isn't exactly in his first youth. He needs support from… How shall I put this? Younger minds. He wanted to stop at fifty. I told him to double it. 'Think of what's at stake!' I said. In the end we've put up ninety-four microsatellites. Of course, I was delighted to be of service. Now, that's enough! No more talking shop! About that dinner… You're so bewitching, Marina Andreyevna. Brains and beauty: the perfect combination. Not to mention your smouldering sex appeal…"

Marina slipped her arm out of his.

"Tell me, Viktor Dmitrievich, how do you have *time* for such… such *exhausting* flirtation? Aren't you supposed to be busy with the affairs of state?"

"For a beautiful woman, I always have *time*. And for a beautiful and *clever* woman, well, I have all night!" said Viktor, squeezing Marina's hand.

Marina was asking herself how much more she could stand of Viktor's nonsense, when they were interrupted by one of those people who take up a lot of space and make a lot of noise: the oligarch Boris Kunko. He had no neck; instead, his square head seemed to sprout from his shoulders; his eyes were small and suspicious, and he was bald, except for a rim of grey hair around the back of his head. For some reason, Marina had a soft spot for Boris. And so, it seemed, did Viktor Romanovsky.

"My friend!" Boris exclaimed in a deep voice, his arms outstretched. Boris and Viktor embraced, a big, all-enfolding hug.

"You know Marina Volina?" said Viktor. "Our president's favourite interpreter?"

"Who doesn't know Marina Andreyevna? She's a star! Good evening, my dear."

Boris offered his sweaty palm, which Marina took.

"Next time you're in London, Marina Andreyevna, please call me. I'll invite you to watch a football match! Have you ever seen one? I thought not! Well, now's your chance. My team – not yet, but soon; we're in negotiation – is called Tatonom Hatspur."

"Tottenham Hotspur," Marina corrected. "Is it for sale?"

Boris waved a hand to indicate that the question was neither here nor there.

"My son, Dima, is going to Eton, while my daughter, Zoya... I swear to God, she's the next Rostropovich. She's studying at Royal College of Music. Zoya, come over here!" Boris waved to a young woman in a long beige dress who was standing alone in a corner.

Zoya reminded Marina of a frightened bird. She winced when her father called her "a genius", held out a limp hand and murmured that her cello-playing was very average and that she would be lucky to get a job in a string quartet.

Suddenly the band belted out the Rolling Stones, and young women in diamonds and emeralds rushed to the dance floor, gyrating suggestively. They were followed by middle-aged oligarchs, who tossed their jackets to one side and began to dance with surprising abandon, turning back the clock and reliving their youth.

Marina excused herself and pushed her way through the clamorous, increasingly drunken crowd towards the beach and the car park, noticed by no one except General Varlamov, who sat alone at a table by the exit.

By nature, the general was an observer, not a participant, a man who prided himself on his powers of observation. He had noticed that the president was sweating much less than usual, that he had been wearing a smart new suit, and that his unkempt private secretary, Lev, had, for once, made an effort.

Volina didn't look too bad either, although her navy suit was on the dull side. The general also thought of himself as a shrewd judge of human nature, and one of the reasons he came to these occasions was to keep an eye out for those oligarchs who were getting too big for their boots, who couldn't resist showing off, who might even be thinking of breaking rank.

The general knew exactly on which side *his* bread was buttered. Serov was not only his president, but also his patron. What was good for Serov was good for Varlamov; it was as simple as that. Of course, now and then the general allowed himself a secret little flutter. One couldn't be subservient *all* the time.

Marina was leaving the wedding tent, one eye on a drone buzzing about in the blue sky, when Varlamov blocked her path.

"So, you went to the Bolshoi after all," he said, letting the remark drop gently, like a falling leaf.

"I did," said Marina. "I changed my mind. A woman's prerogative, wouldn't you say, Grigory Mikhailovich?"

The general gave Marina a cautious look. Was she making fun of him? He could never be sure.

Marina held the general in a solemn, relentless stare. Varlamov looked away.

"At the Bolshoi you met the Englishman who was with Vera Seliverstova. She has a daughter called Anna, a political activist – in other words, an enemy, and very much on our radar." He continued less delicately, "The mother, Vera, is not much better, but at least she's old. You met Vera at the Bolshoi. Were you going to mention it?"

"Of course I was going to mention it. But this is a wedding, and I thought we might, just this once, enjoy ourselves. It's also, in case you've forgotten, a public holiday."

"I don't have holidays," said Varlamov gloomily. He held up his glass to the light, inspecting the champagne. He turned the glass this way, then that, and drank it all in one go. "I went to a fortune-teller the other day. Not the sort of thing I usually do, but the woman is a friend of my sister's. Anyway, this fortune-teller said I was heading into a great storm. She couldn't tell me if I'd come out alive. That's nice, isn't it?"

"Did you have her arrested?" said Marina. Before Varlamov could answer, she added, "That was a joke. You used to laugh at my jokes, Grigory Mikhailovich. But not today. Is something bothering you? Spoiling your fun?"

"Since you ask, yes. I'm not in the best of moods. Why? You want to know why? Let me tell you. My wife spends far too much money. Now she wants to buy this huge ski chalet in Krasnaya Polyana. My teenage daughter won't speak to me because on Saturdays I want her home by one a.m. My ten-year-old son stares at his mobile or his iPad twenty-four hours a day. I get up every morning at five o'clock and go to bed at midnight. I'm going prematurely bald and I've gained three kilos. What else do you want to know?"

"Goodness me," said Marina. "You do need a holiday. If you'll excuse me…"

But the general was not done.

"When you left the Bolshoi, you said something to Franklin in English. Why?"

"I like to show off."

"What exactly did you say?"

"I quoted *Macbeth*. 'And all our yesterdays have lighted fools. The way to dusty death.'"

"Why such pessimism?" asked the general.

"Why not? Life is difficult for Russians."

"You should find yourself a new husband, Marina Andreyevna. I've never met a woman on her own who's happy."

"Is anyone happy?"

The Russian national anthem erupted on the general's phone. He took the call, and Marina slipped away. It was time to go home, time to meet the man who could change her life and set her free.

The road sign "Peredelkino, Rest Zone" always made Marina smile, and so did the sight of her magnificent Afghan hound, Ulysses, who came bounding to meet her through the apple orchard.

10

"You came the back way?" Marina said, leaning against the rickety fence that separated her orchard from Vera's and peering past Clive into the forest and the fading light.

"Yes. And my tail's sitting in a Ford Escort parked right outside Vera's dacha. I noticed him when we came back from picking mushrooms. He's very young. I think he's watching a movie."

"Porn, more likely," said Marina. "I saw him too. He looks about fifteen. Probably a trainee."

Marina spoke in Russian, and she went on speaking in Russian for the whole evening, which was fine with Clive. He understood that she wanted the safety of her mother tongue, and, after all, she had the perfect excuse: they were in Russia.

"You didn't tell Vera Petrovna you were seeing me?" she said as they crossed her overgrown apple orchard in front of the dacha.

"No."

Clive had told Vera that he was going to see Alyosha at the Pasternak Museum, and Vera had pretended to believe him.

"Good. We can only meet like this once. It's not safe. Next time I'll have to think of somewhere else."

Clive was about to say, "There's not going to *be* a next time," when Ulysses came racing across the garden, stopping dead in front of Clive, sniffing at his legs, then licking his hand.

"He's beautiful," said Clive, stroking Marina's beloved pet, a magnificent, huge, lean dog with anxious, watchful eyes.

"He's a pedigree, but he must have run away from home or been abandoned, because I first met him on the rubbish dump by the garage while he was scavenging for food. He was all skin and bones," she said, leading the way into the dacha. "I gave him an old ham sandwich from my briefcase, left over from lunch, and he followed me home. He stood outside my gate all night. In the morning, I decided I had to adopt him. When I'm at work, my neighbour Tonya takes him in. She has three other dogs, and they all play together. Everyone loves Ulysses."

Marina shivered. There was a chill in the air.

Inside the dacha, she lit a fire in the small sitting room, then poured out two glasses of red wine, a present from a Chinese delegation. Rather expensive and rather good, she explained. They clinked glasses. She was wearing jeans and a loose black T-shirt that slipped, and now and then Clive caught sight of a bare shoulder. Her skin shone in the flickering firelight. She looks so young, he thought, so beautiful.

Clive sank into the old sofa and looked around, noticing there was very little furniture – just the bare minimum. Even the bookcase was half empty. Everything about the place was sparse and neat, but not quite lived in, not quite home.

Ulysses shambled over and put his head in Clive's lap, looking up at him with trusting eyes.

"He likes you," said Marina.

"I'm not sure why I'm here," Clive said abruptly. "You're not trying to recruit me, by any chance?"

Marina's whole face relaxed and she laughed out loud.

"The president did mention it… And so did General Varlamov. Are you interested?"

"Not remotely."

"Of course not," she murmured, crouching down to give the fire a prod. "Do they know about this meeting?"

"They?"

"Hyde? The ambassador?"

"No."

"I knew I could trust you."

"Really?" said Clive carefully. "I wonder why. You made a fool of me once. What makes you think you can do it again?"

Marina was taken aback. She stared at Clive, shaking her head.

"You're still angry with me after all these years?"

Yes, he thought, I am still angry… Why? Because we could have had a life together, children… You threw it all away! Because I loved you as I've never loved anyone else. Because… because it's just possible that I still love you, damn it!

Clive kept his eyes on Marina as he sipped his wine. Ulysses shuffled over and lay at his feet.

Meanwhile, Marina took a photograph from the mantelpiece and handed it to Clive.

"You can keep it, if you like," she said.

It was a picture of Alexei, young and healthy, wearing his Russian *shapka* on a snowy day in New York. Clive smiled at the open, confident face of the man who had saved his life, stolen his love and stayed his friend, all in the same summer.

"Alexei liked you a lot. He said you were a good and honourable man. Before he died, he left something for you. I'm so glad I can give it to you after all these years."

Marina went over to her bookshelf and pulled out two nicely bound green-leather volumes: the collected works of Chekhov. Inside the first volume, Alexei had written in his flamboyant cursive script: "To my friend Clive, who thinks and speaks and feels like a Russian."

"Thank you," said Clive, stroking the green leather. "Were you happy with Alexei?"

"Happy?"

Marina sat down in an armchair, facing Clive.

"Yes... Yes, I was," she said. "For the first year, maybe two. I was very happy. And then... And then along came..."

"...the cancer?"

"Monique, a French interpreter. And there were others..."

"I warned you."

"You did... You did, my dear Clive."

He winced at those words.

"You should have married me," he said.

Ulysses moved from Clive to Marina, curling up at her feet.

"Yes," she said quietly. "I should."

This admission came as a complete surprise to him. He sat upright in the sagging sofa.

"Why didn't you?" he blurted out. "I've never really understood... I thought we were... well, perfect together. Perfect in every way. So, what did I miss?"

"You didn't miss a thing," Marina sighed. "It's just that the chasm was too big. I couldn't make the jump, the leap of faith, whatever you want to call it. I couldn't put my parents through the... well, the shame of it. I suppose that was it. Yes, the shame! My parents were old-fashioned Soviets, remember? My father was a Soviet general, my uncle was in the KGB. It was my duty to marry a Russian. It wasn't easy. I gave it a lot of thought... For days on end, I couldn't think of anything else. Believe me, I weighed everything up... If I married you, I knew I'd lose my job, have to start again. I'd be totally dependent on you, which you wouldn't like at all, and sooner or later you'd resent me and stop loving me. That's what I thought at the time. And there was something else... I never told you at the time, but the FSB were asking questions. I'm pretty sure they didn't know about us, but they did know that all my friends were foreigners, and they didn't like it. I was told if I didn't change my ways, I'd be sent back to Moscow. I was under so much pressure, Clive, you have no idea… From my family, from the FSB… I cracked. Alexei was a much easier option. Surely you can see that?"

Marina let out another deep, spontaneous sigh, then turned her back to Clive and faced the fire, holding onto the mantelpiece with both hands. She stood quite still. When she turned round, her face was red from the heat.

"I was sure that you'd forget all about me," she said. "That you'd find yourself a lovely English wife, have five children and be really happy. That's the life I imagined for you… Do you have children?"

"No. And my wife and I are divorced."

"I'm sorry. I really am."

Marina poured more wine, then tended to the fire, finding a big log and placing it carefully in the middle. There was an outburst of spluttering and crackling, and new flames leapt up. Satisfied, she turned and faced Clive and waited.

"So how did you end up in Moscow?" he asked. His voice had softened.

"I was *summoned*… Of course, I should have said 'no'. Alexei warned me to keep away from Moscow and above all to keep clear of Serov. He said it over and over again when he was dying."

"Why didn't you?"

"How could I? The president was in Saint Petersburg for the Economic Forum and the mayor had put me in charge of translation. Alexei was dead. I was alone. And there was Nikolai Nikolayevich, telling everyone how much he'd loved my father, that I was like a daughter to him. The next thing I knew, I was told to pack my bags and move to Moscow. I had landed the plum job: personal interpreter to the president. It was a huge privilege, a very great honour – or so everyone kept telling me.

How *could* I turn it down? What excuse could I give? Nikolai Nikolayevich has always been kind to me. There was no personal animosity. And the regime? Well, I thought I could keep all that at arm's length. Bury myself in language and syntax."

Ulysses let out a big yawn and stretched out his long, shaggy limbs in front of the fire. Marina pushed him away with her foot.

"Don't say anything, not yet… I know I'm throwing a lot at you, out of the blue… And why should you trust me?… No reason… No reason at all… Still, there are some things you have to know. When I accepted the job in Moscow, I thought I knew what I was doing. Being an interpreter, going to conferences, sitting next to the president and whispering in his ear. But it didn't turn out that way. Serov wanted my help in all sorts of areas… Secret areas where he was investigating people he didn't trust: a politician, an oligarch, anyone he saw as a threat. It turns out that languages are very, very useful… Talking French to Swiss bankers in Geneva, or English to lawyers in the British Virgin Islands, or German to disgruntled ex-Deutsche Bank employees with an axe to grind… I helped dig up the dirt. And there's lots of it, Clive, believe me. And some of it has rubbed off on me. I accepted presents. Big ones. Like a villa on the Black Sea."

"Why are you telling me this?"

"Because I want you to understand how I've arrived at this point… this point of *betrayal*… My God, Clive, do you think this is easy for me? Do you think I don't know what I'm doing?"

"Our people won't believe you, Marina. They'll think it's some sort of trap."

"I know your people won't believe me. And you probably don't either. Why should you? I dare say you think this meeting is a set-up. Well, it's not. And I'm no spy. I've been trying to put myself in your shoes. 'Why now?' That's what you must be thinking, isn't it? That's what anyone would think… So let me explain…"

"A Damascene moment?"

"Not at all. On the contrary, it's been a slow, gradual process. I don't know how to explain this… In the end, it was the lying. The bare-faced lying. It got to me. It still gets to me. I feel ashamed. I feel dirty."

Marina picked up the iron poker and poked this log and that, although there was really no need. Ulysses watched her as he lay stretched out, his head on his paws.

"I thought about this culture of lying," Marina went on. "I tried to understand how we in Russia had got to this point. The whole administration lies, from Serov down, and they're proud of it! They have the perfect excuse: 'Everyone lies, the US, the UK, everyone – it's all a game.' But that's the sticking point for me, because *it's not true*. Every country does *not* put lying at the heart of its policy, at the heart of its thinking."

Clive sat forward on the sofa, holding his drink with both hands, staring down at his feet. His boots had lost their shine in the muddy woods.

"But Marina," he said, keeping it formal, avoiding "Marisha" in case she got the wrong idea. "Forgive me, but you *must* have known what you were getting into when you accepted the Moscow job… You of all people!"

"Nothing can prepare you for what happens inside the Kremlin. Nothing. I knew I had to get out, but how? Then you came along."

With a crack like a pistol shot, the fire spat out a burning ember, which landed on the wooden floor. Instantly Clive was on his feet, grabbing the shovel, tossing the charred wood back into the grate.

"You can tell your people," and here Marina switched to English, "about the straw that broke the camel's back. By the way that's a tricky proverb. There's no equivalent in Russian, as you must know – you, the master of idioms. We say 'the very last drop', meaning the drop that overfills the cup." Marina paused and switched back to Russian. "Well, for me there was such a moment. It was the murder of a twenty-year-old boy. My foster son, Pasha. Not officially, but… well, I loved him. He was like a son to me. And I love his brother, Vanya."

In a voice that thinned, now and then, to a whisper, Marina told Clive about her years with "her boys", about the responsibility, the love and, above all, the guilt she felt over Pasha's death at the hands of Grigory Varlamov.

"'Vengeance is mine'," said Marina. "The first page of *Anna Karenina*… Right at the top, remember?"

Clive was shaking his head.

"Marisha…"

"You're the only person who's ever called me that," Marina said quietly. "Alexei called me Marinochka. So does the president."

"Marisha, what *exactly* do you want?"

"I want a new life somewhere far, far away. For me and for Vanya."

"They'll come after you."

"Not if your people protect us. Not if we get a new identity."

"They'll keep on looking for you, you understand that? And if they find you, they'll kill you. To Serov you'd be a…"

Clive broke off but Marina finished the sentence.

"…a traitor. Don't be afraid to use the word. I know what I'm doing. I know the risks I'm taking. But the trick is not to get caught, don't you agree? Listen to me, Clive. We can outsmart them. They're not so bright. Believe me, I know."

"Marisha, it's not a game."

"It is. It's all a game, my dear, dear Clive. I need your help. I can't do this on my own… I can't take even one step out of Russia without official permission. I'm a security risk, you see.

But I'm not asking for charity. I *know* how these things work. That's why I said to you, 'Ask your people what they want.' Did you? Or did you make it up, all that about the satellites? You came back to me so fast. Maybe too fast…"

Clive got to his feet, pushed his hands deep in his pockets and paced the bare floorboards, away from the fire.

"I didn't ask 'my people', because I didn't need to. On the flight over I had a long talk with Martin Hyde. He wants to know exactly how many micro communication satellites Russia has launched and why all at once."

"Ninety-four," Marina said. "We've launched ninety-four microsatellites this year. My source is the deputy prime minister, Viktor Romanovsky. But as for 'why', I'm not there yet. But Hyde is right to wonder… There *is* something going on. The president keeps dropping hints about landing a knockout punch. Serov's words, not mine."

Clive looked at Marina standing there against the crackling, leaping flames. She was a shadow of her former exuberant self, washed out, too thin, but it didn't matter. He felt an overwhelming tenderness for her disillusioned Russian soul. Then, once again she took him by surprise.

"This doesn't have to be about me," Marina said, struggling with each word. She was crouching beside Ulysses and stroking his head. "I don't deserve your trust, your friendship. I get that. I have no right even to ask for it… But think of your country. You're a patriot. My country wants to do you harm, and you can prevent it, if you help me. Think of me as… nobody. I'm offering you a deal. Take it or leave it."

Marina spoke the last words almost in a whisper.

Clive was staring at her, frowning, trying to read between the lines, trying to understand what she *really* meant.

"So, you *did* love me in New York?" he said. "I want to hear you say it… I *have* to know."

"Yes, I loved you, Clive," she said, looking at him, her eyes full of sadness. "But I kept myself in check, held back because I knew it was useless... I was destined to marry a Russian. That was my fate, my *sudba*, and I accepted it."

Marina stood up and arched her back. "Anyway, it was all so long ago. That was *then*. Now we've got more serious things to think about..."

"Is there anything more serious than love?"

Marina was sitting in her armchair, resting her hands on the arms, breathing quickly.

"Don't make this so difficult!" she begged. "I know how these things work, Clive. I need to put something on the table *now*, something that will make your people take me seriously. I can get you a stack of General Varlamov's private emails by Wednesday, the day after tomorrow. Thirty-six hours. Will that do?"

"Do you know what you're getting into? Do you?"

Marina looked at Clive, her eyes desperate, pleading.

"You're the only person I can turn to... Don't you see?" she said. Then she got to her feet and stood in front of the fire. Clive did the same and stood inches away from her.

"I've made such a hash of things," Marina whispered, and then, in a move he remembered so well, she leant forward and rested her head against his chest.

"Marisha," he whispered. "Marisha..." He stroked her hair, her cheek, and, with only the slightest hesitation, they kissed with an intensity that took both of them by surprise.

It would take him days, even months to make sense of his feelings that evening in Peredelkino as he and Marina made love after so long. His feelings of then collided with the feelings of now, and he was overwhelmed. Lying on his back, he shut his eyes. Marina kissed his eyelids.

Later, in the darkness, Marina sat on the edge of the bed, her back to Clive, while he trailed a finger down her spine over the bumpy ridge of bones. A sliver of light came obliquely through the window from the lamp on Leo Tolstoy Street.

"You've got the body of an eighteen-year-old."

"I'm a forty-year-old woman. Clive, listen to me. This is just a one-off. You understand, don't you? We can't meet here again. What time is it? You have to get back to Vera."

Clive bent forward, kissed her back between the shoulder blades and said:

"It was the nightingale, and not the lark, that pierced the fearful hollow of thine ear."

"It was the lark, the herald of the morn," Marina answered, twisting round and laying the palm of her hand against Clive's cheek. Then, with infinite sadness, she added, "Oh, Clive, this is all too little, too late."

They talked on and on, and it was midnight by the time Clive got back to Vera's dacha, where he found her asleep in front of the film they were supposed to watch together: *Ivan Vasilyevich Changes His Profession.* Clive turned the sound off and poured some white wine into one of Vera's glasses – hand-painted with pink roses and surely a survivor from before the revolution. He had just sat down in the frayed red velvet armchair when Vera woke with a gentle snort. Clive muttered something about a lengthy supper with Alyosha, who then insisted on reciting Pasternak, but Vera cut him off.

"I don't like it when you lie to me," she said, looking sternly at Clive. "I'm no fool."

Vera helped herself to a glass of Baileys, her favourite night-cap, and asked no questions. As they stood together outside on the veranda, Clive looked up at the stars, at half-hearted clouds scudding across the bruised face of an almost full moon, at the gnarled shape of the apple trees, which looked like old men. He felt so miraculously alive, born again. He wanted to reach out and pocket the night, whole.

"It's all right," Vera murmured, patting his arm. "You must lead your life the way you see fit. I'm not here to judge you."

Clive took Vera's small hands and kissed them. As he climbed into his Yandex taxi, the Ford Escort parked opposite came to life, and with it, the FSB tail, who closed his laptop. On the drive into Moscow, Clive leant back in the car and tried to digest the last few hours. What surprised him most was that she had felt so familiar: her smell, the softness of her skin, the way she let out an almost frightened gasp as he entered her. It was as if nothing had changed, nothing at all. And yet, Clive understood perfectly that the opposite was true: his whole life had been turned on its head.

11

"What *is* this fixation with Anton Chekhov?"

General Varlamov had walked into Marina's office in the Senate Palace without knocking, one of his many irritating habits. Marina was sitting at her desk, her laptop open, correcting the spelling on menus for a reception the next evening in honour of the German ex-chancellor, now on the board of Gazprom. Reluctantly, she looked up and forced herself to smile.

"Yesterday morning," said the general, sitting himself down in the chestnut armchair, "your friend Franklin took himself off to Novodevichy Cemetery and laid flowers at Chekhov's grave, and then, right in front of the tombstone, he made a speech. Unhealthy, don't you think?"

"He likes Chekhov," Marina shrugged. "At the Bolshoi, he told me he was translating some of his stories."

He also told me, Marina thought, staring steadily at Varlamov, and for once able to put her hatred of the general to one side, that he would help me get out of here and never come back. But everything depends on the level of intelligence I can provide. It has to be first-class. Then, and only then, will *they* get me out. This is what Clive promised after we made love.

Marina stared pointedly at her screen, hoping that Varlamov would take the hint that she wanted to be alone, but the general showed no sign of leaving; instead, he paced about her office, deep in thought. It was a particularly nice first-floor office, with a balcony, a high, corniced ceiling and windows on two sides, so the room was filled with light. The heavy nineteenth-century furniture was not to her taste, so she had ordered a black leather revolving armchair from Italy, which she called her "thinking chair". Oh, and a Nespresso coffee machine. From her balcony, she could see Red Square and St Basil's. Was that the reason General Varlamov kept dropping in? To admire the view?

"Yes, but *flowers*? A *speech*?" the general persisted.

"Maybe he's just eccentric… That's an English characteristic."

Not in bed, she thought to herself, keeping her eyes fixed on her computer screen. In bed, he's gentle and ardent. Last night, I felt desired… It was so surprising, so lovely… His touch, his kisses, all the things I've missed for so long.

Marina's last years had been almost entirely celibate, except for a fling with a German interpreter, which lasted only a few weeks and ended when he wanted to take her to meet his mother in Worms. Otherwise, she had lived like a nun, caring for Alexei. Then, once he had died, she found that she had no appetite for relationships. But now, everything had changed.

"How do you translate soufflé?" Marina asked.

"Soufflé," the general replied with a casual wave of the hand. His mind was on something else.

"That's what I've put. In Cyrillic of course."

Marina's office was in the heart of the presidential administration, which filled most of the Senate Palace, a majestic eighteenth-century building, yellow with a green dome, inside the Kremlin. Just down the corridor from Marina, General Varlamov had a courtesy office, which he could use whenever he pleased, although everyone knew the general was happiest in his penthouse office on the top floor of the Lubyanka, the headquarters of the FSB.

"Maybe Franklin's gay. What do you think?" Varlamov asked suddenly.

"He was married to a *woman*."

"That could have been a front."

"You're too suspicious, Grigory Mikhailovich."

"Yes, yes, I am… My wife says the same. I just thought you might know, that's all. From your time in New York, when you were young and carefree."

Marina searched the general's face for suspicion, even mockery, but found none, which told her that he didn't know about her affair with Clive all those years ago. It was not in her FSB file. In those days, she reflected, the FSB was strapped for cash, and I was a nobody, not worth the expense of a tail.

"In New York, I wasn't exactly carefree," Marina said slowly and with just the right hint of reproach. "My husband got cancer."

"He was unlucky. I've had cancer and I'm fine."

To Marina's dismay, the general pulled out his vaporizer.

"May I?"

"Of course."

The general turned back to his phone and to his operative's report.

"Where were you this morning? I looked for you… No one knew where you'd gone."

"I was running."

At first light, she had driven from Peredelkino to Luzhniki Stadium and timed herself for a half-marathon pace run, pretending this was for real. She ran with a lightness that she hadn't felt in years, completing 21 km in 2 hours 8 minutes 44 seconds. That was 6.1 km/h, a personal best for that year.

"At the Bolshoi, you gave Franklin your card… Why did you do that?"

"So he can call me, in case he changes his mind."

"Changes his mind?"

"About running," Marina said in a helpful, obliging voice. "You told me to ask Clive Franklin if he would like to go running. So I did. He said he was too busy, but you never know, do you? These trade talks might come to a grinding halt, and then he'd be as free as air."

"May I see this card of yours? If you don't mind?"

Marina pulled out her desk drawer, where she kept her business cards and a secret supply of cigarettes for Lev. With a patient smile, she handed Varlamov an ivory name card. He held it between his manicured fingers, read it and turned it over. On one side was Russian, on the other side English.

"How many languages do you speak, Marina Andreyevna?"

"Let's see… Not counting Russian, I speak English, German, French, Italian, Spanish, some Turkish and a bit of Farsi."

"Very impressive," said Varlamov. "But when push came to shove, you bottled out."

"Meaning?"

"On paper, you've always agreed to help us. If I remember rightly, in Geneva you even took a course in basic surveillance. But in practice, you've delivered very little. Almost nothing. Disappointing."

"General," Marina said, keeping the smile on her face, "I'm a linguist, not a spy, and, what's more, I've always kept out of politics. You know that. Nikolai Nikolayevich knows that. We can't *all* be on a war footing *all* the time."

"I'm afraid you're wrong, Marina Andreyevna. We must not let our guard down. Not for a moment. In fact, we need to keep one step ahead. Soon, very soon, we'll impress the whole world with our… our ingenuity."

Marina closed her laptop and leant forward, her hands clasped.

"If there is anything I can do to help…"

"Nothing, thank you. Not *this* time. But who knows? One of these days…"

"As you know, General, I'm always at your service."

This time her smile was genuine. Marina was pleased with herself that for the past fifteen minutes she had been able to keep her loathing for the man in front of her under perfect control.

"Now, about this menu," Marina said, keeping her tone light and good-natured. "Profiteroles? Almost the same in Russian, except we skip the 'e'. *Profitroli*. Would you agree with me, Grigory Mikhailovich, that our favourite food is French?"

Before the general could respond, there was a knock at the door. With scrupulous politeness, Lev announced that the president would like to see the general. And Marina Andreyevna, too. He held the door open for the general, who stopped suddenly to berate the younger man for his sloppy appearance. Jeans? No tie? No socks? Had he forgotten where he was?

"Nope."

The Aubusson carpet muffled the sound of Marina's heels as she followed the general and Lev down the long corridor. By the open gilded doors, Marina nodded at the two armed bodyguards from the Federal Protective Service, and the men nodded back. She was friendly with these elite officers: some she knew by sight, and some by name.

Serov was in his oak-panelled sitting room, watching BBC News, his hand gripping the remote.

"Marinochka, quick. Sit down. I need you to translate."

The BBC reporter was standing against a backdrop of the white cliffs of Dover, his hair flying about in the wind, microphone in hand, speaking straight to camera. "Sergei Yegorov, a former oligarch turned political opponent and vocal critic of President Serov, was celebrating his fifty-third birthday when he was taken ill and rushed to hospital. His condition is critical. His wife says that he was in excellent health and played tennis twice a week. She also said her husband, who is a British citizen, had received death threats from unknown Russian sources."

Marina translated as fast as she could while the camera switched from Dover beach to the lobby of the House of Commons, where the member of parliament for Dover called this "extremely worrying" and wished Mr Yegorov a speedy recovery. Back in the television studio, a security correspondent reminded his audience that Yegorov was the author of the best-seller *Serov's Kleptocracy*, which made him a prime target and, once again, pointed the finger at Russia.

"Prove it!" President Serov shouted at the screen, before turning off the television and smiling at Varlamov.

"Well done, Grisha," Serov said, getting briskly to his feet and patting the general on the back. "Congratulations."

He should have gone straight to Hyde – of course he should. But he didn't.

Clive reasoned to himself that, apart from the exact number of Russian microsatellites orbiting the Earth – hardly classified information – he had nothing concrete to bring to the table. Maybe he never would. Maybe it was pie-in-the-sky bravado? Wishful thinking born of desperation? He would know soon enough, though. Marina had set her own deadline: Wednesday morning. She had twenty-four hours left.

The trade talks at the Ministry of Foreign Affairs were going nowhere, and it was no surprise to Clive, as he sat at the green baize table, that the mood on the British side was subdued. When the Russian chief negotiator abruptly adjourned the talks without explanation, Clive was relieved and positively glad to escape the ministry – a monster building, one of Stalin's gothic fantasies, overpowering in its *folie de grandeur*. On the pavement, in front of roaring traffic, Clive gave just one backward glance at the soaring spires and marble pillars before melting into Moscow and just wandering about. He visited his two favourite art galleries, but, as he stood in front of one painting after another, he kept seeing Marina's green-flecked hazel eyes. There she was in Matisse's *Moroccan Triptych*, in Picasso's *Woman with a Fan* and, most of all, in Argunov's peasant woman. On a whim, and perhaps to put her out of his mind, he disappeared into a cinema and watched a film before going back to his hotel. His phone had been off for hours.

Clive was crossing the hotel lobby, planning his solitary room-service supper, when a commanding voice stopped him in his tracks.

"At bloody last," said Rose, jumping up from a leather armchair. It seemed to Clive the red streak in her messy blond hair was redder than ever, but she looked good in her tight-fitting green trousers and black sweater, a jacket slung over her arm. "You got my text, right? I've cleared it with Lucky Luke..." Clive looked puzzled. Rose smiled. "To lesser mortals, he's Her Majesty's Britannic Ambassador, Luke Marden. To me, he's Lucky Luke."

"What about Martin Hyde?" said Clive.

"Cleared it with Lucky Luke," Rose repeated. Clive remembered what George Lynton had told him: that there was no love lost between Rose and Hyde. "Clive, my new best friend," Rose went on, "the British Council needs you. We're outta here, for crisis talks with Boris. And you're my secret weapon."

Fyodor sat behind the wheel of the embassy car. Clive greeted the driver warmly, and so did Rose, who leant forward and patted him on the shoulder. "Best driver in Moscow," she said. "We're pals, aren't we, Fyodor?"

"Pals," said Fyodor, grinning as he headed into the Moscow traffic.

Leaning her head against the leather seat, her eyes half shut, Rose explained to Clive that the oligarch Boris Kunko, chief sponsor of the British Council, had that morning delivered an ultimatum: Kunko plc was withdrawing its sponsorship of the Royal Shakespeare Company's performance of *Julius Caesar* that Friday, unless Boris's conditions were met, which were, quite simply, a place at Eton for his son.

"It's blackmail," said Rose. "You've got to talk him out of it. Get him to change his mind. It's an all-black cast and totally brilliant, and the theatre is sold out."

"No pressure."

"Don't talk to me about pressure! If we have to scrap the whole thing, I'll have egg all over my face," Rose said.

Clive chuckled.

"What? What's so funny?"

"Nothing… nothing… just a bad habit of mine."

"*What… is… so… bloody… funny?*" Rose insisted.

"I'm a bit obsessed with proverbs… A bad habit. If I hear a proverb in English, I have to find the equivalent in Russian, and vice versa. Ridiculous, I know, but there it is. There's no 'egg on your face' proverb in Russian… The closest would be 'sit in a puddle'."

"Oh. Really? So here's my choice: egg on my face or sit in a puddle… Is that it?" Rose asked as the car drew up outside a converted warehouse on the Savvinskaya Embankment. Opposite them was a flashing blue neon sign with the words HIGH TIDE in huge Latin letters.

Tuesday night was eerily quiet at Moscow's most famous nightclub. The dance hall was shut; only the roof restaurant was open, and it was here, overlooking the Moscow River, under a canvas roof with red-hot heaters, that Rose and Clive took a seat at the bar. From there, Rose kept her eye on the overweight middle-aged man with a shiny bald head sitting at a largely empty table between a brunette in a short silver skirt and tight sequin sweater and a blonde all in black.

"That's him," said Rose. "That's Boris. He owns this place, and a chain of luxury hotels, and most of the dry cleaners and car-wash outlets in Moscow, and millions of acres of forests in the Russian Far East. Now, don't get me wrong. The British Council *loves* Boris Kunko. He's promised to pay for an exhibition of eighteenth-century British portrait-painting at the Tretyakov, and he bloody well better be paying for *Julius Caesar* tomorrow night. Otherwise, we're all fucked."

Now the oligarch was waving at the barman, who knew exactly what to do: open a bottle of Cristal valued at $5,000 a pop.

"Right, Clive, my friend. Let's get stuck in. And just remember this. No egg and no puddle."

Rose took Clive by the arm and marched him over.

"*Privyet,*" she grinned. "Fancy meeting you here."

"Rose! My English rose!" Boris exclaimed, throwing open his arms. "Welcome, welcome. Sit. Drink. You like vodka or champagne?"

"I'll kick off with champagne, thank you. Boris, this is Clive Franklin. Clive, this is Boris Kunko."

"It's a pleasure to meet you, Mr Kunko," Clive said in Russian. "I understand you're a great patron of the arts."

Boris looked puzzled, then replied in English, hammering each syllable.

"You *Russian?* I thought you English boyfriend of English rose."

"He's English, all right," said Rose. "But he's not my boyfriend."

With skill that Clive could only admire, Rose manoeuvred herself next to Boris and somehow managed to place Clive on his other side.

"So, Boris, what's all this about getting cold feet?... That's not right. Clive? Help."

Clive put the question delicately in Russian, but, before he could finish, Kunko was venting in English.

"Play called *Julius Caesar*... Caesar mean *tsar*... You know that? This play I sponsor... if... if... British Council guarantee Dima goes to Eton! That is new deal!"

"Boris, that was never our arrangement," Rose said in her best nanny voice. "You gave me your word."

Boris cut Rose off with a wave of his hand and a shake of his big bald head.

"Dima now in Sunningdale. His English perfect. No mistakes. Winner of chess competition and batman at cricket. After Sunningdale, must be Eton. That is necessary route. Absolutely important to receive official letter from British Council with signature from chairman of council. And please do not forget the..." Boris broke off and turned to Clive.

"...the stamp," said Clive. "As in, official stamp."

"That was never part of the deal, Boris, and you know it," said Rose.

"No Eton, no Shakespeare!" Boris said and banged the table with his fist.

"Mr Kunko," Clive said, this time in English, for Rose's benefit. "I am sure we can work things out... There is always a way, don't you think?" At this point, Clive slipped into Russian. "What a wonderful place you have here. And what a view! I'd love to take a walk on your terrace. Is there any chance... I mean, would it be too much trouble to ask you to show me round?"

Boris hesitated, looking hard at Clive, then he pulled out a packet of cigarettes.

"One cigarette," said Boris, getting to his feet.

On the terrace outside, Clive took a deep breath of the sharp night air: winter was on its way. With a gold lighter the

144

oligarch lit his cigarette. Far below, the dark river slid by, and the lights of Moscow blinked into infinity.

Fifteen minutes later, the men returned to the table. "Mutual understanding," Boris announced. "Friday night we watch Tsar Yulius. And son of Boris will go to Eton." Boris shook Clive's hand warmly. "Now we celebrate!"

Boris glanced at the barman, who hurried over with another bottle of Cristal, already on ice. After a toast to Anglo-Russian friendship, more friends arrived, and Clive and Rose took their leave.

"So, what magic words did you come up with this time?" Rose asked, as they walked down the wide staircase beneath a gigantic Swarovski revolving crystal ball.

"I explained that in Britain we keep things fluid. We don't write things down. We don't even have a written constitution. So, point one: no signed letter or contract. Point two: I asked if his son was bright. He said, 'Yes.' Then I asked Boris if he was a rich man, and he said, 'Very.' So, I told him there should be no problem. All these public schools love a rich parent with a bright son. You could say it was the dream ticket. Point three: on no account should he cancel *Julius Caesar* because the ambassador was planning to give a dinner for Boris at the embassy, and, if that were cancelled, Eton would hear about it…"

"I haven't heard about this dinner."

"Well, you have now. Rose, I had to offer something… I'm sure the ambassador will understand. I'll try and speak to him. There's something else… I don't want to spoil your evening, but Boris told me that *Julius Caesar* is the last thing he'll sponsor for the British Council."

"Bugger. Did he say why?" asked Rose, handing her ticket to the cloakroom lady. Clive waited until they were outside before he answered.

"He wants to spend more time in London with his daughter, and he needs his money. He's been talking to his Russian friends in London… They've told him to buy his way into London society: chuck a lot of money at a lot of institutions, get invited to all the right parties. Boris is going to sponsor everything with the word 'Royal' in it, starting with the Royal College of Music – that's where his daughter studies. After that, the Royal Opera House, the Royal Ballet, the Royal Academy, the Royal Horticultural Society, even the Royal Society for the Protection of Birds. Boris is a breeder of falcons, did you know? He told me they have superb eyesight and kill their prey – other birds – in flight."

"Fascinating."

"He's trying to get out of Russia. Can't you see that, Rose? Anyway, I'm sorry to tell you that, according to Martindale, Serov's about to shut down the British Council, put a lid on all those liberal ideas… So, you won't *need* another oligarch. Just another job."

"I don't want another job," Rose snapped. "I like this one. By the way, you were terrific… Thanks. Thanks a bunch. Beyond the call of duty. And bloody clever… Now, where *is* my pal Fyodor?" Rose kept talking as she scanned the parked cars. Suddenly she spotted the embassy car and waved her arms, shouting, "Fyodor, over here!"

In the back seat of the embassy car, Rose was unusually silent. Clive glanced at her and thought she looked exhausted.

"There are times," she said eventually, "when I think I just can't do this any more. It's too bloody hard. But I'm stubborn, and I feel so attached to this place. Maybe it's because I've got Russian roots. Don't laugh! I know my Russian's crap, but I'm working on it. My great-grandfather was appointed chief artist for the Agricultural Exhibition of the Soviet Union in Moscow in 1939. His son, my grandfather, got out in the seventies…

That's when thousands of Jews left Russia. Grandpa went to Vienna and somehow got to London. St John's bloody Wood."

Clive reached out and put his hand on Rose's arm. He was touched that she had confided in him.

"I'll be gutted if I lose this job," Rose blurted out. "And what if they send me back to boring old London? I'm not done with Russia. I want to see Vladivostok and Omsk and Tomsk…"

Rose was staring out of the window at the relentless flow of traffic even at midnight, at the shops and bars with neon signs proclaiming round-the-clock opening hours, at the pavements still alive with people, at floodlit buildings and fountains, at gigantic, pixelated advertisements, at bright lights everywhere.

"Moscow never sleeps… I love that," she said, turning to face Clive. "Did you see the girl in black next to Boris? Alisa, that's her name. We really hit it off while you were on the terrace. She does events. Pop concerts, music festivals. We've got a date." Rose hesitated. "I'm gay. Did you know?"

"I guessed," Clive said gently.

"I've got a date with Alisa! In this city, every night's an adventure. Another reason why I really love Moscow."

"I do too," said Clive.

At some indeterminate hour of darkness, when even the Moscow streets had fallen silent, Clive found himself staring at the ceiling of his hotel bedroom. He could manage Rose Friedman; Boris Kunko was a welcome distraction; it was Marina Volina who was keeping him awake at night. Could she, would she deliver? With all his heart, he hoped that she would. Not just for her sake, but also for his.

Marina waited until the light was fading before she left Tverskaya 25. In her backpack was her emergency supply of cash, ten hundred-dollar bills, which she'd retrieved from the bookcase, just behind her Oxford Thesaurus. It wouldn't be enough. She took the metro, getting out at Universitet, and found the first of three cashpoints.

She knew the area intimately: the broad avenues with their neatly planted rows of apple trees around another of Stalin's gargantuan gothic fantasies, Moscow State University.

Was she being followed? Of course not. She was just being paranoid. And yet, she kept looking behind. She took a bus, walked some more, then another bus, all the time feeling something cold at the back of her neck. Maxim Gorky Lane was a depressing street of boarded-up buildings. At number twenty-eight, she pressed the intercom three times in quick succession, then twice slowly. She stood back, so that she could be seen clearly by the entrance camera. The door opened.

The lift smelt of urine and was covered in obscene graffiti that included "fuck" in English. Marina got off at the eleventh floor, where a dismembered fridge took up most of the landing. Flat 11A was at the far end of the corridor, and, when she rang the bell, a wary eye peered through the glass circle in the centre of a heavily padded leather door. A whole series of bolts began to unlock, and then the door swung open. There stood Vanya, his jeans so low on his hips that Marina could see the top of his underpants. He leant forward and kissed Marina. She saw right away that his blue eyes were less wary.

Inside the flat, the mess was incredible, with empty Coca-Cola cans and plastic cartons of half-eaten food lying about. All the windows were shut, and the room was unbearably stuffy.

Marina pushed aside some dirty plates to make space for her bag on the table. Carefully, she lifted out some smoked sturgeon, red caviar, bread, butter, a knife, a cutting board, plastic plates, beers, cups and a bottle of vodka.

"Now you're talking!" said Vanya, smiling from ear to ear as he began to eat. When he'd cleaned his plate, Marina handed over a photograph that she had taken of the two brothers five years earlier. It was at Peterhof, against a background of cascading fountains. Pasha had his arm around Vanya, and their heads were touching. Vanya propped up the photograph against an empty beer bottle next to his laptop, and, with his index finger, he stroked his brother's face.

"Vanechka... With these emails, if we play our cards right... together we can bring down Varlamov. Destroy him."

"Really?" said Vanya, backing away from Marina. In a second, his mood had changed, his eyes full of mistrust. "Really? I saw you on the telly, standing next to Serov and Varlamov. How do I know they haven't sent you here, those FSB shits?"

"Vanechka, look at me! In all the years we've known each other, have I ever lied to you? Have I? No one knows I'm here. No one! We're on the same side, you and me. I swear on Pasha's soul. Let's talk business," she said gently. "You asked me if I could find a buyer for the emails. I have."

"Who?"

"Me."

Marina took out a white envelope from her bag and laid fifty hundred-dollar bills on the table. Vanya picked them up and counted them out again, fingering the last between his thumb and forefinger.

"New notes," he said.

"I've been negotiating on your behalf. This five grand is for one day's worth of Varlamov's emails on a flash drive, which I need to take with me. It's bait. If they like what they see..."

"They?"

"You don't need to know. If they like what they see, then you give me another flash drive with the rest of the emails, twenty-three thousand of them, and you get the big bucks."

"How much?"

"Three hundred thousand dollars."

Vanya opened his blue eyes wide, and a smile spread across his face.

"I'm not part of this deal, Vanechka," Marina continued urgently. "It's important you know that. I'm just the broker. Unpaid. The email money is all yours. So, shall we get to work? I need to see what I'm buying."

Vanya sat down in front of his laptop.

"Let's start with you... Why not? I bet you're mentioned somewhere..."

Vanya typed "Volina" into the search box, then tipped back in his chair and burst out laughing.

"'Marina Volina is too clever for her own good...' The dickhead doesn't like you much."

"Who's he's writing to?"

"Viktor Romanovsky, from the office of the deputy prime minister."

"Viktor Romanovsky *is* the deputy prime minister."

"Well, *he* likes you. Look at his answer. 'Not true. And by the way, Volina has the complete confidence of the president.'"

Marina smiled. It was nice to know she had friends in high places. She was going to need them if she was going to get out alive.

"Vanechka, do me a favour," she said. "Put 'microsatellites' into the search box."

Vanya did as she asked, but nothing came up.

Marina trawled through the general's emails for three hours straight, until her eyes ached. Along the way, she made a note of dates and times and gave herself cryptic clues as to what was in the emails. She drank one black coffee after another to keep awake.

Dawn was breaking when Marina woke Vanya. She asked him to put all the emails sent and received on 23 August onto a new flash drive she had brought with her, but Vanya shook his head. He reached up to a tin marked "tea" and pulled out a flash drive.

"No foreign stuff gets into my devices," he told Marina.

The job took ten minutes, and, when it was done, he held up the USB stick between his thumb and his forefinger.

"This is the bait?"

"Yes."

"And if your friends like it, they'll get the rest of the emails, and bring the bastard down?"

"Yes."

By the time Marina got home, it was light. As she climbed the chipped marble stairs to the landing, Oxana raised a sleepy head from her narrow bed.

"My, you're late!" she said, rubbing her eyes. "New boyfriend?"

12

Clive was on edge. It was Wednesday morning, and he hadn't heard from Marina. Was it all bravado? Fantasy? And the one-off, was that something for old times' sake? Clive felt foolish because he had allowed himself to dream that she would pull it off, that he would see her again... that... that...

And there was something else. This "tail" business was getting to him. Even as he ate his breakfast in the world's most majestic dining room – according to the Metropol website – he could not shake off a feeling of unease, and, as he sipped his coffee beneath an enormous vaulted stained-glass roof thirty metres above his head, he kept looking for a sleazy face, a crooked smile. He glanced up at the balcony, half expecting to find a man in dark glasses staring at him. He searched behind the giant candelabra, ablaze with lightbulbs and gilt, for a pair of eyes looking in his direction. And he gazed across a sea of white tablecloths to the gurgling fountain at the far end of the huge room, almost sure that he would see a man, or indeed a woman, leaning against a red alabaster pillar, eyes fixed on him.

Suddenly, Clive lost patience with himself and his fears, and, leaving a half-eaten croissant on his plate, he walked out. He was about to pass through the revolving doors of the hotel for another day of pointless trade talks when he saw Narek, and Narek saw him. The Armenian smiled and nodded. Clive walked over and sat down in the high chair and waited, but this time Narek had nothing to give him, no newspaper or in-house magazine. Instead, he took up where he had left off, about his love for Liza, and the life he wanted to make with her, which was still a pipe-dream, because he had no money and her mother wasn't keen. Mothers are always a problem, Clive sympathized. When Narek had finished polishing, he handed Clive first the left shoe, which Clive slipped on, and then the right. Clive felt something in the toe. He thanked Narek for doing such a great job, gave him a handsome tip and disappeared into the men's lavatory, where he locked the door, took off his right shoe and pulled out a tiny parcel. On the wrapping paper was scribbled: "NB 11.27." Inside, he found a USB stick, the size of a domino, which he slipped into his pocket.

The embassy car was waiting in front of the hotel to take him to the trade talks, and he asked Fyodor to step on it. He felt like an idiot for doubting Marina; she had kept her word. Slipping his hand in his pocket, he felt the USB stick cool against his palm. He rested his head against the back of the seat and closed his eyes. Everything was going well. Too well.

Clive had completely forgotten about the security at the Ministry of Foreign Affairs, and by the time he remembered, it was too late; he was already inside the marble entrance hall, staring at the steel structure shaped like a square arch: the metal detector. There was no escape. He dragged the palm of his hand down the alabaster pillar, leaving behind a trail of sweat. The stone felt cool. That's what I must be, cool, he told himself as he looked at the armed security guards.

Clive passed under the metal frame. When the alarm went off, he looked up at the ceiling, surprised, and shrugged his shoulders at the high-pitched wailing that bounced off the alabaster pillars. The security guards all looked directly at him. Emptying his pockets onto a table, he stared down at a jumble of coins, a Metropol keycard and a USB stick.

The guard held up the memory stick between his thumb and forefinger and called over to his boss, who was sitting at a desk in the corner.

"Do we check it?"

Clive could hear the sound of a prison door shutting.

The head of security glanced up from his iPad hidden under the desk. He was watching a replay of a football match between Spartak and TSK the night before, which had gone to penalties. The head of security looked resentfully at the guard, who was waiting for an answer, shook his head, then stared back at his screen.

Clive steadied himself against the table, then stuffed his keycard and small change back into his pocket. The security guard tossed him the USB stick. Clive caught it.

That same morning, the trade talks ended in a blazing row. The first secretary of Her Britannic Majesty's embassy lost his rag. Right in front of the Russian delegation, he tore up the agenda sheet, relishing the ripping, tearing sound, as he declared, in English, the game was over. As long as Russian tactics were simply to obstruct, the trade discussions were a waste of time. With that, he wished everyone good day and walked out.

From the back seat of a stale-smelling Golf, Clive sent Martin Hyde a text: "Trade discussions have collapsed. Need to discuss. Am especially concerned about JCB diggers and Tiptree jam." He made himself comfortable in one of the big leather armchairs in the Metropol lobby, picked up a discarded copy of the *New York Times*'s international edition and turned to the cartoons at the back. Now and then he slipped a hand into his pocket, to make sure the USB stick was still there.

"Is that it?" said Hyde as he and Clive strolled across Red Square. "Have you told me everything?"

It was early afternoon, and the two men had distanced themselves from the tourists around St Basil's and were heading down towards the river. Hyde's FSB tail, a tall man in a leather jacket, was not even attempting to hide; he kept a distance of about ten metres and didn't even bother to glance at his guidebook. And where is mine? Clive wondered as he looked around. Is it the young woman dragging along the bored child with the balloon?

"I'm quite sure you *haven't* told me everything," Hyde continued. "No one ever does. *But...* you've told me enough. And eventually you'll tell me everything, because you are going to need help."

"I'm just the messenger... This isn't my world."

"Isn't it? We've entered a new era, Franklin, with the internet, social media, hacking... It *is* your world... It's *everybody's* world."

They walked in silence. Then Hyde stopped dead, glanced behind at his tail and looked around. Hyde assumed there would be CCTV cameras on the surrounding buildings, which could pick out individuals but not, he thought, what they were saying. That was the job of the tails, and it was *his* job to make their lives as difficult as possible. Hyde also assumed both tails, his and Clive's, would be carrying the most sophisticated recording equipment, which meant that he had to keep as close as possible to the folk music blaring out of amplifiers or to the guides bellowing through loudspeakers. Yes, Hyde concluded, giving Red Square one sweeping look, this is as good a place as any to have a top-secret conversation.

"Why did you wait so long, Franklin? Why didn't you come to me after the Bolshoi? Or on Tuesday after your meeting at the Ministry of Foreign Affairs? Why the wait?"

"I wasn't sure."

"About?"

"Her. Me. Everything."

Hyde stuck close to a Japanese tour guide, who was booming information through a loudhailer.

"She didn't try to recruit you? Really?"

"No, she didn't."

"Are you in debt?"

"No."

"In love?"

Clive shook his head vigorously.

"Then she's got her work cut out... If that's her game."

"I don't think it's a game. She's not a spy."

"Sometimes these lines are blurred," said Hyde.

They walked in silence towards Lenin's tomb.

"Why is she ready to take such a risk? What does she want?"

"As I've told you, a new life. A new identity."

"And money."

"Money is secondary."

A Chinese schoolgirl came up to Hyde and asked if he would take a picture of her and her school friends with St Basil's in the background. Hyde obliged, as if he had all the time in the world.

The two men kept close to the blood-red Kremlin wall until they reached the Spasskaya Tower, where a crowd had gathered to hear the noonday chimes of the famous clock. Clive and Hyde pushed their way into a group of garrulous tourists. "Finns," whispered Clive, as he stood among the tall, flaxen-haired men and women who were counting down the minutes, eyes fixed on the clock face. Hemmed in on all sides, he slipped the USB stick into the pocket of Hyde's smart suit.

"We need a reason for you to stay on in Moscow now that the trade talks have collapsed," Hyde murmured in a voice that was barely audible against the raucous Finnish chanting. "Any ideas?"

"I wouldn't mind running the Moscow marathon. I've never completed the course. In New York, I collapsed. In London, two years ago, I pulled a hamstring. One of these days, I'd like to cross the finish line."

"What a good idea. And the president himself suggested it. Do put it to your friend, won't you?"

Hyde glanced around. His tail was elbowing his way through the crowd only a few metres away.

"See you at the embassy in an hour," said Hyde loudly, looking in the direction of the tail. He had a certain sympathy for the lower orders of espionage. Now and again you had to throw these foot soldiers a bone. "The embassy, not the residence. We'd like your take on the trade talks."

At the stroke of midday, the Spasskaya Tower clock chimed out four musical phrases, one for each quarter, followed by twelve single notes. Hands shot up, holding smartphones, snapping photographs.

"Did you know," said Clive, "that this clock was designed in 1624 by a Scottish engineer and clockmaker called Christopher Galloway? Britain had good relations with Russia in the seventeenth century."

"He's definitely an odd one, your friend Franklin."

It was Wednesday morning, and Marina had slept for only two hours. Her eyes ached from the hours she had spent staring at the computer screen in Vanya's flat and sifting through General Varlamov's personal emails. And here he was, the man himself, back in her office, uninvited, and this time he had taken a seat in her "thinking chair". Marina leant forward, to object, then checked herself.

"The British storm out of the trade talks... It was bound to happen. So, Franklin has the day off. He wanders around Moscow like some lost soul. He goes to the Tretyakov and moons about in a room full of..." The general hesitated. "Kuindjee?"

"Arkhip Kuindzhi. Wonderful romantic painter. Ukrainian of Greek descent."

"Then he goes to the Pushkin and spends four minutes in front of just one Picasso, a cubist rigmarole. Six minutes in front of a Matisse. Then he sees a film about Queen Victoria and an Indian servant, in Russian, before meeting up with that woman from the British Council, Rose Friedman. She's a lesbian. Did you know? Your friend goes to a nightclub, with a lesbian, on a Tuesday, when there's no dancing, no life. Does any of this sound normal to you?"

"Grigory Mikhailovich, what exactly is 'normal'? He's doing what interests him…"

"Is he? Or is he on some special mission? How do we know? This morning at the trade talks, the British first secretary tore up the agenda, but not before your friend read a summary of yesterday's discussions – first in English, then in Russian – and had the nerve to tell our people that we'd left things out or changed the meaning."

"Had we?"

"Language isn't an exact science. Everything's always open to interpretation! I tell you in all honesty, Marina Andreyevna, he's a nuisance."

"Maybe he was just being thorough. Doing what he's paid to do."

"Well," said Varlamov wearily, "I'm paid to be suspicious."

"But you're right to be suspicious, Grigory Mikhailovich!" Marina said with sudden animation. "We've all got something to hide."

Marina knew what she was talking about. She'd spent most of the night looking into every nook and cranny of Varlamov's personal life. She knew where he had his hair cut (at the Four Seasons), which *banya* he liked (the new one in Malaya Dmitrovka), which football teams his son supported (Spartak and Manchester City), which singer was his daughter's favourite (Beyoncé). She also knew that Varlamov had taken a nice fat commission ($300,000) for helping (i.e. not blocking) Boris Kunko's application for a five-a.m. alcohol licence for his newest nightclub, High Tide – and she knew the general would pocket a great deal more over the years to come. She knew, moreover, that he had a girlfriend called Dasha. But these were trifles. She had found a nugget of pure gold in the general's personal emails.

Marina watched as Varlamov walked over to the window and gazed down at Red Square, his head still, his pale-blue eyes watching and waiting, just like a wolf. Isn't that what Clive called him? The Wolf?

"He's down there now, the Englishman, walking about with the spy, Martin Hyde." Varlamov glanced down at his phone. "They've been standing for four and a half minutes in front of the monument to Minin and Pozharsky. What can possibly be their motive?"

"General, I honestly have no idea. Interest in historical monuments? The pleasure of sightseeing?" The general didn't turn his head and Marina could feel his displeasure. "Or could it be the trade talks?" she asked helpfully. "You said just now that there'd been a row."

"More than a row," Varlamov said. "The talks have *collapsed.*"

"There you have it! Franklin is being debriefed."

"It's possible, but somehow I don't think so."

Varlamov was restless. He walked over to the bookshelf.

"Why so many foreign books?"

"I don't think of them as foreign, Grigory Mikhailovich. I think of them as interesting. You'll find Tolstoy on the top shelf, next to Chekhov's letters. At home I've got a whole Soviet library, which I inherited from my father... All those Russian writers nobody reads any more: Gladkov, Fadeyev, the

Strugatsky brothers. And there's a whole lot of English books in translation that no one reads any more, either. Bernard Shaw, Galsworthy, Jack London…"

The general trailed his finger along the spine of several volumes.

"You have here a whole shelf of books that were banned in the Soviet Union. Now why is that?"

"They're good books, that's why. And maybe they have something to teach us…"

"Such as?"

"I don't know… Not to repeat the mistakes of the past?"

The general turned and faced Marina. There was no animation in his stern face.

"I always trust my intuition. There's definitely something odd about the Englishman. Why don't you call him? See if he won't run with you? And find out what you can."

Marina sighed and shook her head with a weariness that was all too genuine.

"If you insist."

The moment Varlamov left, Marina wiped her chair down with a damp cloth. Absurd, she knew, but it made her feel better. And so did the sight of Lev's bald head poking round her door.

"I've just got time for a fag. And a coffee."

"Lyova, you told me you'd given up for good."

"Just one," Lev said.

While Lev made himself comfortable, putting his feet up on her desk, Marina slotted one capsule after another into her coffee machine; he was a double-espresso man. She handed him a cigarette from the secret supply she kept in her desk drawer. He lit up, closed his eyes and inhaled as deeply as his lungs would allow before blowing out a plume of smoke into the air.

"You'll set off the smoke alarm."

"I've turned it off."

Lev was in one of his rare talkative moods. In between puffs, he told Marina that his years at Stanford University had been his undoing. At Stanford, he'd taken up smoking and online gambling, learnt to ride serious motorbikes and almost killed himself on the Pacific Highway. It was fun at the time, but he didn't miss America at all. He never really liked the place. In his opinion, there was no real culture to speak of, and most Americans had zero sense of humour. After lighting a second cigarette, he told Marina that his life was looking up. He was training with the elite bodyguard service, the FSO; it was the boss's idea. The training was exhausting and took up all his free time, but any day now he would have elite-bodyguard status. And a lot of extra cash. And clout. Everyone loves a strongman, Lev said, closing his eyes. Then he opened them wide and tossed a credit card onto the desk.

"I nearly forgot. Buy yourself some clothes. No limit."

They hadn't always been friends. On the contrary, when Marina had first come to work in the Kremlin, she had kept her distance, making it clear to Lev that she wasn't interested in perks. This didn't go down well. When Lev asked what car she wanted, Marina said she was very happy with her second-hand Golf; she even made a joke about how vulgar it was to drive Porsches and Jaguars and said that the only car to have was either a Prius or a fully electric car (which was useless in Russia because there were so few charging points).

A month later, Lev asked the same question again and she gave the same reply, adding that she was in need of nothing and could live perfectly well on her official salary of 1,596,000 roubles a year, or $25,000, which was a great deal more than most Russian doctors or teachers received. Lev listened to Marina with total indifference and informed her that she was being given a bonus of $50,000 from a special fund within the

Ministry of Foreign Affairs for her outstanding services as an interpreter; he also informed her that she was the proud new owner of a Prius, a personal gift from the boss, but, since she was so fastidious, she could pay for the insurance herself. A week or so later, Marina had found herself alone with Lev in his office as she waited to see the president.

"Marina Andreyevna, let me give you some advice. You can't be half in and half out. It doesn't work that way."

Sometime later they met in the restaurant on the second floor of the Senate Palace. One Friday, over lunch and a good bottle of wine, they discovered they had much in common; their fathers were bullies, while their mothers were secretly religious and only "came out" after the fall of the Soviet Union.

"Were you in the choir?"

"Of course! And you?"

"Of course."

The ice was broken. They understood each other perfectly. They had grown up in dimly lit churches with the smell of incense and icons glinting in the half-light, watching bent old ladies in pinafores and headscarves snuffing out spluttering candles. There was always one person, usually a woman, with a beautiful voice that soared above the others, straight to God, so Marina used to think as a devout little girl. Neither she nor Lev had kept their faith: that was something else they had in common.

"The boss has a very high opinion of you," Lev had said that Friday. "Which means you're going to have a very comfortable old age."

"But that's not why —"

"You still haven't understood, have you? The boss is a very generous man, and you take what's on offer. And you're grateful. Very, very grateful. That's how things work around here. Don't try to be different. Go with the flow."

Then Lev poured out what was left of the red wine and clinked glasses with Marina. Together they drank to a glorious old age.

Before the year was out, the president had given Marina a villa near Yalta in Crimea. It was owned by an offshore trust with bearer shares, and she was the sole beneficiary. The die was cast. She found herself living in a gilded cage with plenty of money and presents she couldn't refuse – and a guilty conscience that kept her awake at night.

13

"It's a trap," said Oswald Martindale that afternoon in the safe room on the top floor of the British embassy. "So *obviously* a trap," he insisted, looking at Hyde, who was helping himself to coffee. The ambassador paced the room with his usual restless energy. Only Clive sat quite still.

Officially, the safe room didn't exist. In his three years at the embassy, Clive had never set foot in this inner sanctum, but of course he had heard all about it. A secret room on the top floor of the embassy's west wing, hermetically sealed by British engineers so that no signals or communications of any sort could get in or out. To enter, you went in naked, so to speak, taking nothing with you: no smartphone or smartwatch, no tablet or laptop, no USB sticks, no earphones, no chargers. According to the ambassador, this was the only space in the whole of Moscow free from FSB surveillance, although Martindale had his doubts. As for Clive, the white walls and functional furniture reminded him of a dentist's waiting room, without the magazines.

"Can't you see? Volina is just pretending she wants out," said Martindale, warming to his theme. "All she really wants is to plant some illegal material on you and make sure that you get caught red-handed, that you're arrested, banged up and eventually exchanged for one of the Russian spies we're holding in London. Your diplomatic immunity won't protect you... they'll find a way around that. They can always 'lose' you for a couple of days, during which you will *not* be having a nice time. But who cares? After all, you're not really a diplomat, are you? Just an interpreter."

"I'm a translator."

"Clive," said Luke Marden, "I'm afraid Oswald's right. It's a set-up, a trap... Call it what you will. We've got half a dozen Russian spies in UK custody at this very moment... This is a neat way to secure their release. You might be worth one or two. Who knows?"

"I don't think it *is* a trap," Clive said quietly.

"Why?" said Hyde. "Why do you believe Marina Volina?"

"Gut."

Hyde smiled. You could never explain your "gut", but over the years it was the only thing he had learnt to trust.

"Let's consider the intelligence so far, as provided by Mrs Volina," Hyde continued. "Number of Russian microsatellites launched in the last two months: ninety-four. That figure is correct, according to my friends in the Pentagon. Today, we have a USB stick with over fifty emails to and from General Varlamov. One day's worth. With twenty-three thousand to follow. Which could be of great interest. Or not. We simply don't know. Remind us, if you will, Franklin, of Mrs Volina's terms?"

Clive remembered only too well how Marina had set out her stall that night in the dacha after they had made love. She had showered and dressed and poured out more wine and stood in front of the fire with Ulysses at her feet. "Here's what's on the menu," she had said. "The amuse-bouche is one day's worth of General Varlamov's personal emails, and that'll cost five thousand dollars. For the starter: twenty-three thousand of the general's personal emails over six months, the last one sent only two weeks ago. Cost: three hundred thousand. For the main course: whatever Serov has up his sleeve... and anything else you need to know. And once I deliver, then you have to get me out and keep me out. Me and Vanya, who gets all the cash for Varlamov's emails. The final cost, and here I am talking about the main course, is to be discussed, and this is where I take my cut. I've got an offshore account in Cyprus. It was a joint account with Alexei, in my married name. No one knows I have it. Not even Varlamov. My account is protected with a password and a memorable date and a security question. How good is your memory?"

Clive gave the assembled company a perfect summary of his discussion with Marina, carefully omitting what mattered to him: that he could not take his eyes off her lovely, sad face and her small, perfect breasts; that he had felt almost drunk with joy as he slipped inside her, while she let out a gasp and melted into him – or so it had felt.

"She doesn't pull her punches, does she?" said Martindale, leaning back in his chair. "Three hundred and five thousand dollars isn't cheap for what she calls 'starters'."

"It's reasonable," said Hyde, who never quibbled about money if the intelligence was good.

"The money's not for her," said Clive. "It's for Vanya."

"In which case," said Martindale with undisguised sarcasm, "he's going to be a very rich young man."

"Before we all get carried away," Luke Marden said, "may I ask if Marina Volina told you just *how* this foster son of hers managed to hack into one of the most secure private email accounts in all Russia?"

"Yes," said Clive solemnly. "She did."

"I'm all ears," said Martindale.

As Clive looked at each man in turn, he felt it was important for them all to understand how close Pasha had been to getting away with it and to staying alive. And so, he retold the story Marina had told him, which she had heard from Vanya.

Pasha had been working out of a small office at the far end of a corridor on the fifth floor of the Lubyanka, and it was there, under General Varlamov's watchful eye, that Pasha had enjoyed his greatest triumphs, hacking into the emails of rich Russians – people like Deputy Prime Minister Romanovsky and the oligarch Boris Kunko – who, according to the general, had ideas above their station. Pasha not only hacked into their emails, but also into their Swiss bank accounts. He dug up enough dirt to put them away for ten years. But, Pasha being Pasha, he could not help noticing security flaws in the FSB's system. For a start, the general had approval month after month from the director of the FSB to keep his USB port enabled with no questions asked. That was slack! Such a strategic facility should have been reviewed on a regular basis. Pasha mentioned this to the general, who told him it was none of his business. This infuriated Pasha. He was the only person who had produced results, who had succeeded where the FSB engineers had failed. If there was one thing Pasha could not forgive, it was a lack of respect, and so he decided to prove to the general once and for all that he was a class act.

One day he got his chance.

It had been a while since Pasha had stepped into the general's inner sanctum, a penthouse office on the fifth floor with a magnificent view over Moscow. Why had he been summoned? For the stupidest of reasons. The general's computer was irritatingly slow. Pasha found himself sitting there at the general's desk, in front of his computer, trying to speed things up, when the general had to leave the room. Varlamov had had prostate cancer, and, even though he was in the clear, he had to pee – often. So, once Varlamov left the room, Pasha decided this was the moment.

Not an easy task. The general and *only* the general could get into his personal email account through a whole series of passwords and security checks. Varlamov's personal email account was open on the screen, but almost before the general had gone out of the door, a time-out kicked in and the screen went blank, except for a narrow, oblong, empty box asking for a password.

It was Pasha Orlov vs the FSB. Pasha knew he had only a few minutes to crack the puzzle. He clicked on "Paste". His thinking was that the general must have had a complicated password that he couldn't possibly remember, and, being too professional to leave this password lying around on a piece of paper, he must have kept it in some innocuous-looking file on his desktop – labelled "Children's School", for instance. If so, he'd be obliged to open this file and painstakingly copy out the password (such a bore), but, once typed in, it could be copied and pasted. (Pasha had hacked a guy who did just this.) He clicked "Paste" but was careful not to press the enter key. The cursor stayed where it was, waiting for a valid entry from the keyboard, which meant that "Paste" had been disabled. Pity, thought Pasha, but hardly surprising.

He had wasted two seconds, but not one of his two attempts at guessing the general's password. Pasha changed tack, switching from the complicated to the dead simple. The password could be something easy, something the general could remember – or, if not remember, then see right in front of him. Pasha found himself staring at a box of Prostacor pills. He read the words on the box: "Natural prostate support. 30 vegetable capsules." Pasha typed in "Prostacor30." (Upper case, lower case and a number.) *Incorrect password.* This was his last chance. In theory, he had three attempts, but in practice, he had two. If he chanced a third and got it wrong, all hell would break lose. Alarms would go off, and he would be facing the rest of his life in prison. He considered his options: "ProstacorVegetable30" or "ProstacorCapsules30" or "ProstacorVegetableCapsules30". His intuition was working overtime. It ought to be "ProstacorVegetableCapsules30". But it wasn't. Why not? Something told him that this pedantic general would set up a minor obstacle even for himself – as a matter of pride. All at once, Pasha was completely calm; his whole being was enveloped with a sense of his own power, his own invulnerability. His head was in a blissful state of absolute certainty: he knew his next move was the right move, the perfect move. Slowly and carefully, into the gaping open mouth of the box, he typed: "30ProstacorVegetableCapsules".

Pasha was in.

On the screen in front of him were the personal emails of General Grigory Varlamov, including one from his fitness instructor, Anatoly. He took a USB stick from his pocket – he never went anywhere without one – made a block selection of the emails and pressed "Copy". Then he downloaded his contacts. There would be a digital footprint, of course, which he had to cover, since ordinarily the paranoid general never let anyone else near his computer.

By the time Varlamov came back into the room, Pasha was on his feet, asking if he would consider a computer update with some fancy new AI software from the United States. Pasha even had a brochure in his hand, which the general brushed aside.

"We have perfectly good AI right here in Russia," Varlamov snapped, sitting down at his blank screen, but for the little oblong box begging for a password.

"Pasha really thought he'd got away with it," said Clive, getting to his feet and stretching his legs. He stared at the three faces in front of him.

"Why didn't he?" said Hyde. "Why didn't he get away with it?"

"He couldn't resist showing off," said Clive. "He didn't like Varlamov, but he knew he had to keep on the right side of him. One evening, the general invited Pasha and the team of FSB software engineers for a drink in his office, to celebrate all the good work they had done hacking into other people's lives – powerful, important people who didn't like Serov. Well, Pasha got drunk and reminded the general he had a fitness appointment at his gym on Petrovka at seven o'clock the next morning."

"Fatal," said Hyde with a shake of his head.

"Yes," Clive agreed. "With one stupid sentence, the boy had signed his own death warrant. Varlamov must have freaked out. In any case, we can assume that he got one of his acolytes to check his computer. He must have found Pasha's digital footprint and the exact time he'd inserted the USB stick and downloaded the emails. After that, it was only a matter of time before…"

"Hubris," Martindale murmured, but not without sympathy.

"The boy was brilliant," said Hyde.

"The boy is dead," said Martindale.

"With the help of our own new AI software, Franklin here has been looking through the general's emails," said Hyde, eager to move on. "Of limited interest, wouldn't you say? Except for one sent from Varlamov to the foreign minister two weeks ago at 11.27 – private email to private email. The foreign minister was pressing for a top-level trade mission to China. Varlamov pushed back. He mentioned a certain 'Plan A'. Not much to go on, is it? Franklin, could we have chapter and verse?"

Clive pulled out a couple of sheets of embassy paper covered in his own neat handwriting.

"This is Varlamov speaking, or, rather, writing," said Clive. "And I quote: 'For the moment, we must concentrate all our energies and resources on Plan A. Once it is completed successfully, we can discuss the other matter.'"

"It could be something to do with Ukraine," said Martindale.

"It could be anything," said the ambassador.

"The word *plan* in Russian also means 'operation'," said Clive. "For example, 'Operation Barbarossa' is *Plan Barbarossa*. 'Plan A' could be some sort of military operation."

"That's very interesting," said Hyde. "Maybe your friend can find out?"

"I hope so," said Clive. "I really hope so." He remembered the confidence in Marina's voice when she had told him, "They're not as clever as they think…"

Hyde stared at Clive for what seemed like an eternity, and it made Clive uncomfortable. When would Hyde speak? When would he come to some sort of decision?

"A lot is riding on this," Hyde said eventually. "Not just for us, but for her. Mrs Volina has given us her terms. That's all well and good. But… and I'm sure she knows this… Mrs Volina is on probation. The general's emails… They're a start. A good start. But if she can give us meaningful intelligence on Plan A… Well, that would put her on a much surer footing. Will you pass this on?"

Marina was five minutes early for her two-thirty appointment at the Aphrodite beauty salon on Petrovka. It took two hours and twenty minutes to colour her hair a rich brown with reddish lowlights and cut it into a sleek bob with a fringe. Feeling presentable, she tanked herself up with a double espresso and walked a few metres down to Dior, where the dress in the window had caught her eye.

An hour later, she walked out with two new work suits, two cocktail dresses, a midnight-blue trouser suit, a white-and-navy polka-dot blouse with a floppy bow, and a long black one-shoulder dress, on sale. The sums involved were, to Marina's mind, stratospheric. She paid for everything with her new black credit card. No limit.

By this time, the Dior manageress was all over Marina, telling her how elegant and beautiful she was and reminding her that she must not forget about shoes. A dress without the right shoes was, said the manageress, no dress at all, but a bird with a broken wing. Right next door was Jimmy Choo, where Madame could get a discount. So Marina went next door and bought one pair of shoes at a price that made her feel sick. She then took a taxi home, buried under her packages, and paused on the landing, where Oxana was sitting in her swivel chair next to her narrow bed. For once, Marina pressed the button for the lift, while Oxana looked on in amazement before demanding to know what on earth had come over her. Why the new haircut? The new clothes? Why so many shopping bags, when she always said she hated shopping? As the lift doors swallowed her up, Marina blew Oxana a kiss.

Marina slept for an hour, then dragged herself out of bed and thanked her lucky stars that she was only on duty for the drinks *before* dinner. Serov didn't need her at the dinner for the ex-chancellor; he spoke fluent German from all his years in Dresden.

And there was a text from Clive. Formal. Official. She read it with a sigh and thought, if only she could be back in Peredelkino with Clive holding her tightly, giving her the illusion that life was beautiful and that she was safe.

Marina put on her new black dress that left one shoulder bare; she hardy recognized herself. Usually these formal dinners in the Kremlin filled her with dread. But not this one. She had a new dress and a new challenge. A week ago, at 11.27, General Varlamov had sent an email to Foreign Minister Kirsanov in which he had mentioned a Plan A.

A for what?

. . .

Inside the Palace of Facets, they all made such a fuss. How many times that evening did Marina hear, "Good heavens, is it Marina? I didn't recognize you." It all started with President Serov, who summoned her over and showered her with compliments. "Now that *is* an improvement..." he said. "New hair, new dress... I like you in black... very smart indeed... You could pass for a Parisienne... You look most attractive, my dear... and you know what?" Then the president leant forward and whispered, "We'll have you married in no time."

"I have no wish to be married," Marina replied, but the president wasn't listening, and moments later he insisted on a photograph with Marina and his guest of honour, the ex-chancellor of Germany. Marina was then assigned to take care of the German VIP. Soon, however, she found herself guide to most of the German delegation as they toured the gilded seventeenth-century chamber with its wall-to-wall frescoes, while the president looked on approvingly. Several people commented that the newly restored chamber looked magnificent. It should, thought Marina, at a cost of nine million dollars, half of which was pocketed. Marina, who had done her homework while her hair was being dyed, pointed out the intricate marquetry of the floor in seven different woods. Eventually, the Germans melted away, and General Varlamov, who had been prowling around the edge of the room, moved in.

"So, you took my advice after all," Varlamov said, looking Marina up and down. "With, if I may say so, very satisfactory results."

"You're most kind," Marina replied. The general seemed pleased with himself, and Marina wondered why – until she noticed his new suit. Italian, she thought. When she saw a flash of red silk lining inside the jacket, she told Varlamov it reminded her of a bird of paradise.

"Bird of paradise? I like that," he said, pushing back his shoulders. The general took another glass of champagne from a passing tray and was handing it to Marina when the Russian national anthem sang out from his pocket. He took the call.

"Thank you," he said. Then he looked at Marina and smiled. "Yegorov is dead... That *is* good news. A toast, I think." Varlamov raised his glass. "To one less traitor in the world."

Marina had never toasted a man's death before. The champagne stuck in her throat, but she swallowed and forced herself to smile.

"His book about our president was pure slander," said Varlamov. "Of course, the West loved it. It was top of the Amazon best-seller list for weeks. Yegorov describes me as the power behind the throne, compares me to Talleyrand... He even calls me shit in a silk stocking."

"That's quite a compliment," Marina said, keeping her voice detached.

"Is it? That's what my wife said. But I don't think it's a compliment at all. Not at all. How's the Englishman?"

"You'll be pleased to hear that I'm running with him tomorrow. He sent me a text saying that now the trade talks have collapsed, he's got time on his hands. We're meeting for a drink this evening to plan our route. I think we'll do Frunzenskaya. Ten, maybe fifteen kilometres, starting at seven a.m. And, by the way, I know the protocol. From now on, you'll have a full report every time we meet."

"So it was *his* initiative," Varlamov mused. "That's interesting... Maybe there's more than meets the eye... What do you think?"

"I'm running with him, Grigory Mikhailovich, not recruiting him."

"Why not do both? Think outside of the box, Marina Andreyevna."

Marina excused herself, reminding the general that she was on duty and the president had asked her to check the seating plan. As she crossed the room, a hand shot out and took her by the arm.

"Well, I never! What *have* you done..." Viktor Romanovsky gushed. "Let me take a long look at you! I can hardly believe my eyes. What a figure inside that elegant gown... My goodness me..."

"I was really hoping I'd see you here," Marina said, pressing his arm. "It makes such a difference to have a friend at these dos."

"I want to be more than a friend. Much, *much* more," the deputy prime minister whispered. Marina forced herself to smile, bracing herself for a stream of unwanted compliments. Much of the world had moved on, she thought, but not Russia, where men still thought of themselves as superior to women, where women could only advance in life with *permission* from men. Would Russia or Russian men ever change? She left the question hanging in her mind as she turned to Romanovsky and said, "Did you know that General Varlamov thinks highly of you?"

"He does?" said Romanovsky, vaguely looking around for the general. "You surprise me."

"Honestly... I often hear him singing your praises... Just thought I'd pass it on... Of course, you two must be seeing a great deal of each other these days... I mean, we live in exciting times."

Romanovsky eyed Marina cautiously.

"It's all very secret, you know."

"I know it's secret, but... Well, it's safe between *us*. I find the name intriguing. Who thought it up?"

"Our foreign minister," said Romanovsky, dropping his voice to a whisper. "Kirsanov likes to show off. He went to the classical gymnasium. Spent years studying Latin and Greek and, as a result, has a thing about Greek gods. I don't know... Something about the underworld appealed to him. I suppose it's logical when you think about it."

"*Ayid...*" Marina murmured with her sweetest smile. It was Russian for Hades.

"Shhh!" said Romanovsky. "You'll get me into terrible trouble... If they think for one moment I've been indiscreet... Even though it's only *you*... Now, when are we having our dinner? My private secretary will be calling you first thing tomorrow, and she won't take no for an answer."

A gong announced that dinner was served. Marina sent Clive a text, collected her coat and left.

They met in the bar of the Metropol, chose a table next to the pianist, who was playing 'I Get a Kick Out of You'.

"Nice dress," Clive said as he helped Marina off with her coat and felt her skin tense at his touch.

"I've come from work... a reception," she said.

They ordered cocktails, surrounded by the lush notes of Cole Porter, and then, in clear voices and well within earshot of the man drinking alone at the bar, they talked about running.

"If you're late, I can't wait," Marina said, pulling out her phone. "Seven o'clock, sharp. At the foot of the stone steps, which you get to from the bridge. Here, I'll show you on the map."

Marina tapped on Yandex Maps and typed in "A = *Ayid*. Source = DPM Rom" without hitting "Find". She gave Clive just enough time to read the five words before she cleared the search bar. Then she typed in "Frunzenskaya", and, as she and Clive studied the map, she thought that Vanya would be proud of her.

. . .

An hour later, Clive found himself back in the hermetically sealed safe room, where the walls seemed whiter and the air stuffier.

"So," he began, and then wondered why everything these days has to start with "So…". "So… The 'A' in 'Plan A' is for *Ayid*. Which means Hades. Plan A is Operation Hades."

"And Volina's source is…?" said Martindale.

"Romanovsky. The deputy prime minister."

The ambassador looked impressed.

"Hades!" scoffed Martindale. "Ludicrous. I mean what on earth does it conjure?"

"Hell? The depths?" said Clive. "Marina doesn't know. But she'll find out."

"The depths," said Hyde. "The depths of the Atlantic Ocean, where you'll find the fibre-optic cables that carry ninety-seven per cent of internet traffic between Europe and the US."

Hyde took a sip of whisky and looked around the table.

"Cut those cables, and we're in darkness. Good name, Hades. God of the dead. King of the underworld. In Greek, it means 'the invisible one'. He's a ruthless god. And hard to detect."

"How long have you known?" asked the ambassador.

"It's just a guess," said Hyde. "But it fits. The microsatellites. The new belligerent stance. This latest assassination, which is, I think, a smokescreen, a diversion from what's happening elsewhere. And now we have an invisible enemy…" Here Hyde paused. "It's the Russian submarines that bother me the most. And the stealth drones that hide in their bellies."

Hyde was quick to explain that he was not talking about the drone nuclear submarine codenamed Status-6, about which Serov had boasted on Russian television, claiming that it had scoured the US coast undetected in order to test American defences. No, Hyde was talking about a new invention, an underwater drone, unmanned and designed specifically to gather intelligence. "Rather like an unmanned spacecraft on the moon," Hyde explained, "this new submarine can 'do things'."

"What sort of things?" said Clive.

"I'm coming to that," said Hyde. "In recent months, a Russian submarine and two, possibly three, 'baby' underwater drones have been annoying the hell out of the Royal Navy by skirting our southern coast – Cornwall, in particular – and just steering clear of our coastal waters, which, in case anyone had forgotten, extend twelve nautical miles from the low-water mark of any coastal state, as defined by the 1982 United Nations Convention on the Law of the Sea. These pesky underwater drones are very hard to detect, especially if you have a navy as depleted as ours."

"Do we have any idea *why* these underwater drones are snooping off the coast of Cornwall?" said Clive.

"I do have an idea. So does Her Majesty's Royal Navy, and so does the PM. In a word, reconnaissance. Which brings me back to your question, Franklin. You asked what these drones can do. They are highly sophisticated robots. They can plant themselves on the seabed and cut cables." Hyde let this last remark hang in the air. "Not any old cables," he continued, "but the fibre-optic cables which carry the data for most of the world's emails, text messages and phone calls. The traffic under the Atlantic, in particular, is huge and conveyed through eight super cables. Policy Exchange has just published a report on all this with a foreword written by an old friend of mine, an ex-NATO supreme allied commander, who says these fibre-optic cables – or 'pipes', as he calls them – are, and I quote, 'the backbone of the world's economy'."

Hyde poured himself a glass of water. The air in the room was dry.

"Let me give you a little background," he continued. "As I mentioned just now – but believe me, it bears repeating – ninety-seven per cent of global communications is transmitted via these underwater cables. Each fibre has the capacity to transmit as much as four hundred gigabytes of data per second. That's a lot of data. And the speed is breathtaking. Here's a statistic I particularly like: one cable containing eight fibre-optic strands could transfer the entire contents of the Bodleian Library across the Atlantic in forty minutes. Quite a thought, don't you think?"

"Terrifying," said Luke Marden, who found this sort of data deeply depressing.

"Only last week," Hyde continued in the same even tone, "the chief of the defence staff gave the PM a briefing, a sort of risk assessment. He said that cutting the fibre-optic cables under the Atlantic would hit the UK and the whole Western economy 'immediately and potentially catastrophically'. His words, not mine."

There was a heavy silence in the safe room. Hyde's grim assessment held that the ninety-four microsatellites were Russia's insurance policy, to keep its own communications up and running while the UK and much of Western Europe crashed.

"And before you even bother to ask," Hyde added, "we in the UK don't even *begin* to have our own satellite capacity."

"So how do we defend ourselves?" said Clive.

"With difficulty. The Royal Navy has been talking about an ocean surveillance ship, but it's still on the drawing board. Meanwhile, Russia has a modern submarine fleet. We don't. We can't possibly patrol all our coastline. They can slip in and out, and there's nothing we can do. If they have an operation in place to cut the cables, we won't be able to stop them, unless... unless we know *when* and *where*..."

Clive was struck by the gravity, not just in Hyde's voice but in his face. The special adviser on Russia stood there unsmiling, grim, his features set in stone. Clive had never been party to a discussion of national security at this level, but he understood that this *was* his world, after all, and this meeting, in the stuffy confines of the safe room, was a call to duty. He had to play his part.

"If I could come in here…" said the ambassador, who was on his feet and pacing about the room. "Relations between Russia and the UK are worsening by the hour. The PM gets back to London this Friday, in time to make a statement to the House of Commons. This murder of Sergei Yegorov… It is… How did she put it? The last straw." The ambassador was looking at Martin Hyde.

"The PM is furious," Hyde confirmed. "There'll be expulsions."

"Thank bloody God," said Martindale, getting to his feet and heading to the sideboard for a drink. "And, with a bit of luck, the Russians will retaliate, and we'll all be sent home… The usual tit for tat… And I won't shed a tear."

"Well, you should," said Hyde. "For us, this is the worst possible news, don't you see? The assassination is a diversion, a sideshow, but the expulsions are a more serious matter." He gave Martindale his sternest look. "It leaves Volina exposed. Clive too… We won't be here to give them the usual support or back-up. They'll be largely on their own, face to face with Operation Hades, god of the underworld… home of departed souls… a dark, dark place… It's the sort of place we'll find ourselves in if those fibre-optic cables under the Atlantic are cut. Of course, I'm assuming this is what Operation Hades is about… It's just possible that I'm barking up the wrong tree, but I don't think so. Anyway, this is where Marina Volina comes in. We need all the details from her… Chapter and verse."

"You know her terms," Clive said, keeping his voice flat, disengaged. "She's waiting to hear back from you."

Hyde studied Clive for a moment, not unsympathetically, and then asked him, politely, to leave the safe room and wait outside. Ten minutes later Clive was back.

"Right," said Hyde. "We accept Volina's terms. Over and above. For one day's worth of emails from General Varlamov, she's asked for five thousand dollars. The money will be in her account immediately. For the other twenty-three thousand emails, she's asked for three hundred thousand dollars. Agreed. We'll pay in daily instalments of fifty thousand, starting first thing tomorrow. As for getting out of Russia and starting a new life, that depends on what Volina can tell us about Operation Hades. If she's instrumental in preventing this attack, then she's out and we'll give her two million. Dollars, that is."

Martindale whistled between his teeth.

"That's as far as we can go for the moment," Hyde said, looking directly at Clive. "Until we see the quality of her intelligence. It's a classic case of what, where and when. *What* is Operation Hades? *Where* will it take place? *When* does it start? These are the only three questions that matter. We have a handle on the *what*, in that all the signs point to an attack on underwater cables. But we have only the vaguest idea of where and when. We think it's Cornwall, and we think it's soon. Which isn't good enough. We need precise information, and we need it fast. Can you make sure Volina understands this?"

"She does," said Clive.

With the serious work over, and a fine sense of timing, Luke Marden pulled a cork on a very good bottle of claret, a Bastille Day present from his French counterpart: Château Margaux, 2002, premier grand cru classé. The ambassador was old school: he genuinely believed that good wine helped to stimulate a good brain. With this in mind, he poured out the deep-throated nectar into four glasses and passed them round.

"Give her till Monday," said Clive, the first sip of wine reminding him of a velvet cloak his mother had once owned.

"Why? What's happening this weekend?" said Martindale.

"She's flying to Crimea with Serov. It's his birthday."

"A golden opportunity," murmured Hyde.

"Why? Why is she doing this?" Martindale asked, leaning back in his chair, tapping the end of his pen on the wooden surface of the table. "Why would she of all people, sitting so pretty in a plum job, part of an elite with access to unlimited money, unlimited luxury, why would she risk her life to get out?"

"She's had enough of the lying," said Clive. "And they killed her foster son. Sir Martin knows the story."

"She's brave," said Hyde.

"Or cunning," said Martindale.

Marina felt there was something wrong the moment she pushed open the heavy mahogany doors of Tverskaya 25, still holding the menu for the banquet (now well under way) and still remembering the touch of Clive's hand on her bare shoulder – a jolt of electricity that had taken her by surprise.

She found Oxana sitting in her rickety chair on the landing, shaking her head and muttering, "This is terrible... terrible." Next to her, on the narrow bed, sat a sixteen-year-old girl with long red hair and freckles. At once, Marina recognized Lyuba, Oxana's granddaughter, who lived in the northern suburb of Mitino with her mother, Sonya. The moment Oxana saw Marina she threw up her hands.

"Marina Andreyevna! We're in the most terrible mess. The police are looking for Lyuba here! Look at her... She's just a child! My Sonya's hysterical. The police came to her flat this afternoon. Mercifully, Lyuba wasn't there. In fact, she was on her way here, to bring me some medication... Sonya made up some story about her daughter being an impossible rebel, that she'd moved out. Then she sent Lyuba a text message telling her the police were looking for her and not to come home. What are we going to do? I can't have her here… and we can't both sleep in this bed!"

Lyuba was sitting on Oxana's high brass bed, swinging her legs. She looked impatient, even bored.

"Grandma, I can sleep anywhere…"

She looks so young and so tired, Marina thought.

Oxana was shaking her finger at her granddaughter. "I begged you not to go on another unauthorized demonstration, but you wouldn't listen, and now they've caught you on CCTV! It's terrible, just terrible!"

"Come with me," Marina said, holding out her hand. "There's a bed in my study, and I've even got spare pyjamas and a toothbrush. Oxana, don't you worry. No one will come at this hour, and we can sort it all out in the morning."

Oxana dabbed her eyes with a white handkerchief. "Thank you, Marina Andreyevna. You're too kind. One of these days, I'll return the favour. And can you please make Lyuba see sense? No more protests!"

Lyuba was no trouble. She wasn't hungry and asked only for a glass of water.

"It's dangerous to go out protesting these days," Marina said in the kitchen as she watched the girl take gulps of water. "What is it you care about so much?"

To Marina's surprise, she began to chant in a low voice:

Just pay the money, kid!
Pay three hundred dollars,
And you'll get a licence.
Don't matter if you can't drive.
Just pay the money, kid.

Pay one thousand dollars,
and you'll get your degree.
Don't matter if you can't write.
Just pay the money, kid.

The girl stopped singing and let out a deep, sad sigh.

"Who wrote that song?" Marina asked.

"Nikita Strelnikov. He speaks… No, he *sings* for all of us. He's in prison, and we've got to get him out. We've got to try everything. On Sunday we marched… hundreds of us, until they brought in the riot police and the dogs."

"Lyuba, I don't want to frighten you, but the police will keep looking for you. You could end up in prison. Your mother could face a big fine. Your mother and your grandmother could lose their jobs."

"I know all that," said Lyuba. "So what? We do nothing? Let Nikita rot in jail? I can't do that… I'm not afraid." Then Lyuba let out a big yawn. "I'm knackered… Thanks for the bed."

Marina fetched a duvet and pillows for the bed in her study. "Tomorrow morning I'm out running early, so you can sleep as late as you like," she said. "Help yourself to anything in the fridge, and when I'm back we'll make a plan."

In the middle of making the bed, Lyuba stopped, and, still holding the duvet, fixed Marina with her green eyes.

"You work for the president, don't you?"

"I do. But I'm your grandmother's friend, and *she*'s my concern tonight, first and foremost. You're safe here, I promise."

Ten minutes later, Lyuba was asleep. The door to her room was half open, and Marina looked in and saw a shaft of light from the streetlamp falling on Lyuba's red hair, which covered her sleeping face. Where does her courage come from? Marina asked herself later as she sat at the kitchen table. Suddenly, Marina felt ashamed that her only aim was to save her own skin and get out of Russia. That night, it took her a long while to get to sleep.

14

It was 7.15 a.m. on Thursday morning, and this was their first run together.

"Is this what you wear in the Highlands?" Marina asked Clive as they ran along the Moscow River opposite Gorky Park.

Clive was wearing baggy brown shorts, a dark-blue T-shirt with a white cross on the back, which he'd picked up in Kinlochleven, and mismatched socks.

"I'm just an amateur. You're the pro with all the fancy kit."

In these last few days before the marathon, the Frunzenskaya Embankment was packed with runners, including two FSB tails who stood out in their ill-fitting tracksuits; one was overweight, and both had forgotten water bottles. Marina kept glancing over her shoulder at the tails.

"When... we're... running..." she said in staccato bursts, increasing the pace and, at the same time, glancing over her shoulder at the tails, "their mics... are... useless. Lev... told... me. Do... we... have... a... deal?"

"Yes," said Clive, surging forward. It felt good to be running again, and good to see the tails behind, struggling. "Yes, to everything. Check your account."

Clive glanced back. One of the tails was closing in.

"I'd like to accept the president's kind invitation and run the marathon... *President's invitation... run the marathon...*" Clive repeated, loudly. "Can you get me a late-entry pass?"

"I should think so," Marina said.

"Make no mistake," Clive suddenly shouted out. "My bounty is as boundless as the sea."

"That's my line," Marina laughed. "Let's try a sprint and give our friends here a run for their money."

"Marisha," Clive said as they quickened the pace. "I'll go mad if I don't see you alone. Think of something, will you?"

Marina was still in her running clothes when she let herself into Tverskaya 25 and checked her mailbox. Inside, she found a postcard of the Gagarin statue and, on the reverse, one word written in capital letters: COURTYARD. But he wasn't there. Marina looked everywhere. She even asked Sasha the handyman, who was bent over one of the giant rubbish bins, rummaging for whatever he could find: an almost-new sweater, a winter coat worn at the elbows, an old microwave or electric blanket, tins of sardines past their sell-by date.

"Yes," said Sasha, pulling on his wispy beard and stroking the head of his mangy hound, Ivan the Terrible. "There was a man wandering about. Check the playground?"

There he was, sitting on the bench by the swings, his hood pulled low over his head.

"So, did they take the bait?" Vanya asked. He had dark circles under his eyes.

"They did," said Marina. "And we have a deal. You're going to be rich, Vanechka. Richer than you ever dreamt of…"

"I don't give a shit about the money," Vanya shot back. "Well, I guess that's not true. Of course I do. But I want the bastard to pay for what he did."

"So do I, Vanechka. So do I. But we need to work together. Do you understand that? I worry sometimes that you'll do something reckless."

"Reckless? Me?" said Vanya, grinning.

"How do I get the money to you?"

"Bitcoin."

"You have a… What do they call it?"

"A wallet. Sure. I'll tell you what to do."

"When the time comes, I'll need your phone to make the transfer."

"Good thinking," said Vanya, impressed with Marina's caution. He pulled out a USB stick from the knapsack at his feet.

"Twenty-three thousand emails," he said, handing her the stick. "There must be enough in this to send him to hell."

"I'll let you know tomorrow. Here. Same time."

Vanya was on his feet, allowing himself to be hugged, when he looked up and noticed a girl on Marina's kitchen balcony. Marina had forgotten all about Lyuba and was about to explain, when Vanya darted through the parked cars towards her.

"Lyuba?" said Vanya, standing right under the balcony. "What the hell?…"

"Vanya!" Lyuba said, leaning over the balcony, her red hair falling across her face. She stretched out a hand and whispered, "I'm on the run."

"That's so cool. Stay there. I'm coming up."

Effortlessly, Vanya climbed the fire escape to the balcony, where he hugged Lyuba while Marina hurried into the building and up the stairs to her flat. At the kitchen table, Marina heard how the two teenagers had met, nine months earlier on New Year's Eve, in the back of a police van after a drugs raid at a gig in Nizhny Novgorod. Vanya had been caught with hash and Lyuba had saved him. In the police station, she'd kept her head, cried a lot and clung to Vanya, swearing he was her autistic brother. Somehow, they'd got off.

Lyuba was a first-class mimic, and she did a fine impersonation of the policeman in Nizhny Novgorod who had questioned her. Vanya had a loud, raucous laugh, which boomed through the flat and filled Marina with joy. She had never seen her Vanechka looking so carefree, so young, so full of life. It had been months – or was it years? – since she had heard such laughter in her sombre flat, and it reminded her of the world out *there*, beyond the Kremlin, a world of young people with lives to lead and dreams to fulfil. And never had she seen such a soft look in Vanya's eyes as he gazed at the girl with a face full of freckles.

"Lyuba can stay at mine," Vanya said, "till things cool down. I've got this air bed. You OK with that?"

"I can sleep anywhere," Lyuba said with a shrug. "But I'd better get out of here, for Grandma's sake, and maybe for yours?" she added, looking at Marina.

"Yes, I suppose it does make sense," Marina said, looking at the girl and thinking to herself that if she and Alexei had had a daughter, she would be about this age. What a beautiful age – so young and so brave.

As Lyuba followed Vanya out of the door, her knapsack slung over her shoulder, she called out to Marina. "Please tell Grandma not to worry. And tell her to tell my mum."

As she passed Oxana on the landing, Lyuba hugged her grandmother. She caught up with Vanya in the car park, and together they disappeared through the courtyard gates onto the eight-lane highway of Tverskaya. Meanwhile, Marina realized she was late for work and hurried to the Kremlin.

General Varlamov was sitting beneath a portrait of President Serov in his penthouse office in the Lubyanka, asking the young operative who stood in front of him why he had failed so dismally.

"It was quite difficult to keep up... Marina Volina and the Englishman were fast... And Misha isn't used to running... At the seven-kilometre mark, he didn't feel well... He had to stop. I kept going..."

"You took that fat slob with you?" Varlamov said in disgust. "Major, you're an idiot."

"Yes, General. But they probably weren't saying anything… I mean, when you're running you don't have much surplus breath…"

"I'm not interested in conjecture, Major. What's on the recording?"

"Nothing… Well, nothing when they're running… Only when they slowed down… When people are running fast, you can't hear what they're saying… Heavy breathing scrambles the words. That's a fact, General. I'm sorry, but it's a fact."

"And what about the fact that we've got the best surveillance technology in the world?"

"Yes, we do… That's true… But it doesn't alter —"

"The best surveillance equipment in the world… You've been telling me this for months, Major." Varlamov leant forward across his desk, resting on his clenched fists. "So what have you got?"

"The Englishman wants to run the marathon. He asked Mrs Volina for a late-entry pass."

"Is that it?"

"No, there is something else."

"Spit it out, for God's sake!"

"It's just something the Englishman said. Actually, he didn't say it. He sang it, quite loudly. It's about bounty and the sea. We googled it. It's a line from *Romeo and Juliet*. Act two, scene two."

"Get out of here!" shouted the general, his fist clenched.

Clive was not about to admit this to anyone, but he felt exhausted after his run with Marina. He was also troubled by a niggling doubt that would not go away, one that he had to put to Marina sooner rather than later. How could he be sure that she was not using him? How? He took a shower, rang room service, ordered wild salmon and "Olivier" salad, and switched off his phone.

He was woken by a loud and persistent knocking. Irritably, he called out to see who it was. "Narek," came the reply. "I believe you wanted me to polish your shoes, sir?" Opening the door, Clive, still groggy from sleep, caught the expectant look in Narek's eye and said, "Yes, of course." He fetched a pair of black loafers. Narek took the shoes and asked what exactly Mr Franklin had in mind. New heels and soles? He held the shoe inches from Clive's face. On the side of his thumb, Narek had written a letter and a number: R 137.

Clive dressed quickly, placed his mobile by his bed and left his room. He walked down four flights of stairs to the first floor and was about to head down a corridor when a voice behind him called out.

"Can I help you, sir?"

Clive turned to see a maid holding towels. She had just come out of the lift.

"How kind of you! I'm looking for room two-three-seven."

"Two-three-seven? That's on the second floor. I'm sorry, sir, but you're on the first floor!"

"Am I really?"

The girl smiled, happy to speak to someone.

"It's easily done, sir. The first floor is closed… All of it! You couldn't stay here, even if you wanted to. There's no electricity or running water. The rooms, well, actually they're all suites… This floor is for the very rich… There's nothing but suites down this corridor, and they're all being redone. Top to bottom. The workmen are in suite twelve this very minute! Working their way up to one-seven-six. Everything's being rewired."

"Of course. Entirely my mistake. You've been so kind. Thank you."

Clive took the lift back up to the fifth floor, waited, then took the stairs back down to the first. There was no sign of the maid. The new carpet in the long corridor was covered in plastic, which cracked underfoot. The faux-marble frame around door 137 was sealed with masking tape. Clive pushed. The unlocked door opened into an oversized sitting room with faux-marble columns. The sofas and chairs, two writing desks and a bar were all covered in dust-sheets. There was the sour smell of fresh paint everywhere.

Open gilded doors led directly to the bedroom and a king-size bed, also covered in plastic and a dust-sheet, but on top of the bed was a fur rug, and on top of the rug was Marina in her grey working suit, a bottle of Veuve Clicquot resting in her lap.

"I come bearing gifts," she said in English, waving a USB stick in the air.

"The tail didn't see you?" Clive asked anxiously. "A baby-faced guy who sits in the lobby, pretending to read a newspaper?"

"I came in by the side entrance and through the bar, where I got this." Marina held up the champagne. "Sorry, no glasses."

"That's fine," said Clive, turning the key in the door. "We'll drink from the bottle."

Clive sat on the edge of the bed, popped the cork and took a swig of champagne, all the while looking at Marina.

"What?" she asked.

Clive took another swig.

"I know what you're thinking, Clive... I know *exactly* what you're thinking... This... You and me... Is just part of my game plan to get myself out? You think... you think this isn't for real... that I'm just using you..."

"Are you?"

"No. *Nyet. Non. Nein. Nah. Non è vero,*" Marina insisted vehemently, shaking her head. Then the certainty drained from her face and she let out a deep, despairing sigh, and her arms fell limply to her sides. "But why should you believe me?" she whispered.

Marina didn't expect an answer. She swung her legs off the bed, straightened her back and reached for the bottle. "My turn," she said, and took a gulp of champagne, wiping her mouth with the back of her hand. "I was such a fool in New York," she said quietly, staring down at her hands. "If it's any consolation, I paid dearly for my mistake. I lived with Alexei's infidelity, and then with his cancer… and sometimes both at the same time… It was a very steep learning curve in patience and tolerance, and it wore me out. Eventually, I just gave up. I thought, 'That's it. I don't want to be close to anyone ever again.' I honestly thought that, until… until Sunday, when you came back into my life."

Clive leant forward. He could feel his doubts melting away. She had always disarmed him; she always would disarm him. In that moment, he knew once and for all that he loved her.

"What do you want?" he asked gently.

"A second chance," she whispered.

Clive placed the bottle on the plastic-covered floor and took Marina's face in his hands. He looked into her sad eyes flecked with green, and he kissed her, lovingly, greedily.

Later, when he looked back on it all, this was the defining moment when he put his full trust in Marina, when he gave himself permission to stop doubting her and to love her.

In room 137 of the Metropol, Clive passed the point of no return.

15

Hyde was furious. He had been trying to reach Clive from the embassy for over an hour.

"Sorry," said Clive. "I turned my phone off and went to sleep. The run wiped me out."

"Get yourself to the embassy now," said Hyde before ringing off.

Thirty-six minutes later, Clive handed Hyde a USB stick with twenty-three thousand of General Varlamov's emails and was much relieved to see a smile cross Hyde's face.

"Good work, Franklin," Hyde said. "Let's hope to God they tell us something. Time is running out."

Once again, Clive found himself with the same cast of characters back in the safe room on the top floor of the British embassy, overlooking the Moscow River with Kievsky station beyond it. Someone had sprayed the room with air-freshener, and it now smelt of pine.

The ambassador took the clingfilm off two plates of sandwiches – chicken, and egg mayonnaise – and passed them around. Clive helped himself to two of each. Why not? he thought. I've burnt a lot of calories in the last twelve hours.

"Right, Oswald," said Hyde. "You start."

Martindale leant back in his chair, tapping the table with the end of his pencil.

"The cruiser *Moskva*, the flagship of the Black Sea Fleet, is heading to Crimea. Right this very minute. The navy top brass has been summoned to the president's birthday party, along with his nearest and dearest, the handful of ministers closest to him. I would say things are hotting up. It could even be a final briefing."

"Final?" said Clive.

"All the signs are pointing to that," said Hyde. "I've already told you that for the past few months we've been monitoring one mother submarine with her baby drones skirting the Cornish coast. Well, she's brought a friend, so now we have two Russian submarines and a whole brood of pesky drones buzzing about. It's clear the Russians want their mission to succeed. If one drone fails, another can take its place. There's back-up. In other words, the Russians are serious."

Hyde paused to let the information sink in.

"Up to now, the Russians haven't put a foot wrong. But this morning, they slipped up. We intercepted a communication from a Russian submarine to its base satellite. This word *Ayid* came up – excuse my pronunciation – not once, but a couple of times."

Hyde stared straight at Clive.

"Put it all together, and it's more than possible that President Serov is holding a final briefing for Operation Hades this weekend. Mrs Volina's intelligence will be… How can I put this? Crucial."

Marina had spent an agonizing afternoon translating expressions of goodwill from the prime minister of Pakistan to President Serov and the Russian foreign minister. The moment had come, suggested the Pakistani prime minister in perfect English, to reimagine the partnership between their two countries in energy, defence and investment. Marina had to force herself to concentrate. Her mind was on the weekend ahead in Crimea and the intelligence she needed to gather in order to get out of Russia.

What if I fail? she asked herself as she walked down Tverskaya at the end of the afternoon, free at last. What if I get caught? Don't go there, she told herself. Think of Clive and his sweet face. She tried to do just that. Taking a moment to examine the plaque on the wall by the entrance to Tverskaya 25, with its profile of her grandfather incised in bronze, she pushed open the heavy mahogany door. An urgent, ugly sound filled the entrance hall.

Oxana was in a terrible state, sitting on her bed, twisting her fingers and letting out terrible, shuddering sobs. Lyuba had been arrested, she told Marina, right there on the landing by the lift, her arms full of flowers. It had all happened just minutes after Marina had left for the Kremlin that morning. Lyuba and Vanya were heading for his flat, but Lyuba remembered that she'd forgotten to leave her grandmother the medication entrusted to her by her mother, so she went back, stopping at a flower shop on the way. She was holding eleven yellow roses when she pressed the bell at Tverskaya 25 and walked straight into the arms of two policemen from Bolshaya Dmitrovka 28. They were looking for her, and they even had a photograph. Of course, the girl was unmistakable with her bright-red hair.

"I can't bear to think of her locked up in a police cell," Oxana sobbed. "Sonya's tearing her hair out. She's desperately searching for a lawyer. But where will she find the money? Where?"

Marina took Oxana's hand and stroked it.

"Oxanochka, calm yourself. I'll think of something. I promise."

Oxana pulled out her handkerchief and blew her nose loudly.

"Vanya," she spluttered. "He saw it all... He was here... Maybe he's still there... out in the car park?"

Marina ran down the back steps and into the back courtyard, where she found Vanya slouched on the green bench by the swings, two backpacks at his feet. As she sat down by his side, she could feel his despondency.

"She said it would take less than a minute... I waited for her in front of Taiga... I couldn't believe it when I saw those policemen go in..."

"Vanechka, you're not safe... We have to assume Lyuba will tell the police about you, about me... She knows where I live. And she knows that *you're* my foster son."

"She won't say anything. She's smart."

"Does she know where *you* live?"

"She hasn't got a clue. And she hasn't got my number either. Here's her stuff," he said, kicking one of the backpacks. "With her mobile. I'm gonna leave it all with her gran. Just chill, will you?"

Vanya jerked his head up. A lock of blond hair fell across his face. Marina took his hand. He had long, delicate fingers, unusual for a man.

"Vanechka, listen to me," she said, keeping hold of his hand. "*Please, listen to me.* With Lyuba arrested, you're not safe in Moscow. You're in possession of top-secret classified information, and if they catch you, then you'll spend the rest of your life in prison. Go to Minsk. Or Kiev – that would be safer still."

"Yeah. And what about you?"

"I'm fucked."

Vanya laughed and pulled the hood over his head.

"You promised, remember? Promised to get the bastard? Well, I don't see much progress."

"We're much closer than you think, Vanechka."

"Really? I saw Varlamov looking smug on TV just yesterday. I think we need some... some Pasha-style thinking here. This whole thing is taking too fucking *long*."

"Vanechka, for God's sake, don't go and do something reckless," Marina pleaded. "I beg you! We have to work *together*, don't you see? You must be patient."

"Patience is for old people! You gotta get Lyuba out. I know you can do it. She's just a kid…"

"I'll do my best," said Marina. Vanya left through the back courtyard gate, while Marina went up to her flat, changed into jeans and trainers and headed for the metro.

Am I losing my mind? Marina asked herself, emerging from Belorusskaya station into the fading sunlight just after seven o'clock. Only two hours ago, she had been making love to Clive on top of a plastic sheet in a room covered in dust-sheets. There was still dust in her hair.

The offices of Justice for All were in a side street behind the station. Marina pressed the buzzer on the intercom and asked for Anna Seliverstova. "Who is it?" said a voice. "It's Marina Volina. I'm an old friend." The metal front door opened, and Marina took the stairs to the third floor, pressed another bell and found herself in a small office where every spare inch of desk space was covered in papers. There were still more files piled on the floor, and everywhere half-drunk cups of coffee and waste baskets overflowing with torn or shredded documents. Two women were sitting behind laptops, typing furiously; neither looked up. Through a half-open door, Marina could hear someone talking in the next room.

"Excuse me," said Marina, "but is Anna here?"

The young woman who looked up could not have been more than twenty, Marina decided. Her brown hair was scraped back in a ponytail, and she wore glasses.

"Hi," she said, before turning towards a half-open door and calling out, "Anna! Someone to see you!" She then turned back to examine Marina, her intelligent eyes blinking behind her glasses. "My God, you're *that* Marina Volina," she said with disdain. "If I'd known, I wouldn't have let you in. You're Serov's interpreter. What the fuck are you doing here?"

"It's OK." Anna was standing in the open doorway, in jeans and a T-shirt with WE WILL ROCK YOU written in English on the front. From beneath her jet black fringe, she stared at Marina with intense, dark eyes. Anna showed Marina into her office, which was just as cluttered as the adjoining room, every surface piled high with papers and files. She removed a pile of documents from a chair and offered Marina a seat.

"Thank you for seeing me," Marina said, sitting down, while Anna faced her, leaning against the edge of her desk.

"How did you get this address?" Anna asked.

"From your website."

Anna laughed.

"I must delete our address… We don't need random visitors."

"This isn't a random visit, Anna."

Marina could see no trace of friendship in Anna's dark eyes, and yet, for five whole years of secondary school, they had been the best of friends. True, at university they had gone their separate ways: Anna studied law, while Marina studied Shakespeare; Anna stayed in Moscow, while Marina escaped to New York. In the years that followed, their paths diverged even further: Anna took on the Russian state, while Marina worked for it. She despises me, Marina thought. So be it. I have a job to do.

It didn't take Marina long to tell Lyuba's story, but it seemed to make little or no impression on Anna.

"There are lots of sixteen-year-olds in prison," she said. "You didn't know that? Really? Where is she being held?"

"The police who took her were from Bolshaya Dmitrovka," Marina said, bridling at the sarcasm in Anna's voice, but refusing to be thrown. "Anna, can you help to get her out? I can pay all your costs."

"I don't want your money," Anna said. "We'll manage… We always manage. Why are you doing this? Why are you sticking your neck out for a girl you hardly know?"

"Her grandmother is a woman I like and respect. And she's been a very good friend to me. And I don't think a sixteen-year-old girl should be in prison."

"Nor do a lot of people. We're marching this Sunday... Mothers against children in prison. Join us..."

"I'm away this weekend."

Anna let out a hard, unsympathetic laugh.

"Of course! It's the president's birthday, and he's having a big flashy party. I've read about it online. You're going. Of course you are..."

They were interrupted by a ringtone. Anna took her mobile onto the small balcony outside her office; when she returned, she was sheet-white and her hand was trembling.

"Nikita Strelnikov died last night in police custody," Anna murmured.

There was a knock at the door, and the young woman who had berated Marina looked in, flustered and anxious.

"Anna, we've just had terrible news..."

"I know," said Anna. "I was so afraid this would happen... We have to get hold of the family right away."

Marina felt she had no business being in the room at such a time, and she got up to leave, but Anna stopped her. "I'll do what I can for Lyubov Zvezdova," she said. "When the police detain sixteen-year-olds, it almost always backfires. The parents go berserk. They get *Novaya Gazeta* and Ekho Moskvy on their side, and Serov looks like even more of a monster... The fact it's against the law is incidental. Leave me the grandmother's name and contact number and... Here, give her my card."

Marina scribbled Oxana's name and number on a used piece of paper, which she handed to Anna. She was staring at Marina, as if she were searching for something in her face, something she had once loved.

"How can you work for…" Anna began, but stopped mid-sentence. "No. Put it this way: when you're singing 'Happy Birthday', take a good, hard look at birthday boy and spare a thought for your Lyuba, who's in prison, and for Nikita, who's dead."

Marina was heading for the door when Anna called after her.

"General Varlamov. Do you know him?"

"Yes, I do."

"What's he like?"

Marina understood that Anna was asking for inside information. It was hers by right, Marina decided.

"Varlamov is relentless," said Marina. "And dangerous. Like a dog with a bone, he never gives up."

"That's what I'm hearing. He's tightening the screws."

"Thank you, Anna, for seeing me."

Was it wishful thinking, or did Marina see a glimmer of warmth in Anna's tired face?

In the outside office, among the files and phone chargers and random leads trailing across the floor, Marina noticed a camp bed in the corner. Is that where Anna slept when she was overloaded with work? From this tiny office, she was taking on the Russian state. How long could she survive?

That evening, when Marina told Oxana that she had spoken to a lawyer and there was hope, Oxana burst into tears.

16

When the general arrived at his office in the Senate Palace on Friday morning, he found Marina's report on his desk. Apparently, she had sent it by email to Lev, who had, most obligingly, printed it out. This annoyed Varlamov. It was as if, at every turn, Marina wanted to remind him how close she was to the president. The report was in bullet points, which Varlamov found disrespectful.

As the palace clocks chimed noon, Varlamov walked into Marina's office, which was empty. The door was open, and her passport was on her desk, so he knew she must be around. What is it about passports? Why are they so irresistible? Especially the photographs. Varlamov looked at Marina's serious, determined face. Not a trace of a smile. Then he looked at her date of birth. She was just forty. A Leo. They shared the same star sign. She was a leader, which was probably why they clashed. Because what was he, if not a leader? Then Varlamov studied the various objects in the room, looking for clues: the suitcase by the door, the black leather swivel chair, a copy of *The Times* on a side table. He made a mental note of the English books: *Sapiens: A Brief History of Humankind, Leonardo: A Biography, Looking for Trouble* by Virginia Cowles. He went over to Marina's desk. There were only two photographs: one of Marina next to a good-looking man in a ski suit, and one of two teenage boys, their arms around each other at Gorky Park.

"Can I help you?"

Varlamov turned around to find Marina standing in the doorway.

"Where have you been? I looked for you earlier this morning... No one knew where you were."

Vanya knew. Marina had met him on the bench in the playground at nine, and together they had transferred a large sum of money from her account to his. Vanya double-checked, and, yes, his Bitcoin wallet was bulging.

And Narek knew. On her way to the office, Marina had stopped by the Metropol to get her shoes polished. Sitting in the high chair, Narek had handed her a crumpled copy of *The Times*. She'd looked and looked again and found nothing, her eye skating over an article about the Perm theatre company that had been touring the UK, performing *Uncle Vanya* in Russian. The last port of call, in mid-September, would be the Minack amphitheatre on the Cornish coast. Marina smiled when she read this and made a mental note to tell Clive. And then she found what she was looking for.

"I was getting ready for the weekend," Marina said. "Packing. That sort of thing."

Marina watched in dismay as the general picked up *The Times*.

"I thought everyone got their news online," he said, turning the pages.

She should have binned it hours ago... What *was* she thinking? Too late now. Would the general notice Clive's words scribbled in English along the margin of the page with crosswords? *Plan A: What, where and when? Final briefing this weekend?*

"It's yesterday's," said Varlamov, tossing the paper to one side. "When you have a moment, maybe you could step into my office, Marina Andreyevna? I'd like to discuss your report."

Alone in her office, Marina found herself breathing heavily. Distantly she heard her phone ping, and she saw a text from Lev: "The boss needs to see you NOW."

Marina found the president in his office, sitting beneath a photograph of himself in the Kremlin's throne room, staring at a flat-screen television on the wall, while the foreign minister was sitting in an armchair, drinking tea and talking to General Varlamov.

"Translate, translate…" Serov said to Marina, pointing to the screen, where Martha Maitland was addressing a packed House of Commons.

"I am now able to tell the house," Marina translated, staring at the furious face of the British prime minister, "that our forensic experts have established beyond any reasonable doubt that Russia is behind the murder of Sergei Yegorov. And, yes, I use the word advisedly… this was murder."

"You can't prove a thing, you stupid woman!" the Russian president shouted at the screen.

The prime minister gave details of the police investigation, which Marina translated as fast as she could.

"We cannot sit idly by and watch yet another assassination from a Russian hit squad on British soil," Mrs Maitland continued, leaning forward on the dispatch box. "And so, I can tell the house that I have ordered the expulsion of eighteen Russian diplomats. They have forty-eight hours to leave."

A crescendo of approval rose up from the packed benches of the House of Commons.

"Such a hysterical reaction… Typical of a woman," Serov said, turning to Kirsanov. "So, Dima… What's our next move?"

"We retaliate, of course, and expel exactly the same number," the foreign minister said with a sigh.

"Excellent," said Serov. "Let's get it out there, right away… Keep up the pressure. Marinochka, what's *he* saying?"

Serov had his eyes fixed on the leader of the opposition, who was on his feet, arguing that we should not jump to conclusions and that the expulsion of diplomats was premature. He was interrupted by cries of "Shame!"

Marina translated with ease. She always found the brawling, braying atmosphere of the House of Commons invigorating and at times hugely entertaining. It was such a far cry from anything you might see in Russia.

"The useful idiot… He does it again," said Serov.

"Order! Order!" the Speaker roared.

"Listen to all that noise!" said Serov, staring at the screen. "Their House of Commons is like a zoo. Look at them… Yelling and shouting… No respect for their leader. It's uncivilized!"

Serov got to his feet and signalled to Lev to turn off the television.

This was Marina's cue to leave. Lev opened the door for her with a slight bow and followed her out. His office was right next door, and here, Marina lingered.

"Lyova, the Englishman has decided to accept Nikolai Nikolayevich's invitation and run the marathon, but he'll need a late-entry pass. Can you fix it?"

"Not a problem," said Lev. "But is he up to it? Are you sure? What's he like, this Englishman?"

"Mr Franklin?" said Marina. She was flustered by this unexpected line of questioning from Lev. "Well, he's quiet. And literary. And pretty fit. We've been out on some practice runs and he keeps up with me just fine."

"You like foreigners?" asked Lev. "I had American friends when I was at Stanford, but here in Moscow all my friends are Russian."

With another bow, Lev showed Marina out of his office and into the corridor, where they both found themselves face to face with Professor Olga Tabakova of the Institute for Longevity.

Ignoring Marina and looking over her shoulder, the professor addressed Lev.

"So, can I go in?"

Lev shook his head.

"But I can't wait all day!"

"He knows you're here," said Lev, closing the gilded door in her face.

It was early afternoon when Marina was shown into General Varlamov's courtesy office at the Senate Palace.

"Take a seat," he said, his thin mouth set hard as he sat at his desk beneath a portrait of Felix Dzerzhinsky, the founder of the secret police under Lenin. She could not help but notice everywhere the photographs of the general with various heads of state – from Azerbaijan, Kazakhstan, Syria and Algeria. Marina had brought a copy of her report with her, and, as the general pored over his copy, she reread her own words and wondered what he found so interesting in the mundane facts she had set before him.

MARINA VOLINA. REPORT FOR GENERAL VARLAMOV.
Run with British translator Clive Franklin. Friday, 15 September.

PLACE: Frunzenskaya Embankment.
DISTANCE COVERED: 10 kilometres.
TIME: 1 hour 18 minutes (slow and steady).

- Conversation almost impossible; breath needed for running, not talking.
- Franklin kept up, is surprisingly fit.
- Now that trade talks have collapsed, he would like to run the Moscow marathon. He thanks President Serov for his invitation and wonders if he can be a late entry.

- Says it seems a pity to leave Moscow with so little accomplished.
- Has spent time with Martin Hyde, who is interested in sightseeing and history.
- Did not enjoy *Queen of Spades* at the Bolshoi on Monday night.
- Is impressed by new Moscow pavements.
- Is looking forward to the Royal Shakespeare Company's production of *Julius Caesar*.

Varlamov let go of the paper and it fluttered to the desk.

"It's a bit thin."

"That was not my intention. But you cannot talk and run at the same time, Grigory Mikhailovich."

Varlamov stabbed the report with his finger.

"What's all this about *Julius Caesar*?"

"A one-off performance by the Royal Shakespeare Company at the Chekhov Moscow Art Theatre. An all-black cast. I'm sorry to miss it."

The general didn't react.

"So, the Englishman is going to stay on. Do you know *why*?"

Varlamov sat calmly, clasping his elegant, manicured fingers.

"As far as I know, he likes it here, and he wants to run the Moscow marathon. He's very keen on fitness, like so many men these days."

Instinctively the general pulled in his stomach.

"Let me tell you something about Clive Franklin." Varlamov leant forward, his hooded eyes fixed on Marina. "I smell a rat."

Marina was saved by a knock at the door and the sight of Lev's bald head.

"I've been looking for you everywhere, Marina Andreyevna. *Legs in hands*. Excuse me, General, but we're off."

Damn the woman, thought Varlamov as he watched Marina hurrying down the corridor while Lev, in a show of courtesy, took her suitcase. As they disappeared down the marble stairs to the helipad beyond, Varlamov felt a surge of resentment towards Marina Volina, and with good reason. She was off to Simferopol with the president *today*, in the new PUM1 jet, while he, General Varlamov, had not been invited to travel with the president and would only go *tomorrow* – and commercial, at that. First-class VIP, but still commercial. These things rankled with Varlamov, who understood perfectly that he had the trust of the president but not his friendship. He had learnt to live with this, and, as a result, his entire attention was focused on being outstandingly good at his job, on cultivating support among the president's inner circle within the Kremlin and making sure that he could never be ignored or overlooked, so that when the head of the FSB retired – perhaps in one or two years – he would be the obvious candidate. I do not need to be liked, he told himself. What matters is that I'm feared.

It wasn't long before the general heard the sound of the president's helicopter taking off for Vnukovo airport with Volina on board. She's getting too big for her boots, he thought. I really must bring her down a peg or two.

It was Friday afternoon, not yet five o'clock, but there was no sign of life in the Senate Palace. It was the same every week. All the president's men and women left early on a Friday to miss the four-hour traffic jams out of Moscow. Not Varlamov. He worked most weekends, and this one was no exception. It was a short drive to the massive Lubyanka building, headquarters of the FSB, where the general had his office on the top floor. There, sitting behind his desk, General Varlamov felt at home, surrounded by FSB officers who knew him and, more importantly, feared him.

Varlamov could feel the same familiar stillness of a Friday afternoon hanging over the FSB headquarters. Most people had left, but not Lieutenant Maxim Mishin, the youngest and most inexperienced of the general's team, and also the most industrious. Varlamov summoned Mishin on the intercom, and, while he waited, he picked up his mobile and glanced at the picture of his wife and children on the screen. Would they miss him this weekend? Unlikely... They were used to his not being around – and anyway, they had their own lives. In truth, he'd never been much of a family man. From his children he expected obedience and respect, but over the years he'd discovered this was hard to come by, since his wife, Raisa, constantly undermined him. She spoilt the children, and herself. In recent years, he'd grown very fond of his daughter, Veronika, and made a conscious effort to get close to her, even taking her to meet her favourite ballet dancer at the Mariinsky in Saint Petersburg. Nothing pleased him more than when she came over to him as he sat in his armchair reading, put her arms around his neck and kissed his cheek. Varlamov put his mobile face down on his desk and turned his thoughts to Marina Volina. Yes, he really must take her down a peg or two. But he had nothing on her: not yet. There was a knock at his door. On entering, Lieutenant Mishin saluted.

Mishin was a young man of medium height, who looked younger than his twenty-three years, with brown hair that sprouted in several directions, a round face, a flat nose and dark, currant eyes. He wore glasses with thick lenses, which magnified his black eyes and made him look fearful. But the lieutenant was not fearful; he was focused and determined never to return to the impoverished life he had known, having grown up in a tenement block in Chita. He worked late every night, was utterly reliable and obedient, a workaholic hoping for promotion and, eventually, a slice of the pie. It was Mishin who, at Varlamov's request, had inspected his computer and found the digital footprint of someone who had inserted a USB stick into the back of the monitor and copied thousands of emails. It was Mishin who had changed Varlamov's password and who had been paid five thousand dollars to keep his mouth tightly shut. And, of course, Mishin knew exactly what would happen to him if he talked. To anyone.

"Lieutenant? I need you to do something now. I want the old file on Marina Volina from her days at the UN. Our people in New York will help you. I want that file this evening. Bring it to me as soon as you get it. Understood?"

An hour later, with Mishin's help, the general was spreading out printed sheets of paper and photographs across his desk. Varlamov liked the feel of paper. All that digital information didn't seem to stick in his brain. He loved glossy photographic paper, which was, in most cases, the genuine article, he reflected, unlike today's digital photographs, which can so easily be doctored or Photoshopped. Ah yes, he sighed, those were the days when a photograph could be counted on as evidence!

Varlamov studied the photographs before him. Volina was so pretty when she was young, he thought. As for Franklin, well, he looked absurdly young, like a schoolboy. One particular black-and-white photograph caught the general's attention: the two of them in a park somewhere. Maybe Central Park? Clive Franklin sitting on a bench, looking at Marina Volina.

Mishin leant forward to take a closer look.

"That guy's crazy about her," he said.

"You think so?" asked Varlamov.

"It's obvious."

The general dismissed Mishin.

A little after nine o'clock, Varlamov was deciding to call it a day, when suddenly his phone pinged. There had been an incident at the Chekhov Moscow Art Theatre, where the Royal Shakespeare Company was performing *Julius Caesar*. Clive Franklin, the British interpreter, had been seriously injured.

.   .   .

"It's nothing," Clive was saying as he sat in the front row of the stalls, looking at his hand, which had a deep-red wound in the heart of the palm. Blood was dribbling down his wrist. On his lap was a theatre programme impaled by a dagger. The programme had saved him – or, rather, it had saved Zoya Kunko, who was sitting next to him.

"What an extraordinary thing to happen," said the ambassador. "I've never seen anything like it. Never. Here, take my handkerchief."

"For fuck's sake," said Rose Friedman, "you're a bloody hero."

"I have personal hospital," said Boris Kunko, standing with his back to the stage and facing Clive, blocking out the footlights with his huge bulk. "Personal hospital is yours. Doctors are yours. Everything is yours… You save my girl from —" Kunko muttered a word in Russian.

"A nasty accident," said Clive. "Do tell them to get on with the play."

The production had been halted, leaving the audience in suspense, except for those in the front rows, who knew exactly what had happened. Most people in the auditorium assumed it was a technical problem, until the RSC director walked on stage and asked if there was a doctor in the house. Even then, some people laughed, thinking it must be a joke, a modernist take on Shakespeare, but the laughter subsided as the anxious director stood on the stage scanning the faces before him, begging for someone to come forward. A man put up his hand.

It had all started so well, Clive told Marina later. The play was set in a modern-day military dictatorship in Africa. The acting was superb, the staging original, and on that evening in Moscow there wasn't a spare seat in the house. The first act had passed without a hitch: the all-black cast played reggae on the steps of a Roman amphitheatre, and the audience clapped and swayed to the music.

The trouble started with the second act. With Caesar dead, Brutus and Cassius were quarrelling about the future of Rome. Brutus hurled a knife at his brother. From London to Liverpool, the knife had skidded neatly across the stage and landed in the wings. In Moscow, it went off at right angles and headed straight for the face of Zoya Kunko, who happened to be the daughter of the play's major sponsor. Years of catching practice on the cricket pitch kicked in, and Clive's right arm shot out; he was holding the RSC programme, and the thick, glossy pages took the hit. Even so, the point of the knife had dug into Clive's palm. Zoya had tied a handkerchief around Clive's hand, which was now soaked in blood.

Clive was ushered out of the auditorium into the foyer, where the embassy doctor, Malcolm McPherson, examined Clive's hand.

"I'm a dedicated Shakespeare fan," said Doctor McPherson, who came from Dundee and spoke with a soft Scottish accent. "I was so excited to see the RSC in Moscow, I can't tell you. Came straight from the surgery, checked my medical bag in the cloakroom… Now how's that for a piece of luck?"

"Clive's a bloody hero," said Rose, looking at the blood-soaked handkerchief.

"The cut isn't so deep," said the doctor. "I think you can get away without stitches. There's always a lot of blood with these surface wounds."

The doctor dressed the wound and wrapped Clive's hand in a clean white bandage.

"You might not need these, but just in case," said the doctor, handing Clive some painkillers.

"I'd rather have a drink," said Clive. Right on cue, Rose handed him a vodka and resumed her place on a bar stool, helping herself to sandwiches meant for the cast and VIP guests.

"Doc," she said. "You do realize, your patient here deserves a medal! He saved the daughter of one of Russia's richest men from *permanent disfigurement*. The dagger was two inches from her face."

"Well, you can tell those actors from me," the doctor said, "they should be using rubber knives."

By the time that Clive had downed his second vodka, he could hear clapping, and then more clapping and the odd shout of "Hurrah!" It was the second interval. Brutus, who was dressed like Papa Doc in a white military suit with dark glasses and knee-high leather boots and brandishing a whip, appeared in the foyer and came straight over to Clive.

"Sorry, my friend… This is a first. Two hundred and fourteen performances and nothing like this has ever happened before. You gonna live, or you gonna die?"

"I'm going to live," Clive said, smiling and trying not to wince with pain at the same time.

"Good man," said Brutus, giving Clive a high five on his left hand. Clive thanked the doctor and insisted on going back to his seat to watch the end of the play.

"Hero!" Boris Kunko boomed at Clive, slapping him on the back at the after-party with the cast. "You absolute hero! You want car? I give car. House? Big house? How many bedrooms?"

Clive's hand was throbbing, and he reached for the pain-killers in his pocket.

"You're not looking so good," said Rose. "Come on, I'll take you back to your hotel. Boris, can we borrow your car?"

"My car is *your* car," said Boris, grabbing Clive's wrist close to the wounded hand and sending a spasm of pain though Clive's arm. "You *keep* my car. Driver wait for you all day, all night. Take you anywhere."

"Just the Metropol," said Rose wearily, and, moments later, she was grateful to find herself in the back seat of Boris's armour-plated, blacked-out Mercedes S600 with Clive in the seat beside her. The hotel was just around the corner, but, as Rose pointed out, why walk when you can hitch a ride in a fancy car?

At the Metropol, Rose saw Clive up to his room.

"Thank you, Rose… What were the odds of this happening? A trillion to one? You couldn't make it up…"

"They always say truth is stranger than fiction."

Clive took four painkillers and went to sleep.

Meanwhile, Varlamov was taking stock behind his desk in the Lubyanka. Was this an assassination attempt that had gone wrong? he wondered as he reread the brief account from his agent in the theatre. Was the target Boris Kunko perhaps?

The general made a telephone call and waited. Moments later he was speaking to the director of the theatre, who gave a detailed account of the whole episode, which he himself had witnessed from a box just above the stage. It was an accident. Varlamov didn't believe in accidents, but since the perpetrator of the "crime" was a British actor, and since the play had resumed after fifteen minutes with no further incident, and since the English translator, Mr Clive Franklin, had personally assured the theatre and the British Council and Boris Kunko that he was not going to press charges, General Grigory Varlamov decided to let the matter drop.

17

Marina woke early on Saturday morning to a sunlit view of the Black Sea, as smooth as glass and a striking blue. She was rocking in a chair that came with the house, listening to the creaking sound of wood on wood, drinking her first coffee of the day, but not in peace, since Olga, the red-faced house-keeper, was asking if she didn't wanted to try the figs, which were wonderful that year. Marina succumbed, tried a fig, and then asked for another. Olga beamed.

It was a charming house overlooking the sea, backing onto a vineyard laid out in terraces cut into the hillside. A small path led down to a beach thirty metres long, which was part of the property, with a jetty and a boathouse where Marina had a speedboat – another present from President Serov. Last summer, she had taken her boatman's licence. Geographically speaking, Marina knew exactly where she was: beyond the hazy horizon lay Turkey; to the east was Russia; to the south-east, Georgia; to the west, Romania and Bulgaria.

This is Crimea, Marina thought, land of grapes and sun. In the nineteenth century, you came here to stave off tuberculosis, like Chekhov, or to while away unwanted exile, like Pushkin. Today, Russians come in their thousands to feel the sun on their backs. Not me. I have an entirely different objective: I'm here to plot perfidy. The Russian word, *verolomstvo*, rang in her ears: a combination of "trust" and "smash". In English, Marina reflected, rocking herself back and forth, you can take your pick between treachery or perfidy. Somehow, perfidy sounds worse, she decided. Either way, it's the sort of thing they kill you for.

Absolutely no presents, said the invitation from the president's office, printed in elaborate script, with a gold border around the edge. Marina was about to disobey.

At half past nine, an official car drew up in front of Marina's villa. The driver had a message: Marina Andreyevna was to bring a pair of rubber-soled shoes and to wear trousers. Marina hurried back to change.

On the eight-kilometre journey to the president's villa, the driver did not draw breath, telling Marina that during the night a guided-missile cruiser called the *Moskva* had anchored a few kilometres out to sea, in front of the president's villa. This was the president's birthday… A red-letter day!

Marina heard her phone ping and saw a text from Lev: he would meet her on the lawn and brief her. She was on duty at ten-thirty.

Twenty minutes later, Marina was standing on a meticulously mown lawn in the warming light of the Crimean sun, facing a three-storey mansion that reminded her of the White House, except that it was a pale yellow. On the flight over, the president had told Marina that his spanking new Villa Nadezhda was an exact copy of the Yelagin Palace in Saint Petersburg, but, of course, on a much smaller scale. It's a house, the president had told her, not a palace, and he had named it after his late wife, Nadezhda.

Marina was curious to see inside the huge lunch tent, which was draped in the white, blue and red of the Russian flag. Inside, she found an army of waiters laying tables for two hundred guests. As she wandered back across the lawn, she saw Lev waving by a fountain. No hurry, he explained. The Indian VIP she was to look after hadn't yet arrived, so there was time for a quick tour of the garden.

They stopped at the ha-ha and stared out over the sparkling sea. On those dancing shards of light bobbed the president's yacht, usually a most impressive sight, but not today, when it looked like a toy in a bath, dwarfed by the flagship of the Black Sea Fleet, the *Moskva*, which dominated the horizon. Through Lev's binoculars, Marina could see the missiles, gunmetal and gleaming, neatly stacked and pointing upwards. Don't go far, Lev said, before disappearing to find out where the Indian VIP had got to and leaving Marina alone on the greenest of grass. Everywhere Marina looked, she saw navy top brass in their distinctive white-and-gold dress uniforms. She was drawn irresistibly to where the president stood, holding court, besieged by admirals and fawning guests, all eager to convey their birthday wishes. Marina spotted the foreign minister and Boris Kunko on the steps of the villa, and sitting on the edge of a fountain, where water gushed from the mouths of dolphins, was the deputy prime minister, Viktor Romanovsky, who had spotted her and was fast approaching.

Looking around for an escape route, Marina caught sight of the newlyweds, Nastya and Igor, and threw herself into Igor's bear hug, thanking first him and then Nastya for the most beautiful wedding reception.

"I was hoping you'd be here," Igor said with genuine warmth. "This is some place, don't you think? They finished it in record time. The paint is hardly dry." He looked approvingly at the yellow mansion gleaming in the sun. "I met the project manager in Moscow. He told me he'd been given an impossible deadline by the president… But when Nikolai Nikolayevich wants something, he gets it. Just like that. Now, if you'll excuse me, we must go and congratulate the birthday boy…"

"Just like that," echoed Marina, taking another cup of coffee from a passing tray and discreetly moving away to sit down on the edge of a fountain and wait for Lev.

A voice from behind startled her.

"Hello."

Marina looked up to see a ravishing young woman in a white summer dress with blue forget-me-nots.

"Sorry if I startled you. It's Marina, isn't it?"

"And you're Katya," said Marina with a smile.

"What do you think of this place… Impressive, no? I mean, look at the size of it! I'm here with Igor and Nastya… I don't know anyone here… I feel a bit lost…"

"You should meet Lev…" Marina began, but to her dismay she spotted Viktor Romanovsky striding purposefully towards her. This time there was no escape. Standing inches away from Marina, the deputy prime minister launched into his usual obsequious patter.

"Marina Andreyevna… What a vision you are this morning! Dazzling… Quite dazzling. Have I told you that I'm putty in your hands? Just putty…"

Then Romanovsky's lascivious eye fell on Katya.

"My, oh my, who do we have here? Am I speaking to the new government adviser on quantitative easing?"

Katya looked puzzled.

"It was a joke," said Viktor, taking Katya's arm. "Shall we have some ice cream?"

Is it going to be like this all weekend? Marina wondered. Nothing but social chit-chat and idiotic banter? And shall I come away empty-handed, my tail between my legs?

She glanced around at the dozens of smiling faces; everyone was in a holiday mood, except for General Varlamov, who stood alone in a corner, eating a peach, the juice dribbling down his chin, which he wiped away, most carefully, with a red silk handkerchief. Marina was thinking that she, too, might like a peach, when the general noticed her and walked over.

"The Englishman was stabbed last night," he said with casual indifference, keeping his eye trained on Marina's face.

"Stabbed?"

Marina's face gave nothing away.

"In the hand. He'll be fine. It really is an extraordinary story."

Varlamov had just finished telling it, when Lev sauntered over and told Marina that the boss was looking for her.

Serov was in an exceptionally good mood, and soon Marina understood why. The head of the Indian navy, Admiral Mahrendra Singh, had just signed a contract that morning for five Russian submarines.

"Now *that's* what I call a birthday present," said Serov, taking Marina by the arm and strolling across the lawn with Lev just behind. "He's here somewhere, the navy chief. That's what he's called in India. Going home today, but I've invited him to tour the *Moskva*. You're coming too. I need you to translate… Lyova, where *is* our Indian friend? Go and find him!"

Lev hurried off while Marina slipped her arm free.

"Nikolai Nikolayevich, speaking of birthday presents…"

From her blue handbag she pulled out her prettily wrapped gift and presented it to the president with a speech she had prepared, wishing him a long and healthy life, and hoping that he would be guided by integrity and common sense in his most difficult job. Serov scolded her for bringing a present, but she could see that he was pleased when he held up a framed photograph of the young KGB officer Nikolai Nikolayevich Serov standing next to her father, Andrei Borisovich Volin, in his Soviet general's uniform. Between them stood a little girl.

"Look at you! Marinochka, you come from great stock. He was a great patriot, your father, and a great soldier. A hero of the Soviet Union and my friend and mentor. Marinochka, you must be very proud."

"I'm proud, of course… but… well, my father was a bully. You remember how I hated the early-morning swimming? He forced me… he literally dragged me out of bed, sometimes kicking and screaming!"

"Andrei Pavlovich was stubborn, I grant you that," the president conceded. "But he had real focus, real determination… And all that swimming, all those early starts, look what it did for you! It taught you discipline and commitment. It made you the woman you are today, Marinochka."

Serov took Marina by the arm and wandered across the lawn, telling her that turning seventy-one was more fun than turning seventy. They were joined, moments later, by the commander-in-chief of the Russian navy, Admiral of the Fleet Vyacheslav Konstantinovich Fyodorov, an imposing figure with a round and very red face who was dressed in a spotless white uniform with four rows of medals. He came to wish the president a very happy birthday and ended up telling a joke that brought tears to Serov's eyes. It was then that Marina remembered what Lev had once told her: Admiral Fyodorov made the president laugh.

Marina was introduced to the admiral and also to his good-looking aide-de-camp with white-blond hair, Artyom Smirnov. She thanked Admiral Fyodorov for inviting her aboard the *Moskva*.

"Delighted," said the admiral.

"Cars will be leaving from the house in exactly one hour," murmured the ADC.

"I've never been on a guided-missile cruiser," Marina remarked to the president, staring at the *Moskva* spread across the glittering surface of the Black Sea and feeling in her bones that something important was about to happen. Whatever that was, it would take place on board this gigantic floating arsenal.

"I just hope I don't let you down. I don't know the first thing about ships, even in Russian... the terminology..."

"You'll manage," said Serov, dismissing her comment with a wave of his hand. "Ah!" he said, spotting Lev, who was leading the Indian VIP across the lawn. "At last. The man himself."

The Indian admiral's uniform was the best of the lot, Marina decided as she took in the swathe of gold braid that hung across the chest of the navy chief. Mahrendra Singh was a handsome and austere man with black bushy eyebrows, who spoke English with a cut-glass accent that put Marina to shame. As they shook hands, and Marina looked Admiral Singh directly in the eye, she thought: You are my passport to the missile cruiser, and I am all yours.

There was majesty in the sheer size of the warship. The navy cutter that brought the president and his party alongside the *Moskva* felt like a dinghy next to the huge grey bulk of the warship. How do you board such a monster? she asked Lev. Easy, he whispered. Just watch. An accommodation ladder was lowered down the side of the ship, and the president, eager to show off his rude health, briskly climbed the steps, followed by Admiral Fyodorov, who puffed a little, and Admiral Singh, who was as nimble as a twenty-year-old. At the top of the steps, standing to attention was the captain of the *Moskva* and the commander-in-chief of the Black Sea Fleet, a big-chested man with orange hair. Serov savoured the moment. He was smiling from ear to ear as he was piped aboard. This was his birthday, and this was his ship. A guided tour followed, led by the captain.

Marina could not believe how clean the ship was, how shiny and slick, with so much high-tech equipment: the masts, the revolving dishes, the long-range radar and the missiles – gun-metal, so sleek and smooth and deadly. As they moved from one deck to another, she found herself disorientated and a little queasy. The red-haired captain of the *Moskva* had a deep, sonorous voice, and he waxed lyrical about the wonders of the warship, which Marina translated into English for Admiral Singh, who now and then corrected her technical terminology with an indulgent smile. It was a relief when the tour ended and the president's party of twelve was shown into the captain's large cabin, where the wood-panelled walls were covered in prints of victorious Russian sea battles and where a dining table stood heaped with refreshments. The captain urged everyone to get stuck in, but Marina held back, taking in the details of the room. At one end of the cabin, a naval officer stood to attention in front of a closed door. Why? she wondered as she made a beeline for Admiral Fyodorov's good-looking ADC, Captain First Rank Artyom Smirnov, who was helping himself to a blini with caviar. Marina asked if he ever got seasick. This broke the ice. It turned out Captain Smirnov had spent six months on the *Moskva*, knew every inch of it and loved it with a passion. Marina felt with a sudden rush of adrenalin: here was the man who could tell her what she needed to know. But suddenly the president summoned her over.

"It's no use," Serov said to Marina, helping himself to a sturgeon sandwich. "I cannot persuade my friend Admiral Singh to stay to lunch. Not even on my birthday!"

The Indian admiral smiled and said that he was needed urgently back in New Delhi, but what a pleasure it had been to tour such a great ship in the company of such an accomplished interpreter. Marina thanked him for the compliment, translating from English into Russian as she went along, but said that Admiral Singh had been too kind; she had struggled, especially with "fire-control radar". When Admiral Fyodorov heard this, he burst out laughing and clapped Admiral Singh on the back, repeating, "Good man, excellent man." Then the blow fell. The president asked Marina to accompany Admiral

Singh back to shore. "Of course," said Marina, feeling a stab of disappointment. The intelligence was *here*, under her nose. She could feel it. "Delighted to accompany Admiral Singh," Marina said, forcing a smile. Here she was, on board the *Moskva*, with nothing to show for it. All she could hope for now was luck ashore, under the tent, maybe over lunch, or tea, or dinner. But luck came her way earlier than she expected. She hardly noticed when Admiral Singh discreetly asked if he could use the men's room and was ushered into the captain's private bathroom. That was when she overheard the president murmur to Admiral Fyodorov: "It's just as well our Indian friend has to go back to India... We need to have our meeting..."

"We certainly do," Fyodorov replied. "Not a moment to lose, as I've said more than once."

So, the final briefing is happening here and now, Marina thought, and it will all take place while I'm ashore. I won't pick up even a crumb of intelligence. Resign yourself to your fate, she told herself, and approached her new friend, the good-looking ADC, asking if she, too, might use the facilities. Perhaps there was another lavatory? Captain Smirnov consulted the ADC to the captain of the *Moskva*, then, to Marina's surprise, he asked her to hand over her mobile, explaining that devices were forbidden in the "confidential compartment", even though she was only passing through. Smirnov led Marina over to the naval officer standing to attention in front of the closed door and whispered something in his ear. The officer nodded, opened the door and led Marina across a windowless room filled with electronic humming from a bank of flickering computer screens. Passing a central table covered with sea charts, he escorted her to a lavatory on the far side. Marina locked the lavatory door and stood quite still, breathing heavily as she realized exactly where she was: inside the lion's den. Lady Luck was smiling down.

Marina emerged from the lavatory and looked for the naval officer, who was waiting for her at the far end of the room, holding open the door, his head turned towards the president and his guests. For a few seconds, Marina understood she had the room to herself. She glanced down at the chart which had some markings in black, but all she had time to read was the title: LAND'S END TO FALMOUTH. The guard turned his head. Marina met his eyes with a smile and walked back into the captain's cabin to retrieve her mobile and meet the penetrating stare of Grigory Varlamov.

It seemed an age since Marina had waved goodbye to Admiral Singh. The hours dragged by. She managed to get a glimpse of the birthday cake in a special kitchen at the back of the tent and even met the French pastry chef from Paris who had been working on it for three days. "*C'est magnifique,*" she said, as she watched the Frenchman in his starched white coat and hat sprinkle gold dust over a one-metre-high replica of the Villa Nadezhda, before spelling out the exact ingredients needed to make the strawberry, raspberry and blackcurrant cream filling and the yellow fondant icing. Marina barely listened. She was thinking of the naval chart in the airless "confidential compartment". She had something to offer Hyde, but not enough.

Thanks to Lev, Marina found herself at Admiral Fyodorov's table, but every time she leant across to talk to him, his big-boned wife, who had a huge emerald on her finger, glowered and demanded his full attention. When Mrs Fyodorov went to the ladies, Marina slipped into the vacant seat.

"Good meeting?" Marina asked with a dazzling smile.

The commander-in-chief let out a deep sigh.

"Still no decision... Oh, these politicians! But I'm a seasoned servant of the state, my dear, and over the years I've learnt to be patient."

"Patience," Marina sighed. "Ah, yes. I'm afraid I have very little."

Fyodorov raised his glass.

"Did I tell you I knew your father? Here's to his memory! A great patriot."

My bully of a father is turning out to be useful after all, Marina thought, and she clinked glasses with the admiral. But her optimism was short-lived.

"And where am I supposed to sit?"

Mrs Fyodorov had asked the question in her most imperious tone, standing behind her husband, her finger with the emerald ring resting on the golden epaulette of his naval uniform. She was staring accusingly at Marina, not just for usurping her seat, but for being there in the first place: the president's interpreter should have been at another table. After all, she was only *staff.*

Suddenly, a Gypsy ensemble burst into the tent, singing and dancing, and everyone started clapping, including the president. Marina had never seen Serov so light-hearted. When the show was over, and before the presentation of the birthday cake, an interval was announced and Marina took a walk across the lawn, feeling increasingly anxious. The day was slipping away. On the steps of the villa, she noticed her new friend, Captain First Rank Smirnov, talking animatedly to another naval officer. On seeing Marina, the captain stepped forward.

"Marina Andreyevna, could I ask a favour? I'm having a bit of an argument with my friend Denis here… How do you pronounce this word?" The captain produced a list of Cornish names scribbled across a piece of paper, with Pentewan at the top.

"I'm not sure," said Marina, but I think the accent is on the second syllable, so that would be *Pentéwan.*"

"And these?" said the captain, stabbing at the scrap of paper.

Marina went through the list – Harlyn, Praa Sands, Polzeath, Perranporth, Pentewan – saying each one out loud, slowly and carefully. "I'm just guessing," she admitted. "I could be wrong," she added. "Maybe check with Google Translate?"

"I shall, of course," said the captain. "I was just surprised to find such odd words… My English is fairly fluent, but I've never come across place names like this. They don't sound anything like London or Manchester or Birmingham."

"Cornwall has its own language. It's part of the Celtic family, like Welsh and Breton."

"I didn't know that," said Captain Smirnov. "Thank you."

"Are you planning to visit these beaches, Captain?" said Marina, keeping her tone casual. "Or perhaps one in particular?"

Artyom shot a nervous glance at his friend. For a moment, the question hung in the air. Then he blurted out, "Maybe one of these days. Denis here is a serious surfer!"

Brick walls! She kept hitting brick walls. Marina felt the frustration mounting as she walked round the side of the lunch tent towards the main entrance. She stopped dead at the sound of Admiral Fyodorov's booming laugh. He was standing three metres away with his back to her, smoking and looking out to sea. Beside him stood the president.

"Why not?" said Serov. "We can say it was the sharks!"

"That's good," Fyodorov roared. "That's really good! Sharks are always biting into cables… Apparently they think they're some sort of eel… It happens all the time."

"Not on this scale," Serov said drily.

"I would still go for seven if not eight. I mean, why hold back?"

"Plausible deniability. Six is quite enough," Serov said emphatically, and the two men wandered into the lunch tent.

Back in her seat, Marina took stock. She was getting there, inch by inch. And time was on her side. The lunch would go on for six hours and the guests would keep on drinking. Indiscretion was on the cards. Just wait.

But the lunch did not go on for six hours. Suddenly, General Varlamov was by the president's side, whispering something in his ear.

"What? You're joking... That idiot..." Serov spluttered, shaking his head. He then got to his feet, summoned Lev and Marina, and left the tent. Meanwhile, the French pastry chef watched in dismay as President Serov hurried across the lawn towards the waiting cars in front of the villa, shouting and gesticulating to Varlamov. Lev loped behind with Marina by his side; neither had a clue what was going on. And what about the cake? Marina wondered. Would they light it and cut it *in absentia*?

It was midnight by the time that Marina got home from Vnukovo airport, and she tiptoed up the chipped marble staircase of Tverskaya 25 in order not to wake Oxana. But Oxana was not asleep, and the moment she heard footsteps, she turned on the light. The next moment, she was kissing Marina's hand.

"Lyuba's free!" Oxana said with tears in her eyes. "Thank you, thank you... Your friend is a miracle-worker... Please, thank her from me, from the bottom of my heart."

"A miracle-worker," said Marina, taking Oxana's hand. "That's a good name for Anna. I'm so relieved for you all. How is Lyuba?"

"I saw her only for a moment, but she seemed fine. She came straight here, to collect her backpack and to look for Vanya. Well, she didn't have to look very far... He was here, on the bench in the playground. I tell you, Marinochka, it was fate! Those two... They seem very fond of each other. I wish your boy could make Lyuba see sense. She says she's not going back to school... At sixteen she can make her own decisions, get a job. I didn't have the energy to argue, but I told her to stay away from here... And I told that boy of yours the same thing!"

"Why did you say that?" Marina asked wearily, longing for her bed.

"They were here."

"Who?"

"The FSB. I can tell them a mile off. They pretended to be from the insurance company and were here to install the latest security, but, when I asked for their ID, they didn't have any, so I told them they'd have to wait while I called our administration, but they left. They wanted to install CCTV cameras front and back, and even on the first floor. Which is really odd, because on the first floor there's just you and that tiresome Zlobina woman. Why would anyone want to have cameras up there? Marinochka, what's all this about? Are you in some kind of trouble?"

It was bound to happen, Marina thought. Sooner or later, Varlamov was bound to put her under his spotlight, not because she'd made a mistake or slipped up, but because it was in his nature to suspect everyone. Snoop as much as you like, she thought. Just try and catch me out! It won't do you any good, because I'll always be one step ahead of you, General.

Marina took Oxana's hands in hers and looked into her anxious eyes.

"Oxanochka, the FSB… they'll be back."

18

On Sunday morning Marina discovered why the president had cut short his own birthday party. It was all over the internet: North Korea had launched another missile test, which had misfired and landed in Russian waters less than a hundred kilometres from Vladivostok. Later that day, Marina watched the president's televised address. Serov told anxious Russians that he'd received a full apology from the North Korean leader: the latest missile launch was a mistake, a regrettable accident that would not happen again.

That afternoon, Marina and Clive ran fifteen kilometres, ending up at Luzhniki Stadium. Marina checked her smartwatch, which logged everything she needed to know about her performance: heart rate, time, calories burnt. Clive was breathing fast. Too fast.

"You don't look so good…" Marina said.

"Not as fit as you…" he said, gasping for breath.

"What is it?"

He waved his bandaged hand, unable to speak, while, at the same time, pulling out dextrose tablets from the pocket of his shorts and chewing on five of them.

"Sorry about that. Forgot to check my glucose level."

Marina looked at Clive sympathetically; she had completely forgotten that he was diabetic.

They collected their backpacks from the lockers by the running track. The two FSB tails seemed taken by surprise when Marina suddenly hailed an old Renault and offered the student driver an insanely generous Sunday rate. Once inside the car, she asked the driver to turn up the volume on the music station. She switched her phone off and motioned to Clive to do the same, then she glanced behind. One tail was on his mobile; the other was flagging down a car.

"God, how I've missed you," said Clive, resting his head against the seat.

Marina took Clive's bandaged hand and kissed it. "Trust you to have such a poetic injury. Tell me what happened."

He kept it short, leaving no one out, including Rose, whom he called a "one-off", describing her exhausting energy, her painful Russian and her appearance: the unmissable red streak in her mess of blond hair, the three rings in each earlobe, the outlandish clothes. Then he glanced behind, saw no sign of his tail, took Marina's face in his hands and kissed her. The kiss went on and on until Marina pushed him away and looked through the rear window. A Ford was coming up fast from behind. Meanwhile, the driver of the Renault was banging the steering wheel in time to music on the car radio, which was so insistent, so pervasive that Marina asked him what he was listening to. "Skryptonite," he cried, grinning into the rear-view mirror. "Best rapper around... from Kazakhstan."

Marina left the driver to it, thumping the steering wheel and shaking his head to the music. She spoke in English, quietly, trying to remember every detail of the past thirty-six hours.

"I've been trying to make sense of it all, but I think I understand... I saw a sea chart of the Cornish coast. I heard the admiral mention cables... We're planning an attack on the underwater cables somewhere off the Cornish coast. And soon. Hyde probably knows all this. That's why he'll be disappointed.

He needs more detail. I'll get it… Tell Hyde I won't let him down… I won't let *you* down," Marina said, touching Clive's arm.

Clive glanced behind and saw that the Ford was caught behind a bus. He took Marina's hand and kissed it. Moments later, they were passing a small park, and Clive suddenly asked the driver to stop.

"Wait here," he said to Marina. "I'll just be a few minutes."

From inside the car, Marina watched Clive as he ran towards a small crowd that had gathered under the chestnut trees, mostly women and children holding homemade banners: "MOTHERS FOR JUSTICE" and "SET OUR CHILDREN FREE". Marina recognized Vera, small and fearless with snow-white hair, holding a placard: "KIDS BELONG AT SCHOOL, NOT BEHIND BARS!" Vera looked overjoyed to see Clive, and then she started laughing as she looked him up and down, and Marina understood that Vera was teasing Clive about his running shorts. It was then she noticed Anna surrounded by children under a tree, and she was about to go and thank her for her help with Lyuba, when Clive hurried back to the car. He had seen the riot police. They came out of nowhere. From the back seat of the Renault, Clive and Marina watched as Anna walked up to the riot police to remonstrate, but there was no dialogue; instead, a helmeted officer grabbed Anna's arms and pulled them hard behind her back, forced her head down and pushed her into the back of a nearby police van. Two other women and several schoolchildren were also herded into the van, heads down and arms behind their backs. Then the door slammed shut, and the van disappeared.

Clive and Marina watched as the riot police moved in to disperse the remaining protesters, with their customary brutality. It was all so depressingly familiar, Marina thought, but Clive had his eyes on a tiny white-haired woman standing alone, holding a banner: "JUSTICE FOR ALL!"

"What can we do?" Marina murmured.

"Not a lot," said Clive. "We have to stay out of this… I'll call Vera later… But Anna, she's on her own. God help her."

Anna had nothing with her: no handbag, no mobile. Once or twice she banged on the door of the police cell, but no one appeared. There was a glass of water on a table and a bucket in the corner beneath a naked, flickering light bulb.

As usual in these situations, Anna recited poetry to herself. It calmed her down, steadied her nerves and gave her inner strength. She knew the whole of *The Bronze Horseman* by heart, and then she switched to Brodsky and Akhmatova, her two favourite poets, both of whom had lived under repression and survived.

Time dragged by. Minutes? Hours? She had no idea, but eventually she heard footsteps and the door swung open. A prison guard barked at her to come out.

"I need my mobile and my bag," she said firmly, looking at the young man in a creased and dirty police uniform.

But she was not led upstairs to the entrance of the police station; instead, the young guard steered her along the corridor to another cell and pushed her in. Moments later, two men in plain clothes appeared. One was young, wore thick glasses and stood to one side; the other sat down at the table opposite Anna. She observed him carefully; he was middle-aged and wore a dark, expensive suit; his blue eyes were clear and unnervingly lifeless, as if made of glass. In fact, they were dead. His blue eyes were dead…

"Anna Lvovna, I'm getting tired of all your antics," the man said, pulling out his vaporizer and puffing a plume of white vapour into the stale basement air.

"I don't know what you are talking about," said Anna. She was familiar with this line of interrogation. "I'm a lawyer and my job is to uphold the law."

"You're a professional agitator."

"Who are you?"

"It doesn't matter who I am. What matters is that you understand that I've had enough. The next time, you'll go to prison for a minimum of five years."

"On what charge?"

"Assaulting a police officer."

Anna threw back her head and laughed.

"And the evidence is?"

The man turned and called out a name. The door opened, and the young man in the dirty uniform stepped inside, holding a photograph. The interrogator took it and laid it down on the table. It showed a young woman with long dark hair. She was holding a stone and trying to hit a policeman.

"That isn't me! Anyone can see it's not me... And look at the background. That's the Winter Palace!... It's not even Moscow!"

Anna sat back in her chair and looked straight at the man.

"What is this? What do you want?" she said.

The man barked again at the young policeman, who disappeared and came back with a second photograph. It was exactly the same photograph, except that this time the young woman was Anna, and in the background was the Bolshoi instead of the Winter Palace.

"Here's your evidence," said the interrogator. "Enough to keep you in prison for three, maybe four years. Possibly longer. Possibly much longer..."

He put his hands on the table and leant forward. Anna could smell an expensive cologne.

"A moment ago, you asked me what I want," he said. "I

want you to stop your disruptive, unpatriotic activities. This is a warning, Anna Lvovna. A final warning."

Anna straightened her back and calmly placed her folded hands on the table, staring at the man in front of her. Her interrogator stared back at her with his dead eyes.

"Your mother... She's quite an age, isn't she? Still trying to cause as much trouble as she can... even though she's in her eighties... We could arrest her any time, you know?"

"On what charge?"

"She does not comply with the new fire regulations. Your mother burns bonfires right in front of her dacha, in violation of new safety rules. She's already been fined once. And her neighbours have complained."

"Which neighbours?"

The interrogator ignored the question.

"Burning bonfires is against the law," he said. "So, where does that leave you, Anna Lvovna?... You who are so keen on upholding the law? Let's move on. I want to talk about your friend, the Englishman."

"Which Englishman?"

"Franklin. Clive Franklin."

"He's not my..." Anna hesitated before continuing. "Clive Franklin was my mother's student. He's not really my friend."

"Very odd... No one wants to be a friend of this man," said the interrogator, drumming his fingers on the table and glancing up at the young man who stood silently in the corner. "I wonder why? In your case I find it particularly odd, since only a few days ago – Monday, to be exact – he came to your mother's dacha in Peredelkino and you kissed him on the cheek."

"I was being polite."

The interrogator almost smiled.

"Is he interested in your... activities?"

"Not in the least."

"Then why did he come to your illegal rally this afternoon?"

"Our rally was not illegal. We had permission to gather in that park. I can show you the documents."

"You had permission for a peaceful demonstration."

"It was peaceful until you sent in the riot police."

"Answer my question. Why did the Englishman turn up?"

"He was there by chance… He saw my mother from the car window. He was still in his running clothes…"

The interrogator leant forward, his jaw tight, his blue eyes clear and cold.

"He was *there*."

Anna held the man's stare.

"I've been here for hours and I want to go home," Anna said in a matter-of-fact voice. "You've no right to detain me any more than you have the right to detain children without charge. I repeat: *children*. Why are you so afraid?"

The man stiffened.

"Put out your hand," he said. Anna did nothing. "Lay your hand on the table, your fingers splayed." Still Anna did nothing. The man glanced at the silent man in the corner, who took a step closer. "Do as I say," said the interrogator, taking out a knife and wiping the blade with a white handkerchief. He was smiling.

Anna did as she was told, laid her hand on the table, fingers splayed. Her whole body was tense, her jaw tight.

The interrogator raised the knife, looking hard at Anna's emotionless face, and then down came the knife with terrible force, right in the V of her index and middle fingers. The point of the knife was embedded in the table, so close to her finger that she could feel the cold blade against her skin. Anna drew back her hand slowly and without tremor. The interrogator grasped the handle of the knife and jerked the blade free.

"In this game, what you need is nerves," he said. "Pity you're on the wrong side. I could use a woman like you."

The muscles in Anna's face were tense, and her dark eyes stared at the man with disdain.

"Let's go back to why you're here…"

The man looked straight at Anna and spoke in an unemotional, threatening voice.

"Think carefully about what I've said. Stop engaging with the opposition. This is your last chance. A lot of people don't even get a warning, so count yourself lucky."

The interrogator took one last puff of his vaporizer and got to his feet. The young policeman was standing to attention and holding the door open.

"Let her go," said the interrogator.

"Yes, General."

The same young man in his crumpled police uniform led her down the long, cold corridor towards a flight of stairs and the light.

"That was Varlamov, wasn't it?" Anna said, glancing at the nervous young face. The policeman tensed his jaw and looked straight ahead.

As Anna stepped into the night air, she felt a familiar chill: a first hint of winter. It was just after midnight, so she discovered from her phone, which had been returned to her by the silent policeman. She stood by the side of the road and put out her arm: a young man in a Volkswagen stopped. From the back seat of the car, Anna posted a message on VK, thanking everyone who had come to the rally, which, she emphasized, was entirely legal. She told her followers that she had been wrongly detained by the police and had now been released. "Onwards and upwards," she wrote, followed by a string of emojis. By a traffic light, Anna opened the car door and dropped her mobile through the slats of a drain.

Marina couldn't get the image of Anna out of her mind, her head pushed down by the police, her arms wrenched back. It made her feel guilty for daring, just for a moment, to be happy and carefree, kissing Clive like a teenager in the back of a car. She arrived home to find Oxana in the back courtyard, smoking.

"They came back, just as you said they would," Oxana said. "This time with all the right ID from the insurance company. Insurance, my foot! They had FSB written all over their grubby faces. Can you believe it? The administration called, telling me everything was OK, and they were from a very reputable security company and needed to install CCTV cameras here, there and everywhere... Sasha followed them around... He can tell you what's what... let's go and find him."

Sasha was by the rubbish skip, inspecting his latest find – a brand-new desk lamp and a good pair of boots – while Ivan the Terrible ran about, sniffing the ground. The caretaker knew exactly what had been installed and where, and he was not happy. He didn't like being spied on.

"If you want to pass unnoticed," he told Marina, "don't go out by the front. Use the back door and hug the wall. The CCTV cameras will miss you. Otherwise, just take an umbrella."

A carpet of brittle brown leaves covered the playground floor. Any minute now, the first snow would fall.

"I wasn't born yesterday," Oxana said, kicking the dead leaves with her foot. "You're in trouble, aren't you?"

"Too many questions, Oxanochka... Too many questions..."

"Lyuba called me. From a public call box. She's still with that boy of yours. Says she's going to learn the guitar and be a songwriter like Nikita Strelnikov."

How will I keep in touch with Vanya? Or he with me? Marina wondered as she walked slowly up the stairs to her flat. Then she told herself not to worry. The alley cat would find a way. She took out her keys, then took a step back and looked up into the CCTV cameras. She wanted Varlamov to know that she was up to the challenge.

It was no one's idea of a pleasant Sunday evening, sitting in the claustrophobic safe room on the top floor of the embassy. They were already tired of coffee and indifferent chicken sandwiches. But this was Martin Hyde's farewell, and Martindale's too. He and his family had forty-eight hours to leave Moscow.

Around six o'clock Hyde had opened a good bottle of claret and handed a glass to each man in the room: the British ambassador, Luke Marden; the political counsellor, aka head of station, Oswald Martindale; the translator, Clive Franklin; and finally he poured a glass for himself.

"I like to give credit where it's due," said Hyde, pacing the room, glass in hand. "Volina did very well, exceptionally well when you consider she's an amateur. It's helpful to know the Russians are planning to cut six out of eight, although that's been our assumption from the start. Otherwise, Volina has confirmed what we very much suspected: that the attack by Russian stealth submarines on the underwater cables is imminent. But where? On a Cornish beach, but which one? And when? We're short on detail."

Hyde was looking directly at Clive.

"I need a location to within ten, ideally five, nautical miles, and I need a date. Is that too much to ask your friend?"

"Is there anything in Varlamov's twenty-three thousand emails?" Clive asked.

"So far, not much," Hyde answered. "Don't get me wrong. Under normal circumstances, I would be delighted to have twenty-three thousand emails from an FSB general on a USB stick. But these are not normal circumstances, and we're looking for specific intelligence. I can't say I was expecting any revelations. Varlamov is a professional. He's not about to let the cat out of the bag in his private emails. When he mentioned Plan A, that was sloppy. Unusually sloppy. From everything I know about General Varlamov, he's a meticulous man."

Cat out of the bag? thought Clive. How funny. For once, the Russian equivalent was identical.

"It took us just seventy-seven minutes to sift through all those emails," Martindale said, looking eagerly round the room. "Here in the embassy, we've got a new piece of software, an artificially intelligent brain that can sift through sensitive information at the speed of light. It's the work of an American company called Text IQ. Very sophisticated. With some lovely neural connections and an ability to triangulate human relationships and associated key words. Shall I go on?"

Martindale was met with silence. To mask his disappointment, he poured himself a full glass of water and drained it.

"How will Marina get out?" said Clive. His question took everyone by surprise.

"Oswald's been coming up with various ideas," said Hyde. "We think her best shot is to tell her office she's going to have a few days' holiday at her house by the sea and book herself on a flight to Simferopol. Then, instead of going to the airport, she can head for Belorussky station and take the train to Minsk. You only need an internal passport for Belarus. In Minsk, one of our agents will be waiting for her, and he'll get her over the Polish border. Luke... You have his contact number? But, basically, this is her call."

"You mean she's on her own?" said Clive. He had suspected as much, but to hear it from Hyde's lips sent a shiver down his spine.

"I'm afraid so," said Hyde. "These diplomatic expulsions mean we can't back her up. But at least she's got you, for the time being."

She's got me for all eternity, Clive did not say.

"We'll keep in touch by email, text, whatever," Hyde continued. "Of course, don't use her name. Call her... call her a Dyson air-purifier."

"Email?" said Clive. "From this embassy? How can that possibly be secure?"

"Because," said Martindale, "we'll be using RSA asymmetric encryption with keys 4,096 bits long. By the time the Russians crack it, which of course they will, it'll be old, old news."

"*Pace*, Oswald," said Hyde, at which point Clive had a sudden urge to ask why Martindale was "Oswald" and he was "Franklin". Once again, Clive said nothing.

"Before I go," Hyde continued, "may I remind everyone in this room just *what* is at stake. As you know, I am not given to exaggeration. I think you all know that if we fail to prevent the Russian submarine attack on our internet cables, then the consequences for our country, for our economy, will be catastrophic. This is war by another name." Hyde turned to face Clive. "Everything now hinges on Franklin and on Volina. It's as simple as that."

19

"Why is everyone so busy all of a sudden? Up all night... Doing *what?*"

Once again, General Varlamov had walked into Marina's office, unannounced and uninvited, waving a single sheet of paper in her direction.

"My agent at the British embassy has just sent me this report," Varlamov said. He began to read: "'Clive Franklin, the English translator, entered the British embassy on Sunday night at 7.16 p.m. and left at 11.14 p.m. The ambassador and Sir Martin Hyde went in earlier, at 6.05 p.m. and 6.10 p.m., respectively, and, as of the filing of this report at 7.06 a.m. on Monday, have not emerged.'"

"The British are unhappy, Grigory Mikhailovich," Marina said wearily. "Diplomats are being expelled. The ambassador has a lot on his plate."

"Why involve the Englishman? What can he add? He's a linguist, and everyone speaks English."

"Perhaps he's helping them with the Russian press releases? Perhaps they just like him... He's one of the team... And he's here... I honestly don't know."

Varlamov was not convinced.

"I think it's something else... I can't put my finger on it..." said the general, taking out his vaporizer. "I need to know *why* Franklin spent five hours at the British embassy yesterday evening. Maybe you can find out, Marina Andreyevna? I don't like all these loose ends."

And I don't like the CCTV cameras you've installed in my building to spy on me, Marina thought.

"Talking of loose ends," she said, eager to change the subject. "What's Professor Olga Tabakova doing here? Still peddling immortality?"

"The president likes her. He trusts her. Why do you ask?"

"He shouldn't trust her," said Marina, "The woman is bogus."

"Oh, come now, Marina Andreyevna. Olga Tabakova is harmless," said Varlamov, heading for the door. "It's all about diet and deep breathing. Don't be distracted by Tabakova. I want you to focus on the Englishman."

"At your service," said Marina with a smile.

Hyde dropped by the Metropol to say goodbye to Clive. He suggested a walk. The two men strolled over to the Alexandrovsky Gardens and the Tomb of the Unknown Soldier. It wasn't the gardens that interested Hyde, but a line of dark-red blocks of stone lying like large coffins one next to the other, commemorating the "hero cities" of the Soviet Union that had fought the hardest and taken the greatest losses during the Second World War. Without looking at the name plates, Clive rattled off the list: "Leningrad, Kiev, Stalingrad – the name plate said Volgograd until 2004, when they changed it... Shall I go on? Yes? Odessa, Sevastopol, Minsk, Kerch, Novorossiysk, Tula, Brest, Murmansk and Smolensk."

"What's the stone?"

"Porphyry."

"It's beautiful," said Hyde. "And without Russia, we might never have won the war. Twenty million dead. But you have to move on from war... You have to make peace work... Russia isn't so good at that. It still sees the West as the enemy. You know all this, of course…"

They walked along in silence, followed by two FSB tails who could not have looked more different: Hyde's tail wore a dark-grey suit, dark glasses and an earpiece, while Clive's was a baby-faced young man pretending to be an ice-cream-eating tourist in a baseball cap and a Moscow-metro T-shirt. Clive followed Hyde into the Okhotny Ryad underground shopping centre and rode the escalators up and down as Aretha Franklin belted out "Respect" over the loudspeakers.

"You're not in this alone. I give you my word," Hyde murmured, holding the rail of the escalator and glancing down at the tails several steps below. "From our end, we'll do everything we can to help you. And the ambassador is here for you. And Rose Friedman. She's staying. Not my favourite person, and, of course, she's not in the loop, but at least she'll be company for you."

Hyde's embassy car was waiting in front of the Metropol. The hotel doorman in his red cape and black top hat held open the passenger door.

"Good luck," said Hyde.

"I don't really believe in luck," said Clive. "I share the Russian view that we can only do so much. Ultimately, we're in the hands of fate: *sudba*."

"I beg to disagree," said Hyde. "We shape our own destiny. The Ancient Greeks understood it perfectly… You know what Heraclitus said? *Character* is fate. Think about it."

"I have."

As they shook hands, Clive noticed that Hyde wore a signet ring, and, for this first time, he wondered about the man. Was he married? Did he have children? Who was he?

Hyde had just settled into the back seat of the car when he caught sight of something or someone which darkened his mood. "Talk of the devil," Hyde muttered.

Rose appeared out of nowhere, her knapsack on her back, wearing skinny black jeans and a leather bomber jacket.

"What the fuck!" said Rose, smiling at Clive. "Fancy seeing you here... I'm doing the tourist thing in case I'm chucked out along with the rest of them. There's just three of us left: you, me and Lucky Luke. The others have all gone, including Sir Martin bloody Hyde..."

From the back seat, with the car door still open, Hyde was staring straight at Rose.

"There goes my job," said Rose, staring at Hyde's embassy car sliding into the traffic, while the charcoal-suited FSB tail melted away. "Not my finest moment. Sorry."

Clive wasn't listening. He was staring at a WhatsApp message from Marina. "Come, my friends, 'tis not too late to seek a newer world."

He wrote back: "For my purpose holds to sail beyond the sunset."

"I need your help, Rose. See that young man over there? The one with the baby face and the baseball cap and the map? I need to lose him. I have to get to Peredelkino."

"*Nyet problem,*" said Rose, who then pretended to say goodbye to Clive with elaborate hugs and kisses. She marched off to flag down a gypsy cab, returned in less than a minute and threw the door open for Clive, who jumped in, leaving the panic-stricken FSB tail running towards a taxi.

"Where shall I drop you off?" Clive said to Rose.

"Oh, no! No, Clive. I'm here for the ride. I can't leave you all alone with that wounded hand of yours. Anyway, I've never been to Peredelkino."

They ducked and weaved through side streets, shot the occasional light and lost the tail somewhere near Victory Park.

"Don't know what your plan is," said Rose, "but that mobile is a tracking device. If you want to disappear, then lose it."

"I don't need to disappear," Clive murmured.

I just need to stay alive, he told himself. Stay alive, finish the job, get Marina and Vanya out of here. And me: mustn't leave myself behind. That's all I have to do. It's a doddle. Get a grip, he told himself.

"Need to see Vera, my old Russian teacher," said Clive. "She hasn't been well."

Clive called Vera on his mobile. She was at home. Ill? Who said she was ill? Just a cough, nothing more... Of course, she would love to see him.

As they hurtled down the Moscow–Minsk highway, Clive made a second call. He would have given anything to be alone in the car. He needed time to think, but Rose was restless and inquisitive.

"So, let's hear it then," she said eagerly as they passed the sign for the "writers' village and rest zone". "Why are we here?"

"You're going to visit the Pasternak House Museum. It's the dacha where he lived. My friend Alyosha is waiting for you... He knows every Pasternak poem by heart. And you'll see the desk where Pasternak wrote *Doctor Zhivago*."

Rose was silent.

"Don't tell me you haven't read it? Oh, Rose." There was deep disappointment in Clive's voice. "On the other hand, what a treat you have in store." Clive looked out of the car window, catching sight of the lake where he used to skate as a teenager. "Make sure you see the drawings by his father, Leonid... He did the illustrations for Tolstoy's *Resurrection* and they've got some in the museum. They're very good. When you're done, Alyosha will bring you to the house of my old Russian teacher, Vera Seliverstova... She hasn't been well."

"And you?"

"I have a meeting."

"How long's your meeting?"

"How long's a piece of string?"

Clive met Marina by the edge of the forest, a short walk from her dacha. She kept her distance, looking around and listening to the stillness that hung over the woods and the dachas and the gardens with their tangled rose bushes. No one was around: no cars, no people. Only Ulysses was by Marina's side, alert, looking out at the birch and pine trees, sniffing the air for rabbits.

"I wasn't sure you'd understand my WhatsApp message," Marina said, staring down at the soggy earth.

"The Tennyson?" Clive said. "It was pretty obvious. *Cherchez le chien.*"

Clive took Marina's face in his hands and kissed her.

"What's wrong?" he said, pulling away.

"Varlamov is closing in."

Marina had paraded herself in front of the CCTV cameras in Tverskaya 25 to make it clear that she was going out. Then she disappeared into the metro, changed trains and platforms several times. Forty minutes later, she emerged from the Arbatskaya metro station and hailed a cab. To avoid the police checkpoint, she asked the driver to take the back road to Peredelkino. As for her phone, she had left it on her kitchen table at home. Clive had left his mobile in the drawer of Vera's kitchen table.

They took the path through the woods, with Ulysses bounding by their side and dashing off, now and then, in all directions. It was getting dark, but Clive could just make out the colour of the leaves, which were turning a hundred shades of brown and purple and red. Autumn always came suddenly to Russia, he remembered, crunching dead leaves underfoot.

"He must have been disappointed, Hyde?" said Marina.

"Not really. Well, maybe a little."

"Of course. But I *shall* get the information he needs. It's right under my nose. I can feel it."

"We don't have much time."

"I know... I know that."

"It's just us. You and me. Ridiculous, when you think about it."

Clive leant against the bark of a silver birch and kissed her again. They walked on. The woods were so still; a deep-red sky was bearing down on tops of trees; nothing moved. Clive thought to himself how much he loved this country and the woman by his side.

Marina gripped Clive's arm. The apprehension... No, that's not right, the *fear* that had been weighing her down had melted away.

"We need to add a few new code words to our little lexicon," Marina said. "We can't always use poetry. It looks too suspicious. Russian painters? Kuindzhi? Repin? Goncharova?"

There and then they worked it out, hidden from view in the scrappy forest. Goncharova had to be happiness. Yes, I'll meet you tomorrow. Or, bravo, well done! If you used Goncharova with her lover, Larionov, then it was even more urgent, meaning, I'll meet you tonight. Kuindzhi was a "no"; Levitan, a "maybe". Repin, the perfectionist, was "more information needed".

Later, they lay on the bed, looking through the dirty window at a thin, pale sliver of a moon. Clive said, "I like these one-offs. They're very, very nice. A one-off, followed by another and another." He kissed her shoulder. "We meet again tomorrow. Goncharova. Promise?"

"Levitan."

"Not good enough."

She lay in his arms, her back resting against his chest, her breasts covered by his hands. She felt a safeness that she had forgotten or perhaps never known.

"What do you think? Is this the calm before the storm?" she asked. And then she told him how much she longed to go to Venice. In particular, Torcello.

Now it was dark. They listened to the silence of the forest. Clive told her what Hyde had said. That she was, basically, on her own. Marina was not surprised. She had always assumed as much. The train to Minsk wasn't such a bad idea.

"Once out, MI6 will take care of you," said Clive, and suddenly he felt ashamed that they, he, the British, were doing so little to help this woman. "None of it will be easy," he whispered.

"Of course not."

"It could all go wrong."

"Obviously."

"When I got your WhatsApp," he said, "I thought you might have some news… Some important news."

"I do," said Marina, turning around to face Clive, her naked body pressed against his, their faces lit by a lamp on the porch. "It's just possible that I love you."

"That sounds a bit tentative," said Clive, scattering kisses across her forehead. "But it's better than nothing, I suppose. As for me, I haven't a shadow of a doubt. Not a smidgen. I love you. *Je t'aime. Lyublyu tebya.* That's about it. I'm not a linguist, like you."

It was half past ten before Clive got back to Vera's dacha, where he found Rose watching an episode of *Sherlock* in Russian. Alyosha, the Pasternak scholar, had gone home, and Vera was asleep in her chair, exhausted after a coughing fit that had nearly killed her, Rose said.

Clive was reclaiming his phone from the drawer where he had left it, when Vera woke with a start. She apologized for being such a poor host, made some tea for herself and opened a bottle of red wine for her guests. Clive asked about Anna and was relieved to hear that she had not spent the night in jail. He raised his glass and gave a toast to the bravest of the brave: Anna Seliverstova.

With a sudden burst of energy, Vera tackled Rose about the new and perfectly dreadful production of *The Queen of Spades* at the Bolshoi. It was a spirited discussion. Rose held her own, and Vera liked her for it.

Clive tried and failed to get Vera to take the medicine he had brought for her. She stroked his cheek and said he was not to worry: hot water with honey and lemon would do the trick.

When Clive and Rose left Vera's at eleven-forty to get into a Yandex taxi, they noticed, under the yellow light of a street-lamp, the baby-faced FSB tail sitting in his white Ford, a few metres from the rickety old gate.

"*Privyet,*" Rose said, giving the agent a wave with her fingers.

20

Marina got a lift back to Moscow with a neighbour in Peredelkino who was glad to earn some extra cash. She went over the evening in all its detail. They had declared their love for each other, so why was she feeling so anxious? This should have been enchanted territory, the stuff that dreams are made of, and yet she was fearful, even frightened. Did love make them more vulnerable? Was that it? There was more to lose, much more… And she had yet to fulfil her side of the bargain.

Marina slept badly and woke before dawn in a cold sweat. Time was running out. It was Tuesday: five days until the marathon.

That morning, in the Senate Palace, she was caught off guard by General Varlamov, who stopped her in the corridor as she was about to lock her office door.

"Yesterday," said Varlamov, "your friend Franklin walked with Hyde in the Alexandrovsky Gardens, past the tomb of the Unknown Soldier, and, as they said goodbye, Hyde wished your friend 'good luck'. I can't get my head round that. Why would Hyde be wishing Franklin 'good luck'?"

"Why *wouldn't* he wish him luck?" Marina said, straightening her back and looking the general in the eye. "Clive's a diabetic about to run the Moscow marathon. When we ran on Sunday, he forgot his glucose tablets and collapsed. It's all in my report, Grigory Mikhailovich. *Of course* he needs luck. Forty-two point one nine five kilometres takes a lot out of you. Excuse me, General, but I need my lunch."

General Varlamov watched Marina double-lock the door to her office and head down the corridor, and, as she walked so confidently, with such a straight back, he felt intense resentment towards this woman who had an answer to everything. Varlamov was in a foul mood, still cursing the incompetence of his operative who had lost Franklin and the British Council woman the evening before, and who, instead of coming back to FSB headquarters, had wasted two hours driving around the south of Moscow.

That morning, Varlamov had brought in Lieutenant Mishin to sort things out. Mishin had tracked Franklin and the Englishwoman through their mobiles. Rose Friedman had spent an hour at the Pasternak Museum, then joined Franklin at the house of Franklin's former Russian teacher, Vera Seliverstova, where they stayed all evening. Where had Volina been? According to Nadia, the lift lady on duty at Tverskaya 25, Marina had been at an excellent production of *Khovanshchina* at the Bolshoi. She had returned home at 11.03 p.m., according to the CCTV in the entrance hall. Nadia, who was paid a nice little retainer to report to the FSB on all activities inside the building, had been shown the Bolshoi programme by Marina, and even her ticket: row five, seat three. Marina had left her mobile at home. Was that an odd thing to do? Not really, when you are going to an opera.

Still, the general was not satisfied. He had come top of his FSB exams because he left no stone unturned; he always asked one more question. Perhaps the lift lady had been shown an old programme and a ticket for another night? This might have been a ruse? Mishin rang the head of security at the Bolshoi and discovered that *Khovanshchina* had indeed been performed at the Bolshoi last night – and that, yes, the critics were rapturous. He also double-checked with the police at the checkpoint just before Peredelkino: Marina Volina's car had not been seen. So, she's telling the truth, Varlamov thought, as he watched Marina's slim frame heading down the corridor, treading ever so lightly. Doesn't she always tell the truth? The president certainly thinks so.

Very soon, none of this would matter: not Clive Franklin, not Marina Volina, not the expulsion of diplomats, not even the Moscow marathon. Very soon, the West would be rocked to its foundations, and he, Grigory Varlamov, would be a hero. He could already picture the ceremony in the throne room of the Kremlin, where, dressed in his FSB uniform, he would stand to attention in front of President Serov, his whole family in attendance – yes, even his rebellious daughter, Veronika, the apple of his eye, who would glow with pride as the president pinned to her father's lapel the medal of the distinguished order "For Merit to the Fatherland, first class".

In the Senate dining room with its elaborate gilt mirrors and red damask wallpaper – and under the watchful eye of a waitress, all smiles and purple nail varnish – Marina ordered salmon.

She couldn't remember the last time she had eaten; even so, as she stared at the slab of pink flesh on her plate, she felt sick.

That morning, she had pinned her hopes on indiscreet revelations from Lev, but he had sent her a text, full of emojis, saying he was up to his eyes, too busy even for a cigarette.

"You want it cooked more?" said the waitress, staring at Marina's slice of salmon. "The president likes his pink."

Marina was alone in the dining room. Two ormolu clocks chimed noon, their high tinkling sounds criss-crossing each other in the silence.

"Cooked?" the waitress repeated. "Cooked more?"

"No… No, it's perfect, thank you," said Marina. She was wondering how she would swallow even one mouthful, when she was startled by the sound of a belly-laugh. They made a noisy entrance, the five men in their naval uniforms, insignia and gold buttons glistening.

"Funny, that's so funny!" said Admiral Fyodorov, his eyes glittering and his round face even redder than usual, as he followed Lev to a table laden with hors d'oeuvres and flowers. With a slightly theatrical gesture, Lev waved his long arm over the VIP table, indicating that the admiral and his colleagues should sit and eat. On his way out, he nodded to Marina. The admiral sat down, still laughing. Then he noticed Marina and threw out his arms.

"Marina Volina! My dear friend! What are you doing sitting there all alone? Come and join us…"

Here's someone who can tell me what I need to know, Marina thought, picking up her plate of pink salmon.

Admiral Fyodorov patted the chair next to him. "You must sit right here, next to me," he said. Marina did as she was told and sat down beside him; opposite sat a face she recognized, the admiral's ADC, Captain First Rank Artyom Smirnov. Marina smiled at the good-looking ADC, and he smiled back, although he did not seem at ease. Marina noticed that he sat stiffly at the table and forced himself to smile at jokes that he didn't find funny.

"Moscow doesn't hold a candle to Saint Petersburg," said Fyodorov. "It's too big and too noisy. Saint Petersburg is so much more beautiful – the city of poets, the city of Pushkin. Do you know Petersburg, Marina Andreyevna? Yes? Well, then, of course you must agree."

Marina shook her head.

"I'm sorry to disappoint you, Admiral Fyodorov, but I prefer Moscow."

There was a howl of protest, and someone said it was time to toast Saint Petersburg. Only if we toast Moscow, too, Marina insisted – and on it went. "The Mariinsky," the admiral said. "The Bolshoi," Marina countered. "The Philharmonic," said the Admiral. "The Conservatory," replied Marina. "The Hermitage," said the Admiral. "I surrender," said Marina.

"What a girl!" said Fyodorov, raising his glass. "Fighting her corner right to the end!"

There were coffee and liqueurs, and the Russian navy did not hold back.

"For how long do we have the pleasure of your company?" Marina asked the admiral.

"If only I knew," he replied. "We're just waiting for our dear president to make up his mind. Let's hope it's sooner rather than later… But once we get the green light, then we're off to the races, my dear girl."

"I hope it won't be Sunday," said Marina, "because on Sunday I'm running the Moscow marathon."

"Are you now? Well, may I wish you the very best of luck," said the admiral, draining a glass of red wine and signalling to the waitress that he would like another. Then Fyodorov leant forward.

"Did you know that the Russian navy is the third biggest in the world, behind the US and China?" he said. "The third biggest! Bigger than the British. Did you know that? You're too young to remember, but in the early nineties we were in a terrible mess… Bankrupt… Rudderless… The West was dancing on our grave. But we have risen from the ashes, and today we're stronger than ever! Let's drink to a mighty Russia!"

Fyodorov was on his feet, his glass raised, clinking glasses with Marina. It was the first of many toasts. Marina hung in there, but to no avail: the admiral gave nothing away. Lunch broke up around three o'clock, and Marina went back to her office. Sitting in her "thinking chair", she closed her eyes and tried to block out the real possibility of impending defeat; she opened them to find Lev standing over her.

"The boss wants to see you."

"Anything in particular?"

"He's in one of his hyper-manic moods. He's been up all night, worrying. Can't make his mind up about this and that. Basically, he just wants to chat. That's what he said. And you always put him in a good mood. He said that, too."

Marina found Serov sitting behind his desk and biting his lip.

"Ah, Marinochka, come in. Tea? Coffee? Lyova, what else do we have?"

"Everything. Vodka. Gin. Martini. Rum..."

"I've just had lunch," said Marina. "Tea is perfect. Thank you."

"Decisions, decisions... Your father was so good at decisions. He told me that the worst thing for any leader was to be weak. It led to so much confusion, so much mess."

Marina said nothing. She wasn't sure if she was supposed to sit or to stand, so she stood.

"Sit down, for God's sake!"

Marina sat in a black leather chair facing the president. She had no idea what he wanted.

"So, how do you think I look?"

Marina was so taken aback she didn't know what to say.

"Meaning what?"

"Meaning what I just said! How do you think I look? My face? My appearance?"

"You look very well, Nikolai Nikolayevich. Much younger than your years."

"And... and... Is that a good thing or a bad thing?"

"Well, most people would say it's a very good thing."

"You're not most people, damn it!" said the president. "Why do you think I'm asking *you*? It's *your* opinion I want, your *honest* opinion."

"Well, since you ask, I think you *do* need some wrinkles. You're a man of the people, and proud of it. Wasn't that your last election slogan? So, you need a few wrinkles, like everybody else. You *don't* want to look like Silvio Berlusconi."

The arrow hit home.

"Jesus, is it that bad? I've paid thousands for this…"

"People would trust you more if you had some wrinkles."

From his desk drawer the president pulled out a hand mirror and examined himself.

"You think I look like Berlusconi… Really?"

Lev had looked up from his iPad, and Marina caught the edge of a smile.

"An honest view at last! Only you have the guts to tell me the truth. You and Lyova."

"You should look your age," said Marina.

"How?"

"Don't use Botox."

Serov was put out. He straightened his tie.

"Who told you?"

"No one. I guessed."

"The professor says I need to look younger for television. And Grisha agrees."

"Well, I don't."

There was a knock at the door. A secretary brought in tea on a tray and poured out three cups, handing one to the president, who told her, sharply, to leave it on the table.

"You were talking about decisions, when I came in?" Marina said, plopping two sugar lumps into her tea.

"Decisions are a bugger," said Serov, pouring some tea from his cup into his saucer. "When my Nadezhda was alive, we talked things over. She always gave me such good advice. Women are such good listeners." Serov put the saucer to his lips and slurped his tea, peering above the rim with a guilty look. "Can't do this with Grisha around. He objects... Says it's what peasants do. I am a peasant. Ha! That's what I told him... Now, what was I saying?"

"About decisions..." Marina said softly.

"Usually, I'm so decisive. No mucking about with Nikolai Serov and all that... But this time I've got my doubts... You see, we're in uncharted territory."

"Uncharted territory?" Marina said in her most sympathetic voice. "Forgive me, Nikolai Nikolayevich, but I'm not sure that I know what that means..."

"You're not *meant* to know."

"So how can I help? Be of service?"

"You can't. I just wanted somebody to talk to. Someone I can trust."

"I'm very honoured, Nikolai Nikolayevich."

The president waved a hand, as if to tell Marina that she could dispense with the compliments.

"This is Uncle Kolya, or have you forgotten?"

"No... no... of course not..."

"Here in Russia we should experience relatively little disruption. At least, that's what Grisha says. But he also says that we won't *know* until it happens. The microsatellites are up and running, but will they be enough? How do I know when it's the right moment to give the green light? There's a lot riding on this, Marinochka... More than you could ever imagine."

"Making big decisions is never easy. My father had a favourite quotation on this very subject. It's from Shakespeare."

"I can't be doing with all your poetry! Your father used to say you'd never get married because you always had your nose in

256

a book. He was wrong… How's that English interpreter? Any chance he'll come and work for us?"

"I'm afraid not."

"A pity. But Lyova here tells me he'll run the marathon… So I may get my photograph after all… Britain on its knees! What were you saying about Shakespeare?"

"I was saying that my father had a favourite Shakespeare quote, which he used when he was trying to make up his mind. It's from *Hamlet*. Part of the great speech, 'To be, or not to be…': 'Conscience doth make cowards of us all.'"

"I never liked *Hamlet*… What's he talking about?"

"Well, Uncle Kolya, since you ask, and, of course, this is just my interpretation, there are dozens of others…"

"For God's sake, get on with it. You sound like a bloody politician."

"Man's fear of death stops him from acting decisively, turns him into a coward."

"Balls, that's what I say! Of course, no one wants to die. But *fear* of death? No… no… It's *overthinking* that does the damage. Overthinking makes a man impotent! Paralysed! And then he behaves… yes, like a coward! Maybe *that's* what he meant, your Hamlet."

"*My* Hamlet? With all due respect, most Russians think of Hamlet as their own. 'He's one of us' is what they say."

"And they're right, they're bloody right," laughed the president. "Everyone knows he's ours. You don't want a drink? I have good wine."

"Uncle Kolya, you must forgive me. I'm in training for the marathon."

"One glass won't hurt you. Anyway, according to French doctors, red wine is a muscle relaxant… You'll run even better, faster… What have we got, Lyova? Something Barton… Lyova's the expert…"

"Not really. I like beer. You're thinking of Léoville Barton, 1990. The Chinese ambassador gave you a case on your seventieth. You liked it. We ordered a lot. I mean *a lot*."

Lev produced three glasses, uncorked a bottle and poured. Serov got to his feet and clinked glasses, first with Lev and then with Marina.

"To your father and his favourite quotation!"

President Serov took a couple of greedy gulps and seemed surprised to find that his glass was almost empty.

"Nikolai Nikolayevich, may I speak in confidence?" said Marina.

"What does that mean? You and I always speak in confidence, for fuck's sake!"

"You asked me to help Grigory Mikhailovich in his enquiries…"

"I bloody well did. Wanted to nail those bastards who've been stealing from the state. Romanovsky. Kunko. Those guys are toast, I tell you. I'm just waiting for the right moment. Timing is everything."

"I brought in Pasha, my foster son, if you remember…"

"That boy was a genius! In line for a medal! If only he hadn't—"

"Yes, well, he told me that, over a two-month period, one billion dollars from the World Cup Development Fund was paid in chunks of a hundred and a hundred and fifty million into an unknown bank account in the British Virgin Islands. I brought this up at the time with Grigory Mikhailovich, who said he'd look into it. Did he… did he mention it to you?"

The president stared at Marina.

"No."

The telephone rang on Serov's desk. He picked it up, said hello, and put his hand over the receiver.

"It's that shit, Romanovsky. Doesn't he have the hots for you? That's what Lev tells me… I better take this call… Thank you, Marinochka. Thank you for coming to see me."

·　　·　　·

That same afternoon, Clive moved out of the Metropol. He said goodbye to Liza. And he had his shoes polished one last time. Narek was unusually talkative and wondered whether his friend Clive had seen the Chagall exhibition at the Tretyakov Gallery? No? Really?

"I can show you the picture of the bride and groom flying through the sky," said Narek, pulling out his mobile. "It's the very essence of love."

But what Narek showed Clive was not a Chagall but a text from Marina: "Decision imminent. Missing you."

21

Martin Hyde had a bad habit of forgetting to drink his coffee before it went cold. The double espresso had been sitting on his desk for over half an hour while he paced the room, looking out of the window and waiting for intelligence from Moscow.

Hyde's office was on the top floor of 10 Downing Street, in a quiet corner at the back of the house, with a perfect view of the garden with its neatly mown lawn, carefully tended flower beds and impressive London trees – an ash, a chestnut and a lime – still clinging to their summer green.

The COBRA meeting that morning had been difficult. Predictably so. In perfect sunlight, Hyde and Martha Maitland had walked side by side across the internal courtyard at the back of Downing Street, hidden from the prying eyes of journalists, to briefing room A in the Cabinet Office. They had walked in silence, anticipating the barrage of questions to which they would not have the answers. The prime minister was in the chair, and her special adviser on Russia was first up.

Hyde got to his feet and scrutinized the men and women sitting around the table; each was there on a strictly need-to-know basis: the first sea lord, the chief of the defence staff, the head of the National Cyber Security Centre, the prime minister, of course, and the foreign secretary, who was always snapping at her heels, along with several other senior cabinet ministers.

Over the years, Hyde had learnt that, where politicians are concerned, it was best to keep things simple: go easy on the detail and, wherever possible, offer three-word sound bites that they could repeat, ad nauseam, in radio and television interviews – or simply tweet.

"Last week," Hyde began, "some of you were briefed by General Wallis, chief of the defence staff, on what it would mean to this country, to our economy, if Russia were able to cut the fibre-optic cables under the Atlantic, which link the UK to the US. From General Wallis, you heard that such an attack would impact the UK and the whole Western economy immediately and catastrophically. We have some new intelligence. This Russian attack on the the undersea cables, codenamed Operation Hades, is now imminent."

Hyde let his words hang in the air.

"How many cables?" asked the secretary of state for defence.

"Six out of eight. That way, they leave two intact for plausible deniability." Hyde paused to let his words sink in before continuing. "It is not an exaggeration to say that we are facing a massive disruption to our way of life and a crippling loss of revenue."

"What sort of disruption?" asked the secretary to the cabinet. "Can you spell it out?"

"I'm coming to that," said Hyde with the firmness of a headmaster. "But first, I think a little background might be helpful. Every day, billions of international trading and financial transactions are transmitted via these undersea cables. Data shoots down strands of glass as thin as a hair at almost three hundred thousand kilometres per second. Each fibre has the capacity to transmit as much as four hundred gigabytes of data per second. That's three hundred and seventy-five million phone calls concurrently at any one time."

Hyde paused for effect and looked at the faces around the table, wondering whether these people had any idea of the gravity of the situation. Clearly not, he decided, when the secretary of state for business, energy and industrial strategy pointed out that underwater cables were lying on ocean beds all over the world and, if cables were cut, then the internet traffic would automatically reroute itself. Surely?

"In theory, yes; in practice, no," said Hyde. "Internet traffic does reroute itself. It automatically looks for alternative pathways. This is an entirely autonomous process. However, if and when there is *too much* internet traffic on the move, which would most certainly be the case if six out of the eight cables were cut, then the pathways get clogged and the internet seizes up."

The home secretary stared at Hyde in disbelief. "No internet?" she said, opening the palms of her hands and shaking her head. "Are you serious? So that means… what exactly? No telephone calls, no email, no social media. What else?"

"I'm afraid that's just the tip of the iceberg," Hyde said, giving the home secretary a sympathetic smile. They were friends, after all. "All online transactions, commerce and services will stop. Banking will grind to a halt, and within minutes this will impact ninety-nine per cent of the population. You won't be able to use your credit or debit card. It's back to cash, but how do you get cash without a card? How do you pay for anything? You don't. So, no petrol, no driving. No salaries, no pensions. No plane tickets, no train tickets, no online shopping. No insurance. No online tax returns. Or exam results. Or study materials. I could go on and on… And, if you get your TV over the internet, your screen will be blank. This is war by another name."

As the word "war" rippled around the table, a sense of alarm filled the room.

"God in heaven," muttered the home secretary, just loud enough for everyone to hear. "You mean we're bloody helpless?"

"Not helpless. Not at all," insisted the first sea lord, Admiral Geoffrey Hutley, a small, resolute man with a shock of white hair and bright-blue eyes. "But we're not up to speed, that's the problem. We need a state-of-the-art ocean surveillance ship now... Where is it? Still on the drawing board!"

"Sorry, everyone, but I just don't get it," said the foreign secretary breezily, keen to make his mark and strike a different tone. (Everyone knew he was after the top job.) "If these undersea cables are shredded, can't we switch to satellites?"

At this point Hyde handed over to the director of the National Cyber Security Centre, who patiently explained that they had done the modelling and, if you used every single available Western satellite, you might just handle ten per cent of the internet traffic that currently passes through six out of the eight cables. More likely, it would be five per cent. Even so, contingency plans were in place to bring all available cable and satellite connections online in an effort to boost capacity, to allow prioritization and reactivity, and, where possible, to limit the damage. With a shrug he sat down.

Hyde hammered the point home: the United Kingdom did not *begin* to have satellite capacity, and a Russian attack on six undersea cables would be crippling.

"Sorry to be difficult, everyone, but all this *still* doesn't make sense to me," the foreign secretary insisted. "Russia needs the internet as much as we do... Why cut off your nose to spite your face?"

"For the past few years," said Hyde with a courtesy that masked his dislike of the man, "Russia has been reducing its reliance on the correct functioning of the internet by setting up its own parallel systems."

"Parallel systems?" repeated the secretary to the cabinet office. "Could we please have that in plain English?"

Hyde explained that in the last twelve months Russia had launched ninety-four pathfinder microsatellites from its Soyuz launch base in Kazakhstan. These microsatellites were able to handle a good part of Russia's internet traffic. Not all, but a sizeable percentage, he told the meeting.

"There's something else," said Hyde. "Russia has developed a well-thought-out contingency plan of its own in case of a major disruption to the internet. Russia is in a position to isolate its telecommunications infrastructure from the global network. This isolation will act as a shield and protect Russia from the ensuing chaos. We in the UK, however, will be knocked off our feet."

"It's madness," said the foreign secretary, pushing a hand through his tangled hair. "They've lost the plot. Why do this and make yourself even more hated around the world?"

"Who can prove it's Russia?" countered Hyde. "They'll deny everything."

"So, what's the point?"

"To disrupt. To unnerve," said Hyde. "That's always the point. And to prove that we're vulnerable."

There was a growing sense of indignation in the room, then fear. Sensing the anxiety, the prime minister took charge and invited the chief of the defence staff to address the meeting. General Wallis was a stocky man with a ring of brown hair around the top of his head and a deep authoritative voice. He had been an infantryman in the Argyll and Sutherland Highlanders, and, to this day, he was never really at home in the highly technical world of underwater warfare. However, he was a good dissembler, and an even better communicator. Wallis was able to reassure everyone that the armed forces had not been standing idly by. The military – the army and, above all, the navy – was fully prepared to counter this aggression. There was a plan in place that could be activated immediately.

"However," Wallis said, choosing his words carefully. "At such a difficult time, we must *not* jump the gun. We still have time… Time to receive additional intelligence, pertaining to… Well, forgive me, Prime Minister, but I would rather not expand on this here in this forum. But I can tell you all that this intelligence is crucial and will greatly strengthen our hand. In other words, it's worth waiting for."

"This intelligence we're waiting for is coming from where?" asked the home secretary, doing her best to keep her voice steady.

"From our agent in Moscow."

"When can we expect it?" asked the secretary to the cabinet.

"Any moment," said General Wallis, looking expectantly at Hyde.

That was hours ago. Hyde pressed his buzzer, and, seconds later, George Lynton appeared, alert, deferential, immaculate as ever in his bow tie.

"Still nothing? No email? No word?" asked Hyde.

"Not a dicky bird," said Lynton with genuine regret in his languid voice.

Across Hyde's vision, with no warning whatsoever, flashed the bright-green wings of a parakeet. He opened the window and peered out: the parakeets were back. Hyde liked parakeets: they brought him luck, and God knows he needed it. He knocked back the espresso in one gulp. The shot of cold caffeine did him good.

22

It was the Wednesday before the marathon, and the clocks all over the Senate Palace seemed unbearably loud. Marina was battling her demons, telling herself not to panic.

The intelligence is out there, she told herself, and you will find it. You'll secure a new life, for yourself and for Vanya, and you'll walk into the sunset with Clive. This story has to have a happy ending. Trust in your *sudba*. Something will turn up.

Marina had spent the morning in the audience room of the Palace of Facets, translating from French into Russian salutations of goodwill from the president of Senegal to President Serov and Foreign Minister Kirsanov. Gifts were exchanged. This was followed by a request for several billion dollars. When Marina got back to her office, she discovered an interloper lolling about in her "thinking chair", smoking and with his feet on her desk.

"Make yourself at home, Lyova. Be my guest."

Lev turned round and grinned. He had no tie on, and the lion's head tattoo was clearly visible on his neck.

"I got this craving for a fag and, for once, your door wasn't locked, so I thought I'd help myself. I left them to it, the boss and the admiral. They're having a real ding-dong."

"Double espresso?"

"You read my mind," said Lev, taking a deep drag on his cigarette. He turned full-circle in the swivel chair and then banged his feet back onto Marina's desk. "I've told the boss he should do meditation. I do it every day. It teaches you how to rise above things. But every time I mention the word, he bites my head off."

"So what's this ding-dong all about?" Marina asked with light-hearted curiosity, handing Lev his coffee.

"Timing. It's all about timing," said Lev, exhaling a massive plume of smoke. "If you ask me, the admiral will get his way."

Suddenly, a high-pitched screech exploded ferociously inside Marina's office, making all conversation impossible. Seconds later, Varlamov stood in the open doorway, his furious gaze directed at Lev. The private secretary swung his feet off Marina's desk and got to his feet, mumbling an apology. He fiddled with his phone, and the noise stopped.

"All government buildings in Russia are no-smoking," Varlamov said icily. "I thought you knew that, Lev Lvovich."

"Apologies," said Lev, reluctantly stubbing out his cigarette into his own personal ashtray, which Marina kept just for him. Casually he picked up his phone and headed for the door, but the general blocked his path. Varlamov had stiffened to his full height but was annoyed to discover that he was still an inch or so shorter than Lev.

"Why can't you dress properly?" Varlamov asked. "You're private secretary to the president of the Russian Federation and you need to look the part. What do you mean by wearing jeans? And no tie! And your shoes… Just look at your shoes!"

Lev looked at his Axel Arigato trainers, which had cost a fortune; so had his Hermès shirt and his Momotaro jeans, but this old man was stuck in a world of suits and ties and wouldn't get it, so Lev said nothing. Marina came to his defence.

"Grigory Mikhailovich, I feel I must point out that at every official occasion Lev Lvovich is perfectly dressed. Here, in the Senate Palace, the president doesn't mind if Lev wears casual clothes…"

Varlamov ignored Marina. He was on the warpath.

"And why are you always playing computer chess?"

"I don't play computer chess, General. What gave you that idea?"

"I see you playing on that iPad of yours, or on your phone. It's one or the other, and it's all the time!"

"I study chess games between computers. That's quite a different thing. Computers are the new champions... computers with neural networks that teach themselves chess. Humans are history."

Varlamov looked at Lev with undisguised contempt.

"Humans are *not* history. That's ridiculous."

Varlamov stood in front of the closed door, waiting for Lev to open it, which he did with icy formality.

"Have a nice day, General," said Lev with a look that could kill.

Varlamov disappeared into the corridor.

"Finish your coffee, or would you like a fresh one?" said Marina. "Now, where were we?" she added, trying to get Lev back on track.

But the spell was broken.

"Bastard," Lev muttered, clearly shaken by Varlamov's attack. "Thanks for the support." He pushed his hands deep into the pockets of his jeans and grinned at Marina. "Sod politics, sod affairs of state and all that crap. Let's take a break. Come and meet the love of my life."

Marina let out a heartfelt sigh. The gods were mocking her.

Lev's new passion was his BMW R nineT, which he parked round the back of the Senate Palace in a corner of the Kremlin courtyard under a custom-made, snug-fitting silver cover.

He pulled the cover off with a flourish.

The bike was a "she". Lev was so proud of her matt-white colour, of her low handlebars and under-bar mirrors, all without a trace of vulgar branding. And the tanned leather seat matched his Hermès wallet. And her engine... oh, her engine... so beautiful and big on such a slim body. "Very sexy," he said, stroking the bike. This lean, mean machine weighed over four hundred pounds, but Lev swore she was light and easy to manoeuvre. Her acceleration was as smooth as silk, and her power... her power was like... was like...

Marina decided to put a spanner in the works.

"Surely," said Marina, "this beautiful bike is begging to be stolen?"

"You're right," Lev conceded. "She *is* begging to be stolen. On the other hand..." He broke off to glance around the Kremlin courtyard at the FSO armed guards – big, burly men wearing helmets and bullet-proof vests and carrying automatic weapons – then smiled. "Not where *I* park her". Then he kissed the metal frame. "We've been to Baikal and back. You know where I'm going next? Paris. It's all planned. I'm leaving this courtyard, right here in the Kremlin, and blasting my way to Paris."

"They won't let you," Marina murmured.

For a moment, Lev looked crushed, like a little boy, then he laughed and slipped the silver cover back over the bike. As he did so, Marina noticed, inside his jacket, a holster with a gun.

"You're *armed*?" she said, shocked. "Since when?"

"Just got my licence," said Lev. "New bodyguard status in the FSO. I'm a crack shot. I'll take you to the range one of these days."

"Please don't. Just take me for a ride on your beautiful motorbike."

"OK. That's a deal. Promise."

They went back into the Senate Palace, passing through security. While Marina passed under the metal detector, Lev handed over his gun to one of his FSO mates.

"Varlamov has a gun," Marina murmured as they climbed the marble stairs. She had seen it. One morning, she met the general at security, and while she handed over a backpack, Varlamov handed over a gun. A Makarov. "Did you know?"

"He does what he likes. He's deputy head of the FSB."

Lev's phone pinged. He glanced down at the screen.

"I can't believe this... The admiral's leaving for Petersburg, and we're heading back to the villa."

Marina caught her breath. The villa. That's it. All the key players are leaving the building, she thought. There will be no one left to talk to, no one to tell me what I need to know. It's game over.

Marina was wrong. The game was not over. On the contrary, as Vanya might have told her, it had only just begun.

That afternoon, General Varlamov was enjoying his *cinq à sept* in the arms of his mistress. His bodyguards kept a discreet distance outside her luxurious apartment on the eleventh floor of the Kotelnicheskaya Embankment Building, one of Stalin's Seven Sisters.

General Varlamov had the perfect cover. With the job came a functional, soulless apartment in the Lubyanka itself, and it was there, so Varlamov told his wife, Raisa, that he laid his head after a gruelling day's work, when he felt too tired to make the long journey out of Moscow to Barvikha.

Everything was going according to plan, Varlamov thought to himself as he watched Dasha, his nubile girlfriend, her blue eyes full of mischief, blowing him kisses as she poured two glasses of champagne. Her white dress was so tight that it reminded him of the clingfilm his wife used to wrap up left-over chicken. He must talk to Dasha about her terrible taste in clothes (so vulgar), but in bed she was delicious – so noisy and unrestrained. Then again, he reasoned, one can't have everything in life, and, since we're never going to be seen together in public, who cares? Let her dress as she pleases. He had agreed to be her sponsor, to pay for the flat and give her an allowance, and she would make herself available whenever he wanted her. The rest of her time was her own.

There was only one rule: no men. When the cat's away the mouse does *not* come out and play, Varlamov had told Dasha, in no uncertain terms. She could invite her girlfriends over for supper and to watch movies on the huge flat-screen TV, also her mother, who lived in a small flat near the university, but no one stayed the night. The general didn't trust Dasha. He paid the porters downstairs to keep a scrupulous list of visitors. And he covered his tracks: he gave his name as Mikhail Grigoryevich Kutuzov – to the porters and also to Dasha. He told her that he was the head of an international construction company. Dasha called him Misha.

"Misha," said Dasha, sliding into his lap. "Thank you for the email…"

Naturally, Varlamov assumed it was for the ten thousand dollars he had sent to her account that morning. He waved one hand in the air, while planting the other on her breast.

"Security," she murmured, kissing his cheek, "is so important. Thank you for caring about me."

She could so easily have added: "The security expert you wrote about in your email… He came this afternoon and did whatever he needed to do while I watched *Game of Thrones*. Very young he was. But they're all like that, aren't they, these software developers?" But she was too busy unbuttoning the general's shirt to go into such detail.

Everything, Varlamov repeated to himself as Dasha ran her long red fingernails through the hair on his chest, was going according to plan. His sky was bright blue. All that remained was to bring down Volina. To knock her off her pedestal.

Dasha's hand slipped into his underpants. Enjoy the moment, he told himself.

The general's wife, Raisa, was enjoying her moment, too, in a fashionable gym on the top floor of the Ritz-Carlton that specialized in Pilates. She was steaming in the sauna, her plump body covered by a towel, her blond hair damp with sweat. She was an attractive woman with good skin and friendly brown eyes, and, as she wiped away the beads of sweat on her eyelids, she thought of the Ruinart champagne she would order when the sauna was over.

She deserved a treat. That afternoon she had been in a total panic after losing her new iPhone, the latest model with voice recognition and God knows what else. She was sure she had put it on the fresh juice bar while she tied the laces of her trainers, but then she knocked over her carrot juice and, by the time the mess was cleared up, the iPhone was gone. She searched everywhere. It had vanished. With each passing moment, she grew more afraid: Grisha would go ballistic. She had already lost three iPhones, and, to be honest, she didn't really understand how they worked. She was always asking her children how to send a video or a voice message, how to set up a group chat on WhatsApp or store a boarding pass. They made fun of her and said she was useless, a dinosaur when it came to technology. Above all, she hated all those ghastly passwords you had to remember. A friend told her to keep everything dead simple. So, without consulting her children or her husband, since they were bound to disapprove, she decided to do things her way.

The moment the iPhone went missing, however, Raisa panicked. She called for the attendant, and, within minutes, everyone was looking under towels and cushions. It was a girl with red hair, who happened to be at the front desk asking about yoga classes, who came to the rescue. She was very young, about the same age as Raisa's own daughter – not more than sixteen – and vaguely Raisa wondered why she wasn't at school, but thank heavens she wasn't, because it was the teenager who, after the most frantic searching, which lasted a good twenty minutes, found the iPhone under the carpet. Raisa pressed a hundred-dollar bill into her hand, which she refused. "I couldn't possibly," said the redhead.

What a relief! Raisa thought, staring at the oblong slab of steel, which felt cool in her palm. Now Grisha would have no reason to berate her. She felt that she had lucked out in her choice of husband. She was still a student at Moscow State University when she'd married Grigory Varlamov, a handsome major in the FSB, but it had never crossed her mind that Grisha would get to the very top of his profession and become a general in the security service. These days they had more money than she had ever dreamt of, and she liked money. She liked the way people smiled at you because they knew you were rich. And thanks to Grisha, there was always plenty of money in her bank account. Recently, he had parked a million dollars in her Cyprus account: a deposit, he had said, for the house he was planning to build in Portofino.

Raisa left the sauna and plunged herself into the ice-cold tub, gasping with shock and, at the same time, feeling a rush of inner warmth and blazing health. Five minutes later, her body pink from the freezing water, Raisa dried herself, patted her precious new iPhone, which lay beside her handbag, and decided it was time for that glass of Ruinart.

The Kremlin was a lonely place without Lev, and so that afternoon Marina was glad to see the ADC to the admiral of the fleet outside her office, looking impeccable in his white navy uniform.

"Captain Smirnov," said Marina with a warm smile. "How nice to see you… But what is it that keeps you in Moscow? I was told the admiral has left for Saint Petersburg."

"Marina Andreyevna," said the ADC with a formal nod of the head. "Yes, well… Of course, I should have left with the admiral. Instead, they've given me a temporary office next to yours, and I'm stuck here while I wait."

"What for?" Marina said lightly.

"Bulgari. They're resetting a diamond brooch for the admiral. It's a surprise wedding anniversary present for his wife. Hugely valuable. Full of diamonds and sapphires, so he can't exactly send it in the post."

The ADC waited a second to see if Marina realized this was his attempt at a joke. She did.

"He must like his wife an awful lot," said Marina. "Or be very afraid of her."

The ADC let out a laugh. "I couldn't possibly comment."

Marina suggested a cup of her most delicious Italian coffee in her office, but the captain shook his head and refused, most politely, explaining that he was up to his eyes in work. With that, he disappeared into his temporary office.

Next day, Marina got up as dawn was breaking. She threw open the windows of her big room and took deep breaths of early-morning air – to fill her lungs with oxygen, to keep up her levels of hope. Later, in her office at the Senate Palace, the thud of a helicopter was unmistakable and took Marina completely by surprise. Ten minutes later, she stood at her office door and watched as the guards stood to attention at the far end of the corridor and the gilded doors swung open, swallowing up the president and his closest advisers. An hour later, knocking on her door was Lev, the man who heard and knew everything.

"That was a quick visit to the villa," Marina said, glancing up from her laptop. "Not even twenty-four hours."

"The boss has ants in his pants. Can't keep still for a second."

"I'm so glad you're here, Lyova. I've been wanting to talk to you about the heating in my office." Marina sat with her hands folded and was leaning forward on her desk. "The radiator must be blocked. In winter, this room is perishing."

"I like the cold," Lev said, making himself comfortable in Marina's "thinking chair". "I grew up in Yakutia… Minus sixty in January. As children, we used to play outside without coats even when it was minus forty. Of course, we were just kids, running around. But even so. Most people would find that hard to believe – minus forty without coats – but it's true."

"I believe you," said Marina, thinking of Pasha and Vanya as boys running around without coats in the coldest weather. "Can you send a heating engineer? Otherwise, I'll have to fall back on a fan heater, which isn't exactly good for the environment…"

Lev wasn't listening. He was looking at the photograph of Pasha and Vanya.

"I remember him," he said, staring at Pasha. "Nice boy. Pity. Marina Andreyevna, why don't you move to a nice new apartment? There's one for sale in my building. With a banya. I can fix the financing and we know the boss will agree."

"I like where I am. The apartment may be old-fashioned, but it has memories. My grandfather lived there… He sang romances in the living room. And there's even a bronze plaque to commemorate him on the front of the building."

"Suit yourself. I'll organize an engineer."

"Thank you, Lyova. You're so kind. You're the only real friend I've got here."

"The boss likes you."

"Yes, but he's the boss."

Lev understood exactly what she meant. You could get close, but never *really* close. There was always a barrier.

"Have a cigarette? On my balcony?"

Lev shook his head.

"Varlamov reported me. Can you believe it?"

"How about a chocolate?"

Lev's phone pinged. He glanced down at the screen.

"I've got five minutes. Then I've got to go. I always love coming here, because it's so peaceful." Lev looked around the room appreciatively. "It's been crazy-busy ever since yesterday."

Marina was rummaging in her drawer for a good box of chocolates given to her by a Swiss interpreter. She looked up and smiled.

"Yesterday?"

"Yesterday evening the boss called an emergency meeting at the villa. They all turned up: the foreign minister, the minister of defence, the minister of the interior... the whole lot of them."

"Not Varlamov?"

"The pain-in-the-arse general was also there. He was late."

For a moment Lev closed his eyes.

"I haven't slept in days... It's total madness. All of a sudden, over breakfast this morning, the boss decides he can't think straight at the villa, with all that water gushing from the fountains and all those birds tweeting – they really got on his nerves – so back we come, and it's been a nightmare ever since. So much tension! So much bad temper! The boss is pacing around like a caged lion, waiting for an update from the admiral. Varlamov and Kirsanov aren't much better. Everyone's on edge, holding their breath. Soon they'll hit the vodka. Or whisky. Kirsanov likes whisky. Whatever they drink, all hell is about to break loose."

"Oh dear, I am sorry," said Marina, passing him the chocolates.

"Sorry?" said Lev. "This whole thing is all your fault! I'm not joking! The boss kept repeating that *Hamlet* quote of yours..."

The one about conscience. The moment we got to the villa, he asked me to get Admiral Fyodorov on the phone. Not any phone, mind you. The special phone, the red one in his study. 'Get me the admiral now!' he says."

"At least you got out of Moscow," Marina said. "Had some fresh air, and a walk in that nice garden with all those statues?"

"You must be joking! I was stuck inside on the bloody telephone, trying to find the admiral," said Lev, reaching for another chocolate. "Ah, caramel dream. Delicious. He was boarding a flight to Petersburg. It was lucky for us he hadn't taken off."

It was Marina's turn to choose a chocolate. "I like coffee," she murmured, consulting the chart.

"So now I've got Admiral Fyodorov on the phone," Lev went on. "And I pass the handset to the boss, who says to the admiral, 'Slava, get the show on the road.' Just like that! 'Get the show on the road.' My God, I wish I could have seen Fyodorov's face. He must have been jumping for joy."

Lev's phone pinged and he glanced down at the screen. "Got to go," he sighed. "Ever since the boss gave the go-ahead, it's been mayhem. No one got any sleep last night. They're all a bag of nerves, waiting for news. 'It's all about timing. Getting our ducks in a row before the deadline.'"

"Ah, yes, the deadline," Marina said, picking up a lemon drop and popping it into her mouth.

"It would have to be Sunday, wouldn't it? I was going to watch you cross that finish line, but I can't be in two places at once, now, can I? We'll be at the villa or here… But we'll be busy, that's for sure. I'll try and catch you on the TV, though. And if I see you, I'll give a cheer!"

"So sweet of you," said Marina, stepping forward and giving Lev a kiss on the cheek. He looked pleased and left.

Marina told herself to do nothing in a hurry. She sent a text, wrote one or two emails, tidied her desk, picked up her sports bag and was standing in the corridor, keys in hand, when she heard voices. She looked up and saw President Serov, flanked by two bodyguards, General Varlamov, Foreign Minister Kirsanov and, bringing up the rear, Lev, all walking towards her.

"Marinochka!" said Serov, hanging back to talk to Marina. "Your father would be proud of me!"

"He was always proud of you, Nikolai Nikolayevich."

Marina sent Clive a text, bringing forward their run by an hour: it was a lovely sunny day and she was leaving the office early. "Don't forget your water bottle," she added. This was their emergency signal.

"You're sure?" said Clive, sprinting down the Frunzenskaya Embankment, glancing back at the fit young minders who were close but not close enough.

"That's what he said."

"Yesterday late afternoon… the green light?"

"Yes."

"Twenty-one hours ago?"

"Yes."

"*Merde.*"

"Why French?"

"Less vulgar, don't you think?"

"I do," said Marina. "I most definitely do."

"Deadline?"

"Sunday."

"Exact location?"

"Unknown."

"I have to see you. Think of something, will you? Oh God, I've got a terrible cramp. So sorry. Got to stop."

Clive could hardly walk, let alone run. He was bent double with the cramp and leant heavily on Marina as he struggled up the steps from the embankment to the road. Once they had reached the top, Marina stopped a cab and helped Clive into the car. She told the driver where to go, then finished her run alone.

Clive went straight to the glass edifice of the British embassy on the Smolenskaya Embankment, where he hobbled into the security booth, grimacing and groaning. It was only once he had been ushered into the safe room by the ambassador that he straightened up and asked for a drink.

23

Sunday makes perfect sense, thought Hyde. Cut the cables on a Sunday for maximum impact on Monday. Defence will be "on weekend".

Luke Marden's encrypted email came through at 12.45 p.m. on Thursday afternoon. George Lynton produced a paper copy, which Hyde took straight to the prime minister. Ninety minutes later, Martha Maitland had convened an emergency COBRA meeting.

"So, ladies and gentlemen," said the prime minister with her exemplary courtesy, looking around the table at anxious faces: fifty per cent women, a statistic of which she was proud. "We have just received intelligence that the Russian attack on the undersea cables is scheduled for this Sunday. As I speak, Russian submarines with their underwater drones are, after several months of reconnaissance, closing in somewhere just outside British waters off the Cornish coast. To launch a disruptive counter offensive, we need six hours: is that correct, First Sea Lord?"

"Correct," replied Admiral Geoffrey Hutley. "But what would really help, Prime Minister, would be an accurate location. As precise as possible. We need to get within twenty nautical miles of our target to be effective. If we can get within five nautical miles, then we're home and dry."

The first sea lord had a lot more to say on this subject, but he restrained himself. How often he had fought his own corner in the last few years in this very room, and how often he had lost. The Royal Navy – the Senior Service – had been relentlessly cut back, starved of cash, with the result he had predicted over and over: we cannot defend our shores. He could have spoken up: yes, of course, and caused a stir. He could have said the Government was in dereliction of its duty. Why? Because, according to the Armed Forces Covenant, "The first duty of Government is the defence of the realm." But now was not the time, Geoffrey Hutley decided, to remind Martha Maitland of this sobering fact.

"Yes," said Hyde. "We need an exact location."

"And we need luck," said the first sea lord.

"You talk as if we're defenceless!" objected the business secretary. "We've got our own submarines. Why don't we use them to hunt down theirs?"

"Because we have too few," the first sea lord said with a heartfelt sigh. "And if we were to deploy them, they might get in the way if we have to increase the level of aggression. We don't want a blue-on-blue situation. Let's keep the field clean."

"So, what are you saying?… That we're sitting ducks?" said the home secretary, her voice rising as she stared hard at the first sea lord.

"Not if we can get a precise location. Then we can neutralize this attack."

"And in the meantime?" said the foreign secretary, looking to the prime minister for an answer.

However, it was Martin Hyde who replied, taking in the whole COBRA meeting with one sweeping look: "We hold our nerve and wait for the final piece of intelligence."

While the COBRA meeting was taking place in London, General Varlamov was sitting in his office at the FSB headquarters in the Lubyanka, reading an email he had received from one of his operatives. "Englishman and Marina Volina went running at 1.30 p.m. At 2 p.m. the Englishman got cramp and stopped. He went to the embassy."

"You mean the residence?" Varlamov texted back.

"No, the embassy. The west wing."

Varlamov took a deep breath and walked over to the panoramic window, through which he had a spectacular view of Moscow, his city and the capital of his great country, Russia.

What is my purpose in life? the general asked himself, staring down at the eight lanes of swirling traffic below. To support the president and to enhance the power and prestige of Russia, came his instant reply to himself. It's my job to make sure we maintain our status as a world power, a nation to be feared and respected. To this end, it's also my job to bring down those enemies, within and without, who want to take Russia in some other direction, reduce our influence, constrain our ambition, build what they call "democracy" and what the president and I call "chaos". I need to be vigilant around the clock. All foreigners are suspect, but what about Volina? Why do I have the feeling that she's up to something? Because Marina Volina is not really "one of us". She's an outsider. And she's too close to Serov for his own good. The woman is punching above her weight. She's a mere translator, nothing more, nothing less, and yet she's always by the president's side. Not good. Not good at all. I've said it before, and I'll say it again. Volina needs to be taken down a peg or two.

General Varlamov summoned Maxim Mishin, and, the moment the young FSB officer stepped into the room, Varlamov declared, "Lieutenant, we've got work to do."

For several hours Maxim Mishin trawled through the CCTV footage at Tverskaya 25. The state-of-the-art surveillance system that had been installed was, in his opinion, a mixed blessing. Whenever there was any movement whatsoever in front of any of the cameras, Mishin would receive a text message and live footage would be streamed directly onto his laptop. This was more video footage than he could stomach, given that there were five cameras, two of which covered the front and back entrances to the building itself, two more that covered the gates in and out of the back courtyard, where people parked their cars, one leading onto Tverskaya, and the other onto a side street, and a fifth camera on the first-floor landing, directly in front of Marina Volina's front door.

Mishin was puzzled by the general's interest in Marina Volina, but, of course, he said nothing. Instead, he watched Mrs Volina coming in and going out, now in a tracksuit, now in a skirt. He watched Volina being nice to one lift lady, Oxana, and less nice to the other, Nadia; and he watched her walking into the back courtyard to find her car, and every now and then staring upwards into the camera with a look of defiance.

"Excuse me, General, for asking, but we could put a tail on Mrs Volina…"

"No, Lieutenant, that's exactly what we can't do."

She was too sharp, too clever, and would almost certainly spot the tail, then go straight to the president. And that might just be that. The president would be outraged and demand explanations, and he, Varlamov, had none. Just instinct. As it was, the general was worried Volina might tell Serov about the CCTV cameras in her building, although his cover was solid: bog-standard security. But a tail, now that was a risk too far. The general was treading on eggshells, and he knew it. He would "watch" her and make sure she knew it. That was as far as he could go. For the moment.

"Where is she this evening? Do we know?" Varlamov asked.

"Not at home," said Mishin. "She left the building through the front entrance at two minutes past six. I called Nadia, the lift lady who reports to us, and she says that Volina has gone to a concert at the Rachmaninov Hall."

That same evening, Clive was sitting with the ambassador in his study overlooking the Moscow River and, beyond it, the walls of the Kremlin. Both men were in a sombre mood, knowing, as they did, that Operation Hades had been launched and everything depended on Marina. Rose Friedman provided some light relief when, to Clive's surprise, she knocked on the door of Luke Marden's study and walked right in. Rose was now living in the residence, so Clive discovered, at the invitation of the ambassador. Safety in numbers, Rose quipped, as she helped herself to a drink before heading off, in her Lycra leggings, to an evening kick-boxing session. She did her best to persuade Clive to join her, to live a little, but he was adamant: he was staying put. The ambassador suggested some fresh air, so they stood outside on the balcony under a threatening sky. It was still light, but the Kremlin walls were already floodlit. A barge carrying coal slid by, sounding its deep, mournful horn. Suddenly there was a clap of thunder, and they hurried back into the ambassador's study, where Clive's WhatsApp pinged with a message from Marina.

> So sorry about your cramp. How are you? Do you need anything? Have left you Goncharova/Larionov book in the InterContinental bookshop. Ask for Maria. See you for the marathon registration tomorrow at 9 a.m.

Clive turned to Luke Marden.

"Could I possibly borrow Fyodor for the evening? Oh, do you have an umbrella? One that folds?"

.   .   .

The risks we take for love, he thought. The reckless, crazy risks.

Everything depended on Fyodor. Clive confided in him that the situation was delicate. First, Clive had a book to collect, and then he had a rendezvous with a married woman, a French lady who was staying in the hotel. Her husband was horribly jealous and, more importantly, was in Paris, so this was their moment. Could Fyodor wait? It might be a couple of hours. Did he mind? And if the FSB tail got nosy, well, just deal with him. Clive pressed five hundred-dollar bills into Fyodor's hand.

Fyodor parked in a side street just beyond the hotel. As Clive got out, a blue Ford with his FSB tail drew up alongside. Clive strolled into the hotel and found the bookshop, where Maria, the sales assistant, was expecting him. The book on Natalia Goncharova and Mikhail Larionov had been put to one side and paid for, Maria explained. Did he know it was the first book about the two of them? Until now, it had all been about Goncharova. No one was interested in Larionov, even though they spent their whole lives together and, of course, influenced each other. But this is one of those rare cases when the woman eclipsed the man. "Women have really come into their own, don't you think?" Maria said, warming to her theme. "Look at Frida Kahlo. She's much more famous than her husband, Diego Rivera." Clive said that women were, on the whole, more capable and infinitely less destructive than men, and with that, he asked for a bag – paper, if possible – for the art book and for his folding umbrella. "No paper," Maria said with regret. "Only plastic." And she gave Clive a smart InterContinental bookshop bag.

Meanwhile, the FSB tail was browsing in the self-help section, trailing a finger over *Rewire Your Anxious Brain*. Maria went over to him and asked if he wanted any help; they had an extensive selection of books. Might he be interested in *The Highly Sensitive Person* or *When Panic Attacks*?

Clive took a seat in the lobby and found Marina's map tucked inside the art book. The tail was sitting in a chair, facing him. Clive took a deep breath and strolled back into the bookshop. The tail also got up and kept an eye on him from the other side of the glass wall. Clive confided in Maria that he had a prostate problem and asked if there was a loo he could use. "Of course," said Maria. "You can use the staff lavatory." Seconds later, Clive disappeared through a side door. He hurried down a flight of stairs and was walking quickly, straight past the lavatory, when he heard footsteps on the stairs. He followed Marina's instructions and pushed open the third door on the left, which led to a rabbit warren of laundry rooms; he kept on going, past the roaring sound of washing machines and tumble dryers, until he found himself in front of another flight of stairs, which led up to a side exit of the hotel, a block away from where the Ford and the Range Rover were parked.

Clive was lucky; it was raining. He put up his umbrella, walked casually round to the front entrance of the hotel and joined a stream of pedestrians heading down into the underpass beneath Tverskaya. When Clive emerged on the far side of the eight-lane thoroughfare, he could see the rear lights of the Range Rover and the Ford, and a man, presumably his FSB tail, talking to Fyodor. Would the driver pull it off? Clive need not have worried. Fyodor produced a pack of cigarettes and, sympathizing with his predicament, offered one to the tail, which he took. "No need to stress," said Fyodor. "Just sit tight and relax." The Englishman was in bed with someone else's wife. What more did he need to know?

At that same moment, Marina had climbed the entrance steps of Tverskaya 25 and reached the landing, where Nadia, the lift lady, sat knitting.

"Back so early?" said Nadia, looking up from her needles and wrinkling her nose as she peered through her thick lenses.

"I'm too old for this contemporary music," Marina replied, tossing the concert programme onto Nadia's table. "I left at the first interval."

"Volina is back," said Mishin, following the live CCTV footage on his laptop. "She's talking to Nadia."

"Find out why she's back," ordered Varlamov. "And where's the Englishman? Find out."

Lieutenant Mishin had answers to everything. Mrs Volina had come back from the concert early because she didn't like contemporary music. He had even taken the trouble to ask Nadia to read out the names of the composers listed in the programme and then double-check with the Rachmaninov Hall. The names Dmitri Kurlyandsky, Sergei Nevsky and Anton Batagov meant nothing to Mishin, but, according to Google, they were not only very contemporary, but also very famous, and the head of security at the Rachmaninov Hall confirmed that they had been playing that evening. As for the Englishman, he texted the FSB tail, who said that the Englishman was in the InterContinental with a friend. A married woman.

"The InterContinental?" said Varlamov. "But that's right opposite Tverskaya 25."

It was the look of pity from the young Lieutenant Mishin that stopped Varlamov in his tracks. The general went over to the window and looked down on the swirling lines of traffic below. Was he going mad? He had nothing on Volina and nothing on Franklin. So far, neither one had put a foot wrong.

"It's raining," said Mishin, looking on his laptop at more CCTV footage of the exits and entrances to Tverskaya 25. "Everyone's under an umbrella. We can't see who's who. But

Volina hasn't moved from her apartment. She's in there. And she's had no visitors."

"If she does, we'll be the first to know," said Varlamov, pulling out his vaporizer.

Clive walked down Blagoveshchensky Lane, his umbrella pressed so close to his head that it felt like a hat. He stopped at the back entrance of Tverskaya 25. Through the wrought-iron electronic gates, he could see the playground, the shed for the rubbish bins, and dozens of parked cars.

He was exactly on time: 8.15 p.m. A ragged old man with an even more ragged dog shuffled towards him, and, without saying a word, Sasha, the bedraggled, bearded caretaker, opened the gate, his mangy dog, Ivan the Terrible, sniffing the ground by his side.

Clive stepped inside the courtyard, pressing a hundred-dollar bill into Sasha's hand, who thanked him and headed back to the rubbish bins. It was almost dark, but Clive could just make out the swings in the playground. He kept to the edge of the courtyard, at times hugging the wall, his face hidden by the umbrella. In the beam of a spluttering yellow light by the playground, Clive reread Marina's note. He studied the different fire escapes and hoped to God he had got the right one. And then he climbed up.

She was there, in the shadows of her small balcony, waiting for him. He kissed her so hard she could hardly breathe. He wanted to dance and sing and throw out his arms, but, of course, he could do none of that. The world was in crisis. But he was in love. Marina opened a bottle of Russian champagne, and they sat together, first in the kitchen, then in the sitting room, and then on the edge of the bed, until…

"We can live in New Zealand," said Clive. "No one will find us there."

"We won't have a choice," said Marina. "They'll have it all worked out. And I'll have to spend time alone before they'll allow you to join me. That's what I imagine."

"It's not what I imagine."

"Let's not think about it now," she said, stroking the side of his face. He smiled into her eyes. Her nakedness was so soft.

"This happiness has set me free," she said. "Do you understand that?"

Clive was careful. And still lucky. It kept raining hard. He left Marina's flat the same way that he came, by the fire escape. Once again, he hugged the wall, and, when the moment came to cross the vision of the CCTV camera and exit via the Tverskaya entrance, he waited until he saw a woman hurrying across the courtyard, also holding an umbrella. He stood beside her as she used her fob to open the electronic gate, and the two of them passed through.

Clive took the underpass and slipped back into the InterContinental through a side entrance; moments later, he emerged through the front door and walked around the corner to find Fyodor and his FSB tail sharing a cigarette.

According to the FSB report, Franklin left the InterContinental Hotel at 11.43 p.m. and got back to the residence at 12.07 a.m. The FSB tail saw no reason to mention that he had lost the Englishman inside the hotel. Instead, he was able to state with absolute certainty that the foreigner had taken the lift to the fourth floor (Fyodor's idea).

Lieutenant Mishin had the bit between his teeth. This was his chance to impress the general, who had told him to leave no stone unturned. At nine o'clock, Mishin started to sift through the CCTV footage from the camera in front of the British embassy. By half past nine, he was standing in front of Varlamov, reading out the FSB operative's email from that afternoon.

"'Franklin got a cramp at 2 p.m. He couldn't walk. Volina helped him into a cab at 2.07 p.m., then finished her run alone.'"

Mishin placed his laptop in front of the general.

"Now... Look at this."

The footage of Clive and Marina running side by side, which had been taken by the FSB tail on his phone, lasted only a few seconds. She turned to him and smiled. Varlamov froze the frame. He had never seen her smile like that. She likes him, he thought. She likes him a lot.

Clive could be seen limping into the security booth on the Smolenskaya Embankment, where he produced his passport. He then passed the security check to the other side. For two steps, no more, he was upright, walking normally, until once again he limped.

"He's faking it," said Mishin.

24

"We don't have a Clive Franklin," the young woman said with a yawn, sitting behind a registration desk in an annexe of Luzhniki Stadium. She had been there since six o'clock that morning, in a Moscow marathon T-shirt with the word "volunteer" emblazoned across the front, and she was already exhausted. For some reason she could not understand, computers played no part in the registration: the names of the runners were printed on reams of old-fashioned paper. "There are twenty-four thousand names here in alphabetical order," she said, holding up a thick wodge of printed pages, "and Franklin isn't one of them."

"It *has* to be there," Marina insisted, reaching over to check the list herself, when one of the FSB tails stepped forward, showed his ID and a letter, and said something to the volunteer, who then called over her supervisor. There was a brief discussion, after which it was all over.

"Right. We do have a Clive Franklin, after all," said the volunteer. "Could I see your passport, please? And your medical certificate?"

"He's fine," said the FSB tail.

"If you say so... Marina Volina. Your ID? Thank you. Clive Franklin, British citizen. You're both C."

"C?" said Clive.

"A is for professionals, B is for the top amateurs, and C is for more or less everyone else. Clive Franklin, you're C105. And you, Marina Volina, are C104. Help yourself to maps."

Inside the annexe of Luzhniki Stadium, the noise grew more deafening with every moment that passed. Marathon runners in their hundreds queued to register, greeting old friends, browsing at the dozens of stalls selling the latest running kit: heart monitors, fitness watches, protein snacks and drinks. Here was everything to keep body and soul together, including massage and kinesiology stations. Should I tape my knees? Clive wondered, before he turned back to Marina.

"Why the suit?"

"I'm so sorry, Clive, I totally forgot to tell you... I never run on the Friday before a marathon. Nor do most runners. It's a sort of superstition... brings bad luck. Let's do a short run tomorrow... Our last training session. Late afternoon. I'm working in the morning. I'll text you with an exact time. We'll just run five kilometres."

"You need to tell me *where*. I need a location."

"Of course you do," said Marina, trying to keep the anxiety out of her voice. "And I'll let you know."

"How soon?"

"Very soon."

Really? Marina asked herself, as she left Luzhniki for the Kremlin. So far, she had run into one brick wall after another. Who was there left to ask? she wondered as she crossed the cobblestone Kremlin courtyard, catching a glimpse of Lev's motorbike under its silver sheet. Silence hung like a mist in the corridors of the Senate Palace; it hung everywhere, especially on the ormolu French clocks with their miniature sculptures of golden swans and mermaids, hairy-legged fawns blowing hunting horns, leopards pulling Diana in her chariot. Where was the tinkling? The chimes? Marina had never known it so quiet.

She didn't know what to do with herself. She walked along the corridor, towards the president's apartment. The two FSO guards were outside on the balcony, smoking. When they saw Marina, they put out their cigarettes.

"Don't worry, boys," said Marina. "I'm not going to say anything. Where is everyone?"

"At the villa."

"For how long?"

"No idea," one said.

"We're always the last to know," said the other. "Maybe tomorrow?"

Marina was walking back to her office, when she noticed a solitary figure in a white naval uniform climbing the grand staircase.

"Don't tell me you're still here?" said Marina to Captain First Rank Artyom Smirnov, her manner sympathetic and smiling. She wondered if this chance encounter might just be her salvation.

"I'm afraid so, Marina Andreyevna," the captain replied, removing his hat. This time Marina persuaded him to come into her office for a quick cup of coffee.

"Bulgari is taking forever," he said, sitting very upright in the chestnut armchair, holding his cup and saucer. "They were supposed to deliver the brooch yesterday, then I got a text saying they'll deliver the brooch today at six o'clock. But will they? The admiral says I'm not to leave Moscow without it. On the other hand, we really do have more important things to do than to worry about a diamond-and-sapphire brooch. We've got a very, very busy weekend ahead. All leave has been cancelled."

The captain stopped himself, as if he knew he had said too much, and got up to leave.

"May I ask you a personal question?" Marina said in a bid to keep him longer.

"Of course."

"Why did you join the navy?"

"Because I'm a patriot and I want to serve my country."

"That's very commendable," Marina said, keeping her voice light. "Why don't we keep each other company over lunch? We seem to be the only people on this floor…"

Captain Smirnov said it pained him to refuse such a generous offer, but, alas, he was chained to his desk.

And so, another door had slammed shut in Marina's face. What else could she do? For over an hour, she walked up and down the corridor and even explored the floor above, just in case she might meet a secretary, a colleague who could be persuaded to talk over a cup of tea. But people were either busy or absent. It was Friday, and the sun was shining, and everyone was eager to get out of town.

Eventually, in the early afternoon, Marina went home. She checked her mailbox in the entrance hall. There were the usual flyers and a postcard of a giraffe. No stamp. The blank side was addressed for Flat 3 and accompanied by a message: 4PM TODAY.

Marina climbed the stairs to the landing, clutching the postcard and sensing the malevolent beam of the CCTV camera on the back of her neck. When she saw Oxana on the landing, she nodded in the direction of the back door, and Oxana hurried after her to the far corner of the courtyard, as far away from the CCTV cameras as possible.

"How did this get into my mailbox?" Marina asked, holding up the postcard with a giraffe.

"Delivered by hand," Oxana explained. "It was inside a pizza box. You see, my Lyubochka sent me over pizza. Oh, that girl does worry me. Won't go home. Won't go to school. Anyway, where was I? Inside the pizza box was this card. It was for flat three, so I put it in your mailbox."

"Thank you. Thank you very much."

And so Marina waved at Sasha and his dog, and kept her head down as she slipped through the back gate onto Tverskaya, where she stopped a car and asked the driver to take her to the zoo.

Marina hated zoos, and the Moscow zoo was sadder than most. The brown bear had hardly any fur; the gorilla lolled about half awake; the zebra stood for hours in the same place; only the birds in the aviary dashed about, twittering. Every once in a while she had taken Pasha and Vanya to the zoo, and the animal they loved most was the giraffe. There were two of them, behind the wire fence, caged but calm, and beautifully languorous.

She kept looking behind and all around, in case she was being followed, but there was no one about. Just a zoo-keeper with a pile of hay for the giraffes.

"Boo," said Vanya from behind. As Marina jumped, Vanya laughed; he had always loved frightening her. Vanya was holding hands with Lyuba. There was laughter in her green eyes, which Marina had not seen before. The three of them sat on a bench beneath the steady, indifferent stare of the giraffe.

"We've got some good news," said Vanya. "Me and Lyuba, we're getting married. But she's gotta finish school, that's what I told her. Get the certificate. Next week she's going home. Back to her mum. And back to school. Sparrow Hills. She's gonna tell them she's been sick with flu, but now she's better. Next May she can take the end-of-school exam. And next June we're getting married. In Tbilisi. That's where her dad lives. I've got it all worked out."

"This is wonderful news," said Marina, and she meant it. She was touched by their youth and beauty and love. Vanya's face was lit up; she had never seen him look so happy.

"Really?" said Vanya. "I thought you were gonna say, 'Don't be daft, you're too young,' and all that crap."

"When it comes to love, I have no advice to give, except to follow your heart. You're very young, Lyuba, but... but... why not? If I have one regret in my life, it's that I was never impulsive enough... always too careful, too cautious, too worried about the consequences. Vanechka, can you and I have a moment alone? Lyuba, would you mind?"

Lyuba wandered off to look at the listless zebras and the sad, moulting brown bear.

"Vanechka, it's your lucky day. You're getting an early wedding present."

Using Vanya's phone, Marina transferred two hundred and fifty thousand dollars from her Cyprus account into Vanya's Bitcoin wallet. He shook his head in disbelief.

"We can buy a house... You gotta come to our wedding. Promise? It's only because of you we met again... You're our fairy godmother."

"No one's ever called me that before."

"I've got something for you... Something really juicy to show you that might come in handy."

He took out his iPhone and showed her a short video: it was General Varlamov having sex with a young woman.

"Oh my God..."

"I've got a video and stills... the lot. We can have a lot of fun with this."

Marina gripped Vanya's arm.

"Vanechka, are you *crazy*? Delete this. Delete all of this from your iPhone... How did you get it? No, don't tell me. Just get rid of it. You're playing with fire, Vanechka. You don't know these people."

"I know that shit Varlamov. I know him inside out. He killed my brother, remember? We can use this to bring him down."

Suddenly, the ringtone on Marina's phone danced into the air.

"Marina? This is Rose Friedman. British Council and all that. Shakespeare forever and a day... Yes? So, where's my friend Clive?"

"How did you get this number?"

"Your card is by his bed. I'm not *in* his bed, by the way. Just staying at the residence, on the same floor as Clive. So where *is* the bugger?" said Rose. "He told me he was going to register for the marathon, then do a quick run with you and be back here by twelve at the latest. We had a lunch date and I'm starving."

"We registered, but we didn't run," Marina said with difficulty. Her mouth was so dry that she had trouble enunciating her words. "I left him in the annexe at the stadium. He said he was going to do a bit of shopping..."

That was indeed the idea, but things had turned out differently. With an empty day stretching ahead, Clive had called Rose, who reminded him they were meeting at the residence at noon for a spot of culture, followed by a spot of lunch, or, said Rose, maybe just lunch. Clive wandered around the vast sports hall festooned with Moscow banners and nearly bought himself a new pair of Adidas trainers before deciding it would be too risky to run a marathon in new shoes. He also decided that he needed to exercise, so he left his backpack with the shop assistant and pounded the track near Luzhniki. It was a beautiful, clear day with a tinge of sharpness in the air, and, for the first time in days, he didn't care about the tail sprinting behind.

After the run, Clive collected his backpack, sprinted up the stairs to the road, stood in the street in his running clothes and, as usual, hailed a gypsy cab. An old Ford drew up. The driver rolled down the window, and Clive negotiated a price to the Sofiyskaya Embankment. He opened the door to the back seat and got in, but no sooner had he sat down than the door opened on the far side and a stranger jumped in beside him.

Except he wasn't a stranger: he was the baby-faced FSB tail who had been following him around for days. Clive reached for the door handle, but there was a loud click as the car doors locked.

His iPhone was in the money bag around his waist, and he was thinking how to reach it, when the fresh-faced youth with pink cheeks held out his hand and, with the hint of an American accent, said:

"Your cell phone, please."

The "please" sounded so odd, almost comical, and the accent was a giveaway: the young man had learnt his English on a diet of American films. Without saying a word, Clive unzipped the money belt and handed over his iPhone. He kept an eye on the streets, noting where they were heading. Then he leant his head back against the worn leather seat and, for a moment, closed his eyes.

Marina's hand was shaking as she ended the call with Rose. Vanya was sitting on the green wooden bench, staring at the giraffe.

"Will you look at those eyelashes?" Vanya said, making a silly face at the animal. "We always loved the giraffes… Pasha tried to climb the fence once. Do you remember?"

"Vanechka," said Marina. "I need your help."

25

Clive was alone in a small basement room somewhere near Taganka. I can't just *vanish*, he decided. Rose will notice, and so will Marina. They'll *do* something.

They had taken his backpack with his passport and his insulin pen and his packet of dextrose. He felt slightly foolish, still in his running shorts, as he sat on the wooden chair at a wooden table, staring at a glass of water.

General Varlamov stepped into the small room, accompanied by a young man wearing thick glasses. The general sat down facing Clive.

"So, Mr Franklin, you know why you're here?"

"I have no idea why I am here," Clive replied. "And I would like to remind you that I have diplomatic immunity and that this abduction is completely illegal. There will be consequences."

"Yes," said Varlamov. "There will. You are going to tell me everything. About your friendship with Marina Volina, and why, on so many occasions, you made a dash to the British embassy, where you went straight to the safe room. To talk about what and to whom? What information were you passing that was so urgent?"

Clive sat quite still, his hands folded on the table. Fear was rising like vomit in his throat.

"Show the pictures," the general ordered, and seconds later Maxim Mishin laid before Clive stills of him arriving at the embassy last Sunday, still in his running clothes. He then produced an iPad and pulled up a video of Clive at the security gate in front of the embassy, crippled with cramp. Then, for just two strides, he seemed to walk normally – until, once again, he buckled.

"You're faking it," said Varlamov. "You didn't have cramp. But you had to get to the embassy fast. Why? What had Volina told you that was so important?"

Now the fear was tasting like bile.

"I can do this two ways," he said, leaning forward across the wooden table. "I can be polite. And I can be impolite. Which means you will feel a lot of pain. It's your choice."

"You have no right whatsoever to hold me here," Clive said, doing his best to keep both the indignation and the calmness in his voice. At the same time, he was trying to remember what he'd been taught at a quick course in London during his embassy years. "What to do if you're arrested…" Keep hammering the illegality, deny everything, and hold on – that was about all that came to mind.

"This is all rather crude, isn't it?" Clive said, being as provocative as he dared. "You've brought me here against my will. I remind you again, General Varlamov" – would that unnerve him, Clive wondered, the fact that he knew his name? – "that I have diplomatic immunity, which gives me the right to see someone from the British embassy. Unless, of course —"

"Unless what?"

Varlamov was on his feet, smelling victory.

"Unless we're going back to the days of Stalin and forced confessions…"

This stung Varlamov. The Stalinist forced confessions were so crude and so passé. Varlamov took a long look at this Englishman and decided he was either a master spy or just a simpleton with extraordinary nerve.

"I can kill you now."

The words hung in the stale air. Who had said them? It was as if Varlamov was surprised that he himself had spoken.

"I know you can," said Clive, with as much indifference as he could muster.

"Or… I can make sure that wonderful ear of yours for our Russian language never hears anything again. Ever. I can make you deaf for the rest of your life. You won't be much use as an interpreter, will you, if you can't hear anything?…"

Clive sat motionless.

"Do you understand what I'm saying?"

Varlamov was on his feet, bending over Clive, looking down on him.

"But of course, in point of fact, I don't have to do a thing. I can just keep you here, locked up without your precious insulin, and you'll die, slowly but surely. Much the simplest."

Clive said nothing. He sat in his chair straight-backed, looking ahead at the grey wall.

"Who did you visit at the InterContinental Hotel yesterday evening?" Varlamov demanded. "The driver said she was a married woman. What was her name? What room was she in? Or perhaps you went somewhere else? Like Tverskaya 25?"

"You're calling at the wrong address," said Clive, quoting the Russian proverb.

Varlamov sat quite still, staring at Clive. Then his fist shot out, smashing into Clive's cheek and knocking him off his chair. Clive clamped his hand to his burning cheek and, still lying on the ground, looked up at Varlamov. Mustering all the anger he could manage, he said, "This is contemptible… I have diplomatic protection."

"Here, you have nothing," Varlamov said, bending over him. "Not even your insulin."

It was the ping that saved Clive. One little high-pitched ping from Varlamov's smartphone. Still flushed from the blow he had landed, Varlamov pulled his mobile from his pocket and glanced down at the screen. He scowled, tapped, scrolled and then looked up at Mishin and spat out an order.

"Let him go."

Maxim Mishin's mouth fell open.

"I'm sorry, General, but…"

"Do what I say!"

"I need my insulin," said Clive, "and my passport."

"Give him the fucking insulin and the fucking passport and let the bastard go," Varlamov shouted, his fist clenched.

At the residence, the security guards kept Clive waiting. He didn't look like the Clive Franklin they had seen earlier. He looked like a drunk who'd been in a fist fight. It was only when the ambassador himself appeared and assured the guards that this was indeed Clive Franklin that they let him in.

"Shit, you look terrible," said Rose, who greeted Clive in the wood-panelled entrance hall.

They called Doctor McPherson, who came immediately, examined Clive and said nothing was broken. Then they called Marina – at least, Rose did, on her mobile, from the ambassador's study with Luke Marden right beside her, reminding her that every word was being listened to by the FSB and so she needed to moderate her language.

"Hi, Marina. It's Rose… British Council… beacon of light and hope. Just to let you know that Clive is back where he belongs, here in the residence. The doc's here, too, thank bloody God. Our friend got himself mugged or kidnapped or both. His diplomatic passport cut no bloody ice. Fancy that! Such disdain for Her Britannic Majesty and this disunited kingdom of ours. We've got no clout any more. Diplomatic or otherwise… What? Can you say that again?"

Rose listened, nodded, then covered her smartphone with her hand and looked at Doctor McPherson, who was examining Clive's bruise.

"Can our friend Clive still run the marathon on Sunday?"

"Run a marathon? Well, that's not what *this* doctor would recommend."

"I have to run," said Clive, who reached for a bag of ice.

"Well," said McPherson doubtfully. "There are no broken bones, and it is only a bruise. Mind you, by Sunday you won't be looking pretty. This side of your face will be black and blue. Tomorrow, you *have* to rest. If I were you, I'd decide on Sunday morning. See how you feel. No sane person would run a marathon in your condition, but…"

"Marina?" Rose said, speaking into her phone. "Thanks for waiting. Yes, he's good to go. But tomorrow he stays put. We'll try and keep him out of harm's way. Not so easy in Mother Russia. Oh, and the embassy has given him a new mobile. He'll text you the number."

Rose said goodbye in her brightest voice and ended the call. Later that evening, sitting in the ambassador's study, she handed Clive a cup of lemon-and-ginger tea.

"Just curious," she said, as she helped herself to a glass of wine. "Was it the Wolf?"

Clive nodded, but at the same time he glanced up at the ceiling, indicating that the room was almost certainly bugged. Rose pretended not to notice.

"Thought so," said Rose. "So, what I want to know is why did the sodding sadist stop?"

"That's good alliteration," Clive said, wincing as he spoke.

The ambassador drove Clive to the embassy, and in the safe room he went through every detail of his inquisition, alone with Luke Marden.

"We'll make a huge stink, that goes without saying," Luke Marden assured him, "but Varlamov will deny he ever set eyes on you. He'll make up a story… You lost your insulin while running and started to hallucinate… Some random thugs mugged you… Something along those lines."

"Of course."

"Why did he let you go?"

"He got a message on his phone."

"Really? Your friend Marina must have pulled some pretty big strings. And thank God she did. You'd better get some sleep. You're on the first flight out tomorrow morning."

"Says who?"

"Martin Hyde."

Luke Marden pushed a sheet of paper across the table.

"Martin knows all about your little adventure."

Clive read Hyde's email. It was unequivocal. The PM needed his services back in London. He was to leave immediately. Clive shook his head and looked the ambassador in the eye.

"I'm afraid you don't understand," he said. "I gave Marina my word that we'd run the marathon together. I gave her *my word*. We're running the marathon together. *Then* I go home, and *then* she gets out. Sir Martin approved this plan, and I'm sticking to it."

"Clive, I don't think *you* understand. Sir Martin's changed his mind. This isn't a request. It's an *order*. If you read between the lines, Martin makes it quite clear that if you disobey, you'll —"

"Get sacked? I don't think so… He's bluffing."

"I'm not getting through to you… Oh dear. Clive, my friend, you're in no shape to run anything… You *have* to leave. You're going home. First thing tomorrow morning. Yes? No? I *still* haven't got through to you?…"

The ambassador repeated his message in Russian, but once again Clive shook his head.

"Please apologize to Sir Martin, but I'm staying put. Unless you're planning to kidnap me and bundle me out unconscious?" Clive tried to smile but his face hurt. "Oh, and please tell Martindale that the safe room really is safe. I have it from General Varlamov himself."

There was a knock at Hyde's door. George Lynton looked in, itching to get ahead of the Friday rush-hour traffic, call it a day, have a weekend off, which, of course, was out of the question. He was also perplexed. There had been no news all day, no encrypted emails from Moscow, and yet his boss seemed less anxious, almost content, as if he knew something.

"Any news?"

"Nothing, Sir Martin. Nothing at all."

"Ah, well…"

Lynton had read about bachelors in their fifties looking for love, but never for one moment did he imagine that this middle-aged romantic surge could apply to his boss, Sir Martin Hyde. And yet, only that morning, he could not help noticing, as he placed a handwritten note from the PM in front of Sir Martin, that his iPad was opened on Tinder. Yes! Tinder! This came as a big surprise to Lynton, who had made it his business to know quite a lot about his boss. The man was a widower. His wife had died of bone cancer. No children. He lived alone. As of today, Hyde was fifty-three years, seven months and ten days old. Everything was perfectly clear to Lynton: Sir Martin Hyde was having a mid-life crisis, thirsting after younger blood. Tread carefully, Lynton told himself as he closed the door.

Hyde got to his feet, his back stiff from hours of sitting. Franklin had got off lightly. No broken bones. Just a punch in the face and a big bruise. It had been a necessary gesture to order Franklin home, even though Hyde knew perfectly well that the man would refuse, which suited Hyde just fine. It was much easier to have Franklin there, in the thick of it, close to the key player in all of this: Marina Volina. Hyde regretted his moment of doubt. Marina was turning out to be worth her weight in gold. But would she be a match for Varlamov? In the end, it would all come down to that. Hyde was not a betting man, but, if he had been forced to take sides, place a bet, in this particular scenario he would back the woman against the man. In his opinion, she had the edge. Why? Because she was *imaginative*. She could pull rabbits out of a hat. Of course, *he* had everything else: the resources, the manpower, the brute force, the interrogation cells. The odds were massively in his favour. And yet, Hyde's money was on the woman.

He let Lynton go around nine o'clock.

"Mind you stay right here in London," Hyde told him. "No dashing home to… Where do you live, Lynton?"

"Anglesey," said Lynton, adding "in Wales" for good measure.

"Ah, yes," said Hyde. "Well, you can't really dash off to Wales, can you? Not exactly next door, is it? Which is good because I want you right here. We've got work to do this weekend."

"Anglesey's beautiful," Lynton said in a burst of nostalgia. "It has a great cultural heritage."

Hyde cut him off. He didn't want to know about Anglesey, or about its great cultural heritage. He wanted to know where the Russians planned to cut the fibre-optic cables underneath the Atlantic. He wanted to know the spot to within five nautical miles.

26

General Varlamov was sitting behind his desk in his FSB office on the top floor of the Lubyanka. In the half-darkness, there was only a desk lamp for light. The sickness in the pit of his stomach had subsided, and he was thinking more clearly now, with the rigour for which he was renowned and which had made him who he was: very powerful and very rich.

The key word was "Englishman". This single word would lead him to his enemy. A single word that narrowed the field to the handful of people who knew anything at all about him. For the tenth time, he read the text that had stopped him in his tracks: "Let the Englishman go unharmed within the next twenty minutes, or this video circulates to everyone in your contacts."

Contacts. This second key word meant only one thing: that Pasha Orlov had not only hacked into his personal email, but that he had also *downloaded* his contacts and almost certainly his emails and stored them somewhere. But where? In the cloud? Or on a simple old-fashioned USB stick? It didn't matter. Before he died, Pasha had shared his secret with someone else.

The general understood that his personal data was now a weapon in the hands of an enemy – someone who wanted to bring him down.

The situation was delicate, to say the least. The vast resources of the FSB were at his disposal, but, in this particular instance, he couldn't draw on those resources without publicizing the compromising material. The video was one thing, and in itself not career-threatening. He wouldn't be the first official caught with a prostitute. But an FSB general who had allowed his own private email to be hacked… Now, *that* was a sackable offence. It might even land him in jail. General Grigory Varlamov had no intention of going to jail. He would find a way out of this mess, one way or another.

The video was only mildly pornographic: Varlamov lying naked on top of Dasha, his head half turned, so he could be easily identified, kissing, fondling. It lasted less than thirty seconds. It's not often you see a picture of yourself naked, Varlamov thought, and he couldn't help noticing that he looked very trim: no flab around the waist. In fact, he had a very nice body: long back, tight buttocks, nothing to complain about. You couldn't see much of Dasha, just a long leg and part of a young, round breast. At one point, you caught sight of her angel face: she looked bored.

Bored or not, she was very good in the sack, he thought, leaning back in his chair, conscious that he was breathing too fast. He was a quick and thorough thinker, a man who had always relied on his wits. His enemy was out there, but without a face. Really? The general shut his eyes and saw a woman's face that looked a lot like Marina Volina. He picked up the handset on his desk and summoned Lieutenant Mishin. Moments later, Mishin entered the room and stood to attention in front of the general, who was sitting behind his desk.

Varlamov fired a series of personal questions at Lieutenant Mishin. Who was he? Where had he come from? Mishin was born in Chita, the son of a single mother, a teacher. His childhood had been poor. He'd won a scholarship to Moscow State University, where he took a distinction in mathematics and, because of this, came to the attention of the FSB. That was five years ago. He was trained in cyber warfare as well as much else. As a lieutenant, he earned a thousand dollars a month.

"If you play your cards right," said Varlamov, staring into the nervous eyes of the young lieutenant, "all that's going to change. You'll get a big promotion: five times the money, not including bonuses. But on the condition that you keep your mouth shut. Everything that passes between us is confidential. You tell no one. Ever. Is that clear?"

"Yes… s-s-sir," stammered Mishin. "It would be an honour to —"

"Never mind about that," said Varlamov, cutting him off. "Meet me downstairs in three minutes. It's a black BMW, registration six-one-six."

It was an eleven-minute car ride to the gigantic Stalin-era apartment building on the Kotelnicheskaya Embankment.

Varlamov and Mishin took the lift to the fifth floor. Varlamov had a key and opened the door marked 5A.

"You're under arrest," the general barked at Dasha, barging past her into the apartment.

"Misha, this is a joke, right?" Dasha asked, looking at Varlamov in astonishment. And then she noticed a confused young man who stood in the doorway.

"Get to work!" the general shouted at Mishin. "Find the fucking cameras."

"The *what?*" said Dasha.

"Cameras, you bitch." Varlamov slapped Dasha hard on the side of her face. "Who installed the fucking cameras?" he yelled. "Who? What game are you playing?"

"You said I had to have cameras… It was *you!*" Dasha said, suddenly screaming and sobbing at the same time. "You told me to expect an expert who was updating the security… I have the email!"

They were interrupted by Mishin, who informed the general that he had found four cameras: two over the bed, one in the bathroom and one that had been placed in the sitting room above the main sofa.

"Shall I disable them?" he asked.

"What do you think?" Varlamov raged. Mishin was about to cut the wires when the general said, "Stop. Can we find out who's viewing the film? Is there a way?"

"Maybe. But I need time…"

"Hurry up," said the general, pacing the room and watching his acolyte at work. A long five minutes passed. Mishin coughed.

"Well?" said the general.

"No luck, I'm afraid. Whoever did this came to the flat with his own laptop and network cable and cameras that are battery powered. He must have connected the cameras to the wireless network. The password is written on the router. Easy. Most likely, he fed the live feed to an iPhone that has no SIM card but is working on Wi-Fi in some public place."

"Where? What public place?" said Varlamov. "We have to find this person. Can't you do that?"

"I don't think so. Whoever did this was thorough. A professional, you might say. Once he's downloaded the pictures, video, whatever, he'll dispose of the iPhone and the laptop. He'll leave no trace."

"No trace…" muttered the general. Suddenly, he was shouting again. "Disable the cameras. Now!"

It was only then that General Grigory Varlamov looked at the tear-stained face of his mistress, at the two lines of black mascara trailing down her cheeks.

"Show me the email," he said.

Dasha produced a laptop and, still sniffling and choking back sobs, she found the email and showed it to Varlamov.

Of course she had thought the email was from him. It was all there: his email address, his terms of endearment, such as "my hot little bunny rabbit", and it was even signed off, "your lustful Misha", followed by a row of kisses. The general read and reread the email, trying to piece together what must have happened. The little shit Pasha had hacked his private email. But Pasha was dead. Before he died, he must have copied the private emails and passed them on to someone. But who? Had Pasha given them to his brother, Ivan? Or to a friend? Or to an enemy of Varlamov's who was ready to pay, and who wanted to bring the general down? Varlamov felt the sweat on his forehead.

"So, it was you who let this so-called 'expert' into this building?" Varlamov said with just a hint of softness in his voice.

"But that's what you told me to do in the email! Go down and tell the porter to let him in – the man from the security company One Step Ahead."

"One Step Ahead... What sort of security company is that?"

"I don't know... I didn't ask... But he left a card..."

Dasha reached over to a side table and gave Varlamov a black card embossed in white. Varlamov read the words "Brother of Pavel". There was a mobile number. Varlamov pulled out his phone and dialled. Dasha looked startled at the tinkle of a telephone somewhere very close... Where? Varlamov moved towards the ringtone. Somewhere on the sofa? He hurled cushions to the ground, and there it was, one of those old Nokia models, tucked in the back of the sofa. Varlamov was still pressing his phone to his ear when his call clicked into voicemail.

"Varlamov," said a metallic, sneering voice. "You're going to Hell. Get ready for the ride."

"I didn't know there was a mobile..." Dasha began.

"Shut up!" shouted Varlamov. He picked up the Nokia and tossed it at Mishin.

"Trace this."

"It's a burner..." said Mishin.

"I said trace it!" Varlamov shouted. But the energy was draining from his voice, and, almost in a whisper, he added, "Didn't you hear me?"

It's a total waste of time, thought Mishin, but he kept his mouth shut.

General Varlamov told Mishin to watch Dasha while he went downstairs to speak to the guard. He was gone for ten minutes. Maxim Mishin had no idea what "to watch Dasha" meant. He sat in a chair, looking at the most beautiful woman he had ever seen. She could not stop crying. He had no handkerchief to offer her, so he went into the bathroom and brought her some loo paper.

"Thank you," Dasha said through her tears, but Mishin noticed that her hand did not stop trembling. When the general came back, she started gulping air and sobbing.

"Shut up!" Varlamov shouted at her. "I can't think properly with all that noise. Now, what did he look like, the man who installed the cameras. What *exactly* did this man look like?"

Dasha couldn't remember, except that he had a beard. Meanwhile, Mishin collected the four cameras and stuffed them in a bag. Suddenly, the general got to his feet.

"Dasha, you're no longer under arrest, so do stop snivelling. Get a grip! Lieutenant, let's get to work and find out who's behind this little prank."

Varlamov strode out of the flat, while Mishin hung back for a few seconds to give Dasha a consoling look, and even a smile.

Marina went from the zoo to the Metropol, stopping on the way at a cash machine, where she used her new card with no limit and her two other cards. She left her car in front of the hotel, slipped her friend the doorman fifty dollars and asked him to fetch Narek, who had just finished polishing a pair of Ferragamo two-tone shoes worn by an overweight Azeri who didn't believe in tipping.

It was Friday, late afternoon, and Narek was killing time. He was waiting for Liza to finish her shift, so they could go for a drink in one of the new cafés in Neglinnaya Street. A Friday night drink with Liza was the highlight of his week.

Outside, Narek found the woman he knew as Marfa standing in a corner of the hotel car park, away from the bustle of the entrance, away from the stream of taxis that dropped off passengers, away from the CCTV cameras.

"Narek, I don't want to alarm you, but you have to leave now. Not just your job, but Moscow. Get a flight out this evening, if you can. Do you have your passport on you?"

"Of course I do!" Narek snorted. "I get stopped all the time by the bloody police, and it's an offence to be without your documents. But... but what's this all about? I can't just leave... What about Liza?"

"You're in great danger, and I've put you there," said Marina. "It's just a matter of time before the FSB come looking for you, either here or at home, which is why I want you... No, no... I *beg* you to leave the hotel and go straight to the airport. Here's four thousand dollars," Marina said, pushing a plump envelope into Narek's hand. "Give me your email and your bank details and I'll send you more money. Another sixteen thousand first thing tomorrow morning. I give you my word."

"For twenty grand, I'll do almost anything," Narek said, feeling the plumpness of the envelope. "I'm in *danger*... You're *serious?*" he asked Marina, looking into her eyes.

"I'm deadly serious," Marina said. "They could kill you. Or lock you up and throw away the key."

Narek retrieved his bank details from his phone and then scribbled them onto his business card, which he handed to Marina.

"And you *must* leave your mobile behind," Marina added urgently. "It can be tracked."

Narek walked back into the hotel, holding the envelope. His hand was shaking. The woman, Marfa, had put the fear of God in him. Suddenly, he felt – was it a delusion? – that he could *smell* danger. At the reception desk, Narek found Liza, who was just ending her shift, and whispered something in her ear.

At first, Liza thought it was some sort of joke. Inconspicuous in her hotel uniform, she stepped out from behind the reception desk, and walked into the centre of the lobby, from where she had a perfect view of the main hotel staircase leading down to the revolving door. Just to the right, she could see Narek's high chair. It was no longer empty. A man was sitting there, looking at his watch and wearing a suit. Even at this distance, Liza could tell that the man was not a foreigner: he was a Russian.

Lieutenant Mishin was not in the Metropol by accident. General Varlamov had sent him there to sift through the CCTV footage from the day the Englishman arrived at the hotel to the day he left. He arrived just in time to see a woman who looked like Marina Volina, although he couldn't be sure, since she had her back to him, having an intense conversation with a short man with dark hair. The woman passed something to the man. A scarf? An envelope? Then she drove off in a Prius. He didn't get the number plate.

Mishin asked the doorman who she was. The doorman said he didn't know her name, but she was a very nice lady who seemed to know a lot of important people and came to the hotel quite often and always gave a generous tip. And the man? That was Narek, the Armenian shoeshiner.

Lieutenant Mishin could feel the hairs on the back of his neck rising. He sensed he was onto something big, something that might catapult him to fame and glory. He stepped into the hotel, found Narek's high chair, made himself comfortable and waited. The shoe box was open, with brushes and polish neatly arranged. Beneath the box he caught sight of something glossy. It was an old Bolshoi programme for the opera *Khovanshchina.*

Mishin waited. And waited. Eventually, he asked to see the hotel manager, presented his FSB ID and said he needed to see Narek right away. Unfortunately, this would not be possible, said the manager. Narek had left for the evening.

With a new sense of power invested in him by General Varlamov, Mishin called the duty office in the Lubyanka and instructed two FSB colleagues to go to Narek's bedsit in Yugo-Zapadnaya and bring him in.

But Narek wasn't there. He was on his way to Sheremetyevo airport, with Liza. They took the metro and the train. At Sheremetyevo, Narek bought a ticket to Yerevan on a flight leaving at nine o'clock that evening. Liza saw him off, waiting as long as she could by immigration control, waving until her friend disappeared from view. Meanwhile, Narek's mobile, like thousands of others, had been left on a seat in the Moscow metro for the cleaners to find in the small hours of the following morning.

Lieutenant Mishin was well into his third hour in that cramped security office at the Metropol, staring at CCTV footage, when he got a text from General Varlamov instructing him to head straight for the Kremlin.

Even at this late hour, the traffic on a Friday night was bumper to bumper on the arterial roads leading out of Moscow. It was the tail end of summer, and everyone was heading for an end-of-season weekend at their dachas.

The duty officer at the Senate Palace was expecting FSB Lieutenant Maxim Mishin and led him through the half-darkness to the first floor.

"Marina Andreyevna's office is the second on the left," he said, pulling out a key. Then he noticed a shaft of light beneath the door. The duty officer knocked.

"Come in," said Marina, who was sitting behind her desk. "What can I do for you, gentlemen?"

"Well… you see… Lieutenant Mishin here…" the security officer blurted out, clearly flustered. "He's been sent here by General Varlamov…"

"Really? And the general forgot to tell me… Well, never mind. How can I help you, Lieutenant?"

Mishin felt himself blushing. Turning first to the duty officer and then to Marina, he garbled an apology and said he had misinterpreted the general's orders. It was all a mistake, a misunderstanding. His fault. Everything was his fault.

"Well, that is a relief," said Marina, getting to her feet, smiling fiercely at the hapless Mishin. "So good of you to set the record straight. Otherwise, who knows what I might have thought? That you were here to steal my personal data. Make off with one of my family snaps?"

Mishin looked round Marina's office. There wasn't a photograph in sight.

"I'm sure the general will tell me what this is all about in due course. Meanwhile, it's late. I'm leaving. And so are you."

Marina locked her office herself and then, standing in the silent corridor, which seemed to stretch forever in both directions, she turned to the duty officer.

"If you ever let anyone into my office when I'm not here, I'll report you to the president. Is that clear?"

It was eleven o'clock when Mishin reported back to the general in his office at the Lubyanka. Varlamov raged.

"What in God's name was she doing in her office at ten on a Friday night? It's as if she knew you were coming. Of course, she's hidden all her photographs… She's protecting the brother…"

As Mishin stood to attention, he had the feeling he was being sucked down into a black hole, one nervous step at a time. But one thing he understood: there was no turning back.

"Right, Lieutenant, let's move on," Varlamov said briskly, with steely determination. "What do we know about this younger brother, Ivan? Let's see. A few years ago, Volina got him an internship at our internet-monitoring centre in Saint Petersburg. Ivan Orlov. A prodigy. Just like his brother, Pavel. Ivan was very young. Sixteen, I think…" The general remembered meeting the teenager. What was it about the boy that had stood out, apart from his brilliance? He couldn't put his finger on it, but it was something specific. "There has to be a file on Ivan Orlov. One with a photograph. Get it. Now," said Varlamov, just as a clock struck midnight.

Lieutenant Mishin kept himself awake all night with endless cups of coffee. The information came through at seven the next morning.

This time, the general warned Dasha that he was coming, and he came alone. It was eight o'clock on Saturday morning, and Dasha opened the door without looking up. She was in jeans and a T-shirt, with no make-up, and her eyes were swollen from crying.

"Why so glum?" said Varlamov, patting her head. "Cheer up… Now, sit down and look at this…"

Varlamov showed Dasha a photograph of Vanya, taken three years ago. "Is this the man?" he asked.

"I don't know," said Dasha, shaking her head. "The man who came here had a beard, but this one in the photo… he's clean shaven… I can't be sure. He had a funny way of speaking… I do remember that."

"His Rs…" Varlamov said eagerly. "He couldn't say his Rs?"

Dasha hesitated, looking down at her hands, avoiding eye contact with the general.

"Yes. That's it. He couldn't say his Rs, which is pretty unusual. Mum always told me that Lenin couldn't say his Rs…"

"Good girl," the general said, leaning forward to embrace her, but she recoiled.

"Leave me alone," said Dasha in a voice that he had never heard before. "I'm moving out. My mum always said: when a man hits you, get out."

"It was a slap, not a hit… Don't exaggerate… Dasha, my little lovebird… Come on, my little pigeon."

But Dasha pushed Varlamov away.

The general left Dasha sulking on the sofa. Sitting in the back seat of his Mercedes as he headed back to the Lubyanka, Varlamov directed his fury not at Dasha, but at Marina. This was all her doing. They were a team, Marina and Vanya. And he would crush them both.

27

It was Saturday morning, 10 a.m. BST, and, more importantly, noon in Moscow. The prime minister had cancelled her weekend at Chequers and sat brooding in her flat at the top of 10 Downing Street. Meanwhile, Hyde was at his desk, staring out of his window, cursing the odd parakeet that flashed past. The telephone on his desk rang.

"Martin? Martha here. Any news?"

"Not yet, Prime Minister."

"Our Moscow agent... You say she's spending the day with Serov? So, we should hear —"

"Any minute now," Hyde said firmly. The prime minister let out an audible sigh and hung up, leaving Hyde to count the hours. Five, six at most, and then they would have no choice but to implement Plan B, which was, they all agreed, far from satisfactory, for the simple reason that it was based on incomplete intelligence. What had the chief of the defence staff called it? A shot in the dark. Don't let the waiting get to you, Hyde told himself. Volina will deliver. The rest of her life depends on it. Needs must and all that. And she's clever and determined. But she needs luck... It always comes down to luck, Hyde thought, as he switched on his television to watch the one-day international in Bristol, between England and the West Indies. Another England batting collapse, he wondered, but no! Number seven had made a blistering century. Well, I never...

Marina could hardly believe her eyes. Sitting at her kitchen table, she'd been checking out the Kremlin news-agency website on her laptop, when she came across a photograph of General Varlamov at a graduation ceremony for FSB cadets; he was watching as the young men and women took the military oath. The place was Saint Petersburg, and the date was yesterday. There was a second photograph of a dinner that evening, one in which the general was sharing a toast with the new graduates. Marina smiled at the sheer audacity of it all. She had no doubt that there had been a graduation ceremony for FSB cadets in Saint Petersburg yesterday, nor that it had been followed by a celebration dinner. But General Varlamov had been at neither. What was he toasting, she wondered? A Photoshopped future for himself, and for all Russia?

It was nine o'clock on Saturday morning. The day before the marathon. This was her D-Day, her make-or-break day. Ever since the release of the sex video and her text to Varlamov, Marina understood that her cover was blown, or would be very soon. The gloves were off, and Varlamov would be gunning for her; and not just her, but also for Clive, and almost certainly for Vanya. Marina felt oddly exhilarated, as if this were the moment she'd been waiting for. And the day had started well – very well. The seven-o'clock text from Lev had come out of the blue and brought good news: the boss wanted her at the Kremlin by ten. They were flying to Kolomna, a town just over one hundred kilometres east of Moscow, where the president was opening an Olympic ice rink. There would be masses of foreigners, and she could practise all her languages, said Lev, adding various emojis. Perfect, thought Marina. Once again, I'll be at the heart of things.

Before she left her flat, Marina crossed the parquet floor and looked out of her window at the street below. The black Audi, which she had noticed last night, was still there, parked right in front of her door. Doing what? She could always leave by the back entrance, either on foot or in her Prius, so this surveillance seemed pointless. But it wasn't. It was intimidating, designed to frighten her and make her slip up. Then she remembered the flustered face of the young FSB agent who had come to her office the previous night and been caught red-handed, and she laughed out loud. But her one overriding thought, she kept to herself: *Fuck you, Varlamov.*

"Apparently, the Englishman was mugged," said Serov from behind the desk in his office, while Varlamov sat opposite him in an armchair. "How is he?"

"Mugged? Really? I had no idea," Varlamov said with a wave of his elegant hand. "I was in Petersburg, giving out medals. Stayed for dinner. Didn't get back to Moscow until five this morning. Took the night train. Excellent. I recommend it."

"Foreign Minister Kirsanov got a furious call from the British ambassador, who said Franklin wasn't mugged at all. Claimed he was kidnapped and it was you who interrogated him, you who hit him."

"Ridiculous. I was in Petersburg, I tell you. There's a picture of me on RIA Novosti."

The president dropped his voice.

"What was the point of this little exercise?"

"Sorry, but this is fake news."

"Really? I don't need any more rogue FSB generals, Grisha. I need loyalty. Do you understand? One-hundred-per-cent loyalty. Don't lie to me!"

Suddenly Serov clapped his hand against his chest.

"I can feel my heart racing… My blood pressure! Lyova, take my blood pressure! The man's a top translator with a diplomatic passport. The foreign minister is livid. And so am I. The Englishman stayed on in Moscow at *my* invitation. Of course, what's done is done and we have to deny, deny, deny… but I needed this like a hole in the head. What on earth was the point? You suspect the Englishman of something? What? Being a spy? Did he confess? Did he say *anything* worth hearing?"

"No."

"Hah! So, you tried and failed. And now, who carries the can? I do! All thanks to you, Grisha. Bravo! Well done! Thanks to you, I look ridiculous. Like some sort of thug. No, it's worse than that. I look like a man who's not in control."

The president was breathing heavily. Then his voice went up a notch.

"Well, let me tell you something, General Varlamov. I *am* in control, and you better believe it! I'm always in control! Morning, noon and night, do you understand? Take my fucking blood pressure!" he shouted at Lev.

"I can't take your blood pressure if you don't sit still."

The president did as he was told, while Lev slipped the cuff onto his arm and pumped.

"One-three-eight over eighty. Perfectly normal."

"Really?" said Serov in a voice that was suddenly small, almost inaudible. "One-three-eight over eighty. Really?"

"Operation Hades is on track," said Varlamov suavely. He was unrepentant and weary of this barrage of criticism.

"Yes," Serov conceded, allowing himself to be sidetracked. "I've just talked to the admiral. So far, so good. The preparations are almost complete. The attack will start in a few hours." Then Serov's eyes narrowed. He wasn't done with Varlamov – not yet. "So, now that you've roughed up the Englishman, he won't run. End of story. And I won't get my photograph… The

Englishman on his knees, gasping for breath… Britain on its knees… Don't you see?"

"He'll run," said Lev. "Marina sent me a text."

"Really? But *how* will he run?" said Serov, looking at Varlamov. "What's his form?"

"Up till now, pretty good. He keeps up with Volina."

"Why do you call her 'Volina'? That's a very odd thing to do. She's Marina. Everyone calls her Marina. It's as if you don't like her…"

"A slip of the tongue, that's all… No offence intended. As for the Englishman, if he can run a marathon, then he can't be badly hurt now, can he? He'll probably romp over the finish line."

Serov came over to the big leather armchair where the general was sitting and bent over him.

"Make sure he doesn't. I want my photograph."

Marina didn't like helicopters, but she had no choice. She was sitting right behind the president in a Mil Mi-8 medium twin-turbine Russian helicopter. They flew over lakes, rivers, motorways, towns and open fields, but Marina noticed almost nothing; she was entirely focused on the matter in hand. In the next few hours, she had to find the missing piece of the jigsaw, discover the location of the underwater-drone attack to within five nautical miles. And then what? What was her exit strategy? I'll think of something, she told herself, feeling her heartbeat quicken. Tomorrow she and Clive would run the marathon, then go their separate ways. For how long? This question to herself hung in the air as the Kolomna kremlin came into view and the helicopter made its descent. They landed with the softest bump, and suddenly everything became clear to Marina. She had two distinct objectives: to obtain the last piece of intelligence for the British, and to destroy Grigory Varlamov. The first depended on fate, the second on herself. As Lev helped her out of the helicopter, there was a new jauntiness to her step.

The stadium with its Olympic ice rink was packed with sponsors and skaters from over twenty countries; there were speeches and loudspeaker announcements, and Marina, who stood by Serov's side for an hour, found herself switching from English to French to German to Italian, and even to Farsi. "Is there any ice-skating in Iran?" she asked an official from Isfahan.

At noon, five hundred Kolomna schoolchildren in folk costumes flooded onto the ice, singing and waving garlands of roses, while journalists took pictures. The president appeared in the VIP box above the ice rink and made a short speech on the great Russian tradition of ice-skating, on heroes and heroines past and present, on the glorious future awaiting the next generation of young skaters. Then, somewhere above the brand-new roof, fireworks exploded into the sky, and the ice stadium was declared open. Over the loudspeaker, guests were invited to a reception in the great hall next to the rink. As of now, Marina was off duty, so Lev informed her.

She joined the flow of people heading for the tables piled high with food and drink, when she found herself a few feet away from a young woman in black leather trousers and with a red streak in her messy blond hair.

"Rose Friedman?" Marina asked.

"A lucky guess, or did you see my name badge?" Rose said, holding out her hand.

"A lucky guess," said Marina, shaking hands, and holding Rose in a steady gaze, which she returned. Somewhere close an FSB tail was listening. Or recording. Or both. "Is Clive really well enough to run the marathon?" Marina asked. "What do you think?"

"What I think doesn't matter a toss! When Clive gets the bit between his teeth, there's not a lot anyone can do. Not even the doc. He told me he was running. Next to you, right? Side by side?"

"That's the idea. Side by side."

Someone was shouting and waving at Rose.

"Oh, Christ... Here we go again. The head of British ice-skating needs help. The man is seriously uncool. Still, duty calls..."

But the large frame of Boris Kunko blocked Rose's path.

"English rose! We meet again! You come tonight to High Tide, yes? We have party!"

"I'm always up for a party, Boris. I'll be there. But now, Boris, I gotta run. *Poka!*"

Marina looked at Boris, then slipped her arm through his. They walked together for a good five minutes, keeping as close as possible to the huge speakers that were booming out Tchaikovsky's *Swan Lake*.

"Boris Borisovich, I'm sorry to tell you, but you're in trouble."

"Big trouble?"

"Everything in Russia is big."

"Better-to-leave-and-not-come-back sort of trouble?"

"That might be very sensible," said Marina, speaking as loudly as she dared above the Tchaikovsky. "Unless you can explain how a billion dollars disappeared from the World Cup Development Fund while you were on the board..."

Boris Kunko turned sharply and stared at Marina, his eyes full of fear.

"Boris Borisovich, I'm on your side," Marina murmured, close to the loudspeaker, inches from Kunko's ear. "Anything you tell me will be in the strictest confidence... But I need information if I'm to help you."

"It was Varlamov's idea," Boris whispered. "He said I should call it my commission, and he would make the arrangements with Romanovsky. We would split the money three ways. But Varlamov cheated me. I provided all the offshore companies, everything, and he shafted me. I got a fraction of the money I was supposed to."

Do I believe him? Marina asked herself. They're all such liars. On the other hand, this makes perfect sense. Pasha himself told me a billion dollars had gone to several unknown accounts in the British Virgin Islands. And in one of Varlamov's private emails, I found a nugget of pure gold: an email from a Panamanian lawyer to Varlamov with an invoice attached and – here's the nugget – lower down the chain, the general's original email asking the lawyer to open a numbered account and to expect significant funds. God bless email chains. What's more, the date fitted perfectly: the general had sent his email a week before a meeting of the World Cup Development Committee.

"Well," said Marina. "Varlamov isn't done yet. He's after you."

Boris pulled back in surprise.

"He is?"

"You know too much. Don't look now but you're being followed. The goon with the glasses just behind me."

Boris turned his head. A nervous young man was staring right at him.

My tail, not yours, Marina thought. But you, Boris, don't need to know that.

"I can help you," Marina said quietly. "In return for a small favour. Perhaps we can discuss this later?"

"Come to High Tide this evening. It's on the Savvinskaya Embankment. Everyone knows it."

Marina was about to say something, when a husky voice whispered in her ear.

"My, oh my, just look at you! Such elegant clothes… This new look of yours leaves me weak at the knees."

Marina turned to face the deputy prime minister, Viktor Romanovsky. When she turned back, Boris had vanished.

"Viktor Dmitrievich," Marina said in a sudden burst of confidence, sensing she was on a roll. "I need to talk to you. I'm worried about Nikolai Nikolayevich, about his health. Do you know Professor Olga Tabakova? She peddles immortality. I'm sorry to say, but I fear she has too much influence over our dear president. General Varlamov won't hear a word against her. But then he has a twenty-five-per-cent stake in her company. I don't think Nikolai Nikolayevich knows this. In fact, I'm fairly sure he hasn't a clue, since the general has taken a lot of trouble to hide this sensitive information. It came to my attention only recently."

It was Vanya who had made the discovery during the long night they had spent together in his flat trawling through Varlamov's private emails. By chance, Vanya had opened an attachment which turned out to be a legal document from a lawyer in the British Virgin Islands confirming the purchase of a twenty-five-per-cent stake in a company called the Institute for Longevity, trading name IfL plc. And the beneficiary? A British Virgin Islands trading company called Volga Enterprises plc. Although nothing was written down in black and white, it was clear that this was Varlamov's offshore vehicle – one of several, no doubt.

"My only concern, you understand," Marina continued, "is how to protect the president. May I speak openly, Viktor Dmitrievich? As far as you're concerned, the general is most definitely *not* your friend, even though I'm aware you may have done business together in the past. In fact, he's accumulated quite a lot of damaging information against you, which, believe me, he intends to use… He's also got it in for your friend Boris Kunko."

Romanovsky maintained total composure as he ambled through the crowd, smiling, nodding at the odd passer-by, but making it clear he did not want to be disturbed.

"Marina Andreyevna," said Romanovsky, choosing his words with care. "You're not telling me anything I don't know. Varlamov has been trying to subvert my nearest and dearest with huge bribes – mouth-wateringly huge. My private secretary is convinced he's even hacked into my emails. Well, I'm a fairly relaxed sort of man, as you know... I'm used to the rough and tumble of political life, but the general is pushing his luck. You're right: we have done a little business together in the past. And you are doubly right when you say that today he is most definitely *not* my friend. I know this. I've known it for a long time and understand it perfectly. But what I don't understand is why *you* are telling me all this..."

The deputy prime minister gave Marina his sweetest smile, but his eyes were as hard as flint.

"Because I want to see the back of the professor..."

"...and the general, too, perhaps?"

"I've got some interesting information about the general that might, just might, make our dear president see him in a different light..."

"Why don't you tell the president yourself?"

"I'd rather it didn't come from me. I try to stay out of politics. The information I'm talking about could be greatly to your advantage. In fact, to put it bluntly, it could save your skin."

"I like you more and more, Marina Andreyevna. You're a woman after my own heart..." He took her arm and led her towards the champagne bar, but they were interrupted by the ravishing nineteen-year-old, Katya, dressed all in white.

"Katya! What are *you* doing here?" Marina asked. Katya shot Romanovsky a flirtatious glance and told Marina that she now had a job in the public relations department of the Russian Parliament, all thanks to Viktor.

Of course, thought Marina. And it was I who introduced them at Villa Nadezhda.

"So you took my advice after all," Marina said, genuinely pleased. "You got yourself a job." A job *and* a sponsor, Marina thought. This girl is going places. "Forgive me, Katya, but I need five minutes alone with Viktor."

"Of course," said Katya, giving Viktor an amorous smile before she sashayed off. Viktor Romanovsky listened intently to what Marina had to say, and, when he learnt about a sex video involving the general and a nubile young woman, the deputy prime minister confessed to being *most* surprised. He always thought of Varlamov as a prude. Of course, it was a grave security risk: no question about *that*.

When the five minutes were up, Katya reappeared, took Viktor, her most valuable possession, by the arm and led him towards the skating rink. Viktor turned back and gave Marina the thumbs up.

Marina walked over to Lev, who was standing by the bar, stuffing an open smoked-salmon sandwich into his mouth. She was about to say something, but Lev beat her to it, squeezing out the words past chunks of salmon.

"You seem very chummy with Romanovsky."

"I always try to be civil."

"He's got the hots for you."

"Not since he's met Katya."

Lev had just swallowed the last mouthful of his sandwich, when his phone buzzed.

"We're off," he said, wiping his mouth with a paper napkin. "The boss needs to get back. There's a lot going on."

They walked through a dense crowd of skaters and sponsors and coaches and Kolomna dignitaries who were there for a good day out.

"About tomorrow," Lev said, coming to an abrupt stop by an Evian water stand and helping himself to a glass.

"What about tomorrow?"

"Your friend, the man you run with, the Englishman… Tell him to watch his back."

"What do you mean?"

"The boss really wants that photo…"

"Photo?"

"Of the Englishman on his knees. In the boss's mind, it's a metaphor for his victory over the British. Get it?"

"I get it," said Marina, feeling her mouth go dry. Lev took her by the arm and said they had to hurry. In the VIP lounge, the president was already waiting. Moments later, they were in the air.

Marina could feel beads of sweat on her forehead.

"I'll drop you off at the Kremlin," the president said through his headset, against the background din of the helicopter. "I'm going to the villa."

Lev shrugged as if to say: Where he goes, there go I.

"You don't need any help, Nikolai Nikolayevich?" Marina asked, speaking into her headset microphone.

"What sort of help? I'm surrounded by Russians. We all speak the same language! But thank you all the same, Marinochka!"

The helicopter touched town inside the Kremlin at 3.07 p.m. As Marina got out, Serov called out, "Big day tomorrow! Good luck! And make sure you cross that finish line ahead of the Englishman!"

With that, they were gone. Marina waved. She waved goodbye to her last hope of finding the location of the underwater-drone attack. She kept her eyes fixed on the helicopter as it soared into the air like some triumphant bird, leaving her standing on the ground, alone and defeated.

28

As Marina left the Kremlin through the Troitskaya Tower, she thought of Napoleon in his bicorn black hat, riding his horse over this very bridge, imagining, poor fool, that he'd conquered Russia. No one conquers Russia. It's too big. When she came to the National Hotel on the corner of Tverskaya, she felt dizzy and leant against the wall. All she could think about was the enormity of her failure. She felt out of breath, winded.

She knew she was a marked woman. She would have to make a run for it. But how? And what if they caught her? The case against her was devastating: passing a USB stick with classified and stolen information to the British. Colluding with the enemy. Passing state secrets. It got worse by the second. Spots were floating across her eyes, blurring her vision. She had to steady herself. Even if, by some miracle, she avoided prison, she would never be allowed out of Russia, and would never see Clive again.

Marina was only vaguely aware that she was walking past the overpriced, over-decorated Ritz-Carlton, when she heard someone calling her name.

"Marina Andreyevna!"

Captain First Rank Artyom Smirnov was standing under the ornate mock-classical portico of the hotel. He was holding an expensive leather briefcase, while the doorman, in his red cape and black top hat, stood in the street, trying to get him a taxi.

"You're *still* here?" Marina said in genuine surprise.

"Leaving now," said the captain, tapping the briefcase. "Bulgari took forever. Still, all's well that ends well. Lev Lvovich told me you're running the marathon tomorrow. Good luck!"

"Thank you. I'm so glad you can get away at last."

"There is one last thing... If you could clear this up. You helped me out in Crimea – do you remember? – with those impossible Cornish names. Well, I'm having another argument with my friend Denis... You met him... Denis says you don't pronounce the 'h'."

Still holding on tightly to the briefcase, the captain pulled out a small notepad from his pocket, which he handed to Marina, and asked her to look at the first page. Scrawled across the lined paper was the word "Porthcurno".

"I'm afraid your friend is wrong," said Marina, handing back the notepad and trying to keep her voice steady. "You do pronounce the 'h'. It's *Porth-curno*, with a 'th', as in 'thought'."

The doorman was holding open the door of a taxi, waiting for a tip from the captain.

"Porthcurno is famous for an open-air theatre," Marina said, almost gaily. "Now what *is* it called? Oh, yes, the Minack."

"Is that so?" said the captain, pressing a note into the doorman's hand. "An open-air theatre? Then a bit more drama won't come as a surprise. Do come and see us in Petersburg, won't you?"

Marina walked into the lobby of the Ritz-Carlton, sat down in one of the armchairs next to an enormous vase full of arum lilies, took out her mobile and called Clive. She got his voicemail, so she left a message, asking him to *please* call her back. Then she sent a text: she had just finished work, and they could do a short run somewhere close to the residence, if that suited him? A couple of kilometres? Just to keep the limbs loose. Half an hour at most. She sat in the armchair and waited. And waited. After ten minutes she sent Clive another text: "Please call."

The next twenty minutes dragged interminably by: Marina checked her phone over and over again, but there was no word back from Clive. Why this silence? she wondered. Why now? There was nothing for it but to call Rose.

"Rose?" Marina said, keeping her voice steady. "This is Marina. How is Clive? Just checking he's all right. I called him, but he isn't picking up."

"Don't tell me you're already back in Moscow!" Rose exclaimed. "My God… We left Kolomna three hours ago, and we're still stuck in bloody traffic. Clive? He's probably asleep… The Doc gave him some pills to help him get some rest before tomorrow."

"He's asleep," Marina said slowly, letting the words sink in. "That's good… I was going to suggest a short run, but of course he should take it easy, after what happened. Well, that's that… Except, well, I've got something amusing to tell him. Perhaps you can pass it on?"

"Amusing? We like amusing. Not much of that around these days."

"It's about Chekhov. I thought it might cheer him up."

"Chekhov never cheered anyone up."

"If he's quick off the mark when he gets back to England, he can see *Uncle Vanya*."

"You want to wake him up for *that*?"

"Of course not, but he's only got a few days to catch it in Russian. I read a whole article about it in *The Times* just a few days ago. A theatre company from Perm has been touring the UK and this is their last week, and they're performing in an amphitheatre called the Minack overlooking the sea… A great location."

"*Uncle Vanya*... Perm theatre company... What more can a man want? Clive knows where to meet you for the marathon tomorrow?"

"He does... Oh, and, Rose... out of interest, what are *your* plans?"

"My plans? Off to London tomorrow with Clive. We both need a holiday. Good luck tomorrow! I'll be there to cheer you on."

Before she left the Ritz-Carlton, Marina took out hefty sums of cash, using three different cards.

Clive woke with a start. For a moment he had no idea where he was. Everything about the room looked strange, even the sunlight. Then he remembered he was in Moscow, in the residence, a guest of the British ambassador. He was lying fully dressed on his bed and someone was knocking at his door.

"Come in."

"Hi, Rocky," said Rose, poking her head around the door and holding out a glass of cranberry juice. "Here's something super healthy to get you going. Then we can order room service. This place works just like a hotel, you know... There's always a cook around somewhere. Huge waste of taxpayers' money, if you ask me."

"What time is it?" Clive said, sitting up in alarm and swinging his legs off the bed. "Seven? It can't really be seven! How long have I been asleep for? Three hours!"

"You were knackered. It's not every day you get punched in the head. Marina thought you might like to stretch your legs, do a bit of running, but you didn't pick up, so she gave me a ring. I told her you must be asleep. She wanted me to tell you something about Chekhov. A play... Let's see if I can remember what she said... Oh, yes. *Uncle Vanya*. In Russian. Perm theatre company acting their hearts out in some provincial theatre.

Mank-something. No, Mink... Wait, no... It was Minack open-air theatre. That's it. I think I've seen a picture of it in the glossy book downstairs on British theatre... Amphitheatre on a cliff... Now, isn't that something to look forward to when you get home?"

Clive was checking his iPhone. Marina had called him two hours ago, twice, ten minutes apart. Then she had sent a text... Then she had rung Rose. Clearly out of desperation. What exactly did she say to Rose? Too much? Did she give herself away?

Clive splashed his face with water, put his hand through his hair and cursed himself in the mirror. You idiot! Asleep when Marina needed you most. You've lost two hours of precious time. Two whole hours. Who knows what this might mean? How many cables can you cut in two hours?

Rose was relaxing in an armchair when Clive hurried back into the bedroom, snatched a paperback from his bedside table and said, "Rose, show me the book downstairs. The one about British theatre."

It was right there, on the round table in the reception room. Clive turned the pages frantically, found the Minack and read that the amphitheatre was on a cliff above the town of Porthcurno on the Cornish coast. He sprinted up one flight of wooden stairs and knocked on the door of the ambassador's study.

"Ah, Clive, come in," Luke Marden said genially. "I was worried about you. How are you?"

"Feeling fine, thank you. I thought you might enjoy this," said Clive. "It's my own copy. A small thank you for having me to stay."

Clive handed Luke Marden a well-thumbed paperback of Chekhov short stories. The ambassador took the book and noticed a folded piece of paper sticking out like a bookmark. On it, he read: LOCATION IS PORTHCURNO.

"Excellent," said the ambassador. "I shall enjoy this. Thank you so much. And by the way, you look rested, which is just as well. You've got a big day tomorrow. And our flight to London is at six in the evening. Forgive me, but I've got to get back to the embassy. Need to tie up some loose ends."

Clive stood in the forecourt and watched the ambassador drive off, still cursing himself and, at the same time, trying to be positive. The intelligence would reach London in twenty minutes. Make that half an hour if the ambassador got stuck in traffic. In half an hour, Hyde would be smiling and the fightback would begin. Clive took several deep breaths and felt better. Tying up loose ends was a nice way of putting it, he reflected.

In the embassy Range Rover, with Fyodor at the wheel, Clive headed west out of Moscow.

The bright-green parakeets were infuriating, dashing about right in front of Hyde's window without a care in the world. Has no one told them we're on the edge of an abyss? Hyde thought, pushing aside his iPad and pressing his buzzer. Seconds later, George Lynton appeared. For once his bow tie was crooked.

"Still nothing?" said Hyde.

"A deafening silence, I'm afraid."

Hyde went back to his iPad.

Lynton caught a glimpse of the Tinder app. He's at it again, the young man thought with a mixture of surprise and dismay. At a moment of national crisis, all my boss can think about is sex.

Hyde left the room abruptly: to see the prime minister, he told Lynton.

He paced the dark-green carpet in the prime minister's office, while Martha Maitland held a conference call on the loudspeaker with the chief of the defence staff, the first sea lord and her minister of defence. It lasted three minutes and fifty-three seconds: enough time for everyone to give their consent to the immediate implementation of Plan A, a no-notice NATO exercise, known to Hyde and those in the know as an NNNE.

"Good," said Martha Maitland, putting down the receiver and folding her hands on her desk. "At last, we can go on the offensive."

"We all know that NATO is leaky," said Hyde, "but an NNNE is the perfect cover for an anti-submarine-warfare emergency response. We protect our intelligence and ruin President Serov's Sunday."

"I rather liked him," said Martha Maitland. "Underneath all that bluster, he seemed *accessible*... He'd lost his wife. I'd lost my husband... I felt there was a bond there somewhere and maybe I could get through to him. Make him see things differently. I know what you're thinking. Women always think they can change people... Maybe we do... Anyway... It was wishful thinking, in any case. Not a mistake I shall make again."

"You remember what to tell the press?" Hyde said to Lynton. "You tell them that a lone yachtsman has got himself into a spot of trouble, and, out of the kindness of its heart, the Royal Navy is activating a search-and-rescue mission. Make sure the press office understands that this is *all* we say. Nothing more and nothing less."

"Got it," said Lynton, heading for the door. But in truth, he was baffled. There had been no word from Moscow, and yet an NNNE had been launched. On the basis of what? He was also baffled as to how his boss had *time* for Tinder.

Sitting alone in his office, Hyde felt pleased with himself. Helping a yachtsman in trouble had been his idea. All it had needed was a little fine-tuning from the first sea lord, who suggested it should be a small craft with no automated information system. So far, Hyde thought with satisfaction, everything was going to plan. Under the guise of an innocuous search-and-rescue mission to help a yachtsman in distress, an anti-submarine-warfare emergency response had been initiated by NATO's supreme allied commander Europe, with a press blackout for twenty-four hours.

The duty officer, Charlie Pence, was looking forward to another episode of *Game of Thrones* on his iPad when the telephone rang in his airy office at the Royal Naval Air Station, Culdrose, near Helston on the Lizard Peninsula in Cornwall. Charlie liked Cornwall, with its blue skies and palm trees. Not that he could see any such exotic delights from his window; he overlooked a row of green-grey hangars, a long runway and a heavy square brown-brick control tower. It would be pretty daft to expect anything else, he reflected, sitting, as he was, in the middle of one of the biggest helicopter bases in Europe.

"Duty officer, Lieutenant Pence," said Charlie, his feet on his desk, one hand holding the handset and the other tapping out G-A-M-E on his iPad.

"Hello, Charlie. It's the operations director here."

"Billy?"

"The one and only."

"All ears," said Charlie, who had a sinking feeling that Billy, the UK operations controller at Northwood Headquarters, was about to spoil his day.

"We're activating the NATO emergency response plan."

"What the fuck's that?"

"That, you plonker, means get airborne in ASW mode for a couple of errant Russian subs."

"You've got to be joking! Our serviceability is a bag of shit!"

"It says on my board that you've got six Merlins available."

"I'll check."

"No, you won't. You'll get your station ops officer on the phone to me ASAP."

"OK. I'll find him."

Legless, most likely, thought Charlie, as he punched the number of the Halzephron Inn into the handset. The pub was famous for having no mobile reception, and, for this very reason, hugely popular with men escaping their wives.

"Halzephron Inn. How can I help?"

"Hello, mate. It's the Culdrose duty officer. Can I speak to Commander Gizzet?"

"Oh, you mean Mikey. I'll get him."

Several minutes passed before a new, cheery voice was on the line.

"Yep?"

"Sir, it's 'Copper' Pence. I'm duty officer. We've been scrambled for a NATO ASW exercise. Sorry, sir."

"Fuck off, Copper. It's my leaving run."

"Sorry, sir."

"Can't someone else do it? We're at peace. Haven't you heard?"

"Sorry, sir. We're on duty."

"Well, what a shitter… OK, get the recall going. I'll see what's left of this lot."

Charlie could hear bawdy laughter and snatches of a raucous singalong, which he knew by heart:

> *When I was young, I asked my CO, what should I do?*
> *Should I fly Phantoms, should I wank cats?*
> *He said it's much the same…*
> *Rota-ry, ta-ry, the Merlin's the bird for me.*
> *She flies so faithfully. Rota-ry, ta-ry…*

Charlie and the rest of the 814 Naval Air Squadron worked through the night at Royal Naval Air Station Culdrose, getting the aircraft fuelled and ready to go: six anti-submarine-warfare Merlin helicopters, three-engined and powerful enough to carry a mixed load of torpedoes and depth charges. Just before the official briefing, which was scheduled for seven a.m., an agitated squadron operations officer hurried over to Charlie, who was outside on the pan, talking to the maintenance crews as they readied the aircraft. He asked if he had seen the commanding officer. Charlie pointed to a hangar where the men were crawling all over Merlin helicopters, carrying out last-minute engineering checks.

"Over there, behind the cabs."

Charlie followed the excited officer into the hangar, where he overheard a brief exchange.

"Sir, I need a second of your time," said the squadron operations officer.

"What is it?" said the CO.

"Sir, Northwood has authorized live ordnance."

"Really? What sort? What about the rules of engagement?"

"Sir, mostly depth charges, some torpedoes. The ROE are just coming in now."

The CO's face was priceless, so Charlie told his mates later. The man looked as if he'd been hit with a shovel when he realized this was no ordinary no-notice NATO exercise; they were using live ammunition.

"Bloody hell," said the CO. "Get the word around. We're going fishing."

Clive was followed all the way to Peredelkino. Fyodor kept glancing in his rear-view mirror at the white Ford that was only metres behind the embassy car.

"Has to be FSB," said Fyodor, "driving up my arse like that."

"They always think foreigners are up to no good," said Clive.

"I told them about the married woman. I hope you don't mind... They asked me a lot of questions," Fyodor said, looking at Clive through his rear-view mirror. "Your black eye... Was that the husband?"

Clive smiled and winced in pain at the same time.

"No. Not the husband. And you did exactly the right thing. Tomorrow's a big day. I'm running the Moscow marathon. And straight after, I fly to London."

One more night in Moscow. Tomorrow he would sleep in his flat in London. At least, that was the plan. And Marina, where would she rest her head tomorrow night? He turned around; the Ford was so close that he could see inside. Instead of his baby-faced tail there were two older, more seasoned men.

Fyodor parked right outside the lopsided gate of Vera's dacha. The Ford went to the end of the road, turned around and came to a stop, facing the Range Rover at a distance of five metres: a stand-off.

Vera fussed over Clive, making him sit in the rocking chair and then examining his face, saying that it was too late for ice or arnica and that by tomorrow the bruise would be huge and black. Then she brought tea and cakes and told Clive that Anna was coming by to look at a court summons that had been delivered by hand that morning. What was the charge against Vera? That she had burnt wood and leaves in her own garden, which was against the law. What law? Vera scoffed.

"Will they put me in prison at my age?" Vera asked Clive, her voice full of scorn. "What do you think?"

Vera had only just poured out the tea when Anna arrived. She was astonished to find Clive in the rocking chair with a black eye.

"What in God's name happened to you?"

"I was mugged," said Clive. "By the FSB."

"What did they want?"

"Information."

"Did they get it?"

"No," said Clive. Then, glancing at Vera, he added quickly, "It was all a mistake. Everything's fine." He rocked back and forth, keeping his eyes on Anna, who pulled up a chair.

"I don't know why I'm saying this to you… It's none of my business… But something tells me you're in over your head. Let me give you a piece of unsolicited advice. Get out. Get out while you can."

"I'm leaving tomorrow."

"I knew it," said Vera, putting a plate of salted cucumbers on the table and looking at Clive with deep sadness.

"I leave tomorrow, after the marathon. That's why I'm here. I've come to say goodbye."

Vera sat down beside Clive and took his hand. "You're going away for a long time," she said. "I can feel it. Wait… wait. I have something for you."

Vera hurried into her bedroom and came back with a bracelet made of animal hair.

"This will bring you good luck," she said, her eyes full of tears.

"Listen to me, Clive," Anna said. "This is *our* fight, not yours. Get out while you can."

Clive smiled and put his hand on Anna's arm.

"Anya, I need your help."

29

What a pity I had to call Rose, Marina thought as she walked up Tverskaya towards her flat. If Varlamov hadn't put two and two together, then surely he has now.

Never mind. Keep going. In twenty-four hours, it will all be over. Meaning what? she challenged herself. Meaning, I'm heading either out of Russia or into a prison cell. It's as simple as that.

At the top of the entrance staircase, Marina found Oxana sitting at her table, her head in her hands. When the lift lady looked up, her eyes were full of tears.

"I've got the sack!" she said, holding a handkerchief to her nose. "The administrator gave me a week's notice. Then I'm out on my ear! What have I done? Nothing! I've done nothing... And now they're throwing me out!"

"Calm down, Oxanochka, calm down," Marina said, hugging her friend. "Let me talk to the administrator. I'll see what I can do."

"Thank you, Marina Andreyevna... Thank you. I need the money... How do they expect us to live on a pension of fifteen thousand roubles a month? I'll never get another job, not at my age... I've been here for eleven years... doesn't that count for anything? And then I've got friends... like you... This job is my life! My life!"

"I'll talk to the administrator," Marina repeated, putting the palm of her hand against Oxana's smooth cheek. "Try not to worry. We'll sort things out, I promise you."

"Thank you," Oxana said between sobs, then she glanced up at the CCTV camera above and headed out into the courtyard. Marina followed.

"Sasha said he looked nice, your friend," Oxana said, once she was outside, among the cars, and safely beyond the range of the CCTV camera.

"He is nice," said Marina.

"Tomorrow, I've got the day off. I'll be there at the finish line to clap and cheer, so watch out for me, won't you? I know how hard you've trained for this."

Marina looked at Oxana with deep affection, and she wondered when they would next meet. This woman deserved a secure, happy old age. She hugged Oxana and said, "See you tomorrow."

"Where are you going?" Oxana asked.

"To see my dog."

The drive to Peredelkino took almost two hours because of an overturned lorry on the Moscow–Minsk highway. A black Audi tailed Marina every inch of the way and came to a stop less than ten metres in front of her dacha. Behind the driver sat a man in dark glasses.

The moment Marina got out of her car, Ulysses came bounding towards her, barking, followed by Tonya, a strong woman who was wiping her big red hands on an apron; she had been peeling potatoes. "Come in," Tonya said, and led the way into her cluttered kitchen, the shelves packed with jars of home-made jam. "You've had visitors. I didn't like the look of them, but what could I do? They said they were from health and safety, carrying out a fire-risk assessment to protect the forest, which meant they had to check all the old dachas, outside and in. They asked if I had a key to your place. Of course, I said no. But they fiddled about with your lock, and in two seconds they were inside. For all I know, they're still there. And just now, there was another prowler, a young man with a hood pulled over his head, nosing about on your veranda. I didn't like the look of him, either. And what's this Audi doing, parked right outside your house? Anyone would think you're in some sort of trouble..."

"Everything's just fine, Tonechka... It's you I've come to see."

"Me?"

"You and Ulysses."

Marina pulled an envelope out of her bag.

"I want you to take this... Don't open it now. Open it somewhere private, somewhere safe... It's money, a lot of money. For Ulysses, so you can buy him food, take care of him... In case..."

Tonya looked down at the thick white envelope that she held in her hands.

"In case of what? Are you ill?"

"No, I'm not ill, but I have to go away..."

"Go away? For how long?"

"I don't know, Tonechka. I'm driving back to Moscow later tonight... Can I drop him back before I leave?"

Marina left Tonya in her kitchen and crossed into her garden with its untidy rose bushes and hollyhocks and weeds. She stopped for a moment at the top of the steps to her veranda. The sun was setting behind the forest, flooding the sky with blood, or so it seemed to Marina.

She switched on the veranda light; nothing happened. Another power cut, Marina thought. Another evening with no electricity. Leaving Ulysses growling on the porch, she picked up the torch she kept on the veranda, let herself in and beamed the light around her sitting room. It was empty. Then she pushed open the door to her bedroom; it was also

345

empty. She turned round to find herself staring into the face of a man. Marina cried out.

"Boo," said Vanya.

"You nearly gave me a heart attack… Vanechka, how could you?"

"You've had visitors…" he said, holding Ulysses by the snout, rocking his head from side to side.

"I know. Tonya told me," Marina said, as she set about lighting a fire.

"I saw the stupid farts come out, waited, went in through the back and then undid all their good work. I did a sweep with a lovely piece of kit that detects all electronic devices. A friend of mine bought it off the FSB. Cost a fortune. But he has a fortune, so who cares. Found four cameras and microphones. Cut the cables. But just to be on the safe side, I flicked the main fuse in the fuse box."

"How did you know I'd be here?"

"Lyuba called her gran and she told us you'd gone to see your dog. I took a cab, paid the driver double and told him to step on it. He checked Yandex navigator: saw there was a hold-up on the highway and took the back roads. Got here about twenty minutes ago. Just in time to see the goons leaving. By the way, there's another geezer outside in a car."

"I saw him. This is the last place in the world you should be, Vanechka."

Vanya kept to the shadows, but his silhouette was just visible in the firelight.

"Anything I can do to help?" Vanya asked.

"Yes. Leave Russia."

"The fucking FSB didn't cover their tracks… wanted you to know they'd been here… left plenty of clues…"

Marina beamed the torch onto the sofa, where a couple of books from her bookcase had been tossed; in the kitchen, she found a cold cup of coffee; in the bathroom, the cap was off the toothpaste.

Then, quite suddenly, Marina understood that this harassment meant nothing at all. It was simply Varlamov flexing his muscles. She was safe for another fourteen, maybe sixteen hours: until the end of the marathon. What was it my old friend Igor said in Crimea, she thought, as we stood together on the lawn in front of Villa Nadezhda? "When Nikolai Nikolayevich wants something, he gets it." Well, the president wants his photograph of Clive on his knees. And if they arrest me now, she thought, then Clive won't run. So, for the moment, I'm safe.

Marina turned on her ancient battery-operated radio, found the classical-music station and turned up the volume. Vanya stood in the darkest corner of the room, invisible. Marina joined him in the shadows, while the music pounded.

"So, did it work? Is the Englishman free?" Vanya asked.

"Yes, thanks to you. He's safe and sound back at the ambassador's residence."

"You sure about that? There's another FSB tail on Lermontov Street, and I saw a bloke going into an old dacha, a real dump with a gate falling to bits. An old lady came up and hugged the guy. That wouldn't be your English bloke? Tall? Lots of black fuzzy hair?"

There was a loud tapping at the window. Vanya darted into the bedroom, while Marina crossed the room and could just make out the outline of Tonya's face peering in through the glass. She let her in.

"I came to see if you were all right," she said, smiling at the blazing fire. "Still no light?"

"No light, but look, I've got a nice fire going, and I have Ulysses."

"I thought you might be hungry," said Tonya, holding out a box of strawberries, a bowl of apple compote and a pot of homemade raspberry jam. Marina gratefully accepted the food. Moments later, sitting on a stool in a dark corner, Vanya was tucking in.

"Vanechka, how will you get back to Moscow? This dacha is being watched."

"There's not much of a moon. Under the cover of darkness. Hitch-hike. Take a bus. Whatever."

"If you go to an airport, you'll be arrested. Everyone will be on the lookout for Ivan Orlov."

"I've got a couple of names. And a couple of passports. You worry too much. Always did."

Marina shook her head and conceded defeat. Vanya always went his own way.

"Where's Lyuba?" Marina asked.

"Back with her mum. But tomorrow, me and Lyuba, we're gonna see you run the marathon… you and your English friend."

Marina knew it was useless to argue; the boy was as stubborn as a mule. He asked for some vodka. Marina poured him a shot. No, that's not right; she poured him two. Before Vanya left, stepping so lightly out of the back door into the blackness, with a piece of paper clutched in his hand, she asked him a question she had never asked before.

"Vanechka, do you like dancing?"

"Who's that?" said Anna, jumping up from the kitchen table where she was sitting opposite Clive and telling him about Varlamov and her interrogation. She opened the back door onto the orchard, but no one was there. At her feet, she found a piece of paper.

"It's for you," she said, handing the note to Clive.

They met in the darkness by the fence at the back of Vera's apple orchard. Neither carried a torch or a mobile. The only sound was the distant drone of an aeroplane heading for Vnukovo airport. A shaft of light from Vera's kitchen fell onto a cluster of magnificent lupins, and the beam of light showed Clive the way to the summer house – if you could call it that, a wooden cabin round the back of the dacha.

Inside, Marina sat close to Clive on a wooden bench surrounded by a broken bicycle, an electric kettle without a plug and an upturned table with a missing leg. Outside, it was pitch black. Vanya was right: there was no moon, although every now and then there was a break in the clouds and a shaft of platinum light would beam down onto the pines and tangled undergrowth.

"You kept your promise... Hyde knows everything he needs to know."

"No, he doesn't. And nor do you. Clive, you're not running tomorrow. You're not well enough. You're flying to London. With the ambassador. Tell him: he must go with you. It's my guess Varlamov won't dare to stop you if you're with Luke Marden."

"Why the sudden panic?"

Marina told him about Kolomna, and about Lev and his warning: *The Englishman... tell him to watch his back.*

"Difficult when you're running."

"What's the matter with you, Clive? Don't you understand?"

"We're running the marathon tomorrow. End of story. Now, more to the point, how are you getting out? What's your plan?"

"My plan," said Marina, trailing a finger down Clive's cheek, "is... My plan is..." Then she broke into song. "We'll meet again, don't know where, don't know when."

"God almighty," Clive murmured.

Marina rested her head against Clive, wondering whether she would ever do this again: lean against him, feel his arm around her shoulders, his kiss on her forehead.

"Don't run tomorrow," Marina said, giving it one last try.

"I had a dream," said Clive.

"Oh, *please.*"

"Let me tell you about my dream," he said, stroking her forehead, a gesture she would always remember. "We were in Torcello together. And I don't know why but I couldn't get J. Alfred Prufrock out of my mind. I kept hearing over and over, 'Let us go then, you and I…'"

"In Russia, happy endings are few and far between, my love."

"Say that again."

"In Russia —"

"No, no. Just the end."

"My love."

30

So far, so good, thought Vyacheslav Konstantinovich Fyodorov, admiral of the fleet and commander-in-chief of the Russian navy, as he sat in the windowless operations room two floors below street level inside the Admiralty Building in Saint Petersburg. The bank of flickering screens in front of him told him everything he needed to know about Operation Hades. It was going well. The two Belgorod-class special-mission submarines were exactly where they were supposed to be. *Kamchatka* was getting herself into position seventeen nautical miles off the Cornish coast; *Vyborg* was already in position, a mile closer to the shore, and had already deployed its first drone, a five-metre mini-submarine nicknamed by the crew "*Vyborg*'s bastard son".

A nerdy, bespectacled captain second rank, an AI specialist who loved getting technical in front of his superiors, was summoned from his computer screen to give the admiral a blow-by-blow account of what would happen next.

The drones know exactly what to do and where to go, the captain explained. They've been programmed in advance, months earlier in fact, during the extensive reconnaissance phase of the operation. Each drone goes straight to a preordained point on the seabed where the multi-strand fibre-optic cable is lying, and, guided by its own inertial navigation system and also by an AI-driven optical system, the drone locates the cable and squats over it like a praying mantis before deploying a hydraulic arm that fastens onto the cable a saddle-shaped charge designed to cut right through it in three hundredths of a second. The drone then withdraws about a hundred metres and waits, hovering just above the seabed thirteen nautical miles off the Cornish coast, near a town called Porthcurno. At the designated time, the drone initiates an audible firing code and detonates the charge. Within seconds, the drone accelerates automatically towards the detonation point, passing through swirling muddy clouds of disturbed sand with one aim in its artificial mind: to photograph the cut. When this is done, the drone turns hard to port and heads back to its mother submarine with, if the captain second rank may be allowed to suggest, a certain satisfied grace.

Delighted by this vivid description, Admiral Fyodorov hailed each drone as a hero deserving of a medal. He praised the perfect precision and declared the entire operation a monumental tribute to Russian science and engineering.

It was now the turn of the rear admiral in charge of the Northern Fleet, a submarine man through and through, wiry and thin, who talked Admiral Fyodorov through the stages of Operation Hades. The *Vyborg* was first up: three drones from the belly of the submarine would cut three underwater cables at exactly the same time, but spaced far apart to avoid interference from detonations. Then all three drones would rejoin their mother submarine and the *Vyborg* would slip away into deeper waters, leaving the *Kamchatka* to position herself and cut three more underwater cables. Admiral Fyodorov could watch every detail of Operation Hades via a tracking screen in the ops room.

Of course, if Fyodorov had had his way, they would have launched Operation Hades two months earlier. The British were totally consumed with trying to find a new role in their post-Brexit world, and this was an ideal moment to catch the enemy off guard.

Enemy? Did I say enemy? Yes, I suppose I did, thought Fyodorov. Well, that's what they are, the British and the Americans, with their sanctimonious lectures about liberal democracy and their bloody sanctions. It's high time they understood that Russia is a world power, equal to China, equal to the West. It's high time *we* called the shots, and that's exactly what we're going to do with Operation Hades. At long last! I was beginning to despair. The president kept getting cold feet. To be honest, I was surprised to get the call when I did. I was convinced Serov would keep dragging his feet – another week, another month. Why now? I said. He gave me a very odd answer. "Hamlet," he said. Who? "Hamlet," he repeated, "as in Shakespeare." One of these days I must find out what he meant.

The admiral looked up at the sudden burst of clapping; the naval officers who had been sitting for hours hunched over their computer screens were on their feet, laughing and smiling. Captain First Rank Artyom Smirnov, who had arrived from Moscow a few hours earlier, hurried over to his commander-in-chief with the news that the *Vyborg* had risen to periscope depth and sent a signal via satellite: *Vyborg* mission accomplished.

"Excellent!" cried Admiral Fyodorov, clapping his ADC on the back.

By the time Clive got back to Vera's dacha, she was asleep in an armchair. But Anna was wide awake, sitting in front of her laptop at the dining table. When Clive walked in, she tilted her head to one side and ran her fingers through her sleek black-brown hair.

"Picking mushrooms in the dark?"

Vera woke up with a start.

"Goodness me, what time is it? Have I been asleep all this time? Clive, you're still here… and Anna…" Vera beamed with pleasure. "You two would make such a lovely couple."

"Mama," said Anna. "Have you no eyes in your head? That seat is taken."

And even then, in spite of himself, Clive searched for an English equivalent, but he drew a blank.

The FSB tail reported that Marina Volina's dacha had been plunged into darkness – there must have been a power failure – and that she had lit a fire (which could be seen through the window). He reported also that she had one visitor, a neighbour called Tonya, and that at midnight she had dropped off her dog at the house of this same neighbour and driven herself back to Moscow in her Prius, to the High Tide restaurant and nightclub on Savvinskaya Embankment.

A big queue had formed at High Tide, with people pushing to get in and being repulsed by two bouncers with earpieces and muscles. The security guard stopped Marina, made a call and then let her in. The FSB tail attempted to follow her, but was stopped by the same bouncer, who was unimpressed by his fake ID and told him that everyone these days pretended to be FSB and that he could go fuck himself.

Only the pretty girls get in, thought the FSB agent, as a young redhead in a miniskirt came up to the bouncer and gave her name as Lyuba. The bouncer spoke into his walkie-talkie. The girl was let in, and so was her boyfriend, who had his face hidden under a hood.

The FSB tail reported that Marina Volina had emerged from High Tide at 2.05 a.m. In his rear-view mirror, he saw the Englishwoman from the British Council tottering out of High Tide shortly after Volina, very unsteady on her feet, before she got into a British embassy car. The driver, Fyodor, one of ours, confirmed that the woman was drunk. Marina Volina drove herself to Tverskaya 25, arriving there at 2.25 a.m.

The Englishman, on the other hand, had left the dacha of Vera Seliverstova at 11 p.m. in an embassy car, arriving back at the British residence on the Sofiyskaya Embankment at 11.43 p.m.

Why no more news? Admiral Fyodorov kept asking, as he paced the operations room in the bowels of the Admiralty. What's holding them up? Why isn't the *Kamchatka* deploying her drones? What's the problem?

No one seemed to know.

Some technical hitch? Or outside interference? The admiral instructed his ADC, Artyom Smirnov, to get hold of the Russian observer at NATO headquarters in Brussels. Impossible, came the reply. The man had turned his phone off. It was, after all, the weekend.

Fyodorov swore under his breath and prowled in front of the bank of computer screens, searching for answers. Meanwhile, Captain Smirnov fielded anxious calls from the president's private secretary. A wave of anxiety surged through the bunker; the smiles vanished. Admiral Fyodorov paced the ops room, ordering coffee, which he didn't drink.

Operation Hades was aborted on Sunday morning at 5.33 a.m. Moscow Standard Time. It was an agonizing decision for Stanislav Kuznetsov, commander of the *Kamchatka*, who was in charge of the top-secret special submarine operation.

It had all begun so well. Commander Kuznetsov had received the following message from the commander of the *Vyborg*: "All good. Three cables cut. Drones safely back on board. Leaving now. Good luck." Everyone in the *Kamchatka*'s control room had burst into applause, not only because the news was good, but also because the *way* the intelligence was transmitted, from submarine to submarine, was revolutionary and a purely

Russian idea. A young officer from Kaliningrad had devised a code that you could transmit underwater and was based on the sound made by whales in the deep. To the enemy, these mournful whale cries full of yearning would be just that; to the Russian commanders of the *Vyborg* and the *Kamchatka*, however, they were coded messages of national importance.

The *Vyborg* had performed impeccably. Now it was the turn of the *Kamchatka*. Commander Kuznetsov wanted her to shine. The adrenalin was pumping as he sat in the control room of his Belgorod-class special mission submarine, manoeuvring her into position. The drones were ready to be deployed, ready to cut three more underwater cables. We're almost there, Kuznetsov thought.

Then all hell let loose.

Kuznetsov was taken completely by surprise when the Cornish waters above him filled with the penetrating sound of an aggressive anti-submarine stance. What on earth was going on up there "on the roof"? Why, at this precise moment, was the Royal Navy stamping all over his patch? So far, there was no sign of British submarines, but warships were transmitting powerful sonar beams into the depths. It wasn't rocket science to assume that aircraft were involved, joining in the fun, dropping hundreds of active and passive sonar buoys. This was the last thing he'd been briefed to expect.

Kuznetsov was not a man to panic. He sat in his control room, staring at his operations screen and listening to the soft hum of machinery and the muffled movement of men. And something else. Ever so faintly, he could *hear* those British sonars penetrating the depths. The commander weighed up his options. On no account was he to get caught. Those were his primary instructions. Now, all of a sudden, there was a very real risk of detection and signature identification. On top of which, he had not yet been able to get into position. He was in serious trouble, and the chances of being caught in this myriad of interlocking headlights were just too great. He was off.

Thirty minutes later, the *Kamchatka* received a radio signal from headquarters that NATO had launched a no-notice exercise in the Cornish waters. "You don't say," muttered Kuznetsov.

An hour later, in deeper waters to the south, the *Kamchatka* rose fleetingly to periscope depth in order to raise its UHF mast, and a dejected Commander Kuznetsov was able to send a coded signal back to operational headquarters in Saint Petersburg: Operation Hades had been aborted. Three undersea cables had been cut instead of six; or, to put it another way, five fibre-optic cables lay intact on the seabed, when there should have been only two.

31

At 6.35 a.m. on the Sunday of the Moscow marathon, a presidential cavalcade of cars and outriders swept through the arch beneath the Borovitskaya Tower into the Kremlin. Why the president had chosen to drive and not to fly in the helicopter from his villa outside Moscow to the Kremlin, no one dared ask; he was in a furious mood. Serov hadn't slept at all, nor had Lev, who was struggling to keep awake in the back of the presidential limousine – an Aurus Senat, one-hundred-per-cent Russian and made at a cost of a hundred and forty thousand euros, brand new and armour-plated, of course, which explained its weight of six and a half tons. These facts, which rattled around in Serov's head every time he settled himself into the back seat of the limousine, usually made him purr with pride. Not today.

If the president hadn't been so preoccupied, he might have noticed that all over the city the preparations for the marathon were under way: the route was being cordoned off with ropes, while tow-trucks under the watchful eye of police were removing any stray cars. Organizers in their bright-orange PVC coats were putting up hydration and first-aid stations and toilets along the 42.195-kilometre route. But the president noticed nothing. Grim-faced, he stepped out of his car into the Senate building and strode down the long corridor with a deliberate, angry tread, passing through the open gilded doors without so much as a nod to the guards who stood stiffly to attention. In his office, he slumped into the leather chair behind his desk and put his head in his hands. Then he looked up at Lev, who had retreated to his spot in the corner of the room, and told him to get hold of Admiral Fyodorov.

Moments later Serov was shouting into the telephone: "What did you say? What did you just say? Someone leaked this end? Someone told the British? This end? Why not your end?... Someone in the Admiralty could have told the British! You don't leak? The Russian navy doesn't leak? It's always politicians who leak? Go to hell!"

The president ended the call. His hand was shaking.

"Call Marina."

Lev was about to say, "Don't you think it's a bit early?" But one look at the thunderous expression on his boss's face made him change his mind. Anyway, he knew that Marina was an early riser. Lev called her on the president's telephone and told her she needed to come over at once. A car was on its way.

Marina closed the front door of her flat, wondering if she would ever open it again. She wore a tracksuit over her running clothes and was carrying a backpack. On the landing, she found Oxana at her table, drinking tea and sighing over her impending dismissal. It was not yet seven o'clock. Marina crouched down beside her.

"Oxanochka, I need your help. Now, listen very carefully. And if it's too much to ask, then you must say so."

"Too much to ask?" Oxana said indignantly. "There's nothing I wouldn't do for you."

Twenty-eight minutes later, Marina, in running shoes and a tracksuit that covered her shorts and her marathon shirt and bib, was shown into the president's office, where she found Serov sitting behind his desk, looking blankly into space. At first, he didn't seem to recognize the woman who was standing before him. Then, in a tired, defeated voice, Serov announced, "It's all over... aborted. Stillborn. Like a dead child."

"I'm so sorry, Nikolai Nikolayevich," Marina said sympathetically, "but I don't know what you're talking about."

"Listen, listen to this," Serov said urgently, handing Marina an iPad. "The link... Press it and tell me exactly what they say!"

Marina tapped on the link. "Lone yachtsman in trouble off Cornish coast," Marina translated. "The Royal Navy has launched an air-sea rescue mission."

President Serov banged his fist on the table.

"Air-sea rescue, my arse. A full-blown no-notice NATO exercise! That's what they launched! The British knew. Someone tipped them off."

Serov sank into a chair and clamped both hands over his thick shock of white hair. He stared through Marina.

"We were betrayed," Serov said quietly, his fist clenched on the desk. Then he repeated the words, but this time he was shouting. "We were BETRAYED!"

Never had Maria seen Serov so angry.

"May I ask a question?" Marina said gently. "Is it possible that this was coincidence? Just bad luck?"

"I don't believe in bad luck!" the president shouted. "I don't believe in good luck either. I believe in efficiency! The leak came from someone, and until we find out who, everyone is a suspect! Kirsanov, even Grisha, even Fyodorov! Yes, even Fyodorov. After all, it could so easily have come from the navy. Why not? From the navy, or the foreign ministry, or the FSB, or right here in this room. Maybe it was you, Lyova?"

"Lyova?" Marina asked incredulously.

"Next you'll be saying it was Marina Andreyevna," Lev muttered irritably. Serov glanced at Marina, shook his head and turned away.

"How much damage?" the prime minister asked Hyde across her kitchen table. It was a quarter past six in the morning. Hyde had managed to catch three hours' sleep in his nearby flat in Cowley Street before returning to Downing Street just after four a.m. There, he had found Lynton waiting for him with details of three huge power surges on the internet and a best-guess impact study, which Lynton had compiled himself with help from an army of all-nighters spread across government. "It gives a rough idea of the chaos out there," Lynton had said, handing over the slim document, too tired to smile.

Just after six o'clock, against the palest of sunrises, Hyde had climbed the Downing Street stairs to join the PM in her top-floor flat for coffee and toast.

"Damage?" Martha Maitland repeated. "How much?"

"Considerable," said Hyde. "Three cables cut. Thirty-five per cent of our internet traffic through the fibre-optic cables is now looking for a new way across the Atlantic. The full impact won't be felt till tomorrow. And it will be considerable. Brace yourself. When the financial markets open tomorrow, there will be chaos. But how much chaos? We have no way of knowing. That's the honest truth. We're in uncharted waters. About a fifth of the displaced internet traffic will automatically find another way through... but the rest will join a queue, so to speak, or come to a grinding halt. We're already feeling some pretty nasty side effects."

"For example?" the prime minister asked, her voice tense.

"Flight data has been compromised. No flights in or out of the country for today and possibly tomorrow."

"What else?"

"The hotline is down between us and the United States."

"So, I can't talk to the president?"

"You can… and must. Our people are working on it now…"

Hyde poured himself more coffee from the cafetière. He liked the way the PM, in the privacy of her own kitchen, always made proper coffee. "For the moment, our agencies can't talk to each other. Not good… not good at all. Counterintelligence has been working all night on what to expect."

"What else?"

"The banking system will… will be suspended."

"What?"

"Hopefully not for too long, but no one can make any transactions for today. By lunchtime tomorrow, the whole country will all be asking what on earth is going on. You need to get in there first and make a statement. By tonight at the latest."

"We've had several briefings chaired by you, Martin, on contingency plans…"

"Which were never going to be foolproof, because we could only guess the extent of the damage. What really matters now is how quickly we can repair the damaged cables. This will take time, although, thanks to our Moscow agent, we might get there a lot quicker than otherwise. The work has already started. Meanwhile, Prime Minister, we must fasten our seat belts. It's going to be a very bumpy ride, but above all there must be no panic."

"I don't panic, Martin. You know that," said Mrs Maitland with a touch of irritation as she raised her coffee mug to her lips.

"You'll face a very hostile House of Commons. And MPs will want answers."

"Asleep on the job… that sort of thing? I can hear it now," she said with a contemptuous chuckle. "Let's get a statement out there, right now. Why wait? I don't want to mention the cables… Not yet. We can hint it's a cyber attack, don't you think? Just so everyone knows we are aware that things are not quite right. Then tomorrow I'll make a more detailed statement to the house. I might just mention one cable... One cable has been cut... And then, bit by bit, over the course of twenty-four hours, up it to three. Or should I bite the bullet?"

"Bite the bullet," said Hyde. The prime minister smiled. Hyde was a good and truthful friend.

"Thank God it's Sunday," she said. "That gives us a little more time."

The prime minister looked squarely at Hyde. "And thank God for so much else, don't you agree? We've been spared a national disaster, thank the Lord, but no church today, I'm afraid."

"I agree. It could have been much, much worse."

"We've had a great escape, a *deliverance*," said the prime minister, buttering her toast. "Our lives, not just here in the United Kingdom, but in Europe and in the United States... *all our lives* would have been blighted – yes, blighted – for weeks, even months if Russia had completed Operation Hades. We were hours away from untold misery for millions. Our Royal Navy, with the help of our NATO allies, was able to force the Russians to abort their hostile mission. Three cables have been cut. This is serious, of course, and the consequences are grave, but they are *temporary*, and the damage is nothing – I repeat, nothing – to what might have been."

Outside, light rain was falling and the wet streets of London were empty. Over the road in St James's Park, the pelicans were standing on their favourite rock while the raindrops pricked the surface of the pond.

"When does Clive get home?" the prime minister asked.

"Tonight."

"Let me know when he's landed, won't you? I don't know why, but I'm anxious. We owe him a lot. Perhaps some sort of award? What do you think?"

"I'm not sure he'd like that. He's a very private person."

"We mustn't forget the Russian woman. Maria something?"

"Marina. Marina Volina."

"How will she get out?"

"That's not really the question."

"Martin, what on earth do you mean?"

"The question is, *will* she get out?"

"Everyone is suspect!" the Russian president repeated, looking around the room wildly, barely noticing Marina, or Lev, who was checking his phone.

"General Varlamov is here."

"Send him in!" said Serov. "The more the merrier."

General Varlamov walked in and stopped for a moment, surprised to see Marina.

"You've heard?" said Serov. Varlamov nodded. "So, what do you think? Was it a mere coincidence, just *bad luck*?"

"According to a local radio bulletin, a lone yachtsman was in trouble…"

"A lone yachtsman in trouble triggers a no-notice NATO exercise!" Serov shouted. "Is that what you're telling me? Do you think I'm a complete idiot?"

"That's not what I'm telling you at all, Nikolai Nikolayevich," the general insisted in his smoothest voice. "The lone yachtsman story was, of course, bluff. The British were tipped off, but not before we'd cut three underwater cables. Make no mistake, this will cause considerable damage."

"Our target was six! Stop dressing this up as some sort of success… It's a botched operation. Our aim was to cripple the West. That is not going to happen. And I'm holding you responsible. You were in charge of coordinating this operation. You blew it!"

"We were almost there," said Varlamov in a firm, unapologetic voice. "Our microsatellites are working very well, by the way."

General Varlamov was not about to show any remorse, nor any anxiety. His composure irritated Serov, who resumed his seat behind his desk.

"General Varlamov, Operation Hades was aborted halfway through!"

"Nikolai Nikolayevich, the question is, surely, who told the British? A NATO exercise of this kind takes between six and eight hours to launch, so the British must have received the intelligence yesterday afternoon."

The general was determined to take charge of the conversation, to wrest it from the over-emotional president, to reassert his standing, his importance.

"The FSB will launch a full and exhaustive investigation, leaving no stone unturned," Varlamov began. "Where the honour of Russia is at stake, you can count on us. Nikolai Nikolayevich, I need not remind you that our resources are considerable. We shall put everyone under the microscope. And I shall have an answer for you within twenty-four hours."

Varlamov's steely nerve and air of authority seemed to calm Serov.

"Don't let me detain you, General," said Serov, resting his hands on the leather surface of his desk. Under his breath he muttered, just loud enough for everyone to hear, "Get on with it!"

Lev was holding the door open for Varlamov when the general stopped and turned to face Marina.

"Do you always go to a nightclub the evening before a marathon?"

Marina looked only mildly puzzled.

"I'm sorry, General, what has that got to do with anything?"

"Everyone is under the microscope, and, as we all know, time is of the essence. While I've got you here, Marina

Andreyevna, may I just ask… How did *you* spend yesterday afternoon?"

Marina looked the general straight in the eye. Her voice was steady.

"I sent you my report by email at six o'clock this morning, General. Maybe check your inbox?"

"And where were *you* yesterday afternoon?"

The president's question took everyone by surprise.

"Me?" said Varlamov.

"Yes, you."

For a moment Varlamov was flustered. The president was asking him, the deputy head of the FSB, to explain himself, to give details of his whereabouts in front of subordinates. This was undignified.

"You! Where were you?" the president persisted.

"Where I always am. In my office in the Lubyanka, or on my way here. Where else would I be at such a critical moment?"

In bed with Dasha, but he could hardly tell them that. He had sent round fifty roses and ten thousand dollars in cash, and Dasha had changed her mind about leaving. With Operation Hades under way, Varlamov had nothing to do but wait. He needed distraction, physical pleasure that would help to pass the time, calm his nerves, make him feel very good about himself. Dasha had provided all that and more.

The president leant forward, his hands resting on his desk, his eyes on Varlamov.

"You understand, Grisha… heads will roll?"

At that moment, an ormolu clock chimed, and Marina looked at her watch.

"Nikolai Nikolayevich… if I'm late, I'll be disqualified… with your permission…"

"Go," said Serov, dismissing Marina with a wave of his hand. Then, more urgently, he repeated, "Go!"

Marina raced down the corridor and took the marble steps two at a time. She had almost reached the door when she heard Lev's voice.

"Wait for me!"

He caught up with her, breathless.

"The boss doesn't want you to miss the race. We'll take the bike. She's itching for a run."

In the courtyard outside the palace, while Lev pulled off the silver cover of his beloved bike, Marina peeled off her tracksuit and handed it to a guard, asking if he would be so kind and take it to her office. She stood in the cobbled courtyard of the Kremlin in her running shorts and tank top with bib number C104.

"You're running the marathon?" said the guard, looking at her bib, impressed. Marina nodded. The guard raised a fist and sang out, "Break a leg!" – to which Marina gave the classic reply, "To hell!" Then she sat behind Lev on his gleaming white machine, her arms around his waist.

32

Clive was where he was supposed to be, waiting for Marina in the starting corridor of the Moscow marathon beneath a huge loudspeaker and a television camera on a crane. He was surrounded by hundreds of runners limbering up, tilting their heads to one side, shaking down their hands and legs, touching their toes, stretching their quads and their hamstrings, talking and laughing and itching to go.

Clive had followed the instructions in the welcome pack and attached his bib, C105, to his T-shirt with the safety pins provided. He had also read through the leaflet, which explained that his time and distance would be recorded by a tracking chip inside a little black strip on the bib. On his wrist he wore the animal-hair bracelet that Vera had given him. The bracelet was supposed to bring him luck, but would it? Clive considered the challenges ahead. First, he had to survive the marathon. Second, he had to make the evening flight to London. Would they stop him at the airport? They could, Luke Marden had admitted, the evening before, but he thought it highly unlikely, especially since he, the British ambassador, would be by Clive's side all the way to London. Well, thought Clive, standing in his running shorts near Luzhniki Stadium and waiting for Marina to appear, either I will get on the flight to London, or I won't, but somehow, with a diplomatic passport, I'll get home eventually. What about Marina?

The two FSB tails stuck out like a sore thumb, with their shiny new running shorts, shoes, socks and even wristbands. Clive decided to call them Boris and Gleb.

"Is this your first marathon?"

The FSB agents looked stunned. There had been no training for a situation like this. Their job was to follow. In secret. Not to engage in chit-chat in broad daylight with the subject of surveillance.

"You're not called Boris, are you?"

Silence.

"Or Gleb?"

Silence.

"They were the martyred sons of Vladimir the Great, you know."

At this moment, Marina ran up to Clive, breathless and "sorry to be late". Then she noticed the FSB tails.

"Well, hello again," she smiled. The men turned away and tightened their shoelaces.

"Boris and Gleb," whispered Clive, making a note of their bib numbers: Boris was C206, and Gleb was C207.

"Really?"

"No. It's a bad habit I've picked up from Rose... She likes nicknames. But we know these gentlemen, right?"

"We certainly do. They're the A-Team."

How can I defend myself? Clive wondered, as he watched Boris and Gleb limber up. These men were all muscle. And why is Marina so light-hearted, when the whole of the rest of her life hinges on what happens today? She looks as if she doesn't have a care in the world.

A voice came booming over the loudspeaker, first in Russian, then in English: would the elite runners please come forward. At exactly nine o'clock, a gun went off and the top marathon runners, in bibs with surnames but no numbers, surged forward to the shouts and cheers of the crowd.

"We don't go for another thirty minutes," said Marina, jumping from one foot to the other. "At ten past, it's the best amateur runners in 'A' bibs. At twenty past, it's the runners in 'B' bibs. Then we go at half past."

"Fucking hell!" A voice rang out from the crowd. Rose was leaning over the barrier, staring at Clive. "That bruise is black," she said, half awake and yawning, in black jeans and a dirt-black T-shirt, her eyeshadow from last night smeared under her tired, small eyes.

"You look horrible," she told Clive.

"So do you."

Rose was munching on an energy bar, holding a map of the route.

"Right," she said, stuffing the energy bar into her pocket. "Nurse Friedman on duty. I promised Lucky Luke I'd do the last-minute checks. OK with you, Marina? Good… Insulin? Glucose meter? Testing strip? Dextrose? All good?"

Clive gave her the thumbs up.

"Nurse Friedman here needs to know you've understood the procedure that I've been drilling into that thick skull of yours over breakfast. Marina, you need to hear this, too. Clive, spit it out."

"When I run, I burn glucose much faster, so I need less insulin, about thirty to forty per cent of my normal intake. One small injection should do it. Two injections is more than enough. I have three on me, just in case. And I carry a sweet drink. If I burn too much glucose, I pass out, so I need to stop every half-hour to prick my finger and check my glucose level using the glucose meter and the testing strip. How am I doing?"

"That's a pass," said Rose. "Need to check your insulin pen. Make sure you haven't left it behind." Clive produced the pen from his pocket and held it up. "Neat little thing,"

Rose said, taking the pen, and while she was turning it over in her hand, Marina tottered backwards. Clive caught her.

"What happened?"

"Some idiot knocked into me. The sooner we get going the better."

"Here's your pen," said Rose. "And say hello to the famous Café Pushkin, right? Best whisky sours in town. Good luck, you guys."

"Marina! Good luck!" shouted a familiar voice from behind the barrier.

Marina turned in dismay to see Vanya a few feet away, his arm around a smiling Lyuba. "You shouldn't be here..." she whispered and turned away.

When she turned back, Vanya and Lyuba had gone.

The president raged against Varlamov for a full five minutes.

"You realize what all this cost? Billions... I gave you a blank cheque... The FSB, the navy... I said, 'Do whatever it takes!'... That's what I told you all: you, the FSB, the navy... 'Spare no expense!'" Here the president slapped his forehead with his hand. "You're an idiot! And I thought I could count on you! Never in a million years did I think that you, of all people, would screw up. Who leaked? Grisha, you need to get to the bottom of this. Fast. I need a head on a plate, do you understand?"

The biblical image was no accident. Serov's grandmother had been a devout member of the Russian Orthodox Church throughout the Stalin years, and, in secret, she told him Bible stories in terrifying, bloodthirsty detail which appealed to Kolya immensely. His favourite was Salome bringing in the head of John the Baptist on a platter.

"I understand perfectly, Nikolai Nikolayevich."

Serov was suddenly calm and speaking softly.

"Good... Good. Because that head will be yours, General, if you don't find out who did this."

The president turned up the sound on the flat-screen television on the wall of his office in time to hear a Russian newsreader announce that the United Kingdom was experiencing internet connectivity problems, which a Downing Street spokeswoman described as "temporary".

"Temporary connectivity problems!" Serov snorted. "Don't let me keep you, General. You have work to do."

Varlamov left the Senate building in his black BMW and told his driver to take him straight to the Lubyanka.

"Sorry, sir, but the road's closed. It's the marathon. We'll have to make a detour."

"The marathon hasn't started yet," the general said imperiously. "You will take the usual route."

And they did. When the police officer saw the number plate, he saluted and unclipped one of the metal barriers lining the marathon route, and the BMW crossed the empty road to the other side.

Varlamov always thought better in the FSB headquarters. This was his natural home, and within a year he would be top dog. The president had said as much. The future was looking extremely bright, provided he did not mess up.

Over the years, the general had known many spies. And traitors. How could he, General Grigory Mikhailovich Varlamov, apply his considerable knowledge to the matter in hand? It was not straightforward, because, for the first time in his life, so his emotional quotient told him, he was dealing with amateurs.

Of course, he could be wrong. The traitor could be wearing a navy uniform; or a suit and tie, sitting behind a desk at the foreign ministry; or with a special pass round his neck, standing in the president's office, tieless and without socks; or even here, walking the corridors of the Lubyanka...

Go back, he told himself. Go back. To the moment when Marina showed her hand. Let the Englishman go, or else… Those had to be her words. But why did she show her hand at that particular moment? To save the Englishman, of course. He is her weakness, her Achilles heel. In order to save him, she had to blow her own cover. How touching! But how did Volina know that Franklin was with me?

"They're a team: Volina and Franklin and Pavel's brother, Ivan," the general said out loud. He pressed the intercom on his desk and summoned Lieutenant Maxim Mishin.

Mishin entered, carrying a slender file of papers. He was nervous; he had failed to arrest the Armenian shoeshiner, and he knew this would count against him.

"In your text, you said you had two new pieces of information?"

From his briefcase the lieutenant pulled out a Bolshoi programme for *Khovanshchina*. On the second last page, below a Credit Suisse sponsorship advertisement, a few letters and numbers had been scrawled: *H 15*, and then *T 25 1502*.

"*H 15* is a seat number. *T 25* is —"

"Volina's address. Tverskaya 25. And 1502 must be the entrance code?"

Mishin nodded and stood rigidly to attention. He had a lot of ground to make up.

"It would indicate, if I may suggest," Mishin said carefully, "that Volina wasn't at the opera at all. She sent the shoeshiner, Narek, in her place, and they met up later so that he could give her the programme."

"Have you found him yet?"

"He flew to Yerevan on Friday night. Armenian Airlines."

"I don't care *what* airline he flew," Varlamov snapped. "At the Metropol you saw him talking to Volina. She tipped him off, of course… He had a friend, you said? A receptionist? Bring her in!"

"I went to her mother's house yesterday. Liza Ushakova left at five o'clock yesterday morning on a flight to Bodrum. I checked the passenger list. She was on it."

"Your incompetence is beyond belief!" Varlamov exploded. "They *both* got away. Bravo, Lieutenant. What else?"

Mishin placed a piece of paper in front of the general, a transcript of Marina's conversation with Rose Friedman at half past three on Saturday afternoon.

"I've already seen this," Varlamov said. "We know the Englishman is obsessed with Chekhov. So?…"

"The Perm theatre company is performing *Uncle Vanya* in the Minack open-air theatre. The last performance of the season is next Wednesday. You told me to leave no stone unturned, so I looked up Minack on Yandex. It's an amphitheatre on a cliff above a Cornish town called Por… Por… I'm not sure how you say this… Do you pronounce the 'h' or not?"

"Get on with it!"

"Porthcurno."

"What?"

"Porth-curno. Or Port-curno, whichever is correct in English… Anyway, the Minack theatre is above the beach. I don't know why, but I thought it might be relevant."

"And you were right, Lieutenant."

I have her now, the general thought to himself. Nikolai Nikolayevich has made it clear he doesn't believe in coincidences. And nor do I.

"Oh, and there's one more thing," said Mishin. "The British ambassador has booked himself on the same British Airways flight as Clive Franklin and Rose Friedman."

"Well, that won't do him any good at all," said the general, half closing his eyes and leaning back in his chair. He would pick them both up, the Englishman and Volina, because holding the Englishman would unnerve Volina and make her crack more easily, and through her he would get Ivan, too, and put the hacker away in Russia's toughest prison, where he would do years of hard labour and most likely die of tuberculosis. He would interrogate the Englishman for as long as he could get away with, and he would exact his revenge. Varlamov knew how to break a man from the inside. But the Englishman's real pain, which would stay with him every moment of every day, would come from knowing the fate of Marina Volina. By the time she confessed, the general had decided long ago, Volina would never interpret again, or even remember a single Shakespeare quote. She'd be lucky to remember her own name. They would park her in a home for the disabled somewhere near Saratov.

Three runners kept looking at Clive. Why? What had he done to deserve their attention? Two of the men, wearing bibs C98 and C99, were, in Clive's opinion, typical marathon runners, long and lanky, but the third man, C100, was a hulk, the sort of person you don't see running a marathon: thick-set with bulging biceps.

"Those Three Musketeers," said Clive to Marina in English. "Why do they keep looking at me?"

"It must be your black eye."

Clive relaxed.

"So," he said to Marina. "What are you aiming for? A personal best?"

"Hardly. No disrespect, but you're not Mo Farah."

"Don't hold back because of me," Clive urged. "Go for it!"

Marina glanced behind her at the FSB tails who were inspecting new Garmin fitness watches.

"And leave you at the mercy of Boris and Gleb?" she murmured. "No way. I need to watch your back."

Marina edged away from the tails, jumping up and down, twisting her neck, loosening up.

"Our friends here," she said in English, nodding towards Boris and Gleb, "will want to strike while the iron is hot."

They looked at each other and understood, instinctively, that in that exact moment, drawn by a linguistic compulsion, they were thinking the same thing. The Russian idiom was almost identical: *Kuy zhelezo, poka goryacho!* (Forge the iron while it's hot!)

"I'm in your head," Clive whispered, "and you're in mine. We're meant for each other, don't you see?"

Over the loudspeaker, a man's voice called on all those in Cluster C to assemble at the start. A gun went off and the mass of runners surged forward like a river breaking its dam.

They were off.

"It's started," said Lieutenant Mishin, glancing down at his phone. He was standing next to the general on a Lubyanka balcony overlooking the six-lane road below; normally it was clogged with traffic, but today the thoroughfare was completely empty, except for soldiers who lined the route in front of the vast Lubyanka building. Mishin was surprised to see the general smoking. Not vaping: smoking.

"When all this is over," said Varlamov, taking a long and deeply satisfying drag on his cigarette, "you'll get a personal recommendation from me. Lieutenant Mishin, your star is rising."

Clive and Marina ran side by side, with Boris and Gleb following a few metres behind. The route was lined with volunteers in fluorescent yellow vests; many were standing behind trestle tables piled high with slices of orange and paper cups of water.

Thirty-five minutes into the race, in front of the glittering glass skyscrapers of Moscow-City, Clive stopped to prick his finger and check his glucose levels. All good.

They resumed running: Clive and Marina in front, Boris and Gleb behind. But not for long. They were passing through Krasnaya Presnya Park when C98, C99 and C100 made their move. The three runners muscled in ahead of the FSB tails, elbowing them aside, the hulk taking his place directly behind Clive, the other two flanking Clive and Marina, boxing them in. Boris and Gleb were impotent: they tried several times to regain their designated place behind Volina and the Englishman, but each time, they were elbowed aside.

"What's going on?" Clive said to Marina in English, breathing hard." Who *are* these people?"

"Kunko's men. Watching your back. Just run."

Kunko's head man, the hulk in bib C100, had always said it would be a doddle, and it was. With fifteen thousand dollars in his back pocket and no ID checks on the day of the marathon, he had no problem persuading three friends, all C-category runners, to part with their running bibs for fresh, crisp dollars. Instead of running the marathon, these same friends were now sitting in a local coffee shop, staring at all the money in cash and planning the holiday of a lifetime.

"Boris and Gleb don't look too happy," said Clive, glancing behind at the FSB agents, who were running hard and, at the same time, speaking urgently into their mobiles.

What *is* their plan? Clive wondered. Keep running. No, better still, talk to Marina. Say something.

"Are you listening?" he said.

"No."

"I said, why is Kunko doing this?"

"He owes you one. You saved his daughter from permanent disfigurement, remember?"

Clive stopped again, for old times' sake, outside the Ministry of Foreign Affairs – where he had wasted so much time and energy – to check his glucose level, while the Three Musketeers formed a human shield. The glucose levels were holding up, but, as Clive had been warned by Doctor McPherson, they could skyrocket at any moment under intense physical pressure. Pretty soon he would have to inject. Never mind, he told himself. Focus. Focus on what Boris and Gleb have in mind. Will it be a gun? Or a knife? Or a needle?

Nothing happened. Clive ran past the White House, which was gleaming in the sun, and passed the towering statue of Peter the Great in a skirt, wondering whether it was a false alarm, after all.

Two and a half hours in, and they were hugging the Moscow River, almost at the halfway mark: Clive and Marina, the Three Musketeers, and Boris and Gleb at the back, all pounding down the Sofiyskaya Embankment opposite the red-brick walls of the Kremlin. Clive slowed as he approached the elegant building set back from the road with a Union Jack fluttering high on a flagpole. Luke Marden was on the balcony, a pair of binoculars pressed to his eyes. Clive waved, and a moment later the ambassador waved back. And still the FSB tails were shut out, forced to run several metres behind the three muscular men, who showed no sign of fatigue.

Now they were crossing Tverskaya and Marina glanced up her street. Would she ever see her flat again? She grabbed two slices of orange from a trestle table along the route and gave one to Clive. A volunteer shouted encouragement: "Go, go, go!" Marina had no energy to reply; she just nodded her head.

On Tverskoy Boulevard, they came to a stop in front of Café Pushkin. Marina hated the sham nineteenth-century building with its overblown interior, but foreigners loved it, and the doorman, in his top hat and cloak, made a fortune from tips.

The Three Musketeers surrounded Clive as he opened the pouch around his waist and pulled out his injection pen. At the same time, Boris crouched down to tighten his shoelaces, and, from his sock, pulled out a blowpipe, which he aimed at Clive's calf. But the hulk, in bib C100, had not taken his eyes off Boris, and, with the lightness of a boxer, he sprang forward and pushed Clive out of the way. The dart hit the ground. A second dart followed, missing Clive, but hitting C100 in the arm. The big man staggered and crumpled. A volunteer rushed forward and asked if she should call an ambulance.

"He's the shithead who's going to need an ambulance," said C99, grabbing Boris from behind and, in one powerful movement, twisting his arm back, kicking his legs from under him and throwing him to the ground. Gleb was frozen to the spot, terrified. He opened the palms of his hands to show he had no weapon, while Boris lay on the ground, moaning.

"You dropped this," said Marina, handing Clive his insulin pen. Except it wasn't his pen: it was a substitute, and filled with Rohypnol. Marina remembered how deftly Rose had made the switch before the race began. Clive injected and sank to his knees. Musketeers C99 and C98 helped him to his feet and carried him into a side street.

"Can't go without Marina," Clive said, slurring his words.

"I'll follow very soon, my love," Marina whispered in his ear.

C100 was back on his feet, his whole body fighting whatever chemical had been shot into his super-fit organism. He managed to steady himself and staggered after his colleagues.

Boris was also on his feet, but he could only stand up for a few seconds before he collapsed against the barrier, staring in disbelief at his tormentor, C100, who was *walking*. What had gone wrong? According to the "alternative" weapons experts at the FSB, the blowpipe tranquilliser could bring down a rhinoceros. Meanwhile, the volunteer had summoned an ambulance, and the sound of a wailing siren grew louder. Still, the marathon runners came pounding by, watched by shouting spectators holding placards, and almost no one noticed Boris, who was clutching his dislocated shoulder, his face contorted in pain.

"Don't lose the Englishman!" Boris shouted at Gleb, who promptly jumped the barrier and followed the receding figure of C100. Volunteers were helping Boris into an ambulance, while nearby spectators were wondering what on earth was going on. As another wave of runners came by, all eyes, within seconds, were back on the race, and the memory of Boris was consigned to the back of an ambulance.

A few hundred metres away, in a side street, neither the ambassador nor his driver seemed at all surprised to have a semi-conscious Clive Franklin deposited in the back seat of the embassy flag car by Kunko's men. The Jaguar then set off at a sedate pace, the Union Jack fluttering on its bonnet.

Meanwhile, Marina continued her run. She had never *not* finished a marathon, and today would be no exception.

"Gone? What do you mean gone?" General Varlamov shouted into his phone. "Where? In a British embassy car? Well find the fucking car! Send out an alert to the traffic police, to *all* the police. It's not exactly invisible, a British embassy car with a British flag."

Varlamov turned to Mishin, his eyes bright with anger. "They've lost the Englishman. Lieutenant, I want you to take charge. Get out there and find the car. Alert the traffic police. And the airports. I'm not done with Franklin yet. And Volina? Where is Volina? Ask those idiots. Ask them where she is!"

In less than two minutes, Mishin had the answer.

"The Englishman stopped outside Café Pushkin, near the thirty-kilometre stop, twelve kilometres from the finish. Assuming Volina is still running, then —"

"What do you mean, 'assuming'? What do our agents say?"

"The Englishman had protection: three bodyguards pretending to be runners. When one of our agents tried to bring him down, as instructed, he was… assaulted, thrown to the ground. He's on his way to hospital, sir. With a dislocated shoulder. And when the Englishman collapsed…"

"What did you say?"

"He collapsed."

"And the photograph? I told them to get a photograph…"

"I'm sorry, sir, but the Englishman's bodyguards made that quite impossible…"

"Impossible is not an FSB word. Do you understand that, Lieutenant?"

"Yes, sir. Franklin injected himself and collapsed. Nothing to do with us. And his bodyguards carried him to the British ambassador's car, which was waiting in a side street. One of our agents got a photograph of the number plate, and of the Englishman in the back seat. Asleep or unconscious."

"Volina didn't go with the Englishman?"

"No. Our agent saw the British embassy car turning into the Novy Arbat and, in my opinion, it's heading for Domodedovo airport."

"And Volina? Where is she?"

"We're pretty sure she's still running. Don't worry, General. Our agent will catch up with her."

33

Marina could feel Varlamov breathing down her neck. She gave a nervous backward glance, but there was still no FSB tail. She could jump the barrier, dive into a side street and make a run for it. Where to? If she went home, for sure they would be waiting for her. Anyway, she didn't have her passport on her. Nor her phone.

I'm on my own, she thought.

In the deep pocket of her running shorts the prepaid "burner" given to her the night before by Vanya, in High Tide, against ear-splitting techno music mixed by one of Moscow's top DJs, was vibrating. She pulled it out and pressed "accept".

"What's your ETA?" asked Vanya. Marina slowed and, still panting hard, told him she'd just passed the Bolshoi and the thirty-five-kilometre mark. She had another seven kilometres to go and her speed was somewhere around seven minutes per kilometre, so, at this rate, Marina reckoned she should reach the finish line in forty-nine minutes.

Eight minutes after Clive was carried into the back of the embassy flag car by Kunko's men he was lifted out again, this time by the ambassador and Fyodor, who put him onto the back seat of an old Nissan that was waiting in a side street. Sitting in the driver's seat was Rose Friedman. The man next to her jumped out of the car.

"You'll be fine," said Doctor McPherson as he held onto Clive, who was groggy and unsteady.

The embassy driver, Fyodor, tapped on Rose's car window. He was smiling. Rose jumped out, gave Fyodor a hug and whispered, "Don't blow the money all at once." Then she resumed her place behind the wheel. The Nissan headed west out of Moscow.

Don't blow the money all at once. Rose's words rang in Fyodor's ears as he followed the ambassador back to the flag car, trying to get his head round everything that had happened in the last twelve hours. For a start, he was ten thousand dollars richer, all thanks to Rose Friedman, whom he'd picked up at High Tide at two o'clock that morning. She was pretty drunk, or so he'd thought, until miraculously she sobered up and suggested a farewell walk in the garden, since she was leaving the next day. Under a pale crescent moon, Rose made her pitch in awful Russian, but somehow her meaning was crystal clear, and Fyodor agreed to her proposal. Rose handed over the cash there and then. Ten thousand dollars. Enough to get him out of Russia. Maybe even enough to get him to London, where he might get a job with an oligarch. What had the FSB ever given him? Nothing. Not a rouble. Only threats.

Fyodor adjusted his chauffeur's hat and, with the ambassador sitting primly in the back seat, headed for Domodedovo airport.

The general was directing operations from the back of his BMW twenty metres from the finish line. He was feeling better. The British embassy flag car had been spotted by the traffic police on the MKAD heading for Domodedovo airport, exactly as Mishin had predicted. Varlamov had dispatched his lieutenant and Major Ivanov of the Moscow police with orders to stop the flag car.

On the outer ring road, siren wailing, the police car tore along at a speed of two hundred kilometres per hour, until it passed the Jaguar with its fluttering Union Jack on the bonnet – at which point it pulled back and nestled right behind the Jaguar, which was keeping strictly to the speed limit.

"We're being followed," said Fyodor.

"To be expected," said the ambassador. "And any moment now they'll pull us over."

Lieutenant Mishin's instructions were clear: stop the embassy car, detain the Englishman and send the others – the woman from the British Council, Rose Friedman, and the British ambassador, Luke Marden – on their way. He had practised saying their names in English, slowly and clearly, after listening to the correct pronunciation on Google Translate.

The ambassador would kick up a stink, the general had warned Mishin, but the lieutenant must stand his ground. No apology and no explanation. Of course, Luke Marden would be furious at the apprehension of a British citizen with a diplomatic passport. He might even call the Ministry of Foreign Affairs, but it was Sunday, and their offices were shut. Did he have the private number of the Russian foreign minister? Unlikely, but even if he did, and even if the ambassador got through to the foreign minister, and even if the foreign minister called the president and the president called the general, he, General Grigory Mikhailovich Varlamov, would not pick up. Not this time. Not until he'd got what he wanted out of the Englishman.

Varlamov had personally checked the British Airways flight bookings: Clive Franklin and Rose Friedman had made their bookings almost a week ago on the 16.05 BA flight to London. The ambassador had booked his flight that morning: the very same morning that Operation Hades had been aborted.

Was the ambassador going home to celebrate? Or to protect Franklin? Well, nothing and no one could protect Franklin from the ice-cold fury of General Grigory Varlamov.

"What?" said Varlamov, pressing his phone to his ear as he sat in the back of his black BMW twenty metres from the finish line.

"The ambassador was alone in the car," Mishin repeated.

There was silence. The general said nothing. Eventually he murmured, "I see."

But he didn't see, at least not yet, although he could almost touch the explanation; it was right in front of him, a mirage shimmering in the distance.

"Yesterday in Kolomna, who did Volina speak to?"

"I don't have the report with me, General, so this is from memory," Mishin began hesitantly. "She spoke to the British Council woman, Rose Friedman, and to Boris Kunko. She also spoke to Deputy Prime Minister Romanovsky and to the girl who was with him, Katya Bogdanova."

"And last night she went to the High Tide nightclub, which is owned by…?"

"Boris Kunko."

Varlamov, who had been leaning against the headrest of the BMW, eyes half shut, jolted forward.

"Get hold of Vnukovo airport… Speak to air traffic control. You're looking for a jet that belongs to Boris Kunko. It does not leave. Is that clear? And get yourself down there. Franklin is on that plane."

General Varlamov was irritated to discover that he was sweating. He was a fastidious man and he detested vulgarity, especially when it concerned the human body: marks of sweat, odours, a badly shaved chin; in women, lipstick poorly applied or smudged mascara, and for a split second he thought of Dasha, of her terrible dress sense and delicious, pliant body.

Rose got to Vnukovo airport within the hour, but not without incident. As they drew near, Clive, who had been sleeping against Doctor McPherson's shoulder, jerked his head up and looked around.

"Where are we?" he said, his words thick on his tongue. "The marathon... Why aren't I running?"

"There, there... You'll be fine," said the doctor. "Just a little knockout punch... No long-term effects."

"What am I doing in this car?" Clive said, struggling to keep his eyes open. "Where's Marina? I can't leave Marina."

"Marina will be fine," said Rose.

"Swallow these," Doctor McPherson ordered, pressing two tablets into Clive's hand and holding out a bottle of water.

Clive did as he was told. Whatever was in those pills, they made him as docile as a lamb until they were inside Kunko's private jet. As they were about to take off, however, Clive, sandwiched between Rose and the doctor, woke up with a vengeance and, with a supreme effort of will, started unbuckling his seat belt. "Marina," he kept saying. "I will not abandon Marina." There was nothing for it but another injection, which Doctor McPherson administered with a jab to the thigh. Clive woke somewhere above Tilbury Docks.

"What news?" Varlamov shouted into his phone above the noise of loudspeakers and the chanting and cheering for runners as they drew near and crossed the finish line. If the general had not been so preoccupied, he might have noticed a pretty young redhead looking adoringly at the hidden face of a young man in a hood, but Varlamov noticed nothing, not even the ambulance that had moved a few metres closer to the finish line.

"I've been talking to passport control," said Mishin, over the phone. "They took off thirty minutes ago. Two passengers with British diplomatic passports: Clive Franklin, who was not feeling well, and Rose Friedman. There was also an English doctor, McPherson, and Boris Kunko and his daughter Zoya. The immigration officer said the passports were entirely in order."

"Have they left Russian air space?"

"No. But, General, if you don't mind my saying so, I think it's too —"

"Shut up."

Mishin was right. It *was* too late, and Varlamov knew it. Only the president could order the interception of a civilian aeroplane within Russian airspace. And why would Serov do that on the basis of such circumstantial evidence?

"Where are you?" said Varlamov.

"On the MKAD, heading for Vnukovo. About twenty-five kilometres away."

"Turn around and get back here. Fast."

The general could hear Mishin shouting something at his driver, and then he heard the sound of a police siren. Varlamov liked the sound of sirens.

The FSB tail had caught up with Marina, just as she thought he would. Gleb must have taken a shortcut in a car or on a bike and then rejoined the race. It was to be expected. His job was on the line.

Marina could hear schoolchildren chanting the name of their school and of their teachers who were running the marathon. "Sparrow Hills! Sparrow Hills!" "Petya! Ira! Xenia! Keep going!" "Well done! Bravo!"

The Nokia vibrated. Marina read Vanya's text on the go: the Wolf was waiting for her by the finish line.

Also by the finish line, an unusually large crowd of young spectators were pressing against the barriers, and more and more young people kept coming in response to all the messages that Vanya and Lyuba had been sending out since dawn on VK, Twitter and WhatsApp about a flash climate-change protest that afternoon at the finish line of the Moscow marathon. Nothing political. Only climate change. And bring a banner!

General Varlamov was just behind the barrier, with a perfect view of the finish line. But something was disturbing his concentration. Directly opposite him, across the track, was a young couple, a redhead and a man in a hood; the man was staring at him. He couldn't see much of the face, but he could feel the force of his stare. How dare a stranger look at him in such an invasive manner? Then the hood fell back, and at once General Varlamov knew who it was.

Ivan looks just like his brother, the general thought, as his hand slipped inside his jacket, where he could feel the cool steel of his Makarov. He thinks he's got away with it, the little shit. Look at the smirk on his face.

Vanya and the general locked eyes across the marathon track. It was a contest of wills, and the general lost; he was the first to turn away. He could feel a ray of heat, of *hate-heat*, beamed right at him. Absurd, Varlamov told himself. The boy's a nobody. I can snuff him out with the snap of my fingers. This is ridiculous. When he looked back, Vanya was gone.

But the redhead was still there, waving a handmade banner with bright red writing: ~~LOVE~~ CO_2 IS IN THE AIR. On her T-shirt was a photograph of Nikita Strelnikov and his guitar, and she was shouting, "Sparrow Hills School!"

Through a crowd of screaming schoolchildren, the general made his way back to the BMW, where he found Mishin who had just arrived, pleased with himself that he had covered twenty-eight kilometres in just twelve minutes.

"Arrest the girl with red hair, the one over there," said the general. "And this time don't mess up."

"On what charge?"

"Just do it!"

Vanya was the first to notice the man in a light-grey suit pushing his way through the crowd, heading towards Lyuba. He was sitting in the front seat of an ambulance close to the finish line, next to Anna Seliverstova and her friend Lena, the ambulance driver. Lena was a big woman with dyed-orange hair who had lost track of the number of times bloodied and unconscious young Russians had been lifted into her ambulance on a stretcher. Her husband Sergei was the medic, and he usually sat next to her in the front, but on this occasion, to make way for Vanya and Anna, Sergei had been relegated to the back of the ambulance, where he sat uncomfortably next to an oxygen tank.

Vanya guessed the man in the grey suit was FSB; he had seen him talking to Varlamov. He rang Lyuba's mobile and willed her to pick up, but there was no way she could hear the ringtone. *Pick up!* Vanya begged Lyuba, who had moved closer to the finish line and was jumping up and down, chanting, "Petya!... Ira!... Xenia!... Sparrow Hills!" Lyuba was doing everything he had asked her to do, shouting her head off for her school and her teachers. "Don't worry about me," Vanya had told her more than once. "I'll be fine." Meanwhile, the mobile tinkled in her pocket.

Vanya knew he would never get to her in time, and he watched, helpless, as Lieutenant Mishin put a hand on Lyuba's shoulder. The girl looked surprised. She glanced over towards the ambulance, and then reluctantly followed him.

"Shit," said Vanya, opening the ambulance door, but he was stopped by Anna.

"You'll blow the whole thing if you go after her," Anna said. "You've got a job to do, Vanya. And so do I. Lenochka, start the siren."

"But why, Anya? What's the reason?" said Lena, her plump hands resting on the steering wheel. At the same time, she glanced at her famous friend, whom she had known since childhood, and knew that she would do whatever Anna asked.

"Lenochka, just start the siren," Anna said urgently, her eyes fixed on the man in the light-grey suit who was leading Lyuba towards a police car. She knew his face. He had been in the room when Varlamov interrogated her. He had stood in the corner, silent. And here he was again, the typical apparatchik with a face like a ferret: small in stature, smartly dressed, ambitious, eager to please. Varlamov's acolyte is moving in for the kill, she thought.

The ambulance siren shattered the air, and neither Lieutenant Mishin nor anyone else noticed a young man slip out of the front seat of the ambulance and disappear round the back. But a few minutes later everyone noticed the polar bear that had somehow leapt over the barriers and was now prancing in the cooling-off zone, adding to the carnival atmosphere. The polar bear even posed for a selfie with an exhausted runner.

Marina was less than fifty metres from the finish line. Gleb, the FSB tail, in bib C207, was right behind.

Shouts turned to screams. Hundreds of schoolchildren started jumping up and down, chanting in a crescendo of enthusiasm: "Petya!... Ira!... Xenia!... Petya!... Ira!... Xenia!... Sparrow Hills School!... Sparrow Hills School!..."

"Go closer," said Anna. The ambulance edged forward, siren wailing.

Marina crossed the finish line and so did the teachers, and, as they did, a roar went up. For a second, Marina held her arms in the air, shutting out the world and her fear. Then she saw Varlamov standing by the barrier. Still breathless, she made her way to the cooling-down area, where runners were lying on the ground, gasping, kneeling or taking selfies. A volunteer handed her a warmer, and Marina wrapped herself in the silver sheet. Another volunteer gave her a medal.

Meanwhile, the FSB agent in bib C207 was bent over, gasping, his eyes fixed on Marina. Suddenly the polar bear bounded forward and took C207 by the hand and started to dance to Isaak Dunayevsky's 'Sports March', which was blaring from the loudspeaker. The FSB tail tried to shake off these unwelcome advances, but the bear would not leave him alone, bobbing up and down right in front of his face, making it hard, even impossible for him to keep Marina Volina in his sights.

Still holding her silver warmer tight around her shoulders, Marina walked over to a white-haired lady with smooth cheeks standing behind the barrier and holding up a hand-painted sign: PLANET BEFORE PROFIT. On her head she had a Happy Birthday Moscow cap, and over her shoulder, a backpack.

Then came the crash. A section of the barrier tipped over under the weight of screaming schoolchildren as they rushed forward to mob their teachers. Marina and the elderly lady were almost knocked to the ground. Oxana steadied herself, took off the backpack and handed it to Marina, who had lost her silver warmer in the crush and was penned in on all sides. Somehow Marina was able to pull a tracksuit jacket from the backpack, zip it over her marathon bib and take the cap from Oxana's head. Suddenly, she looked like everyone else in the crowd. The two women exchanged looks, then, with surprising force for a lady her age, Oxana burrowed her way back into the raucous crowd.

The second crash was even louder than the first. As another part of the barrier fell, hundreds of children were suddenly rushing forward, spilling onto the track just beyond the finish line. Marina caught sight of a banner with the slogan: THE CLIMATE IS CHANGING! WHY AREN'T WE?

Then a new chanting began. It was almost a song, surging upwards with magnificent force, "*Save our forests! Save our Russia! Save our planet!*"

Suddenly a cry went up, and the schoolchildren broke off their singing and made way for a stretcher. A white-haired lady in her seventies had fainted right at the feet of Lieutenant Mishin, who was asked to move out of the way by Sergei, the medic.

By now General Varlamov was tired of being pushed and jostled by the crowd, and so he took refuge in the BMW and summoned Mishin and his other FSB agents to join him. He studied the flushed face and fearful eyes of the agent in the C207 running bib and reminded him that his job, his *only* job, was to tail Volina.

"What makes me think you lost her?" asked the general.

"Sir, I'm really sorry, but there was this fancy-dress polar bear in my face, and then the stampede…"

The FSB agent prepared himself for a dressing down. Instead, the general went quiet. In moments of genuine crisis Varlamov did not explode; on the contrary, he became ice cold and had absolute clarity of thought.

Varlamov turned to Mishin. "The girl with red hair?"

"She's under arrest, sitting in a police car."

"Good," he said. "Through her, we'll get the criminal, Ivan. As for Volina, she can't get away. Her passport is biometric, and all her personal details are on there, including her security status, which doesn't allow her to travel abroad unless it's authorized by the Ministry of Foreign Affairs. She needs official clearance. There's no way she can leave the country."

"Unless she takes a train to Minsk on her internal passport."

Varlamov looked at Mishin, whose pupils seemed enormous through the thick lenses.

"Good thinking," said the general. "Send an immediate alert to Belorussky station. Tell the guards to be extra vigilant. And circulate Volina's photograph. Make sure it's *everywhere*. At all railway stations and airports, and with the traffic police. Volina will be trying to get on an aeroplane, or a train, or sitting in a car, and we are going to find her. Tell the head of security at the station that I want our transport police to board every train going to Belarus, and tell them to carry out a second round of checks once the passengers are in their seats. Tell the head of the transport police that he can have all the reinforcements he needs. The next few hours are crucial."

Mishin had pulled out his phone and was already stabbing at the screen.

"If she makes a dash for Simferopol and her villa," said Mishin, "we can pick her up at Sheremetyevo this evening."

"Put a trace on her mobile."

"I have."

Varlamov decided he could not wait; he needed to get to Serov right away and expose the bitch, Volina. Even without a confession, his case against her was overwhelming. He decided to take Lieutenant Mishin, who might be useful.

The general was about to tell his driver to take them to the Senate Palace when he heard the loud and unmistakable ringtone of the Russian national anthem. Varlamov looked down at his phone, and only then did he see that he had five missed calls from his wife. The general got out of the car and, shielding himself from the screaming teenagers, pressed the iPhone to his ear. Raisa was hysterical. She didn't know how to break the news, but someone had hacked into her bank account and taken all her money. All *his* money. One million dollars. Last Wednesday.

"Last Wednesday!" shouted the general. "And you only notice four days later?" Raisa fought back: of course she didn't check her bank account every day. Who does? In fact, she barely checked her account at all. Why should she? It was always full of money.

Varlamov shouted at Raisa, called her an idiot and threatened divorce as he ended the call.

A strange feeling came over the general. He realized that he was being hunted like an animal. He slipped his iPhone into his pocket, and the tips of his fingers touched a scrap of paper that had not been there before. It was the torn-off end of a marathon flyer with a message scrawled in capital letters: THERE'S NOWHERE TO HIDE.

The general could feel beads of sweat breaking on his forehead. He pulled out a perfectly ironed white handkerchief from his pocket and mopped his brow, and, as he did so, all sound fell away: the raucous shouting and clapping from spectators, even the whirring blades of a helicopter overhead – all this evaporated as he stood in his own silent world. And in that moment, he understood, with perfect clarity, the immediate danger he faced. His enemy was a vigorous young man, a black belt in the martial arts of cyber warfare, out to destroy him.

Varlamov felt himself alone in space, floating, with nowhere to go. He was, for the first time in his life, lost, desperate, unable to defend himself. He stared blankly at the ambulance – an old GAZ, siren blaring – as it shuddered off into the city.

While hundreds of children were chanting slogans to save the planet, Marina had slipped unnoticed into the back of the ambulance where she found herself alone with Oxana, who was lying on the stretcher. Marina kissed Oxana's hand, then she changed into a tracksuit and was reunited with her passport, her wallet and her phone. She looked out of a window to see where she was. At that moment Oxana sat up, her face flushed with excitement, and pulled out a pack of cigarettes. Marina stopped her.

"Make me a promise? If I save your job, you'll give up smoking. Is that a deal?"

Oxana's eyes filled with tears.

"You're going away, aren't you?"

Marina banged hard on the small partition window through which she could see the driver, Lena. The ambulance stopped opposite the crenellated red brick walls of the Kremlin, and Anna opened the back door.

"Anything wrong?"

Marina looked straight at Anna. The raw animosity was gone. There was something new in her eyes: suspicion, perhaps, but also curiosity.

"This is where I get out," said Marina.

"But this isn't Belorusskaya station."

"I'm not taking the train."

"You can't fly to Minsk. They'll arrest you."

"I'm not going to Minsk. Change of plan. Thanks for everything."

Anna stared hard at Marina, then reached out and put a hand on her shoulder.

"I don't know what your plan is," said Anna, "but good luck, my once-upon-a-time friend."

"Keep this for me, will you?" Marina said suddenly, pressing her marathon medal into Anna's hand.

Anna stood by the ambulance and watched as Marina disappeared into the underpass and re-emerged the other side, where she showed her pass to the security guards at the Borovitskaya Tower. Then she passed under an arch, which reminded Anna of a mouth: a gaping Kremlin mouth that had just devoured Marina.

34

The corridors were quiet. It was Sunday after all. Marina walked right past her office door. At the end of the long corridor, the gilded doors were shut, and two FSO guards were standing to attention. She recognized one of them; his name was Bogdan.

"Could I see Lev Lvovich, please?" she said to Bogdan. He smiled and opened the gilded door. In a corner of his office, Lev was sitting on the floor, meditating. Marina coughed loudly.

"Lyova, I have to see the president. I have to see him right away. It is of the utmost importance."

"Did you finish?" Lev asked, jumping to his feet. "Yes? Bravo! Are you sure you want to see him? He's in a filthy mood… But then, you can't really blame him. His pet project has just blown up in his face. Then Romanovsky brought even more bad news just now. I don't suppose you've got any glad tidings? No? I didn't think so. You look exhausted. How did the Englishman do? Does the boss have his photo?"

"No," said Marina. "But I've brought him something much better than that. A head on a plate."

"That should cheer him up," said Lev. "He's called a national security meeting in an hour."

"I need ten minutes."

"He's all yours."

Lev followed Marina into the president's office and took up his usual place in the corner. Serov was staring out of the window.

"What is it, Marina?" Serov said, turning around, with none of the usual warmth in his voice. Marina took a deep breath.

"Nikolai Nikolayevich," she said, standing before the president, keeping this as formal as possible. "As you know, I have always steered clear of internal politics and intrigue. But when you asked me to help with your investigations, I was happy to oblige. However, I now find myself in possession of many disturbing facts and... well... I could never live with myself if I didn't tell you what I know about General Varlamov."

The president listened in silence as Marina laid out her case against General Varlamov. She was very methodical.

"Let's start with the man himself," she said. "He's got fingers in many pies, as you know well. First: fraud. He's been stealing from Russia; he's been stealing from you, Nikolai Nikolayevich. The general helped himself to a billion dollars from the World Cup Development Fund. He had partners, of course, but he was the main beneficiary. The money went into an account in the British Virgin Islands, and from there it went to Panama. I have the details. Second: extortion. He acts as protection for a dozen businesses, including Boris Kunko's nightclub, collecting several hundred thousand dollars a month from each client. Again, I have all the details. Third: security. There's a video of him having sex with his girlfriend, Dasha; as of this morning, it's been widely distributed. He's definitely a security risk."

"I know about the video," said Serov. His voice was thin, tired. "I've seen it. Romanovsky was here earlier. He also told me that Grisha's email has been hacked."

Marina dropped her voice. This was the moment.

"Nikolai Nikolayevich, all of this is secondary to a deep suspicion that I feel honour-bound to share with you. I do not have definitive proof, but I swear on my father's life that I believe your friend Grisha is the mole. And what's more, he wants your job."

Serov scowled and moved away from the window towards his desk. He spoke quietly and deliberately.

"What makes you think that?"

"Operation Hades is aborted. Forgive me, Nikolai Nikolayevich, but in the eyes of your own senior ministers, you have failed. Before long, the general will suggest that perhaps you should consider retiring, and that it would be logical to designate as your successor your old and trusted friend, Grigory Mikhailovich Varlamov."

Marina stopped speaking and let the room fill with silence. Lev was staring at her, and so was the president.

"From the outset, I believe the general did not want Operation Hades to succeed, in order to discredit you. He had endless opportunities to meet with the British political counsellor and resident spy, Oswald Martindale. In fact, two weeks ago they were together in your villa when you met with the British prime minister. But, in my opinion, the general used a different route. He passed classified information about Operation Hades to your enemy and oligarch in exile, Sergei Yegorov, who was living in England and who passed this information on to the British. General Varlamov and Sergei Yegorov were working together against you. When the general felt he had given the British enough to go on, he had Yegorov killed under the pretext he was a danger to you. Am I right it was the general's suggestion to eliminate Yegorov?"

"It was very much Grisha's idea. He said the man was undermining my authority."

Lev kept his eyes on Serov.

"There's one more thing," said Marina in a low, deadly voice. "It comes under the heading of 'deception'. General Varlamov is a major shareholder in that bogus Professor Tabakova's longevity company. You didn't know? Really? Nikolai Nikolayevich, my point is that Grigory Mikhailovich is not what he seems."

Serov was now sitting behind his desk, the tips of his fingers drumming on the shiny mahogany surface against the background ticking of the ormolu clock.

The intercom buzzed on the president's desk. Lev lurched forward and picked up the receiver.

"It's General Varlamov," said Lev.

"Send him in," said Serov, sitting upright in his chair.

General Varlamov strode into the room, but when he saw Marina in her tracksuit, he stopped dead. His eyes jumped from Serov to Lev, then came to rest on Marina.

"So," said the general, "she's got here first. Let me guess... Marina Andreyevna's been making up lies to discredit me. Am I right? Yes? Can't you see she's doing this to save her skin?" Varlamov then pointed a finger at Marina. "This woman is a traitor. She told the Englishman, Clive Franklin, about Operation Hades, and Franklin told the British ambassador, who passed it on to London."

The president stared at Varlamov.

"General, you seem to forget that she had no access to classified information. She was at none of our meetings."

"She was on board the *Moskva*. She even passed through the confidential compartment."

"We were all on board the *Moskva*. And Marina was never alone."

"Maybe it wasn't on the *Moskva*. Maybe it was at some other social occasion... She's always by your side, Nikolai Nikolayevich. Thanks to you, Marina Volina moves in the highest circles and has every opportunity to gather this intelligence... All that I know is that *somehow* she found out about Operation Hades," Varlamov said emphatically. "She found out and passed it on."

"Maybe it was *you*," said the president, staring at Varlamov. "Maybe you told your girlfriend, and your girlfriend told the

British. I've seen the video, Grisha. It's quite something. I see it's been forwarded to a great many of your email contacts. Including your wife."

Varlamov checked his phone and saw that the video had indeed been sent three minutes ago to dozens of his contacts. Already there was a WhatsApp message from his sixteen-year-old daughter, his beautiful Veronika. "I hate you," she had written, in words and without her usual emojis. "I never want to see you again."

Varlamov kept his voice steady.

"I don't deny I have a girlfriend. But she doesn't even know my name."

"I don't care about the video!" Serov said in a burst of anger. "You betrayed me! You betrayed Russia!"

Varlamov was about to speak when Lev stepped forward to show Serov something on his phone.

"The icing on the cake…" said Serov, in a trembling, high-pitched voice. "Your hacked emails are all over WikiLeaks. Posted four minutes ago… Can you see how ridiculous this makes us look? The FSB? Russia? And me? I'm a laughing stock…"

The president picked up the receiver and murmured a terse instruction. Two armed guards arrived in the room and saluted.

"Arrest the general."

The soldiers looked stunned. Varlamov stared at Serov, his eyes full of reproach. Serov stared back, unforgiving. Already, Varlamov could hear his daughter shouting in his ear, in her high-pitched voice, full of fury: "I hate you. I never want to see you again."

General Varlamov reached inside his jacket and pulled out his Makarov. For a split second, he pointed the barrel of the gun at the president, then swung the gun towards Marina. He fired. Marina fell. And so did Varlamov.

Lev had pulled out his own Makarov, aimed at Varlamov's head and shot the general dead. At the sound of gunshots, more soldiers burst into the room, their guns pointing wildly, only to stop dead when they saw the body of General Varlamov sprawled out on the floor, legs twisted, and Marina, unconscious on the ground, blood pouring from her neck.

"An ambulance... Get an ambulance!" the president shouted at Lev, who was crouching on the ground beside Marina, pressing his handkerchief to her wound. Lev could feel warm blood on his hand.

"Please, Marina Andreyevna," he whispered. "Hang on."

That same afternoon, at an emergency meeting of the security council, General Varlamov's chair was empty. The president, pale and clearly shaken, announced that there had been a terrible accident. General Varlamov had been cleaning his new pistol and the loaded gun went off by mistake. It was a tragedy, a terrible loss to the nation. There was a buzz of astonishment at the meeting, but no one dared to question the information. The president, barely able to get the words out and trembling with emotion, admitted that he was devastated to lose such a close and devoted friend.

Eventually, President Serov mastered his grief and addressed the national security meeting.

"We are gathered here today," said Serov, "to discuss how to deal with the current crisis. Three fibre-optic cables under the Atlantic have been disabled somewhere off the southern coast of Cornwall. We don't know how, but already the United Kingdom is pointing the finger at Russia."

There was a murmur in the room, and words like "outrageous" and "fake news" and "Russophobia" echoed around the room.

Serov had no intention of mentioning Operation Hades, which was known only to a handful of people, some of whom, it was true, were sitting round the table. But they were no fools. If they wanted to keep their jobs, they would keep their mouths shut.

"What is our response?" the president asked, leaning forward in his chair, his tired eyes flashing. "As your president, I shall look the British prime minister in the eye and say, 'How dare you accuse Russia? Where is you evidence?'"

"It's pure provocation," said Foreign Minister Kirsanov with as much indignation as he could muster. "And anyway, what's all the fuss about? Britain is still connected to the United States."

"That's right!" said the president. "It's pure provocation! Is it our fault if the United Kingdom cannot protect its cables? It may have been a case of bad maintenance. Who knows? Perhaps it was fishing nets, or even sharks, or a combination of the two?"

The room was stunned. Nobody knew whether to laugh or not.

"Are there really sharks in the English Channel?" said the deputy prime minister, Viktor Romanovsky.

"It's not the English Channel," said the foreign minister, who distrusted Romanovsky. "Cornwall is almost on the Atlantic. Look at a map."

The president got to his feet and brought the meeting to a close. Only Foreign Minister Kirsanov stayed behind.

"Nikolai Nikolayevich, what happened?"

"Grisha was the traitor. Marina found out and came to tell me. Grisha shot Marina and Lev shot him."

"My God, is she —"

"Alive," said the president. "But only just. We don't know if she'll survive."

By Monday, not only the United Kingdom, but much of Europe and the east coast of the United States were experiencing acute internet disruption. Millions of businesses were affected. The London and New York stock exchanges were suspended for the day. Streaming services went down; debit cards ceased to work, and cybersecurity companies went into overdrive to protect key government infrastructure.

The prime minister was able to report to the House of Commons that there had been some damage to three undersea internet cables, but that repairs were already under way and traffic was being successfully rerouted via other cables and satellites.

In Moscow, Lieutenant Maxim Mishin gave evidence in a closed hearing. Mishin said the general was of unsound mind and pathologically obsessed with Marina Volina, who was quite clearly innocent. The fact that Lieutenant Mishin did not altogether believe this was neither here nor there. He wanted promotion. Which he got. He also made it his business to secure the immediate release of the schoolgirl activist, Lyubov Zvezdova. He didn't want any black marks against his name.

A lot of questions were left hanging in the air. Who had hacked into the general's email? Who had filmed him and his girlfriend? Mishin said the general had suspected Vanya, the youngest foster son of Marina Volina and the brother of Pasha, the prodigy whose death was not accidental after all, so Mishin told the closed hearing. General Varlamov had ordered the boy's murder. It got murkier and murkier.

Nevertheless, General Varlamov died with his reputation not only intact but enhanced. There were eulogies in the press, hinting that the general had been involved in undercover work fighting terrorism, and there were rumours that he had died in the line of duty. Deputy Prime Minister Viktor Romanovsky spoke at his funeral, which was broadcast live on Channel 1. Lieutenant Mishin could be seen just behind Varlamov's widow,

Raisa, who wore a black veil and stood next to her sobbing daughter. Mishin was a special guest: he had been there, inside the Kremlin; he had heard the shots.

For seven months, Marina fought for her life. There were endless complications and moments of near death. Every Sunday the president sent her flowers. On the first Sunday, he enclosed a handwritten note: "To my brilliant, clever Marinochka, who unmasked the traitor in our midst. With eternal gratitude."

Lying in her hospital bed, Marina had plenty of time to relive the moment she'd been shot. From the moment Varlamov had stepped into the room, Marina could feel his fury and his sense of impotence once he realized that Serov believed her and not him. Varlamov understood that he was finished; Marina knew this. She also knew that he had a gun and would use it. She had told herself that she must yank her head one way or the other, to the left or the right; she chose the left, and the bullet missed her jugular vein by three millimetres. And thank God for Lyova. She was lucky. No... It was more than luck. It was *sudba*.

Lev visited her once a week and sat at the end of Marina's bed, chewing gum. People were asking after her, he said, high-up diplomats like the German and British ambassadors. The official line was that she'd been hit by a car and was recovering in hospital. And, thanks to Lev, Oxana was allowed the occasional visit: the first thing she told Marina was that she'd given up smoking; she was vaping instead. Oxana agreed to move into Marina's dacha in Peredelkino as a paid caretaker, to look after the garden and check on her neighbour, Tonya, and on Ulysses. Over the next few months, Tonya and Oxana became great friends, walking their dogs and keeping each other company during the long winter evenings; in fact, Oxana made friends with everyone, including Vera and even Anna.

Marina was sad to miss Vanya and Lyuba's wedding in Tbilisi, but she saw the video on WhatsApp. Weeks later, Vanya sent her a postcard from Buckingham Palace and said they were starting a new life in London. He promised to send his new address; she was still waiting. Once again, the alley cat had disappeared from her life.

Marina also missed the wedding of the year – the biggest splash anyone had seen in a long time – when the deputy prime minister, Viktor Romanovsky, married Katya. The bride looked ravishing in a dress by Valentin Yudashkin that cost twenty thousand dollars (she had wanted Victoria Beckham, but the foreign minister said it was no time to be nice to the British). The Russian edition of *Hello!* magazine had exclusive access, and Oxana brought a copy to the hospital, so Marina had plenty of time to admire the teenage bride and her handsome groom, who was old enough to be her father and looked every bit a future president. On social media, people were talking about Katya as the first lady of Russia.

35

In June the following year, Marina Volina was discharged by her doctors. She was frail and thin. There had been endless setbacks, and for three months she'd been fed with a tube.

The doorman at the Metropol didn't recognize her when she dropped by the hotel, looking for Liza. She had left, the manager told Marina, and not just the Metropol but Russia, for a new job, front of house, in a five-star hotel in Yerevan.

President Serov was shocked by Marina's appearance when, at last, she came to see him in the Senate Palace.

"You need a holiday," he said.

"I was thinking just the same," said Marina. "Nikolai Nikolayevich, I have a favour to ask."

"Anything, my Marinochka. Anything."

"Declassify me and let me go to Italy. I've been in hospital for seven months. What harm can I do?"

And so, Marina Volina locked up her flat at Tverskaya 25 and went abroad. She sent postcards to Oxana from Rome, where she was living, and also to Lev, with her address: Via Gregoriana, just above the Spanish Steps, next to the Hassler and the Villa Medici. As a favour, President Serov asked the head of military intelligence to check, which he did, and he was able to confirm that Marina Volina did indeed live in Via Gregoriana and had made friends with a retired Italian diplomat and his wife who invited her to parties on their roof garden. In the spring, Marina sent Lev another email, telling him she was going to visit all the main cities of Italy, starting in the south, in Lecce, then on to Naples and Pompeii, bypassing Rome for Florence, then Siena, then all the northern cities – Ferrara, Verona, Vicenza and Padua, and finally Venice. The head of foreign intelligence asked Serov for instructions: what level of surveillance would Marina Volina require? Leave her alone, said the president. Let her go.

Serov had other things on his mind. For much of the past year, the president had disappeared from public view, brooding incessantly over the treachery of Varlamov and the failure of Operation Hades. Night after night he woke in a cold sweat, hearing the voices of the British and NATO gloating over their victory, over the incompetence of Russia. The last laugh will be mine! he swore to himself. It was time to look to the future. Where could he, Nikolai Serov, make his mark? Leave a glorious legacy, never to be forgotten? Eventually, he put it to his defence minister and to Foreign Minister Kirsanov. Was it not time to protect Russian borders from insidious and creeping Western influence? Hit the West where it hurts? Humble NATO? The very same NATO that had stopped Operation Hades in its tracks and was still breathing down our Russian necks? It was time to strike back!

One morning, as Serov walked along the Aubusson carpet towards the gilded doors of his office in the Senate Palace, it came to him, with blinding clarity, what sort of action he needed to take for the glory and security of Russia. The quote from *Hamlet* popped into his head unbidden: "Thus conscience doth make cowards of us all…" Well, he, Serov was no coward. Sitting behind his desk, he summoned Lev, who was dressed even more sloppily than usual and looked thinner, sadder. Lev missed his friend Marina, and these days he spent every moment of his free time blasting down country roads on his beautiful motorbike, feeling the wind on his face.

"Get me a map," said the president.

"What sort of map?" Lev drawled.

"A map of Ukraine."

On the tiny island of Torcello in the Venetian Lagoon, a couple who had finished eating a good lunch were walking slowly towards the eleventh-century basilica. The man was tall with dark curly hair, and he held the woman tightly by the hand. It was once again September, another Indian summer, and warm sunlight slanted across the lagoon.

"I never thought..." said Marina.

"You never thought what?" said Clive.

They had been together for just a few hours.

"I never thought... No, that's not right. I never expected to be..."

"To be what?"

"Happy."

Clive took her hand and kissed it.

"And I never thought I'd see you again," said Clive.

Over lunch he had told Marina his side of the story. General Varlamov's death had been in the press, but there had been no mention of Marina and for weeks Clive thought she was dead. After almost a month, Anna called and told Clive that she'd heard through the diplomatic grapevine that Marina had been run over by a car and was in hospital in a critical condition. Then, a day or two later, Anna called again with an update, explaining that her source was Oxana in Peredelkino and that the car story was fake. Marina had been shot. But she was alive.

"I'm not a bit surprised," Rose said to Clive when she heard the news. "She's one tough lady."

It came as a shock to Clive – and also to Martindale, who was very put out – to learn that Rose was working for Hyde and was his undercover agent in Moscow. That September, her number-one job was to get Clive out in one piece. Which she did. As for the Tinder wheeze, it was her idea. She described to Clive how she and Martin Hyde had spent an amusing hour in the residence in Moscow setting up their alias profiles on Tinder, putting their discovery settings to within one kilometre and then swiping for half an hour until they matched: Stafford Knight meets Mary Bingham. Their safe channel was open, and Rose could tell Hyde everything he needed to know. On that Saturday afternoon, while Clive slept and missed Marina's calls, Rose, thanks to her secure Tinder channel, wasted no time and passed on the location of the Russian attack. The ambassador doubled up, sending the same information a few hours later, but that extra time was crucial, and Rose was the heroine of the hour. In gratitude, the prime minister held a private "thank you" ceremony in her flat at the top of 10 Downing Street and pinned a medal onto Rose's purple silk shirt. Clive was there. So was Hyde, who brought the champagne and kissed Rose on the cheek. And then Hyde took Clive completely by surprise when he produced a gold Moscow marathon medal, sent to London by special courier from the offices of Justice for All. In her note, Anna explained that it was Marina's medal and she wanted Clive to have it. The gold disc dangled from a red, white and blue ribbon; when Hyde hung it round Clive's neck, Rose and the PM clapped, after which Rose gave a little speech in flawless Russian, which was, for Clive, the last straw.

"I'm so glad the medal reached you," Marina murmured, as the basilica came into view. Torcello was almost deserted: high marsh grasses rustled in the wind, and now and then a sand-piper shot out, squawking. "And your book?… The Chekhov short stories?" Marina asked.

All good, said Clive. Hyde had found him an agent and within a week he had a publisher. The book was selling very well, especially online, and he'd bought himself a new pair of boots from Clarks. On the day Clive had bought his boots, he'd bumped into Fyodor, the British embassy driver, sitting behind the wheel of a Bentley on a double yellow line outside the Ivy in Kensington High Street. Fyodor was looking very pleased with himself, and he told Clive that he had a job with an oligarch who lived in London. Who? Clive had asked, although he already knew the answer. Boris Kunko. Who else?

Clive was holding Marina's hand.

"You're happy," he said. "And so am I. Let's go and see the Black Madonna."

"Don't tell me you've become religious?"

"Never! But I like churches for their art, and we can light a candle to Alexei. I think he'd be pleased that we're…" Clive hesitated. He didn't want to push his luck. "Together." On a holiday, he thought, in Italy, who knows for how long? But at least Marina's out of Russia, and she doesn't have to watch her back or get a new identity. She can be herself and start again.

The Venetian-Byzantine basilica was almost empty, except for a couple with a baby and the odd person praying or just sitting in a pew, admiring the mosaics that shimmered in the gloom. A shaft of light came through a stained-glass window and fell in a pool on the stone floor. Marina and Clive each lit a candle and watched for a moment as they flickered and spluttered; and they remembered Alexei. They sat for a while in one of the wooden pews, then walked slowly round the church until they came to the vaulted apse, one of the jewels of the eleventh century. The dome was covered in gold mosaic, which, even after all these centuries, gleamed in the half-light. Below were figures of the twelve apostles, and above, dominating everything, a serene, elongated figure of the Virgin Mary, dressed in black, holding the Christ Child, her left hand touching his tiny feet, her right hand pointing towards his heart.

"She's called the Virgin Hodegetria," said Martin Hyde, stepping languidly out of the shadows. "From the Greek. It means 'she who shows the way'. We all need guidance in these troubled times, don't you think? Delighted to see you are fully recovered, Mrs Volina. Our debt to you is immense. But I fear President Serov is about to go on the warpath, and once again we may need your help. May I invite you both for a drink? Even dinner?"

ACKNOWLEDGEMENTS

Two friends started this long journey with me and stayed the course to the bitter end, and, without their expertise and total commitment, this novel could not have been written. One of these friends wishes to remain anonymous, but it does not alter the fact that to him, and to Ilya Kachaev, my debt is immense.

Other friends were unstinting in their help. My profound thanks go to Paul de Quincey, Ksenia Pletner, Ben Amado, Alexis Ashot, Tamara Joffe, Chris Alexander, Olga Shurygina and Dicky Wallis. You saved me from many egregious mistakes and gave me the confidence to go forward.

Friends and occasionally strangers came to my rescue at short notice, and I thank them all for their kindness and enthusiasm: Francesco Goedhuis, Louis d'Origny, Alexandra Dieterink, Chris Barter, Timmy Pleydell-Bouverie, Rob Bates, Simon Giddins, Grace Cassy, Rachel Polonsky, Alina Isachenka, Irina Abdalyan, Sir Tim Berners-Lee, Charlie Ward, Mikki Mahan, Jeffa Murray, Apoorv Agarwal, Luke Harding and the late Michael Markham.

I owe more than I can say to my erudite and exacting publisher, François von Hurter, for his leap of faith, and for his expert judgement in steering the book towards its final form. Huge thanks also to Gillian Stern for her incisive and inspired editing; to my agent, Natasha Fairweather, for her steadfast support; and to Bryan Karetnyk, for his scrupulous copy-editing.

Finally, my greatest debt of all is to my son, Spencer, for his faith, not only in the story, but also in his mother; for his astute criticism of the manuscript, which he read and reread in its various drafts, and, above all, for his steely encouragement, without which this novel would have remained a "work in progress".